EQUATORIAL

Book Four of the
ETHER COLLAPSE Series
Written by RYAN DEBRUYN

Cover designed by MiblArt.

MOUNTAINDALE
—— PRESS ——

TABLE OF CONTENTS

Acknowledgments

Thank you for reading this book and giving me the opportunity to live my dream. I can't wait to see where this journey takes us.

RECAP

It's been a while. This time it's probably my fault, and for that I can only say, it's the bloody apocalypse. Still, here's what I've gone through so far.

In case you've forgotten, I'm Rockland Barkclay, and its short form Rocky is rather fitting as I think I'm at my Rocky bottom. Sorry... I joke so I don't cry. Finding a severed arm and leg wearing the clothes of your family might have that effect on you too. But, I'm getting ahead of myself—I should start at the beginning.

The planet literally came to life after a wave of blue hit us from space. That substance is called Ether and seems to have rebooted some ancient deity that governs a system that is reminiscent of some of my favorite RPGs. And just like in those games, Ether brought with it a power to make us superhuman. It's not all sunshine and rainbows though, but perhaps my last paragraph made that clear.

It also brought buildings, cars, and most existing infrastructure to life. Mutated the wildlife to terrifying monstrous creatures. Imported monsters from elsewhere, and more or less brought about an apocalypse on Earth, decimating the population of eight billion to less than a billion in the months since. Perhaps it wouldn't have been that bad if monsters and animated buildings were all we had to worry about.

Unfortunately, some of those animated buildings are sapient, and some of the humans aren't friendly. Oh right, I better not forget to mention the race of mechano-humans or the undead-loving Void God Apep. Just when I thought we had dealt with those last two threats, they seem to come back, like a cockroach infestation.

I personally destroyed some of Dahrix's—the leader of the Mechanolords—minions in the early days, and destroyed his beacon, but he just found others and made more. Me and my group went toe to toe with a rotting corpse of a human, Apothis, and I'm not only talking about his appearance. On a side note, was Apothis named after Apep or…? Anyway, we had help for that fight, and sure, we kind of died during the encounter but we managed to remove the threat… temporarily.

That vagary brings me to my latest 'heroic deed.' I stood next to the underside of the pinky toe of the converted Empire State Building, named Empire, and tried to find my family amidst the ruins of New York. If you haven't caught the tone, or the rather obvious severed limb section, I didn't walk out of there with my mother Nadine and sister Lacy. No, after the Mechanolords, under the control of Dahrix, joined the battle I found my family, and got front row seats to their executions.

I've fled that terror with my pet, Azoth, and while I miss my Ancestral Companion, Selaphelia, deep in my heart I know she was too good for me anyway. She deserves better, and I hope she will find it.

If you want to join me, be my guest,

Rockland Barkclay

P.S. Okay, so I wrote this two months ago shortly after the 'end' of my world. I'll admit, it's a little dark and depressing, but I can also now admit that was my headspace at the time. Let's just say I am glad someone helped pull my head from my ass.

PROLOGUE

Etherless Void—Guild Collective Armada

Dahrix sat in his captain's chair, listening to the imbeciles debate the next steps of the mission. His metal hand gently massaged a stress ball as a coping mechanism to being subjected to this farce.

After he failed to kill Rockland Barkclay and the beacon was destroyed, Dario, the Guild Prime, had chosen to place all the guild heads in charge of the mission. Like democracy had ever succeeded...

"We are passing numerous Planetary Gods as we rush to the place of the Flow Ridians. We should be stopping and studying them. There could be a more defensible planet closer to Helion Prime," Hectar insisted, for the seventy-second time.

Dahrix felt his coolant circulation increase for the seventieth time. Dario must have known how much Dahrix hated democratic processes. The Guild Prime had assigned the perfect punishment, it seemed.

"Listen, child, if one good thing came from Dahrix's complete failure, it's that we now know for certain that the Flow Ridians were not lying about the Epic level wildlife, golems, and creatures on their planet. We have allowed you to launch probes at the planets we pass, but any delay now may cost us the time we need to fortify the prize!" Tirahnya spat.

"I must agree with Tirahnya. If one of the probes returns a sign of life, we will have to reassess the situation. But so far, the planets are practically space rock," Geb said.

The fact that no one addressed Dahrix was a power play. The three bunglers always voted together and overruled his votes against—everything. Although annoying, Dahrix dealt with similar situations in the past, and like then, refused to give away any of his intentions. He sat silently and conversed with his ship and crew through their shared interweb.

<Lieutenant, how much time is the launching of probes adding to the journey?> he typed.

<By my calculations, it has already added two days and four hours to the journey. I have projected an addition of three weeks, two days, and twenty-one hours by the time we reach the target.>

His closing fist destroyed his stress ball in a foamy, stringy explosion. One of the nearby technicians came by to clean up the mess and hand him a new ball. He 'stretched' his neck and continued to listen as the conversation changed to invasion tactics.

They were two months into the journey toward the planet the Flow Ridians had called Earth, and his three fellow guild leaders were currently hypothesizing the best attack strategies with what limited information he had provided. These three were utterly useless. Dahrix would need to do this himself, and had already been using the secondary beacon to remote in secretly.

<Lieutenant, do we have more contacts for humans in shops other than Fiscal Flats or Aretrean Bazaar?> Dahrix typed while listening to Tirahnya bemoan their lack of surprise.

<We have seen groups, sir, but have been unable to make contact. The Hertasi Huts has a few humans who hold regular meetings in its facilities. They have been unresponsive to our attempts to contact them.>

<Lieutenant, I would like to change tactics. Attempt to follow them after they enter the shop. Each group likely must meet a trader to access the private rooms. I want to know what they discuss before the meetings. We may not be able to recruit them, but there may be other ways we can cause further unrest,> Dahrix responded. His mouth curled up at the corners and he saw the other three leaders jolt in their seats.

These imbeciles really believed they were in charge?

***

Egypt – Gaia – Three Months After the First Ether Wave

"You're telling me that the Library of Alexandria has risen from the Mediterranean Sea?" Maat asked while holding out his hand to receive the looking glass.

"Not just the Library, Maat. There is a loose network of buildings that float above the water. It's like an entire city now hovers there," Adom said as he used the contraption to zoom in and out.

Maat looked at the Great Pyramid of Giza. "And the robotic men, the sea serpent?"

"Still engaged in their pointless war," Adom responded and handed the looking glass over.

Maat held it to his own eye and immediately saw a static blue with fuzzy shapes behind it. He began using the focusing twists on the device to zoom past the interior shield that both protected and trapped them.

The day after the Ether struck, the Pyramid had come to life. Maat had woken up to find a faintly glowing blue dome surrounding it for a few miles in all directions. Maat had grown up in the shadow of the Great Pyramids of Giza, and each had been weathered, worn and near collapse. Now three months later, it was flawless, shiny, and glowing as it projected this domed blue field. In the three months since the wave, they had discovered that it formed adequate protection against the newly evolved creatures outside, but they had yet to discover a way to exit themselves.

A vast portion of the buildings in the city of Cairo that were outside the shield were converted to golems while the buildings inside of the shield remained standing. Those golems had instantly turned on the people who had once lived within them—attempting to kill them.

Luckily, many of those people fled into the dome created by the Great Pyramid of Giza, which saved their lives. Still, the interior wasn't entirely safe. After that second day, creatures began to attack, which, of course, had led to the discovery of levels and classes…

Maat had become one of the leaders of the 'pod' due to his group's heroics in those early days. While there were some other strong groups that also hunted for food and protected the people, his group was still one of the brave few that had entered the swirling portal set into Abu Rowash. To his utter astonishment, the interior of the pyramid through that portal led to some other world, called a dungeon, and while they often fought inside the dungeon to gain levels, they had yet to conquer it. They hadn't even cleared the first floor yet, because they refused to attempt the boss battle.

Too many other 'strong groups' died trying to fight the creature or whatever else was inside. Instead, Maat chose to gain strength in fights they could win. Perhaps once his group gained fifteen more levels and reached apprentice level thirty, they would give it a try. He turned to Adom. "What about the robotic man who flew into the dome and is now trapped in here with us?"

"He's sticking to his story of not knowing how he got here. He says he is from London originally, and that his group there accepted help through some sort of transporting shop device. He is certainly stronger than anyone in here with us, but honestly that just means that massive serpent creature is even stronger still…"

Maat nodded and looked north. They were going out to grind for more levels today, but that massive white snake that kept lunging out of the Mediterranean Sea didn't bode well for the power gap between the people in here and out there. If he was honest with himself, he truly thought that thing could flatten them all, Abu Rowash protection or not...

A particularly large boom erupted from the north, followed by a reptilian screech. Maat shivered. "Keep an eye on the battle and let me know if something changes."

***

Toronto – Gaia – Three Months After the First Ether Wave

Sela's jaw clenched tightly. Rockland had been gone for a moon already, and despite her best efforts, she hadn't been able to deal with Frankie Cocozza. The Territory was under constant threat of attack from the nut job and his Apep-generated minions. They had been forced to evacuate their positions in Toronto and solidify all defenses back at Algonquin. Of course, the scumbag had sent hordes of undead on a nearly endless crusade since their retreat.

The issue was that the deranged psychopath was being fed troops from multiple dungeons.

Sela attempted to track down the dungeons in Toronto, but had been forced to give up when she discovered a Territory. She had urged the Grotto and their swelling numbers to act, but because of Rockland's constant conquering of new Territories, they had refused. Of course, their reluctance gave Frankie the ability to roam free and collect more servants. Sela growled as she held her hand to the ground and solidified the pit traps that the people of the Grotto had cleared of bodies after last night's battle.

She breathed out and admitted her actual annoyance was with the inability to travel to Atlantis. She needed a party of people willing to go, but also needed Rockland. But no, the moron was traveling across Canada, conquering Territories. They knew his location because each newly established Territory informed them of its founding. Still, the council refused to side with her and send the ship to collect him.

Oh, they sent the ship, but only after a week of organization. The Grotto was full to bursting, and each new Territory Rockland captured had allowed some of the less powerful in the Grotto to be moved out safely. However, the volunteer process took time. By the time they arrived, Rockland had moved on. In some people's minds, it was also the reason they were staying ahead in food stores against the constant siege-like attacks…

When she saw that man, she was going to slap him. Or kiss him. She was undecided.

They had tried to pass multiple messages including some from his family, but she couldn't be sure he received any. He had no radio, and the people he left behind in the Territory hadn't had any idea how powerful he truly was.

During times that the ship wasn't ferrying survivors to the new Territories, it was assisting in the Territory's defense. Or on some rare occasions, it would run supply drops to people still trapped by golem encirclement. Sela came up with that particular idea after the fateful trip to New York. They had a ship that could circle the globe in one hour. So, they calculated drops to within a meter of the intended target. The ship had dropped supplies into every nearby school quest that they could afford, but, unfortunately, the Territory could only spare so much.

Yes, the rescue of others could wait until they were certain that they themselves were safe. The Territory itself was growing in strength and defenses, but so was Frankie…

For the hundredth time, she considered just turning into a Raven and leaving. She knew what direction the two birdbrains were heading. She could meet them in this BC and give Rockland a piece of her mind.

Instead, she knelt on the ground and fixed the defenses, hoping he would come home soon. She couldn't help but worry that his continued absence was somehow her fault. Had their relationship been a bad choice?

What if he blamed her for the deaths in New York? Still, she couldn't understand how he would go to all that trouble to save his family and then abandon them...

CHAPTER ONE

When you're only good for fighting, you find yourself in a never-ending battle.

Steam rose from Azoth's back and Rocky could see the same misty vapor intermingling with his Dark Cloak skill. All three of the living creatures in the battle-torn clearing heaved in as much air as they could hold and sized each other up with narrowed eyes. This was the twenty-fourth Territory Rocky had entered, and across from him stood a mutated grizzly bear that dwarfed even Azoth.

Grizzly Bear
Master-Ursa
Level 12
Health Points: 1,212 / 6,825
Active Skills: 9
Passive Skills: 9
Territorial Boss

The grizzly bear was at a relatively low-level compared to some of his other recent fights, and thanks to Azoth and experience, they were the first to make their move. They had been fighting together without mental communication for almost two months. Azoth began circling to his right and Rocky moved to his left. The bear chose to follow the more threatening form of Azoth with its eyes, and that gave Rocky all the time he needed.

He willed his Envenom skill to coat his blade from his inner Poison Pool, and then charged a single stack of Dark Blade onto his Soul Sword. Using a horizontal slash from the Seraphim Sword form, he sliced his blade through the heel of one leg of the bear and continued his run to try to disable the other hind leg. As soon as he struck, the bear roared and began to turn, but Azoth roared before rising onto his back legs. Azoth shot both of his wings out like they were the hood of a king cobra, which halted the grizzly's turn as it reevaluated the threat of the chimera. But since it had already begun its turn, Rocky's pet fell on the side of the turning bear and bit into the front shoulder joint as his tail began pin-cushioning into and out of the bear's side. Unfortunately, Azoth's poison was currently recharging so these were more akin to bee stings then deadly attacks.

Not that I don't have a full bottle of chimera poison in my bag of holding...

Rocky managed to swipe the other back leg of the bear as it turned, and due to the injuries and Azoth's added weight, the back legs crumpled under the bear. The bear clearly had some regenerative abilities, because while Rocky's poison and Dark aura attempted to pulse up and spread, something kept it at bay. A familiar red glow came over the bear a moment later and it managed to stand back up with Azoth still clinging onto its back. Rocky groaned at the fourth use of its Aura skill. It somehow closed all wounds and simultaneously enraged the grizzly, increasing stats.

"Disengage, Azoth," Rocky ordered as he dropped half of his Ether pool into his sword. He thrust out at the opposite shoulder from where Azoth leaped away and released his four stacks of Dark Blade. Azoth pumped his wings and crested over the grizzly as it slid across the snow, frozen moss, wood chips and mud of the 'clearing.' Unlike the other four times that Rocky had used this skill to help them disengage, this time the remaining health and inherent Ether of the bear wasn't able to weather his strongest attack. Ten feet into the slide, the front edge of his thrusted Dark Blade broke the fur and skin before puncturing right through the bear and out the other side.

"Finally!" Rocky crowed as he tried to determine how long that fight had actually lasted.

Rocky collapsed onto his butt as the conquer notification flashed into the bottom right corner of his vision. Azoth joined him with heavy steps and laid down with a large huff. Through the bond, Rocky felt pride and exhaustion from the chimera. He was still beyond frustrated by his skill tree's lack of a 'speak with animals' skill. Despite reaching level thirty-one, he still hadn't been able to uncover something like that, and after two months of near constant grinding, he missed talking to his stalwart friend even more.

Congratulations, you have successfully conquered a new Territory.
The Grizzly Den has been captured due to the death of its leader. Would you like to take ownership of the new Territory?
Yes | <No>
Would you like to place the Territory onto the Market?
Yes | <No>
Would you like to condense the Territory into a Territorial Sphere?
Warning! A transfer of this sort will sustain losses.
<Yes> | No

Rocky chose the final option and condensed the Territory into a sphere. He was in one of the national parks that was on the western side of what used to be Alberta, and there weren't a great deal of survivors in the area. In fact, most of the survivors Azoth and he found nowadays were in a designated safe area that had access to a dungeon or a shop. He had to assume that a great deal of others died of starvation or in a desperate fight against the golems that 'protected' them, but each time he set up a new Territory, there were still quests being offered nearby.

Maybe someone was getting food to those people inside the encirclement?

Rocky recognized his mind's attempt to wander down that dark chain of thoughts and he consciously reminded himself that he was still finding groups. Right after losing his family and fleeing the battle of New York, Rocky had begun fighting any creatures or Territories he could find. He admitted to himself now that he hadn't been in a good mind space after that tragic battle. He somehow won all those early fights, but the state of Azoth and himself after many of them had been a close thing. Truthfully, he would have welcomed death in those first few weeks.

"Dark thoughts lead to dark destinations," he mumbled under his breath while also allowing himself to assess his former head space.

It was so bad that Rocky even avoided the survivors inside schools after he saved them. He would simply destroy the golem encirclement and fly off. To make things worse, he refused to restock on his potions or any lifesaving items when he found shops. He would have likely continued along that path still if it hadn't been for a group of hunters he stumbled upon as they fought for their lives...

***

Azoth crashed into the twenty-five-foot-tall moose and Rocky leaped out of the saddle to begin laying into the beast.

They had been flying west, and had likely crossed into Manitoba, Minnesota, or North Dakota from Ontario. From the air, Rocky had made out the telltale flash of skills splashing against something in a copse of trees. Azoth must have noticed it too because he was already banking without Rocky's knee directions. That was when they managed to catch sight of a party attempting to retreat from the huge, pointy-antlered beast as they fired skills off blindly behind them.

Two blood stains on the light dusting of white snow told the story of how successfully it was going. Azoth dove without prompting and Rocky loaded his blade with five stacks of Dark Blade.

Once they successfully killed the aggressive moose and looked around, they found they had been too late for eight of the ten in the group of fleeing survivors. Rocky was about to mount back up when one of the two survivors grabbed his arm. Rocky tried to pull his arm away, not wanting to talk to other living humans, but found that his strength was missing.

"Gary, come heal this guy, I don't think he even realizes he got gored!" the man holding his arm said. Rocky looked down to find a hole in his stomach. It wasn't bleeding, and instead it looked like some sort of blood-covered snake was protruding from the wound. "Hurry, Gary, I can't hold his arm and his innards inside him if he keeps struggling."

Rocky felt a wave of something wash over him and somehow that cooling wave allowed his brain to process the massive amount of pain his body was in. He slumped to the ground and passed out a few heartbeats later. When he woke, he found out that his earlier assumption about eight of the ten dying was wrong.

Seven people sat around a nearby fire that Rocky could feel the heat of on his right side. As soon as he opened his eyes and tried to sit up, a hand pressed into his chest.

"Not just yet. I think the external injuries are healed but I, *or the system*, only just now managed to remove an internal bleeding debuff." Rocky allowed the man's strength to push him back down because he felt that he could overpower whoever this was if he needed to.

Azoth was napping somewhere nearby, and Rocky could feel his pet through his weaker bond. In comparison to when he had his ring, the connection was pathetic and didn't allow communication. Still, he learned some tricks, and pulsed something down that bond to let Azoth know it was time to leave. Azoth woke up and the cracking snow told Rocky his pet was standing. The head of the man pushing him down snapped up at a point to Rocky's left and his eyes looked fearful for a moment. "Can you tell your pet to lay back down? It's rather intimidating to have a beast like that staring at me."

"I woke him up so we can continue on our way…" Rocky mumbled. He sat up, forcing the unidentified man off his chest and pushing him back a few feet. Rocky didn't Analyze the man because he didn't want to be responsible for him or his surviving group. Every person who he helped either died or, in the worst cases, turned out to be an enemy.

"Can you talk for a moment? You don't exactly seem to be in a healthy place…" the man started but increased his volume when Rocky got to his feet. "You would have died if I didn't heal you. You owe me!"

This man must be Gary, the healer the other original survivor had called for. Rocky wanted to point out that he saved Gary's group and so that likely made them even but swallowed the words. How could he talk about saving people? He hadn't even been able to protect his family. That slight hitch in Rocky's walk was all Gary needed and he shot to his feet to interpose himself between Azoth and Rocky.

"Look, I just don't want you to continue on this path and kill yourself. You are the highest level person I or my group has seen. I know you likely have been through something terrible…" Gary said but faded off as Rocky's eyes hardened when the words veered into an area he didn't want to remember.

"Could you come with us back to the school we're staying at? Maybe use your pet to help us survive?"

Rocky shook his head. He couldn't help anyone. Another of the group members interposed himself at the headshake and the other five joined a blink later. Azoth growled menacingly but the people didn't move. One even turned and pointed a finger at the massive manticore.

"Listen, you big black cat-thing, if you want your owner or whoever this man is to die, then help him leave right now. If you want him to get better and heal then come back to the school with us," the man, currently pointing a finger at Azoth's terrifying bulk, stated.

Rocky tried to walk away after Azoth had changed sides, but he couldn't leave his pet who had followed the group of men. Head down, Rocky trudged along after the group as they made their way back to the north of the moose battle. The corpse itself had been partially butchered sometime when Rocky was out cold, and each man carried a full basket of meat. The rest of the corpse stayed where it was, as Rocky's apathy to the world overwhelmed his inner miser.

Perhaps an hour or two after, the group walked onto a campus for a hospital. A chipped and faded blue overhang covered a carport. The word 'SANFORD' was spelled in white letters half on and half above the flat-topped overhang. Two white posts with the words 'Clinic' and 'Medical Center' supported this roof, and Azoth walked toward that structure, accompanied by the seven-person group.

As they grew nearer, Rocky could make out people cooking on makeshift barbecues, fire pits, and smokers. After studying the seven-story building and windows behind the carport, he went back to looking at the ground and following Azoth. That was when a scream kicked his heart into overdrive, and he pulled out his sword.

Gary spun on him and held up two hands in a universal gesture of, 'it's okay, calm down.' The screaming woman who had jumped back and away from her barbecue was already being calmed by another member of the group. Her eyes were on Azoth and slowly softened as the man talked her out of her initial fear-filled reaction. Rocky returned his sword to liquid and tried again to convince Azoth to leave through their bond. The Manticore ignored whatever Rocky was managing to convey, and a moment later Rocky felt kicked-up grit strike his downturned face as Azoth took off and winged into the distance.

"He is just going to hunt, Rockland," Gary said, his hands still raised to keep peace. Rocky screamed then and, for the first time since his family's deaths, he cried. Azoth's bond, while still there, was fading further and further away. He hadn't realized how much he had been leaning on that connection in the last few weeks, but now that it was gone, he crumpled to the ground. No longer able to hold back the tears.

Gary came over and wrapped Rocky into his arms. At first, Rocky tried to push the man away but only succeeded in weakly shoving at him. "Rocky, you need to talk about this, or it is going to eat you alive. If we go inside, can you tell me what happened?"

Somehow, Rocky ended up staying with Gary for a week and, even more strangely, Gary talked him back to something resembling a human again. Rocky couldn't have pinpointed what broke through to him and allowed him to begin healing, but he could remember the man's words that he repeated to himself daily since.

"Do you know how much negativity we see on a daily basis?" Gary had asked and Rocky could only blink, not understanding where this conversation was going. "Even before the crash of this Ether, we were sensationalized by horrible tragedies and would read article after article about the worst possible things happening across the entire world.

"Do you know why I am telling you this?" Gary finished and Rocky shook his head. "Picture yourself as a container of some sort, maybe a glass or perhaps a bucket. The more negative you hear about or see, the more you fill your bucket with that emotion. Simultaneously, you're also filling your bucket with the positive you see. Still, if that bucket is filled with more negative than positive, you're more likely to view everything in a bad light.

"For example, your pet Azoth there," Gary continued and pointed to the manticore snoozing in the sun outside of Rocky's window. "People could view him as a monster, but from your facial expression and his own actions, he is anything but. Still, because of the negativity in this current world, we are predisposed to think of something like that as a deadly enemy. Still, with an open mind and *mindfulness,* we can change people's perspective through action and speech. Do you understand what I am saying yet?"

Rocky shook his head again and Gary smiled before trying again. "Don't worry. Perhaps it's easier to use the classic glass half full metaphor. Because we have all heard that idiom. The glass half full saying has lost a great deal of meaning because of its flippant usage. So, let me try to return it. If your bucket is filled with negativity, you are more likely to see a glass that is half empty and the liquid that you're consuming will soon run dry, leaving you with nothing. If you are in a positive headspace, you're more likely to celebrate the liquid you have left, cherishing each sip, and thus call it half full."

Rocky raised an eyebrow, seeing that analogy from a fresh vantage.

"Good. Now picture your bucket that you are filling with negativity or positivity as your mind. Is there a way to recognize what you're putting into that bucket?"

Narrowing his eyes and thinking, Rocky eventually nodded and even spoke for the first time that session. "Well, it's pretty easy to see when something is negative or positive…"

"I completely agree, Rocky. So, what if I told you to categorize things coming in or things that you say into one of those two categories. Could you?" Rocky nodded. "Could you acknowledge the negative and let it go—filter it out? Or, better yet, do you think you could flip a negative to a positive?"

"Maybe?"

It took almost thirty more minutes before Rocky fully understood what Gary was trying to get him to do. It could almost be described as a silver lining that he was supposed to look for and point to. Whenever he consciously found that positive, the response from Gary would also be positive. While those responses were a little forced in the current environment, Gary continued practicing with Rocky.

"So many people have died," Rocky said, skirting the subject of his family's demise.

"That's true, but what has the rest of humanity gained?" Gary prompted.

"Stats, skills, and the constant fear of death…"

"Close, Rocky. Repeat the first bit and add superhuman gains to it. Then keep repeating it until you can see that side of it. See the wonder and let some of the negatives slide away. Remember, *dark thoughts lead to dark destinations.*"

At some point in that week, Rocky had placed a Territory sphere on the ground outside and converted the hospital which had access to a shop already into a Territory. That had been his first Territory and the start of his current quest to not only get healthier, by untangling his 'Chidi' but also to create more safe spaces for humans.

CHAPTER TWO

Rocky shook off his reminiscing and butchered the grizzly. When he was finished, he took a quick dip in a nearby shallow river to rinse himself off. After the rinse, he tied his long hair back in a samurai knot over his head and brushed out his large, unkempt beard with his fingers. Now 'clean,' he placed the butchered meat into his bag of holding and began returning in the direction of Calgary atop Azoth.

He had created a Territory on the University of Calgary campus, but even after three Territorial orbs, he wasn't able to fully encapsulate the entirety of the myriad buildings and residences. The University had housed twenty-three thousand survivors before he placed the sphere and it had not one, but two dungeons that were already a part of the campus. It hadn't had a shop, but Rocky was confident that one would likely end up there in the future.

While he never liked to stay long in any one area now, instead choosing to go challenge other Territories and find other pockets of survivors, he had decided to stay nearby a few extra days, ensuring that he set up the school grounds as best he could. The survivors inside were an interesting group with a great deal of hunters and crafters working together to keep guns, armors, bullets, and food provided for everyone.

Calgary was his fourth Territory, including Algonquin Valley, and he planned to continue into BC after dropping this orb off. The true benefit of him creating these Territories had been a surprise. Thanks to a Red Quest, his main Territory had been awarded a Greater Perk and they had selected a Guild Hall and Tower. Little did Rocky know that Greater Perk would continue to bear fruit in future Territories. Each one he started got a miniaturized version of the Guild Hall and Tower, which then allowed the residents to join Meliora, and see quests for humans needing aid nearby.

Azoth slowed to a hovering stop under him and Rocky blinked, trying to understand what his pet had seen that drew him up short. They had gotten into a few high-speed chases with other flying creatures, but Azoth's bulk and Rocky's Dark Blade skill usually convinced other airborne predators they were too challenging to be prey. Still, when he saw what had caused Azoth to stop and hover this time, he shouted, "Turn around, now!"

In the distance, lowering itself out of the stratosphere was 'The Scourge,' which was a massive battleship that technically belonged to Rocky. He hadn't expected it to make it out here so fast considering the notices of attack he kept receiving on Algonquin's behalf. In the early days, he had just ignored those messages, and now because they had successfully warded off so many attacks it was even easier to do so. The Territory could handle a few monsters without him.

Still, seeing the ship all the way out here nearly stopped his heart.

Despite the steps he had taken to better himself, he wasn't ready for the people on that ship. He couldn't bring himself to go back to Algonquin Valley and see it without his family. Azoth listened to his request to fly away, which likely meant Sela wasn't aboard the ship, because she would have felt Azoth and been able to talk with him. Thinking of the woman in question made his heart clench tightly but he needed more time.

Or maybe you're just worried you'll lose her too…

Rocky stopped that thought cold and peeked behind him. He noticed the ship continued its descent toward Calgary and didn't alter course, which likely meant they hadn't seen him. At least they weren't following him and Azoth. Trying to ease the pain in his chest, he opened his screens to look over his latest conundrum of where to place his newest skill point from level thirty-one.

Rockland Barkclay Level 31
Class: Journeyman-Dark Chimera Knight
Level 9 Strategist
Class Skills: Dark Blade, Dark Mend, Soul Blade, Dark Cloak, Shadow Clone, Knight's Resolve, Knight's Quest, Poison Pool, Chimera Bones, Chimera Skin
Health Points = 820 / 820
Dark Ether Pool = 500 / 500
You have 10 stat points and 6 skill points to distribute.
Stamina – 66 (Strength of Body +10) (+4 Stat V)
Strength – 69 (Strength of Arms +20) (+4 Stat V)
Agility – 74 (+4 Stat V)
Dexterity – 69 (+4 Stat V)
Intelligence – 50 (+4 Stat V)
Wisdom – 66 (+4 Stat V)
Charisma – 68 (+4 Stat V)
Luck – 22
Weak Skills
Non-Class Combat Skills: Ether Cleanse – 21
Common Skills: Barter – 8, Fall – 18
Profession Skills: Actor – 5, Cook – 22, Grooming – 19, Herbalist – 24, Miner – 1, Teacher – 20, Trader – 5
Moderate Skills
Non-Class Combat Skills: Combatant – 11, Ether Channels – 34, Ether Manipulation 35, Stealth – 51, Swordsmanship – 44
Common Skills: Camouflage – 7, Endurance – 19, Perception – 48, Sneak – 49, Tracker – 39, Trance Meditation – 33
Profession Skills: Butcher – 41, Enchanting – 15, Skinner – 41
Strong Skills
Non-Class Combat Skills:
Common Skills: Analyze – 22

Profession Skills:

—

!Chosen Skills!
Chimera Knight Skill Tree
Tier 1
Poison Pool
For each venom/poison the Chimera Knight suffers
and survives, he gains immunity. The toxic makeup of
that poison will be added to his Poison Pool. In time,
the Chimera Knight can add his unique venom to
strikes or weapons. Do be careful; as Chimera Knight,
not all poisons can be survived.
5 / 5
Skill gained, "Envenom."
Envenom
Create an applicable venom from your Chimera
Venom. This venom increases in strength with each
additional poison and venom added to its base.

—

Tier 1
Knight's Resolve
Increases the knight's resistances against all elements,
poisons, and venoms.
5 / 5
Passive buff gained, "Stalwart."
Stalwart
Stalwart increases elemental, poison, and venom
resistances by 50%.

—

Tier 2
Knight's Quest
Increases the Etherience received from completed
quests.
Passive buff received, "Questing."

5/5

Questing

At 1/5 Questing, buff increases Etherience received from completed quests by 5%.

—

Tier 3

Chimera Skin

The skin of a Chimera is far stronger and durable than most other creatures. There are few creatures in the EtherVerse with more inherent Ether than a Chimera. This skill provides a Chimera Knight with increases in defense as well as resistance against all extreme temperatures.

5/5

Skill gained, "<u>Chimera Skin.</u>"

—

Tier 3

Chimera Senses

The senses of a Chimera are otherworldly, and some would even claim that a Chimera can hear in the void of space.

<5>/5

Passive skill gained at 1/5, "<u>Chimera Senses.</u>"

—

Tier 3

Chimera Bones

Increases the density of the Knight's bones while reducing their overall weight. Each point in this skill will increase Bone Density and reduce weight by 20%.

5/5

Passive skill gained, "<u>Chimera Bones.</u>"

—

! Available Choices !
Tier 2

Knight's Action
Allows the user to increase an attack or perform a dodge at double their usual Strength or Speed. Skill gained at 5/5, "Knight's Action."
0/5

—

Tier 2
Chimera Rejuvenation
Since Chimeras are an amalgamation of multiple creatures, they possess a drastically increased healing factor. Some Chimeras can even regrow internal organs.
0/5
Passive buff gained, "Chimera Rejuvenation."
Chimera Rejuvenation
Can heal from the most grievous of wounds if health points remain. Increased natural Ether healing and spell healing by 100%.

—

Tier 2
Dark Poison Fog
The fog from your Dark Cloak ability will be able to gain the poison and venom effects from your Envenom skill. Breathing this fog will cause a poison debuff on your enemies.
0/5
Skill gained at 5/5, "Dark Poison Cloak."

—

Tier 3
Knight's Training
Training done under a legendary Chimera Knight increases the absorption rate of students. Doubles all effects of all skills relating to Teaching.
0/5
Skill gained at 5/5, "Mentor."

–

Tier 3

Knight's Protection

Allows the legendary Chimera Knight to conjure an unbreakable bubble around a target for one second per level in the skill. This skill has a seventy-two-hour cooldown.

0/5

Skill gained at 5/5, "Knight's Protection (5s)."

–

Tier 4

Knight's Oath

The Knight can link himself to one individual per point in this skill to a maximum of five. If those individuals are damaged, they will trigger a Dark Mend skill from their own Ether pool immediately.

0/5

Skill gained at 1/5, "Knight's Oath."

–

Tier 4

Knight's Charge

If the Knight is mounted on his Chimera, they can increase their momentum and speed by 100% for each point in this skill. All momentum is transferred to the target the knight collides with and not to the Chimera or the Knight.

0/5

Skill gained at 1/5, "Knight's Charge."

–

Tier 4

Chimera Blood

Increases all stat points by ten percent for one hour once every day.

0/5

Skill gained at 5/5, "Chimera Blood."

—

Rocky looked over his skills again and felt that somewhere on the Chimera side of his skill tree was the stronger connection to Azoth. One that would allow him to talk to Azoth again. In fact, a hidden option similar to his Dark Cloak was on the fourth tier of skills. Filaments from Chimera Bones and Skin in tier three combined with filaments that lead off the top of Senses in tier three and the side of Blood in tier four. So, he needed to place points into Senses and Blood before the hidden skill was unlocked.

Should I place points in Blood or Senses first?

He deliberated between the two as Azoth continued to fly further west, away from Calgary and its University. Yet more importantly, away from 'The Scourge.' They headed to the final Canadian province in this direction, before the Pacific Ocean. Since Rocky had liberated a Territory in what he assumed to be the other provinces, this was the only one left to complete a sweep to the west.

As they flew and he considered his options for skill points, he kept his eyes peeled for any large safe zones that had apparent populations within that might need saving.

A few hours later, he had seen many standing buildings but none with signs of life or ringed by golems. As for his skills, he still hadn't made a final decision. If he went with Blood, he would gain a more powerful skill and access to the fifth tier, but something about Senses screamed at him. He waffled for a few more moments before deciding on Chimera Senses.

It seemed much more likely to lead to a connection with Azoth, right?

That unlocked another two skills in the fourth tier.

—

!Available Options!

Tier 4
Chimera Combination
Combine class skills into a single, new, more powerful skill once every five days. Each point in this skill reduces cooldown by a single day.
0/5
Skill gained at 1/5, "Chimera Combine."

—

Tier 4
Chimera Strike
Increases the penetration of an attack against inherent Ether or Armor by 100% per each point in this skill. Costs 15 Ether.
0/5
Skill gained at 1/5, "Chimera Strike."

Two more powerful options. Still, when something required four skills to unlock, he just felt that it was going to be devastating. So, he tried to ignore these new options. The only thing that would have gotten his attention was a 'speak to animals' skill. Maybe that was another reason he hadn't tried to open tier five skills yet...

He closed his screens for now and found a very different world in his eyes. It was somewhere near December or January, and there was snow on the ground as far as he could see in all directions. However, now he suddenly could see different textures upon that snow. Places where snow drifts accumulated and other places where the wind had blown it thinner. He had long since gotten used to the cold at the altitude Azoth flew, but ever since he took the Chimera Skin option, he found that the cold didn't bother him. Yet, up here, after selecting Senses, he could distinguish between temperatures in pockets of air. When they passed through them, it was like a tingle on his skin that seemed to indicate decimal degrees of difference.

His ears even made out sounds of creatures below them and at times he caught smells wafting all the way up to them on the winds.

"Azoth, is this how you always see, and feel the world?" he asked as a smile settled onto his face. This was something he would have to get used to, but a warm reassurance from his bond told him that he would!

CHAPTER THREE

Rocky's senses continued to adjust to the setting sun and night's wildlife volume. It was like a changing of the guards in a way. The flying predators Azoth and he had been avoiding all day headed to roosts and treetops. Dark shadows then slunk out of caves and deep forests.

Despite still being able to see relatively well just from the moonlight, Rocky pointed to a lone building that still stood below them. "Azoth, that looks like an urgent care clinic or a library. Let's go check it out."

He hoped that there wouldn't be dead bodies inside, and was relieved when they landed to find unbroken glass windows with a clear view into the space. The industrial blinds were open and despite the blackness inside, with his improved senses, he could feel that it was empty. The double doors that led inside were dead bolted but a thinned version of Dark Tidings made quick work of the steel, allowing him to pull open the door.

Using Dark Cloak added a grayscale overlay to the interior of the building, and Rocky discovered that they were in a small used bookstore. It was one of those mom-and-pop type places where old hardcover books lined shelves and large leather chairs, currently covered in thick layers of dust, capped each row of books. He could almost smell that musty library odor and somehow it still relaxed his muscles.

A loud rattling came from the doorway and a glance made him roll his eyes; his pet was trying to force his bulk through the doorway.

"There is a delivery door around back, buddy.

"Did you get stuck and need my help getting back out?" he added as Azoth increased the rattling of the door frame, attempting to reverse directions. Rocky moved over and untangled the manticore's feathers, which were far harder and sturdier than a regular bird. "Now go around back and I will open the delivery door."

They spent the night in the delivery bay after that, because it got Azoth out of the snow and his pet couldn't get any farther into the building. Rocky was very tempted to go search the shelves for a good book, but as soon as he leaned into Azoth to relax, he fell asleep.

***

Rocky grilled the bear meat over a portable fireplace and smiled as he added some salt and pepper from small leather pouches that he pulled from his bag of holding. His cooking skill was increasing slowly, but he was probably prouder of its growth than any other skill he currently possessed. His problem seemed to be that he often started cooking and then got distracted by other tasks. Out here, when it was just Azoth and him, he only had to worry about his inner demons, and the meat. Cooking somehow became therapeutic every morning, a moment to tackle his inner thoughts and wrangle them into a positive goal for the day.

Azoth nudged him, reminding Rocky that he liked his treat-meat blue-rare. Smiling, he removed the seared piece from the grill with the tip of Dark Tidings, formed into a dagger, and threw the meat to the manticore. A pulse of warmth returned across the bond as he threw on another bear steak and salted the top side for his pet. After six more 'treats' for Azoth, Rocky plated his medium-rare cuts of bear steak and tucked into his breakfast.

He opened the metal delivery door and jumped back as a pile of snow fell in toward him. Blinking, he studied the fresh white of the world. It must have snowed a foot or more overnight, and soft white flakes were still floating down from the sky, adding to the already large snow drifts a micrometer at a time. He stared out at the pure white and took hold of his mental mood like Gary had coached.

"At least it won't be as cold out there if it's snowing," Rocky said and heard Azoth growl-whimper behind him. "Come on, buddy, I guarantee the air will be less cold than that day I thought my face was going to crack."

That got Azoth to chuff, and with a few more encouragements, he slunk out of the delivery area and into the snow beyond. Rocky mounted up and Azoth stopped jumping from foot to foot and pumped his powerful wings to bring them into the sky. Rocky touched his ear and his nanoweave under armor face guard covered up to his nose. Then he pulled out his nanoweave beanie from his bag and pulled it down over his ears.

He was certainly thankful for Knight's Resolve for helping him ignore fifty percent of the cold, and Chimera Skin for acclimatizing him to extreme temperatures. Still, this morning he was most thankful to the under armor for keeping him from being damp on top of the chill. Somehow the fabric acted like a scuba suit, insulating him from not only the air up here but also the moisture when it was snowing.

As Azoth winged away from their stop for the night, Rocky scanned the horizon, looking for some of the more recognizable mountains that would help him navigate British Columbia. The ski resorts were still particularly noticeable because of the areas that were cleared of adult trees. It looked almost like veins on the hills and mountains he passed. Perhaps that was why he located a ski resort he believed used to be Whistler.

It was tucked in with a group of other mountains, and from this distance, Rocky could make out a few posts with snow-covered signs that had probably been too small to convert to golems. He tapped Azoth on his left side and the big guy veered more south, and within another half hour they could see the ocean and a large island off the coast, which likely was

Vancouver Island. The signs of schools and broken houses became more common as they grew closer to one of the largest Canadian cities before the crash.

Then what looked like abominable snowmen moved into view as what could only be golems covered in snow meandered around a grouping of buildings. The buildings had flat roofs that were cleared of snow and Rocky assumed there were survivors here. As they grew nearer, he blinked. Instead of surrounding the buildings like he initially assumed, the golems were all formed up on a single side, facing the direction Azoth and he were arriving from.

There had been a few cases in the past where the size of the campus didn't allow the number of golems to fully ring it. Like in Toronto at York University, but in this case the golems were numerous and bunched close together. Behind the golems, silhouettes of humans on the cleared rooftops looked in their direction as well. Rocky turned as much as he could in the saddle he was strapped onto. There wasn't anything behind him but more snow. He leaned out and looked down. Nothing under them.

He scratched his head but didn't signal Azoth to land yet. Instead, he passed over the buildings and the people atop their roofs before continuing further into what clearly had been a populated city. Some snow-covered golems remained on this side of the standing structures, but they wandered aimlessly and didn't appear to ring the area he would have classified as the school. He signaled Azoth to descend and after about a thousand feet, he noticed evenly spaced poles with a rope strung between them. The golems on this side seemed to be patrolling beside the guide rope.

"Azoth, try a fly-by over that rope and near that large golem," Rocky shouted and indicated which side of Azoth he was indicating with a tap of his hand. Azoth banked and flew by two times before Rocky added, "Okay, try landing in the space beside the rope."

The golems didn't attack them when they touched down, and Rocky examined the posts and rope using Analyze.

Stainless Steel Post
Quality: Poor

The rope was similarly plain and so Rocky pointed back in the direction of the school grounds. "Azoth, I'm going to go talk with those survivors. Go hunt for something and I will call you using a mental pulse when I know they won't attack us."

They parted ways and Rocky pulled out a pair of snowshoes that had become more and more helpful since the onset of winter. Gary's group had been making the snowshoes in preparation for winter. Rocky had spent some additional time getting them more set up with a Territory and a few dungeons to make sure they were truly ready. Thus they gifted this pair to him. He couldn't help but smile as the snow squeaked beneath them and he followed the rope line back to the cluster of school buildings.

"Halt. No sudden movements or we will open fire," a voice commanded from somewhere in front of him. "I haven't seen you before, where did you come from?"

If it wasn't for Rocky's new senses, he wouldn't have been expecting the shouted words. With them, not only did he see the texture difference between the snow mounds and the white blankets the speaker was under, but he could also hear them breathing. He raised his hands above his head and turned toward the man slowly. The muzzle of some sort of rifle was trained on his chest, but Rocky was relatively sure that the ballistic bullet wouldn't be able to pierce his current armor, and skin. Even if it could, he had survived far worse injuries than a bullet over the last two months.

He could still hit your head, imbecile...

"I'm from the east and have been saving humans from golems on my trip west." Rocky pointed behind himself at the wandering golems who were patrolling along the rope line. Then with slow motions he changed his point to encompass the school behind the guards, where he knew more golems lined up. "Admittedly, this is the first time I have seen whatever is going on here, and you all probably don't need my help." He scratched his nanoweave beanie, and tried to give them a sheepish look.

"I was just coming to offer it anyway," he finished flippantly.

Some whispering broke out from the white blanket mounds and Rocky was surprised when he heard the whispers as clear as day.

"Should we tell him to go away? Or bring him to the student council?"

"He didn't immediately try to attack us..."

"Doesn't mean he means us no harm. He could have already attacked Emily Carr, UBC, or Simon Fraser..."

"No way! We would have heard something over the radio! Let's bring him to the council and they can decide what to do with him."

Someone in the back stood up and Rocky finally was able to Analyze the heavily garbed individual.

Spencer Hamilton
Journeyman-Madman
Level 8
Health Points: 520 / 520
Active Skills: 12
Passive Skills: 6

"Follow me," Spencer shouted and began moving back toward the school buildings. Rocky was surprised when he saw and heard eight other such groups hidden in and around the grounds. He wanted to ask questions of Spencer, but after his first attempt at small talk and the continued silence from the man, he wasn't willing to try again.

The people here had quite a bit of security and were on a hair trigger. If the whispered conversation told him anything, it was that they expected attacks. But who were they defending against?

Spencer climbed a set of metal stairs and opened a set of steel double doors on the side of a gray building. It kind of looked like a hockey arena and Rocky glanced around, noticing that between this and other standing buildings there were literal city blocks of space. He scratched his head, trying to figure out what school this was and how come he didn't know it, if it had such a big campus.

Once he was inside, he realized he was, in fact, in some sort of sports center. He could still smell the lingering stale sweat he associated with hockey, basketball, and other such sports. He also recognized the large, white brick hallways as something associated with such facilities. Off these hallways there would be numerous team rooms, therapy rooms, and multiple access points to the inner arena or arenas.

He took in a deep breath, relishing in the memories of a past life those smells brought.

"Okay, I'm going to need you to hand over all your gear and uncover your face before I bring you in to see the council," Spencer said as two additional guards that had been standing inside and beside the four doors moved to flank Spencer. Now that the original guard was taking off his own cold weather gear, Rocky could tell that he was dealing with a young man. To his relative surprise, the two guards that offered their support were also young.

He shrugged and touched his ear before removing his beanie and putting it on the floor beside him. Once his beard was free of the face shield, he took a moment to un-mat it before removing his leather armor and stacking it to the side as well. He wasn't too worried about any one piece of gear, since he was the one who enchanted these sets for himself and he had backups in his bag. Spencer and the two guards blinked.

"Is that all the gear you were wearing? How did you not freeze to death?" one of the guards asked, his voice a mixture of skepticism and awe as he glanced between Spencer and Rocky.

"Don't ask me, Dave. The guy literally came from the rope leading into the city schools, but claims to have come from the east. I'm leaving it up to the council to make sense of," Spencer responded and pointed behind Rocky toward a side tunnel that likely led to the arena this building housed. "Come on, follow me," Spencer added with a turn.

CHAPTER FOUR

To enter the arena was a slightly surreal moment for Rocky, who actually played in numerous such places in the past. The hallway they walked used to be a Zamboni entrance onto the ice. Halfway down the hall, he found himself looking at hockey boards but instead of ice, the space had large planks of hardwood that were clearly made to fit the floor of the oval-like space. He assumed that the boards could be removed and that somewhere in the building was a basketball court as well. The tiered seating was green and the familiar yellow paint on the concrete stairs brought a small smile to his face. There was only one level of seating and no upper bowls like people might expect to see in large, professional team arenas.

At the far side of the oval from their entrance, there was a slightly raised stage that appeared to be made of the same composite hardwood as the floor Rocky now squeaked across. Up on the stage, there were tables facing away from him and into the stands. From his vantage he thought he counted fifteen people sitting at the table. In the stands outside of the boards, there were additional people seated and one person standing at the center of the stairs. He was standing at the bottom and clearly addressing the council through an area where the plexiglass had been removed. Rocky's ears easily picked out what the man was saying as soon as they entered the Zamboni tunnel.

"The University of British Columbia needs some new sets of gear that are more appropriately scaled for the level of our hunters. The gear your dungeon created for us in the past was fine for Apprentice ranks, but now at the Journeyman levels, our hunters need something stronger."

Rocky rounded the corner and Spencer ushered him into a seat just outside the doorway off the playing surface. So, he got to watch the council look at each other before all the eyes settled on a woman in the middle of the table. The looks carried hints of concern and while the woman sat with her arms folded in front of her looking nonplussed, he thought he could see some tightening in her jaw. He Analyzed the speaker and the woman.

—

Arthur Sones
Apprentice-Trader
Level 23
Health Points: 160 / 160
Active Skills: 0
Passive Skills: 5

—

Jessica Benli
Journeyman-Adventurer
Level 12
Health Points: 480 / 480
Active Skills: 7
Passive Skills: 1

—

Despite the tightness in her jaw and around her eyes, she still carried a calming aura. Maybe it was the way everyone looked to her for an answer, but Rocky immediately felt himself liking the woman. She had long dark hair, skin the color of milk chocolate, and she looked athletic. Like she could stand up and play a few games of basketball or soccer and be right at home, no matter the sport.

"I'm afraid we don't have gear that is higher level than the gear we sent back with you a few weeks ago. While the dungeon is gaining levels consistently, it still isn't producing gear at the quality you're requesting—"

"Do I need to remind the Fraser Valley Council that it is UBC and our hunters that provide you with most of your food? If our hunters are put at risk because we can't armor them correctly, then we may need to stop some of our more dangerous hunts…" Arthur intoned, his voice attempting to sound saddened but coming across threatening.

Jessica's lips pressed together tightly, and Rocky heard her knuckles crack as she clenched her fists. He expected an outburst from the twenty-something year old woman, but she took a deep breath before smiling.

"Perhaps, you would like some of the hunters from UFV to help? We could take some of the night shifts for your dungeon." He felt an eyebrow raise at Jessica's words. First because of the acronym that clearly stood for University of Fraser Valley—it almost seemed like she was using it because Arthur had used his acronym for University of British Columbia. Did some of the old rivalries between the schools still exist?

Still, there was clearly more than just school rivalry going on, and the other byplay happening Rocky couldn't understand. He could, however, understand that Arthur was representing one faction in the area and Jessica another. Clearly, they traded goods for the betterment of each group, and just as clearly that relationship was at a tipping point.

He listened to the two continue but eventually tuned them out. It was almost petty to listen to after a time. He did discover that Fraser Valley had stores of food from nearby farmlands they had smartly seized in the early days of the apocalypse but since it was winter, those were dwindling. He also learned that UBC had access to the ocean, and a relatively protected area between Vancouver Island and the mainland, which gave their 'hunters' access to an abundance of fish with very little risk, but again the winter was hindering that endeavor. Fraser Valley obviously had a dungeon that dropped a great deal of locked gear, whereas UBC had a dungeon that contained a great deal of edible creatures.

He couldn't help but shake his head at the two. The fact that they were acting as two separate groups instead of one large entity bothered him. It was discouraging how often he ran into this. Toronto had been his first such experience but since then, every large group of survivors he met usually clutched their resources to themselves and protected them jealously from humans and monsters alike. He assumed it was because everyone still expected the other shoe to drop, another disaster to strike, and he couldn't blame them, he supposed. He was just grateful that once he established a Territory and the people had an abundance of resources, they seemed to be more capable of sharing.

Then again, I never stayed around long enough to ensure they didn't return to their old ways…

Somehow through the conversation, the two agreed to a set amount of locked gear in trade for a shipment of fish and meat. As soon as Arthur sat down, Spencer climbed the stage and whispered to a man on the wings of the table. The man glanced at Rocky and then stood up. "A man who claims to come from the east has requested a meeting with the student council."

Rocky Analyzed the man who was standing. He had neatly parted gray hair and wrinkled skin. For him to be sitting on something called the student council seemed slightly strange, but he supposed there was no age restriction on learning. Still, when he came up as a level twenty-one Educator class, he couldn't help but grin as he stood up. Flint, the Educator's name, motioned for him to move to the spot the last man had occupied, and Rocky could clearly make out disgruntled muttering and a few insults from the others who he must have just usurped in line.

"Where exactly from the east did you come from, and how did Spencer, a western guard, find you?" Jessica asked, leaning forward in her chair to study him. At first, she looked skeptical of his story, but his level likely made her question that particular stance.

"I'm from the Algonquin Park area, in Ontario. However, most recently from the University of Calgary." Whispering broke out from behind and in front of Rocky as the students and the council began speculating on the truth of that last statement. Instead of continuing, he stood there and waited for silence. He didn't need to prove anything to these people, nor could he, if he was honest.

Jessica raised a hand and silence eventually fell again.

"Your claim seems a little far-fetched, Chimera Knight. How exactly were you able to come so far west?" she asked once the room grew relatively silent.

"Before I answer that, I would like to know how you managed to keep the golems from ringing that pathway out there or ringing your campus like I've seen most other places?" Rocky countered.

"That's simple. One of our campus buildings got destroyed in the early days by some sort of roosting bird creature. When the golems ringed our campus, they chased away the creature, but we discovered that pieces of that building still held whatever power wards the golems away. So, we simply used chunks of that building to herd the golems while simultaneously connecting ourselves to other groups." Jessica waved her hand as if what they had discovered wasn't incredible. Rocky felt his eyebrows climb up to his hair line throughout her description.

"Well, that was extremely resourceful," he began, under his breath. Despite not wanting to be impressed, he found himself unable to not comment on the ingenuity they had displayed. "As for how I got here, I have a pet manticore that flew me across the continent." He waved his hand in the same gesture Jessica had done. Jessica's face broke into a wide smile at his mimicry and Rocky felt some of his stress melt. He knew he liked her on first impression for a reason.

"Well then, Rockland—"

"Rocky will be fine," he interjected.

"Okay Rocky, I will need to meet your pet for proof. But why have you come so far west? If you found other groups of survivors, why not make yourself at home there? You're clearly high-leveled, and any group would be happy to accept you."

"I've created four Territories in the 'provinces' I passed through and planned to create one here as well. Territories—"

"Hold on a minute, sir. We have a Territory just east of us, that's why we herded all the golems over there. They currently protect us and the other groups of survivors from the huge white wolves that are inside. Are you trying to tell me that you can kill creatures like that and conquer a safe zone?" Flint interrupted Rocky, and Rocky couldn't help but smile as he pulled the Territorial orb from the grizzly den out of his bag of holding.

"Yes, to most of your questions, but not exactly to the safe zone. It creates an area that is safer, but not safe. And also, no to me needing to kill those creatures to start a Territory. I just need to place this on the ground, and I can create a Territory that's approximately a thousand square acres." The grizzly den had been about double that size, but most captured orbs only gave half the original size once placed again.

Murmurs broke out, and suddenly the angry insults and mutters from behind him turned into curious speculation. Or excited exclamations. Rocky just smiled and turned to Jessica. "Would you like to meet my pet Azoth before or after we establish the Territory?"

***

"He's huge!" Jessica said as she reached up to stroke Azoth's barrel chest through his thick, black lion's mane. Rocky shook his head and passed on the 'that's what she said' joke that had been presented. Azoth's purring was vibrating the rocks under him, and he wanted the praise to stop so he could set up the Territory already.

Rocky's impatience stemmed from the hours below in the arena listening to the council discuss plans for their new Territory, as well as listening to everyone bring up petitions or grievances they had with Fraser Valley. To truly capture the frustration of those petitions would be difficult to explain, but Rocky sat through five people who felt that they should be given a piece of the broken building on Fraser Valley's campus so they could go reclaim their houses. There was a part of him that wanted them to be allowed to Darwin themselves out of the current world by the end of those arguments.

"Sorry to interrupt the preening, but the sooner I set up the Territory, the sooner you will have contact with the others to begin requesting the aid you might need," Rocky interjected and got some side-eye from Azoth for his troubles.

The council jumped back and apologized multiple times to Rocky, who almost laughed at the show of Canadian culture.

"Alright, I should be right back." Rocky jumped onto Azoth's back and together they approached a spot approximately midway between the multiple intact buildings in the surrounding area. Listening to the petitioners and the council, Rocky had discovered that there was a collection of multiple schools and one hospital in Abbotsford, which was the city they currently resided in. There was a small lake that he could see from the roof of the current village and Jessica had indicated it as the best place to initiate the orb.

North of Mill Lake was Career Gate Community College, and south was Abbotsford Hospital. North and east were Sprott Shaw College buildings, and then southeast was where the UFV campus resided. Jessica claimed that there were many other groups that all functioned as a part of UFV's allied group, and she even claimed there was another campus closer to what used to be an airport.

The distance from the roof to the lake was less than a kilometer and was a short hop for Azoth with Rocky on his back. Still impatient, he slid off Azoth's back and immediately touched the orb to the ground. He was going to begin scrolling through the questions on autopilot when he realized that the very first question was different.

Are you sure you want to place a Territorial Orb near Akela's White Forest?
<Yes> | No
Warning: Placing a Territory next to an existing Territory can be viewed as an act of war by the inhabitants.

Since Rocky planned to attack the white wolves in that Territory anyway, he selected yes and that populated the next screen of choices.

Would you like to start a Territory centered around where this orb is placed or would you like to adjust the boundaries on the map?
Yes | <Map> | Cancel

Rocky selected the map and moved the large circle to encapsulate from Fraser Valley to as near Vancouver Island as he could manage. He noticed that whenever the circle touched ocean it would vanish, so he pulled it back and clicked accept.

What is the name of your new Territory?
<British Columbia>

As soon as he named the Territory, the ground began to rumble, and spectral tentacles shot out of the earth in the rough shape of what Rocky knew would be a Guild Dome and accompanying stunted tower. Stunted only in comparison to its far larger original that resided in Algonquin Park. Then Rocky was awarded a few quests he expected, but also a few notifications and quests he hadn't.

CHAPTER FIVE

Congratulations. You have completed a quest.
Hidden Quest
Personal Quest
Conquer a Territory
Vanquish a leader, boss, or super spawn, and claim a
Territory for yourself.
Rewards:
Territory Awarded
10,000,000 Etherience (+2,500,000 Knight's Quest)
Etherience has been increased since the owner already
has a leader class.
Great job, Leader!

—

Preservation of Life Champion Quest
Hidden Quest
Atlantean Net Generated
Secure the British Columbian Survivors
You have given the British Columbian Survivors a
higher chance of survival. Thanks to you, 212,159
survivors now reside inside the boundaries of a
Territory.
Rewards:
21,215,900 Etherience (+5,303,975 Knight's Quest)
Increased Reputation with Survivors
Atlantean Statutes, Preservation of Life, Section XIV

—

Congratulations! You have reached level 32 and 33!
2 stat points and 2 skill points awarded.
50,580,125 Etherience remaining until level 34.

—

You have initiated a Territorial War with Akela's White
Forest!

—

Congratulations! You are the first person on Gaia to capture 10,000 square acres of land in the form of Territories.
A teleportation pad has been set up between all Guild Domes and Towers.
Temporary Title awarded: Land Baron (waiting on confirmation)

—

Rocky felt his heart soar reading the first few notifications. Conquering Territories was a very fast way to gain Etherience, especially once paired with his Knight's Quest skill. Which was great news because of how much Etherience he needed. After the grind of over three hundred billion Etherience from level twenty-four to twenty-five, he had worried that the next level would take double that. Instead, the Etherience needed had dropped down to four hundred thousand from level twenty-five to twenty-six, and he had begun leveling faster again. He assumed that this was common, and meant that the Journeyman Ranks contained two difficult areas of leveling before one could advance to the Master ranks. Two of what Sela had termed 'the Grind' in the Apprentice ranks.

Remembering Sela and the teleportation pad was what made Rocky's heart sink as he reached the end of the new notifications. Rocky hurried to mount back up onto Azoth. His heartbeat was pounding as Azoth took to the sky. His mental mood was certainly better than it had been when he had run from the Battle of New York, but if his clone refusing to obey any of his orders was any indication, he wasn't ready to go back. Not yet.

Lately I can't even summon the clone without it trying to attack me...

"Let's start killing those wolves, Azoth," Rocky said and pointed in the direction where he could see the backs and fronts of many snow-covered golems. Azoth took off, but after a few wingbeats, Azoth's normal cadence of ups and downs changed, and Rocky's pet began beating his wings erratically. "You okay, buddy? Hey, what the—"

Something was suddenly beating Rocky around the head, and if the strange flapping gusts of wind were any indication, it was a bird. He formed his sword and turned to dissuade the attacking predator, only to be facing a human-sized black raven that he recognized instantly. He swallowed the lump in his throat and closed his eyes for a moment. Guess he didn't have a choice about when he was ready for this particular reunion.

His stomach instantly began doing backflips, and his throat tightened as Azoth began coasting back down to the ground. By the time Azoth landed and Rocky slid from the saddle, he couldn't have told you if he was happy to see Sela or upset. His emotions were just that much of a quagmire. Still, when he rounded Azoth to find the tall, well-toned woman scratching his pet's black fur, he landed on reluctantly jubilant. He still felt like he was going to be sick, and tears leaked from his eyes, but the smile that came onto his face was genuine as well.

Rocky opened and closed his mouth several times, trying and failing to form words around his constricted throat muscles. Finally, Sela turned to him, and the look she wore instantly drained that smile right off his face. Her lips pressed together, and her brows furrowed as she pointed at Rocky.

"You have been gone for more than two moons!" Sela said, her voice quiet but strong. Her eyes closed and her head fell a moment after. "I did not think you would stay away this long…" she mumbled toward the dirt.

"I'm sorry, Sela. I couldn't face the Territory and the people in it after—after what happened…" Rocky still couldn't bring himself to say those words. At night, he woke up in a cold sweat whenever he recalled his brain's snapshots of his family's limbs on the ground. Those limbs and the surrounding blood was all that Rocky could find of his family after Dahrix's attack.

Sela's head flashed up and she studied his face. After a moment she tilted her head, and asked, "You cannot face the Territory because of your family's missing limbs?"

"I just can't. Okay, Sela? I failed, and whenever I try to picture returning to Algonquin Gorge, my entire body begins to sweat." Rocky wiped his forehead, and his hand came away drenched despite the cold. If this conversation was with anyone else, Rocky likely wouldn't have even admitted that much, but with Sela he went a step further. "I can't bring myself to add their names to that wall. I'm getting better, thanks to some—"

"Wait, what wall would you have to update? The one outside of Maximus?" Sela interjected, her voice sounding confused, which surprised Rocky. Couldn't she hear the hurt in his voice? Why was she interrupting him? Yeah, sure. He was about to tell her he was getting over it slowly and healing, but cutting him off seemed a little insensitive.

Maybe she's over me. I ran away for two months, and we were only together for like a week. What did I expect?

He froze, looking at her with his mouth hanging open. He closed it and wet his lips before trying to answer that rather blunt question. Yet, he just made small noises when he tried to force the words out. Tears threatened to overflow from his eyes and the lump in his throat felt solid and substantial. After what felt like a full minute but could only have been a second, he nodded his head and looked away. While he liked Sela, maybe even loved her, he couldn't bring himself to let her see him cry. Not after her rather callous interjection, which likely meant that their relationship had moved to platonic.

"What in the Nine Rainbow Realms is going on? Do you not know that your family lived? Or are you thinking of putting someone else's name on the Wall of Remembrance?" Sela asked as she scrutinized Rocky's face.

Rocky tilted his head and studied her face. The words replayed in his head on a loop, but they didn't have true meaning, yet. His family lived?

Did she just mean Benoit? Because he assumed that part, but he didn't want to face his brother-in-law after failing to keep Nadine and Lacy safe, either. His stomach did somersaults now just thinking about 'Daeric Nallo,' his brother-in-law's chosen name after the crash. No, Sela wasn't one to waste words…

"What do you mean, Sela?" Rocky croaked out. He could feel metaphorical fingers grasp onto the small hope she was offering. He swallowed saliva that invaded his mouth as he waited for her response.

"Your family is alive and in the Grotto! Have you thought that they were dead this entire time?" Sela hesitated, looking torn between running to Rocky and hugging him, and being frustrated with him. When he fell on his butt, and tears really began pouring down his face, she made the decision and rushed to him. She slid on the ground and wrapped her arms around his head.

"I'm sorry, I thought you knew they were alive. Your shadow clone was the one who brought them to me, after all… I wish I had known… You must have been going through so much…"

Rocky only made sense of some of her words as she allowed him to cry into her shoulder and chest. The dreams he had woken from in a cold sweat often depicted him dropping their beat up and mangled bodies at her feet. In those dreams, he tried to talk to her and failed; tried to cast Dark Mend on Nadine and Lacy, but nothing happened. He thought it was some sort of inner guilt manifesting. To find out that it had been his shadow clone trying to tell him something…

No wonder it hasn't been doing anything when I summoned it. It's been trying to force me to see something.

Its miming acts and fists took on a very different meaning with this new realization. It had often pointed back toward Algonquin Valley, or held up two fingers before pointing in that direction. It had even gone as far as trying to spell their names in the dirt, but as soon as Rocky had seen the letters, he angrily unsummoned the clone which was a part of himself, but also not. Sela had told him that it was a part of his subconscious and he just assumed that meant it was trying to force him to face the tragedy.

The tragedy that I believed had occurred...

His body temperature went from cold to scalding hot, and he stood up with Sela still on his neck. "So, my sister's arm and my mother's leg?" he asked pointedly as he grabbed Sela's shoulders and held her away to look at her eyes.

She looked away for a second before meeting his eyes with her shimmering blue ones. "They have robotic prosthetics right now, but we have a few healers in the Grotto that are leveling up and may get a skill that will regrow limbs..."

Rocky pointed back toward the spectral vines that were currently constructing a Guild Dome and Tower. "Can we use that to teleport back, right now?" he asked, his excitement throwing all trepidation and caution out of his body.

Sela shook her head. "The pad on this side isn't formed yet, so we can't use it until construction is done. And even then, we would need this tower to store up some Territorial Etherience, first..."

The structure would take twenty-four hours to finish construction, which wasn't too long of a wait. But Rocky didn't want to wait. His family was alive. Rocky turned to Azoth. "If needed, can you make the flight back to Algonquin in one go?"

Azoth chuffed, which Rocky took as an affirmative. He turned to Sela and asked, "Can you make the flight in your raven form?"

She blinked and looked at Azoth and Rocky before realization came onto her face. "You must not have found a skill that lets you hear Azoth yet." She pointed to the large black manticore. "He just told me that he could carry us both back and still have energy to hunt." Sela reached into a pocket and held out a ring. "I've had this for about a moon, and kind of forgot about it."

Ring of the Amalgam
This ring was created when four creatures were fused together to create <u>Skandranon:</u> The Algonquin Chimera. This ring was the core they fused around.
Soul Link V
If the owner of this ring has an amalgam as a pet, this ring will create a Soul Link between them. Soul Link allows the owner and pet to communicate telepathically (when in range), feel each other's location, and send out distress signals that can be perceived no matter the distance.
Soul Link will also link the pet's soul to its owner, allowing a deceased pet to resurrect at the owner's location. Resurrection can take days or years depending on the Ether concentration of the area and Ether required to revive the pet. Resurrection can only be used once every ten years.

Rocky took the ring in shaky hands and slowly slid it onto his finger. He felt the link he always had with Azoth tingle as the enchantment sent a pulse of Ether along it. In his mind's eye, he watched the unseen but tangible connection gain a hollow tube of blue Ether.

<Rocky hear Azoth?> his pet asked, his voice just as deep and simultaneously childishly simple as Rocky

remembered. He smiled and felt a new batch of tears leak from his eyes as he nodded.

<Good. Rocky stink, need bath badly. Azoth want to fly back too and see family. Sela says Rocky need bath too…> Rocky's smile faded off his face as Azoth filled his head with his thoughts. He held up an arm and sniffed his armpit…

Yep, they were right… he did need a—

A howl that was shortly joined by a multitude of other howls cut off his thoughts, and the strange reunion between his pet and him.

"Oh, right…" he muttered. He had completely forgotten about a war he just started with Sela's news of his family.

The nearby Territorial Leader has issued a challenge and is attacking your newly formed Territory. Defeat the Territorial Leader of Akela's Den or risk losing your new Territory.

CHAPTER SIX

Sela, who could read his notifications, frowned and looked in the direction of the howls. "If we kill the Territorial Leader and take its orb, we should be able to use its secondary effect to gain enough Territorial Ether to teleport back to Algonquin…" she suggested.

A part of Rocky didn't want to wait a single moment now that he knew his family still lived. Yet, it would likely take Azoth a minimum of eight hours to reach the Gorge and now that he remembered the war he just started, he couldn't really just leave the people of Fraser Valley or the other schools to fight the wolves alone. Right?

He sighed before nodding to Sela when she looked back at him and together, they turned to Azoth.

<Azoth revenge mom.> Azoth growled in confirmation of his readiness.

His pet's eagerness to fight reminded Rocky that he had deliberately avoided a few Territories that they had flown over on the way here. They had specifically avoided packs of creatures, and a few plant-based Territories. The latter only after they had entered a Territory in Manitoba and the foliage within had tried to kill them. They hadn't even managed to move into the area by more than twenty feet before they were forced to retreat from a vine that didn't seem to understand personal space. Azoth's reminder of the Steel Wolfpack was a sobering thought.

"We may want to get some help…" Rocky suggested. In response, a large thumping beat of a crash came from the direction of the wolf howls and golems.

"Orr," Rocky drew out the word as his eyebrow raised, "they will attack the non-sapient golems and we can attack the pack one at a time." He grinned wildly and realized the opportunity UFV had created for them by herding the golems together. Sela didn't smile back, her face almost looking upset as Rocky mounted onto Azoth. He held a hand out to Sela, who seemed to pause for a moment before taking hold and swinging up behind him.

Why had she paused? Maybe he was imagining it.

It was a short hop for Azoth from the frozen lake to the battle, but in that time they gained enough height to get a feel of the wolves and the battlefield below. There were seven in total engaged with the golems who had the numerical advantage, but were clearly losing out in terms of power. All seven of the wolves seemed to exude some sort of smoke from their backs and thanks to Rocky's Chimera Senses he could hear the crackle of the snow and perhaps soil underneath the golems as the fog struck them. Azoth circled overhead and Rocky felt the change in temperature of the area on his skin. His breath fogged out in front of him in a thick mist and instantly formed ice crystals.

What is that fog? Liquid nitrogen....?

<Azoth, land near the edge and stay away from that fog,> Rocky sent his pet as he guessed at the wolf's skill. As Azoth performed a wingover and changed his path to the side, Rocky Analyzed the largest wolf he could see.

Lesser Wolf of Akela
Master-White Fang
Level 49
Health Points: 7400 / 8300
Active Skills: 13
Passive Skills: 12

All the other wolves' information was the same, with slight variations in levels or skill distribution. The leader wasn't even present? Rocky felt himself begin to sweat, but thanks to the extreme cold, he also felt that sweat freeze in his pores.

As soon as they landed on the eastern edge of the fight, he turned to the dismounting Sela. "The leader wasn't with this group. Any idea where it would be?"

Sela slid off the saddle and shook her head. "No, I didn't see it either, but it might not be attacking?"

Rocky joined her on the ground. "I think that fog is freezing anything it touches. I don't think we can attack them from melee range. If we get too close, the golems will attack us too…" he stated.

Sela nodded and turned to Azoth. A moment later Azoth growled but flew back into the sky. Rocky gave Sela a questioning look.

"I asked him to scout from above and look for the leader," she supplied.

It sure is going to be helpful being able to direct him like that again!

Rocky's lip quirked up at the thought, but he couldn't dwell on it too long thanks to the large rumbling growls of the wolves. Instead, he nodded and asked, "Any ideas on how we should fight these things?"

Sela, who had been wearing a straight face, turned away slightly to face the battle. A smile bloomed on her face finally and the effect was somewhat menacing. "You aren't the only person to have leveled up."

Rocky Analyzed her as she held her hands up toward the sky.

Selaphelia Ardensai
Journeyman-Dark Druid
Level 23
Health Points: 775 / 775
Active Skills: 7
Passive Skills: 3

She had gone up at least fourteen levels since he last saw her, and since she was nearing the end of the first grind in the Journeyman ranks, she was about to hit a breakthrough. He watched as a ball of purpley-white formed in the air sixty feet above the nearest wolf. The ball grew until it looked to be the same size as the sun, which was above it in the sky. Then a huge beam of the same purplish energy lanced down and struck the entirety of the wolf.

Rocky felt his eyes widen comically as the wave of heat hit him. "What was that?!" he asked, his question reactionary as the purple afterimage of the beam began to fade.

"Moon Fire," Sela called over her shoulder. The snow all around the wolf had completely melted and the brown and gray earth beneath was steaming. The wolf itself no longer spewed the white fog, and instead had licking purple flames lightly coating its body.

Rocky's Analyze told him that its health was falling periodically from just below half. That kind of damage didn't go unnoticed, and the wolf leaped out of the crater in the snow and locked eyes with Sela.

Rocky triple charged his Dark Blade and added Envenom onto it as well. He hoped he wouldn't have to fight it in melee range where Envenom would be effective, but now that the fog wasn't spewing forth, he was hopeful that if he did have to, he wouldn't become a popsicle. He released the three stacks in a horizontal slash and watched the three phantasmal blades slowly grow farther apart until the bottom two collided with the wolf's open jaws.

He was congratulating himself when the wolf's teeth glowed red and sucked in his two blades. The force of his Dark Blade still halted the wolf's forward motion for a moment, but it began its charge again as soon as the phantasmal projections were gone. He groaned when his third blade chopped the head off the two golems that had been chasing after the lesser wolf. He recharged three stacks of Dark Blade but held it on his blade this time as he began to run at the wolf.

Sela's summoned vines grabbed at the loping wolf's paws and Rocky could hear the pings as the vines broke like musical instrument strings. Just as he and the wolf were ten feet from each other, he entered Stealth and Dark Cloak simultaneously while jumping to his left. When his foot touched back down onto the hard-packed snow, he summoned his shadow clone and hoped it would work. He felt the Ether in his pool drop but didn't see his clone. Mentally shrugging, Rocky brought his sword up above his head and slashed at the creature's leading foot just as it pinged through another vine.

His blade bit, the combination of Dark Blade and its new levels too much for the lesser wolf's inherent Ether. He felt the blade tremble slightly in his hand in a sensation he wasn't yet used to. It almost felt like the blade was salivating at the blood that now coated its length.

The strike didn't cut through the limb, but the black poison of his Dark Blade quickly spread. The wolf whimpered but continued toward Sela, who was still the larger threat after her Moon Fire skill. Two steps later, it collapsed as all four of its legs became rigid. Rocky caught a glimpse of his clone with two daggers sunk deeply into the creature's back as it tumbled and sprayed up snow.

"What was that?!" Sela asked, her tone nearly mirroring his original question to her.

"Poison Pool, I think," he responded as he glanced at the notification in his combat log that showed the debuff he had just inflicted on the wolf.

Poison Pool
(Hemotoxin, Latrotoxin, Urushiol, Necrotoxin, Cytotoxin)

Potent Hemotoxin – This venom destroys blood cells and skin tissues. It causes internal hemorrhaging. Max damage is 10 health per second. Lasts a maximum of thirty seconds.

Potent Latrotoxin – This venom causes severe muscle pain and spasms. This may cause the nervous system of a victim to function strangely. Max damage is 1 health per five seconds. Lasts a maximum of seven days.

Potent Urushiol – This poison causes an allergic reaction in most victims and severe skin rashes, if applied to the surface of the skin. If ingested or injected, the victim can suffer severe itching and burning in the location. Max damage is 1 health per five seconds. Lasts a maximum of three days.

Potent Necrotoxin – This is a Hemotoxin variant that can cause dermonecrotic lesions. This venom can cause the breakdown of muscles and even organs if applied to areas. Max damage is 30 health per second, if applied to vital organs. Lasts a maximum of thirty seconds.

Potent Cytotoxin – This venom can destroy healthy cells within the body. This can slow the healing of wounds significantly. Effects: Reduces natural healing of a wound to zero for a maximum of ten days.

Current cumulative venom effect: 15-45 damage per second for thirty seconds, reduced recovery, and partial paralysis.

All potent-ranked venoms or poisons grant immunity to similar toxins for the Chimera Knight.

Rocky and his clone finished this first wolf off as it lay twitching on the ground. He looked to the other six still engaged with the golems as he swept the loot and corpse into his bag of holding. He felt the weight of this corpse despite it being reduced by ninety percent.

Sela must have noticed him flinch slightly because her frown returned as she said, "Put it in the Territorial Inventory for now," as she walked up.

She opened a screen right after and wolf-whistled at it. Rocky glanced at the screen as she sidled up beside him. It was the information on his Poison Pool skill.

"That's an impressive skill," she complemented.

"When it works, it's great, but trust me, it wasn't pleasant getting each of these poisons to the Potent rank." Rocky watched Sela's mouth twist and she hurriedly looked away from him.

<Wolves suddenly attacking gray building!> Azoth shouted into Rocky's mind. He assumed Sela's too because she glanced in the direction Azoth was indicating. They both turned to look back and began sprinting over the snow in unison, abandoning the current fight to the golems. They could easily see the backs of the wolves as they tore literal holes in the Abbotsford Center's aluminum siding. People fired from the roof of the building at the four wolves that were attacking, but if the skill-infused strikes were doing anything, it was difficult to tell from this distance.

The truly heart-stopping part for Rocky was that he could see the white fog streaming to the ground from where they were, running over the snow.

<Azoth, come pick us up, land in our path!> Rocky mentally shouted as they continued to try to close the few miles between them and the building.

<Azoth distract!> his pet responded and Rocky watched in horror as Azoth dive bombed the wolves. From here it was hard to tell the exact size disparity, but it was clear that Azoth was still smaller than the wolves. During Azoth's assault, Sela and he continued to charge forward.

They arrived just under a minute later and saw that Azoth had made the right decision. Thankfully, Rocky's pet had chosen to stay airborne instead of landing or coming to pick them up. The wolves had been forced to circle up against the threat Azoth represented, and each pass by the manticore was punctuated by leaping wolves. Rocky Analyzed all four and found the leader along with three female wolves, which were called Lunas.

Fae Wolf of Akela
Master-Dominator
Level 49
Health Points: 7,912 / 10,333
Active Skills: 13
Passive Skills: 12

—

Akela
Master-Pack Sire
Level 73
Health Points: 15,000 / 15,000
Active Skills: 25
Passive Skills: 5

As Rocky and Sela looked on, they noticed that Akela had some sort of self-healing skill. They watched him glow white before multiple cuts on his back from Azoth closed over. The three Lunas were circling Akela, some guarding his throat while others attempted to leap up and strike Azoth out of the air on each pass. Rocky glanced at the Abbotsford Center and saw Jessica mobilizing a great deal of people on the building's flat roof. A quick head turn in the direction of the other nearby buildings showed him even more people on-route.

"Sela, are they bunched up enough for Moon Fire to strike them all?" he asked, and Sela held her hands up above her head in response. Rocky charged his sword with both Dark Blade and Envenom, hoping to incapacitate all four of them after their freezing auras were negated.

The purple orb of Sela's Moon Fire formed and grew in the sky and Azoth made one more pass at the group which helped keep them close together. The circle of light lanced from the ball and met something pure white midway to the ground. The white semi-sphere grew brighter as if it was being fed from Sela's spell. The interior of the dome filled with the white fog and relatively quickly the four wolves were occluded from Rocky's view. Then multiple beams of blue shot from inside.

Before Rocky could blink, a beam struck Azoth, and Rocky felt his pet's pain as the beam collided with his underbelly and then his wing as he banked away in reaction. Another beam targeted Sela and Rocky shot an arm out, pushing her away as he tried to simultaneously dodge in the opposite direction.

The blue beam missed Sela but caught his arm and shoulder before he managed to extricate it. He found a layer of frost coating the nanoweave under armor and his leather gloves. His skin under the shoulder armor, and his arm itself, were entirely numb. For a moment, he feared that the interior was frozen solid but when he bent his elbow, he found that it was just a layer of frost on the surface.

Thank Gaia for Chimera Skin.

<Azoth, are you okay?> he sent.

<Azoth fine! Wing no fold. Come to Rocky,> his pet responded.

Rocky breathed a sigh of relief and returned to assessing his own damage. He could feel a deep heat from inside of his arm begin pushing back the numbness and a quick check of the area in his mind's eye showed him that the heat was coming from the Ether Channel there. Whether this was due to his passive Knight's Resolve or a combination of Ether Channels, Knight's Resolve, and Chimera Skin didn't matter as he assessed the direction of the other beams. The siding of the building and even some of the roof was covered in a thick layer of ice that looked more similar to a glacier than Rocky liked. He couldn't see any human popsicles at the edge and hoped that the people up there had ducked behind cover in time.

A glance at the reinforcements showed Rocky that a few people hadn't managed to dodge the blast as the survivors attempted to crack them out of their ice prisons. From this distance, it was impossible for Rocky to assess if they were still alive. The other beams seemed to have missed people altogether or been aimed poorly as he couldn't see any targets in the angles he thought he recalled them traveling along.

The white dome came down and the fog inside coalesced over each of the three Lunas, giving them a layer of white armor, and an extra two tails each. Akela was still glowing white, and Rocky assumed it was one of his skills strengthening the three others. The ballistic shots resumed from the roof of the Abbotsford Center and Rocky watched as they seemed to sink into the white armor. The health of the three Fae Wolves didn't drop and he growled. This was going to be a much more difficult fight than he originally believed.

Howls sounded from the direction of the battle between the non-sapient golems and the six lesser wolves. The noise caused Rocky to peek in that direction. His blood froze as he saw six of the beasts loping toward them behind Azoth.

CHAPTER SEVEN

At least I know now where the beams that I thought missed us went...

The six wolves running in near unison over the snow toward them made Rocky tense. Each footfall seemed to send a small shudder through the ground under them. A glance behind him showed Akela and his three Lunas begin attacking the building again, as they tried to get to the people firing from the roof. In less than ten seconds, they were going to be between the Territorial boss, his elite Lunas, and those six minions.

Five booms behind Rocky interrupted any strategy he was beginning to form. He turned back around to find snow spraying up from the ground. What looked like five large green meteors crashed to earth. In the semi-transparent screen of snow, those rocks seemed to shimmer and move. A blink and some snow dispersal turned the rocks humanoid, and the figures unfurled into large golems holding weapons. Multiple other thumps sounded as smaller gray, brown, and black meteors formed craters on the ground as well.

"Glad that the reinforcements have arrived," Sela stated as she turned back to the four larger and stronger wolves nearer the building. Rocky, however, looked up at the sky, hoping he wouldn't see what he knew had to be there. There, up in the sky, was the Scourge starship. His heart stuttered because if it was here, what was defending the grotto?

"Sela, isn't that going to cause the creatures to mutate like it did in North Bay?! Also, what about the defense of my family in the Grotto?" Rocky shouted his worry. He realized he hadn't worried about the ship being above Alberta the previous night after the assault notifications, but honestly everything had changed ten minutes ago. Sela looked up just as the battleship turret began ionizing and discharging blasts into Akela's group of four wolves.

"In North Bay, we were attacking a Territory. Here we are defending our own Territory, so I don't think we have to worry. Also, the attacks on the Territory are evenly spaced out, so we have been making use of the ship for missions right after a successful defense." Sela shrugged but then pointed toward the dome shield that was back up around the four wolves. "We really need to find a way to lower that protection."

That addition brought his mind back to the fight.

The dome didn't extend all the way to the ground, so Rocky settled on melee combat at the same time Sela must have and together they charged toward the towering wolves. The Lunas and Alpha continued to tear and claw at the metal of the Abbotsford Center. The freezing fog from the Lunas was diverting to the armor they wore and Rocky hoped that meant its effects would be similarly dismissed as what Sela's Moon Fire skill had accomplished earlier. Using his Soul Blade, he slashed at one of the Luna's feet, just below the wispy white armor. The blade sunk into the foot and his Dark Blade skill, along with Envenom, began spreading from the minor cut.

He ran to the next target, hoping he could afflict each of them before they turned on him. He scored a small cut on all four of the creatures before he opened his combat log and checked their ailments status. Two of the four were fully afflicted by all of Rocky's poisons, but Akela and one of the Lunas had only been hit with the Cytotoxin. Azoth's black bulk struck Akela from the ground as Rocky watched, and the two large predators became a tangle of limbs. He grit his teeth as he watched his friend's wings pump furiously as they rolled. Thanks to Azoth's heroics, the battleship's barrage managed to strike one of the paralyzed Lunas.

Rocky assessed the reason for the change and realized that the shield was centered around Akela.

<Azoth, try to push Akela away from the three Lunas!> he mentally shouted to his pet before he charged at the single

Luna who was turning to protect her Alpha. He slashed at the back leg of the Fae wolf and watched as the white gossamer fog sparked against the dark black of his skilled blade. His weapon rebounded and Rocky rolled with the new opposing force, trying to avoid stabbing himself. The two Fae wolves that were afflicted by his poisons and venoms were turning into blinding light displays as continuous ballistics, beams, and skills sparked off the foggy armor. However, each strike seemed to dissipate a small portion of that thick white fog, and he thought he could see red coating some areas of their fur.

Sela's vines tripped up the remaining Fae wolf as she attempted to attack Azoth, and that pause allowed Rocky to regain his feet and close back in to try another strike. The blade parted flesh and this time the Latrotoxin and Urushiol took hold, which caused both an allergic reaction and muscle spasms to occur. Sela, in the form of a large black sabretooth, leaped onto the skull of the spasming wolf and bit down into the base. Rocky continued past, leaving this creature to Sela, needing to help Azoth with the Territorial boss.

<Azoth, are you okay?> he mentally shouted and received mental grunts and growls in return. The fact that Azoth wasn't giving a running commentary worried him, and the mental whimper that came next made him pull out an Ether Draught, chug it, and charge his Dark Blade with everything he had. The jumble of black and white separated and Azoth stayed in a heap for a split second too long. Rocky instantly reabsorbed all his stacks of Dark Blade and used the Ether to cast four Dark Mends on his pet. That bottomed out his pool but to his relief, the spells took hold, meaning Azoth was alive.

The Ether headache tried to force Rocky into unconsciousness, but he refused to let the blackness at the edge of his vision have any foothold. Akela panged off what appeared to be a pane of glass that suddenly formed in mid-air. The boss bounced back to the ground just as a red Fireball exploded into the beast's side. Akela howled before starting to glow white. The flames licking at him shrank until they puffed out of existence, but two more Fireballs crashed home one after another. Thanks to the white fog coming off the boss, Rocky watched as the dome shield adjusted angles, focusing on the direction of the fireballs instead of the ballistics and starship's lasers.

Some of those projectiles sunk home now, but they didn't seem to damage the beast significantly. Rocky chugged three more Ether Draughts and watched as a few stacks of Toxic Blood jumped onto his interface. He didn't care.

Akela's back was to him and he could see where the dome ended. He ran forward, sprinting at his top speed as two Fireballs splashed over the dome shield, and the fires of the other two winked out. Rocky got below the wolf just as his Ether ticked up enough to allow him an eighth stack of Dark Blade.

He side-stepped twice and then leaped straight up, while simultaneously thrusting his sword out. When he felt he had his maximum velocity behind his thrust and jump, he released the eight strikes on a seventy-degree angle right at the stomach of Akela. The leading edge of his Dark Blade spun into the fur and muscle there. Then, as if the blow was a drill in hammer mode, the other eight edges crashed into the first, causing the powerful skill to dig into the inherent Ether. Rocky's shadow clone appeared out of thin air, launched itself into the front leg of the beast and began stabbing daggers into the limb as fast as it could.

Akela began to glow white again and Rocky groaned, having seen this particular skill cancel multiple others already. He shook his head, trying to clear the headache and sludge-like feeling from his brain. That was when a golden crown clamped around Akela's snout, head, and neck. The white glow that had been building to blinding again faded and Rocky was grabbed from behind and dragged away as a lightshow exploded down onto the beast from the ship. It was like watching fireworks in reverse. He glanced behind him to find Sela still in her sabretooth tiger form, dragging him back.

That glance also showed him the corpses of three Fae wolves and six lesser wolves a fair distance behind them. He closed his eyes and allowed the back of his head to rest on the snow under it, the ice cold temperature feeling good and easing his raging headache slightly. He focused on his breathing and entered meditation to further mitigate some pain as his Ether slowly ticked back up.

While he couldn't see the fight anymore, he could hear the constant percussive beats of numerous weapons discharging and impacting. According to that sound, Rocky didn't think Akela would survive the barrage that seemed to have no end.

***

"Sorry Rock, we need to take stock of the housing available in this Territory, as well as the number of people. Then we need to negotiate with the dungeons already on the premises and see which ones, if there are any, should be Cardinal dungeons. Plus, we need to appoint a leader, and give everyone the chance to join Meliora." Zippo ticked items off on his finger as he spoke. When he finished, he looked to Smith who nodded.

"Sorry Rocky, we need the Scourge on standby for at least the next twelve hours. Maybe longer, depending on what's in the area," Smith added with a disapproving frown.

"That's okay, Rockland has a few things that he needs to hear about before we head back to the Territory anyway. We will wait for the Guild Dome to finish and then use the teleport feature," Sela said while patting Rocky on the back.

"That is going to be a really useful tool for us moving forward, especially with the war against Frankie and Apep," Zippo said offhandedly.

Rocky felt his eyes widen and his intense worry return. Wait, the attacks were Frankie and Apep, not monsters? Sela must have given Zippo a look because his cheeks flushed, and he hurriedly turned away to go attend to something else. Smith offered a rather scathing look at Rocky before he followed Zippo.

"Is Smith mad at me?" Rocky asked Sela.

"He is not the only one, Rockland. We did not know why you had just left, so most people are confused at best, and at worst… let us go with…not happy." Sela reached out to pat his shoulder, thought better of it, and shook her head. Instead, she motioned to Azoth who was recovering nearby. "Let's go sit with Azoth, he needs to hear some of this news as well."

Rocky held up a hand and moved to loot all the wolf corpses first. When he looted Akela's corpse, a notification popped up instead.

Congratulations, you have successfully conquered a new Territory.
Akela's White Forest has been captured due to the death of its leader. Would you like to take ownership of the new Territory?
<Yes> | No
Would you like to place the Territory onto the Market?
Yes | <No>
Would you like to condense the Territory into a Territorial Sphere?
Warning! A transfer of this sort will sustain losses.
Yes | <No>

"Sela, if I choose to take ownership of the wolf's Territory, will its borders just get added to British Columbia's Territory?" he asked, and simultaneously remembered how nice it was to have a guide who knew much more about this world than he did.

"Yes, it will get added, but if you do that, we might not get enough Territorial Ether to teleport to Algonquin Gorge when the Dome finishes," Sela answered. Rocky selected yes after her answer. He didn't plan to wait for the teleport back. With Azoth or the Scourge, they could be back within six to twelve hours, anyway, so why waste the opportunity just for some Territorial Ether? As soon as the screen flashed off, a new golden notice popped up.

Congratulations to Rockland Barkclay. He is the first leader on Gaia to conquer and confirm ownership of five Territories. Title of Land Baron granted.

Sela read the notice and her frown deepened. She sighed and looked sharply at Rocky.

"That just got sent out to the entire planet, and believe me that isn't always a good thing…" she told him as she began stomping toward Azoth. Rocky closed the world announcement with a sigh and was rewarded with a second explaining the title, this time in the system's standard blue.

Land Baron
You own enough land to be considered a member of the nobility. This title gives all land held by the owner a 10% boost in Resources. This title also increases luck by one point for each Territory owned.

—

Congratulations. You have completed a quest.
Hidden Quest
Personal Quest
Conquer a Territory
Vanquish a leader, boss, or super spawn, and claim a Territory for yourself.
Rewards:

Territory Awarded
10,000,000 Etherience (+2,500,000 Knight's Quest)
Etherience increased since the owner already has a
leader class.
Great job, Leader!
36,988,743 Etherience remaining until level 34.

The two pieces of good news wouldn't likely balance out the bad news that Sela had just pointed out. If everyone on the planet just saw the notice, not only would they be rushing to snatch up Territories to get their own titles, but they may come to attack him and take his. He might not have cared much earlier today, but now that meant his family was in more danger. He threw the gear and crystals from the other wolves into his bag of holding, not bothering to look at the locked gear yet. He had learned early on that getting his hopes up on gear wasn't a great idea.

When Rocky looked at his pet, Sela was petting Azoth, and her hand as well as his feathers seemed to be glowing green.

"New skill?" Rocky asked awkwardly to break the ice.

"Yeah, it's called Rejuvenation. It's more of a pick me up than a heal, but it helps the body increase its healing factor a bit." Sela looked to Rocky as he came to sit down. Azoth was lying beside her, his body flat to the ground and his wings spread wide. This pose helped his pet's wing rearrange broken bones in a less painful way, but the light mewling told Rocky it wasn't painless. He cast eight Dark Mends onto his pet, renewing their pain-dulling effect and adding even more healing speed in response.

<Thanks Rocky!> Azoth said with a purr and Rocky felt his eyes mist up. It was so good to have Azoth back in his head. He looked at the ring and his pet before sitting down and joining Sela in petting him. It was almost like he could forget the last two months. Like it hadn't happened—

"So, let's start with the news that will affect you and Azoth," Sela began, looking at Azoth as he lifted his head and opened his black eyes. "Azoth, you're a father!" Sela crowed, her voice sounding truly excited.

Rocky blinked rapidly. That wasn't even possible. Azoth had never even met another Chimera. "How could—"

<Black Beauty has kits?> Azoth mentally exclaimed, and Rocky stuttered to a stop.

Black Beauty—wait, did he mean Pink Princess? The large cat I saw hunting in Algonquin Valley?

"Yes," Sela answered and patted Azoth's head, "but her name is now Shiva, and she is my pet. Still, she had thirteen kits about two weeks ago."

<Rocky, we go home?> Azoth asked in a way that made Rocky think he meant instantly, and not eventually.

<Soon, buddy,> he responded. Sela still had the other piece of news and after Zippo's slip of the tongue, Rocky thought he knew what it pertained to. If it was Frankie attacking the Territory, putting his and Azoth's families at risk, then he felt they might need to make a detour.

The only question was to where…

CHAPTER EIGHT

"Zippo let it slip earlier, but Frankie Cocozza has managed to capture Toronto. We have evacuated all of the citizens that we could find, but we suspect that he has multiple dungeons providing him and Apothis a never-ending stream of minions. We think he even captured the Territory that was near that place which housed animals." Sela instantly broke the bad news after the good, creating an unfortunate sloppy joe.

Just like that, his suspicion was confirmed. He felt his stomach turn over on itself and his forearms numb as his hands clenched. He took a deep breath. His family was still alive.

"You… *We* haven't managed to stop or even slow him down in the two months I have been gone?" Rocky saw her look after he started and changed his wording as quickly as possible.

"*We*," Sela made a motion that didn't include Rocky, "came close a great deal of times but *he* is like a cockroach, and as long as *he* survives the encounters, *he* comes back. Sometimes *he* gets out of situations *he* should not…" Sela stated, her voice cold and her inflections clear. "Plus, if *we* had your help, *he* probably would not still be threatening the Territory and *we* could be exploring Atlantis!"

Rocky blinked. So clearly she felt a certain way about the whole situation. He chose to pet Azoth with numb hands as he tried to digest Sela's words and her mood. Right now, the old Rocky wanted to play his blame album on a loop, just like she was doing, but he couldn't allow that.

Be mindful…

He closed his eyes and took another deep breath. To start, he acknowledged his part in the current situation and rejoiced in all the people he had helped by creating the Territories across Canada. Sela had been advocating for finding Atlantis since the early days of the Ether crash, so he dismissed that side quest for the immediate need of keeping his family safe.

His 'failures' to be there in the past didn't mean that he couldn't do something in the present.

They, Azoth and him, could help the Territory against Frankie. In fact, it was almost like *they* had used the last two months to train themselves to do so. He opened his eyes and looked at Sela, mind made up.

"Anything else?" he asked, changing the subject with his inflection. He hoped that the rest of the news would not be as bad. Sela gave him an odd look, perhaps seeing his resolve or wanting to stay on the topic of Frankie or Atlantis, but he couldn't be sure.

"Well," she began after clearing some hair from her face. "Ragnar has been training the citizenry of the Grotto, and Maximus has hosted three tournaments. I also placed a final dungeon in the south to be our fourth Cardinal dungeon. Her name is Leesoo and she is a Realm dungeon." At Rocky's questioning look Sela continued, "It just means that she creates life-like areas in an alternate dimensional space and each of these Realms acts like a world with quests and objectives. Some of the young gamers compared it to virtual reality."

"That's interesting," Rocky emphasized. "I hope the 'death' numbers haven't put us in any financial troubles," Rocky continued, hinting for Sela to go into the state of the Territory as a whole.

"Not really. We have had two more protection auras 'time out' and subsequent monster attacks to repel, and have also helped the Territory at your hospital and Saskatoon with repelling their invasions too. So, we used those unique boss monsters and minion corpses to bank deaths with our Cardinal Dungeons." Sela nodded her head in his direction, the motion likely an admission of using the same negotiation tactics he used the first time.

"So, the Territory is doing well?" he asked, and she shrugged.

"For the most part, but now with that *world announcement*... I'm worried that Frankie or others will begin attacking us on multiple fronts if they find the other Territories." She hung her head after that admission and Rocky saw how tired she was from the weight of the ongoing invasions.

"Okay, so what's your thinking on how to deal with it?" Rocky asked and Sela looked up sharply, her eyes lighting up despite her mouth forming a flat line.

She licked her lips and nodded. "We did actually find Atlantis—" Rocky blinked, realizing that her earlier mention of the ancient city was more meaningful than he thought. "—but I haven't even been able to get a glimpse of it. It's impossible to approach by sea or air."

At his raised eyebrow, she continued. "Some sort of large white sea serpent keeps trying to swat the Scourge out of the sky if we take the water route. I've tried in my raven form and the size and number of airborne predators around the city is massive. I think the only way we will be able to get close is overland from the south or north..."

"But if we did manage to get there, we could likely find something to help us?" Rocky asked, not seeing the correlation.

Sela nodded, but her face was pale. She clearly wasn't confident in that answer but was willing to hold on to hope. He didn't respond after that and instead checked out the cleanup efforts from the battle. The sun had just fallen but an orange light hung on the horizon, reminding them of 'Odin's' promise to return tomorrow. The Ottawa Knights were currently helping to repair the jagged rips in the walls of the Abbotsford Center, and near their hulking forms, humans swarmed over the wolf corpses, butchering them.

"How did the golems manage to enter the school grounds of Fraser Valley?" Rocky asked, realizing that they hadn't been able to leave the Scourge in Toronto.

"On a Territory, schools, hospitals, and libraries no longer offer protection from golems," Sela answered as she yawned. Rocky nodded, but as these things often go, joined her in her yawn a moment later. It had been a long day and they should probably get some sleep.

Jessica was overseeing the repair job on her arena and Rocky stood up before motioning for Sela to join him.

"Let's go see if they have a place we can sleep," he said and motioned to the UFV leader.

"I thought you said that the Territory would help regulate the land around it and keep us safer. It appears that it caused the wolves to attack!" Jessica said by way of greeting. Rocky could tell she wasn't happy with him and all he could do was shrug. This fight had likely caused the death of some good people, people she knew, but it had also given the survivors of British Columbia a safe zone which could provide a better life for all of them.

"I didn't know about the war feature for abutting Territories, and am sorry that I didn't give you warning, but you now have an extremely large Territory which includes the forests of those wolves for hunting. That likely means you won't have to rely on the fish from Vancouver to feed your people. Your hunters will be able to hunt in relative safety compared to before, as well," Rocky responded. This world was wild and fierce since the crash, and thanks to his new mindfulness he was able to see the good that came out of the situation, over the tragic deaths.

Jessica didn't seem to see it his way, but she didn't sling any further accusations. Sela stepped forward after a brief silence.

"Hello Jessica, I am Selaphelia Ardensai, co-leader with this idiot." She motioned at Rocky, making it clear who the idiot was, and he just shrugged. "Is there anywhere that we can rest for the night?" she asked the woman after she managed to get a smile out of her.

"Yeah, there is a campus right there, across the parking lot." Jessica accompanied her words with pointing at what appeared to be a condominium complex. "Will all of your people need accommodations for the night, or will they stay on the ship?" she asked Sela with a quick motion at the Golem Knights.

Sela chuckled. "The ship is going to check in with each group of survivors nearby and see what they might need. So, anyone on the ground here helping will likely need a bed to sleep in, as the ship will not be returning 'til morning. I have a large tent we could set up, if you do not have enough spare rooms."

Jessica shrugged and pointed at a collection of buildings less than a mile away. "If we can't, Sprott Shaw College or Career Gate Community College will have spare spaces. For now, you two head over to our dorms and tell Mandy what you need. She'll set you up in a room—"

"Two rooms," Sela interjected, and Jessica looked to Rocky, who tried to school his face but likely failed as he felt his stomach do an uncomfortable somersault. It had been easy to forget while sitting beside Azoth that he had left her alone for two months, but that one comment really drove home her current feelings on the situation. He couldn't blame her, and he forced a smile onto his face. She had every right to be over him, and their brief relationship. In fact, they hadn't even spent a full week together, and it was unfair for him to assume that meant a relationship to begin with.

<Azoth, are you up for a little trip tonight?> Rocky sent his pet as Sela and he trudged over the hard packed snow to the condominium-like structures.

<Azoth always ready, where go?> his pet responded jubilantly.

***

It was almost morning by the time Rocky and Azoth made it to the Toronto Zoo, and instead of the orange of the setting sun, Rocky was flying into the pink of a rising one. Last night, he and Azoth had both consumed an Elixir of Shortened Sleep which allowed them to be fully rested for the flight, but also increased Rocky's Toxic Blood debuff to three stacks. He was slightly concerned that making this attack with the lowered effects of potions might cause it to fail, but his plan didn't require him to fight large groups of enemies. Not if his last experience with Apep's dungeons was anything to go off.

Azoth touched down and Rocky patted him on his shoulder before sliding from the saddle.

<Thanks for the ride, buddy, but from this point on, it's just going to be me,> he mentally sent to his friend. If his plan was to work, he needed to sneak into the Territory and quickly find a dungeon entrance. <Stay close and I will call you if I need you, okay?>

<Azoth can sneak. Azoth good sneaker,> his pet responded and Rocky just shook his head before motioning up to the sky. <Fine. Azoth stay nearby, and sneak through sky.>

Rocky smiled before using Dark Cloak and Stealth and running toward the Zoo grounds. While in the air, they had crossed into and out of the Territory a few times, which would have alerted Frankie, but if the notice was anything like the ones he got in Algonquin Valley, they weren't overly specific. He hoped that the constant barrage of notices would frustrate Frankie into turning them off.

Between one step and the next a notification popped up for Rocky.

You are entering a Territorial Zone of a sapient being or group. If you continue, they will be alerted to your presence. Depending on your intentions or their mood, you may be in danger.

This was the most dangerous part of his plan. If this Territory functioned like his, it would show anyone who accepted the quest a gold line that led right to his location. He needed to be inside of a dungeon before people arrived. He rushed to what used to be a field for keeping grass-fed animals and sped to a raised mound of earth through the high grass. From the air, Azoth and he had seen an opening on one side of this mound and Rocky sprinted into it, crossing his metaphorical fingers. He wasn't disappointed.

Welcome to the "Spawning Ground 3."
You have entered in a group of one, suggested group size 1-5.
Good luck.
Level: 5++
Age: 90 Days
Best time: 10:15.33
Clears: 1
Ether Concentration: Moderate
To exit the Dungeon, leave the way you came in.

Rocky walked carefully down a short path and into a large cavern at the bottom. He was still in Stealth and Dark Cloak which allowed him to hug the wall of the cavern to avoid the horde of zombies in the center. This cavern was large, easily a hundred meters in diameter, and it had numerous other exits off it, but all the pathways tilted back toward the surface. Rocky climbed the wall and tried to locate an exit from the room that led deeper but didn't find one. That likely meant that he was in the 'final' chamber of this dungeon. The name of the dungeon was confirmation enough for Rocky, and he began looking at the space using his Ether Manipulation.

Right in the center of the room was a collection of energy that screamed brightly to his mind's eye. He analyzed one of the undead minions and wasn't shocked to find the same zombie minions that Apep had used before.

He formed his sword and charged two stacks of Dark Blade before unleashing the skill to carve through the Apprentice rank undead that bunched together in the center of the room. The two blades reciprocated their way through the dungeon minions as if they were snowmen, and he felt his gorge rise at the sound of squelching blood and the smell of rotting organs. The zombies died in droves and instead of waiting for the corpses to rise again as abominations, Rocky rushed forward and began digging into the area of the floor that his Ether Manipulation highlighted.

The blood-stained dirt parted beneath his fingers and after about a foot, he found the Dungeon Core he had been expecting. He hurriedly pulled it out of the hole and dumped it into his bag of holding.

He wasn't fast enough because he heard it shout, <Unhand my minion, human!> before he managed to get it fully into the bag. After that, he deactivated his Dark Cloak and summoned his shadow clone. Now was the part of his plan he wasn't completely confident in. If this Territory acted like his, then the leader would be summoned to defend the dungeon from an intruder.

In Stealth, Rocky moved back to the wall and away from the gore that wasn't reabsorbed, thanks to the dungeon no longer existing. All he needed to do now was wait…

***

Rocky decided to climb the wall and dig out a small space to sit while he waited and his clone did the same. His plan was simple because Frankie could just send an army of creatures into the dungeon, and this position would provide a quick exit in that case. Yet, if Frankie arrived with that army, he should still have a chance to assassinate the man.

After about half an hour, Rocky finally saw movement down the tunnel across the space from him. Large abominations rushed into the area, reminding Rocky of Apothis and he quietly sucked a breath in, hoping that Frankie wouldn't have allowed Apothis, Apep's minion, to take the leadership role of this Territory. This whole plan hinged on Frankie's arrogance.

Soon the entire room was filled with abominations that shambled over the gore, sometimes scooping up a bunch of the ground remains and popping it into their mouths to eat. Admittedly, Rocky was disappointed. His plan revolved around the contracts with his dungeons in Algonquin Valley. They could call on the owners and creatures of the grotto for assistance. Either Frankie had just sent abominations to check out the area or he had sent them to flush out anything inside and he was waiting outside of the dungeon right now.

Or perhaps he doesn't have contracts with his dungeons, idiot! Perhaps my assassination plan wasn't completely thought out…

Rocky thought of his intentions to find another dungeon, which conveyed those plans to his clone. Together they exited the dungeon with slow and deliberate care. The actual Zoo grounds were quite a bit deeper into Rouge National Urban Park, and Rocky wasn't sure if heading there would be the best choice or if he should leave and try something else. He didn't even know if Frankie was currently in this Territory. Still, the lack of an organized defense was also an opportunity.

When he was back on the surface, Rocky didn't discover a second army or Frankie waiting for him. He frowned, and reworked his plan. If he could destroy more dungeons, that would severely hinder Frankie in the future. So, he decided to start there.

<Azoth, can you find another dungeon entrance?> he asked his airborne pet.

<Azoth can smell three other areas, much rotting meat…> Azoth responded, sounding slightly confused as to what Rocky was looking for.

With a bit more prompting and a few flyovers, Azoth led them to another area that appeared to be abutting what used to be a flowing creek. The water of the creek smelled awful to Rocky's new senses, and he had to wonder if Azoth had found a dungeon or some sort of run off from a butcher's yard. The water itself was milky white and if anything lived beneath its surface, Rocky wouldn't want to meet it.

On both sides of the river, numerous mounds of earth, sand, and rock were pushed up to create cave entrances that dripped water from the ceilings. Rocky confirmed that his clone was with him by mentally asking it to flash into sight, and then they both entered the dungeon.

Welcome to the "Spawning Ground 4."
You have entered in a group of one, suggested group size 1-5.
Good luck.
Level: 5++
Age: 61 Days
Best time: 1:15.33
Clears: 3
Ether Concentration: Moderate
To exit the Dungeon, leave the way you came in.

About three seconds later, they stopped directly in front of a pool of water. Its depth was indeterminate because of its chalky white color. Rocky, who was already trying to breathe exclusively through his mouth to avoid the smell, tasted the rot and decay in the air instead and almost gagged.

The puddle of water had about four feet of open air above it that seemed to be a doorway into a room. A sound like rain on a lake came from that opening, which made Rocky very hesitant to enter the sludge. Not only was it likely carrying numerous diseases, but he also couldn't see anything that might be under its surface.

He tested the walls as a climbing option to enter the next area but found that the sand to soil composition and perhaps the dampness of the area made any handhold he tried break away in clumps. The light in this dungeon seemed to come from small white rocks that were embedded in the sandy walls and his handfuls of the stuff pulled down three or four of the things. He tossed the glowing stones into the white water, and they plunked in before sinking a foot or two and settling.

Rocky still couldn't see the bottom but the water now glowed, and the light had stopped shifting half a second after the rock made contact. That timing confirmed that the water itself wasn't very deep. Remembering the heavy water from the dungeon in Chalk River, Rocky attempted to Analyze this liquid. Nothing came up and he sighed, resigning himself to having to enter the sewage-like pool.

Just to be sure, he mentally sent his clone first and saw the strange hollow-looking places where the clone's feet entered the murk while holding stealth. Rocky held his breath, but nothing happened, so holding his nose he joined the clone and used his Ether Manipulation to try to spot enemies and the dungeon core.

The enemies made themselves plain when they splashed through the two feet of water, and he instantly felt his gorge rise at the sight of these zombies. He now knew why the water was that chalky white. The skin and muscles of these creatures were so soggy and bloated that it appeared to be sloughing off them. Each creature's hair was falling out, and the strands that did remain were plastered to their heads. A glance at the domed ceiling showed drips of water falling at relatively regular intervals, which had accounted for the rain sound. The zombies in this room area moved even slower than normal and all of them were already below half health.

The state of the two dungeons he had just found made him extremely skeptical that anyone had been here to maintain this Territory for a long time. Again, at the center of the room, he found a glowing mass with his Ether sight. Using the same tactics of a double stacked Dark Blade, Rocky cleared this dungeon, before digging out the core from the bottom of the murky pool.

<You'll pay for—>

Rocky stuffed the stone into his bag of holding.

As soon as he removed the core, though, he felt the dungeon shudder, and he realized that without the core holding this place together, the loose sand and soil was going to collapse above them. Together, he and his clone stomped out of the dungeon and were forced to jump into trees to avoid the abominations that stormed straight into the entrance mere seconds after they exited. Rocky couldn't stop a smile when he heard the crash and saw the bank of the creek erode and collapse. The area formed a small lake the exact size of what the domed central room used to be.

It was well into the morning when Rocky finished clearing the other two spawning grounds and, by that time, he could feel his anxiety climbing. Where was everyone? Surely Apep had spawned some sapient mobs, and armies of more than just the thousands of zombies and the hundred abominations he had avoided most of the night.

Warning! An army has crossed your Territory's boundary!

Algonquin Valley has numerous sapient creatures and minions crossing the border! Push back these invaders or risk losing your Territory.
20 Sapient beings, 1 Territorial Boss, and 200,000 undead creatures have crossed the threshold.

Merlin's glorious gray hair, they must have marched through the night too! I bet as soon as Frankie saw that notice...
Wait, Merlin's what?

CHAPTER NINE

"As fast as you can," Rocky encouraged as his pet strained under him. "The Scourge is still going to be away and so are all of the Golem Knights, Adam's golems, Sela, and even Zippo!"

<Stinky human wants more speed... Azoth fart and it no help!> his pet answered sourly, clearly letting Rocky know that they were already at top speed. He had to wonder if it was his increased stats or his Chimera Senses that allowed him to not feel ill in the slightest from a speed that had made him throw up in the past.

The large trees of Algonquin that Rocky had seen last surrounded by charred and desecrated earth appeared on the horizon. It had been maybe fifteen minutes since they left Toronto, and Rocky silently marveled at the speed Azoth was moving. Even by plane before the Apocalypse, this trip would have taken at least forty-five minutes. He began an apology to his pet but froze when he heard the unmistakable sound of battle from within the trees. Considering they were still many miles away, Rocky blinked—his senses were extremely sharp compared to before.

About five minutes later, Rocky and Azoth crossed the boundary of the Territory, and they could clearly make out the flashes of light that depicted skills, and projectile bombardments, amongst the deep shadows in the trees. Not even a minute later, they were looking down on the Grotto and a fight that he was having trouble processing. Four massive abomination champions held groupings of trees lashed together to form shields but looked to be stalled in their tracks. From among the ranks of zombies, small suns bloomed continuously as what could only have been plasma grenades exploded.

From the top of the rock walls of the Grotto, hundreds of turrets trained on the abomination champions from staggered heights. Rocky scratched his head as he tried to find a place that he would be helpful in the current slaughter. He was just thinking about a way to perhaps set fire to the corpses so they couldn't rise again when four twangs sounded in unison. Rocky turned to watch as four trebuchets launched clay-like jars over the walls. The jars crashed and splashed into the undead and the next plasma grenade caused the liquid to catch fire with a *whoomp*.

Rocky's mouth fell open as thousands of undead turned into melting candles. The Grotto had clearly acclimatized itself to these constant attacks. He almost deemed his presence here unneeded when he remembered the twenty sapient beings and Frankie. He scanned below and noticed a few retaliatory spells coming from under the canopy of trees.

<Azoth, would you like to hunt with me?> he mentally asked, relishing in the return of this option.

<Azoth like food, but Azoth no think this time for——>

<No, dummy. I meant let's kill the people at the back of this undead army.> He rolled his eyes. Maybe relishing was the wrong word.

<Oh, why Rocky not say so…?>

Azoth circled back and dove into the trees a fair distance from the original battle. Rocky summoned his shadow clone again and the three of them began stalking toward the combat. He triggered Stealth, but left Dark Cloak off for now.

Just as they were starting to hear the humans under the canopy, Azoth sent, <Sela says she here, with metal bird.>

Rocky sent back an affirmative, and told the birdbrain to try to convey their current location and plan to Sela. He assumed it wouldn't be clear, but he hadn't thought to ask for a radio from her in BC. Once Rocky spotted the backs of the group of humans and other creatures, he ducked behind the nearest tree before peeking back out.

He didn't bother to count the assorted races present, knowing it would be twenty-one. Instead, he tried to find the greatest threats that he knew would be there. Right near the center of the creatures, he found Frankie, Apothis, and Frankie's pet geomancer. He kept Analyzing the other minions, just to try to understand what the Grotto faced.

Apothis
Level 11
Master Necromonger
Health Points 531 / 8,500
Boss

—

Frankie Cocozza
Level 22
Master Apep's Chosen
Health Points 9,950 / 9,950
Territorial Leader

—

Jack Fan
Master-Mage
Level 15
Health Points: 1,200 / 1,200
Boss

—

Frankie was the highest level, which surprised Rocky a great deal. Still, each of the others except the pet geomancer were dungeon bosses. That meant that these were all creatures spun back out from Apep, and they were outside of their dungeons. If he remembered correctly, dungeon bosses outside of their dungeons suffered penalties after death.

That's why those four dungeons were so weak. Frankie took everything here!

Every boss was of Master rank, which did worry Rocky, but he did have some tactical advantage. He knew that Apothis was the one that was currently controlling the abomination champions and he could also see that a strong breeze may end his life. If they managed to kill him, then the full might of the Territory would be freed up to defend against these other threats. He recalled the last fights he had with Apothis and shivered.

Those two fights hadn't exactly ended in resounding victories for Rocky. The first time he was thrown around like a child's ragdoll toy, and the second time he had sacrificed the entire group to win. Could this time be different? He chided himself for the negative thought and started looking for solutions.

Mindful…

He just needed to take out Apothis. After that, the rest wouldn't likely have the ability to keep resurrecting the hundreds of thousands of undead in the clearing. Of course, last time he had tried to sneak up and assassinate the man, he had become his puppet—so it was probably not going to be as easy as his thinking made it seem.

The hum of the arriving battleship above him caused him to act sooner than he probably would have. He pulled out a jar from his bag of holding and drizzled a tiny amount of the liquid inside onto Dark Tidings.

"Jack, Verimy, and Prentor, take that thing out of the sky," Frankie ordered casually, and Rocky jumped into action. He needed to be a distraction. Not only were there people he cared for on that battleship, but they also needed it to defend against the incoming invasion.

In addition to the jar, he coated his Soul Blade in the poisons from his Poison Pool as well, while simultaneously activating Dark Cloak and four stacks of Dark Blade. The distance was less than fifty feet, but Frankie must have either heard him coming or seen his clone like he had in the past, because he turned around when Rocky reached the halfway point. That was when a two-ton manticore plowed into the bosses from the east and any warning Frankie was planning to give was drowned out by shouting.

Rocky lunged out and managed to sink the tip of his blade into Apothis before a red bubble expanded out from the boss. The bubble flung Rocky back, but as he flew, he noticed that there were also two daggers embedded in Apothis' chest. Two of the nearby bosses began to move their hands and glow, and Rocky prepared to dodge when he hit the ground, but instead the two touched Apothis and he glowed as well. Rocky glanced at his notifications to find that they had cured his venoms and healed any damage he and his clone had just done. Rocky growled when his health returned to five hundred and thirty-one points but he, along with Azoth, had successfully distracted the group from the battleship.

As Rocky watched, the health of Apothis ticked down, and he smiled. Manticore poison wasn't so easy to cleanse…which was why he still hadn't applied it to himself.

Thuds began sounding as minion golems and the Golem Knights LALO-jumped into the fray.

"Rockland, it's so great to see you and your over-sized chicken!" Frankie crowed before he began to glow. Strange insects that were some sort of mix of beetles and ants began erupting from the ground all around the group of twenty and Rocky sneered as he got to his feet.

<Azoth, time for you to get out of here!> he mentally screamed at his pet as he noticed many of the summoned creatures target the manticore. The bosses he had careened into were also picking themselves up from the ground. This battle was about to turn the other way.

That was when a large black sabretooth hopped down out of the canopy, carrying a rider who was throwing large red Fireballs. Sela and Zippo had arrived! Unfortunately, that still didn't even the odds, but it certainly made them slightly better.

Rocky got into his stance just as the nearest bug chose him as its target. He Analyzed it.

Beetle Ant
Journeyman-Warrior
Level 15
Health Points: 1,250 / 1,250
Active Skills: 3
Passive Skills: 5

The beetle glowed red and exploded forward, catching Rocky by surprise, but his much higher stats, combined with his Chimera Knight skills, allowed him to track the ant's trajectory and slash at it. His blade cut into the chitin of the creature and neatly severed its head right where it segmented and joined the beetle shell. Shots and skills began lighting up the trees, and Rocky checked their sources to find hundreds of his people in the trees around them. Shields, heals, and retaliatory skills flew from Frankie's side, but if the Grotto's people were hit, Rocky didn't notice.

He continued to slash his way through beetle ants as he tried to close in with Apothis or Frankie. Those two were the greatest threats to his people in this battle. A wall of earth occluded both from his view when he got back within ten feet of them, and he knew they were likely about to try to escape as Sela had warned him.

"Sela!" he shouted into the din of the battle, and he smiled when the box the geomancer had just created stopped sinking into the ground. Without hesitating, Rocky climbed onto the roof of the dirt box and charged his blade with all the Ether in his pool. Then he thrust downward, releasing the eight stacks into the center of the construction, praying that the three enemies would be trapped inside.

His drill-like blow quickly shredded the earth box, and Rocky, who expected to hear a surprised shout from inside, looked down to see nothing. His head turned in every direction, trying to find where the group of three could have gone. His heightened nose picked up a smell in the air which reminded him of motor oil, but not quite. He couldn't place where he had smelled this particular odor before.

His skill was still screaming against the stones and dirt when the tide of the battle shifted. Apothis must have been out of range because the abomination champions began falling to their knees as the bombardment became too much. Military tanks with people riding them streamed out from the southern Grotto wall. He watched in fascination as groups of approximately five to ten began engaging with each boss that remained. One person charged directly at the humanoid bosses and another individual cast a few skills on them as the others and the tank repositioned the fight. The bosses were definitely sapient as he could hear them threatening, surrendering, and even cursing in some rare cases, but there was also definitely something more at work here.

The tanks were easily able to reposition any ongoing fights and within a minute, each pocket of fighting was spread around the area. Not one of the bosses seemed to remember that they had a group of twenty other Master classes to rely on. Individual fighters began dumping skills into the fray and Rocky, who didn't really have any precision skills, chose to watch his people clean up.

Whenever one of the bosses summoned a large skill or minion, the groups would back off and a Golem Knight would step in to control the Master class boss for a time. In some other cases where the bosses began to charge large scale skills, a silencing skill locked them down. The remaining abomination champions each had one of the Knights raining down blows, and a quick Analyze told Rocky they were about to fall as well.

Rocky felt himself grow anxious as the battle continued toward its rather obvious conclusion. If the Master class bosses didn't work together, then they were going to be slaughtered in what a gamer might call a zerg.

In one case, one of the bosses turned itself into a massive rock creature that reminded Rocky of the Thing from Fantastic Four. Instead of one of the Golem Knights stepping in, he watched as the tank had spells layered onto her. He recognized the golden armor he had gifted Victoria easily, once it and she grew to be approximately twenty feet tall. It was tough to tell if she actually grew, or if the spells created some kind of gigantic avatar. He also recognized the spells as the spells and skills Sela once described to him as the specialty of the first group of exiles from the Grotto.

"The coordination of teams has certainly gotten better," Sela said, as she stepped up beside Rocky. "I thought you were going to wait and teleport back with me this afternoon?"

Rocky scratched his neck and opened his mouth to respond. A yawn escaped his lips instead and he tried to cover his mouth in embarrassment. "Sorry, Sela. I went to assassinate Frankie at his Territory in Toronto. Turns out that he wasn't home…" Rocky motioned around himself at the final four pockets of battle.

"Is this going to be a new theme with *you*?" Sela said, her words dry and disappointed. Rocky looked at her, then at the battles again before shrugging.

"Rockland, you know I would have come with you, *right*?" Sela asked and this time her voice was more sincere. He snapped his head back around but she wasn't looking at him anymore. Rocky felt sweat break out on his arms at the tone she had used. He had almost felt she had meant the two months and not his recent trip to Toronto, or maybe he was projecting. It was hard to tell when she was no longer looking at him.

"Guess I got used to being alone, in my previous life," Rocky whispered, and added a sheepish shrug. "I will make sure to include you—" he began more sincerely but was cut off.

"Look who's back," the whiny voice of Derik broke into Rocky's apology. "It's past time for us to have a council meeting with *everyone* present," Derik finished, his clear emphasis highlighting Rocky.

"Let me clean up the loot and gather these corpses here, and then let's have that meeting," Rocky responded, adding some false joviality to his voice, which seemed to throw Derik out of his pompous stride.

"Good, there are many issues that need to be addressed! Also maybe take a shower and clean that beard and hair," Derik stated unnecessarily.

Rocky moved over and patted Derik on the shoulder with an overly cheerful, broad smile. "I'm sure you've done a fantastic job with them until now. I can't wait to hear what issues remain. Let's say we meet in two hours at City Hall so I have time to *shower*."

He didn't need two hours here, but he did *need* to see his family. Before Derik could continue his snark, Rocky walked away toward the hole in the ground that likely contained a clue to how Frankie, Apothis, and the Geomancer escaped.

Sela joined his walk and stared down into the hole with him. "Something keeps helping him escape no matter what we do…"

Rocky felt a groan escape his chest, but he leaped down into the hole to try to discover something he might have missed from above. The smell was fading from the hole and he wondered if it was Apothis' necrotic flesh.

Congratulations, you have successfully conquered a new Territory.

Frankie's Menagerie has been captured due to the conquer of all four Cardinal Dungeons. Would you like to take ownership of the new Territory?
<Yes> | No
Would you like to place the Territory onto the Market?
Yes | <No>
Would you like to condense the Territory into a Territorial Sphere?
Warning! A transfer of this sort will sustain losses.
<Yes> | No

The Territorial orb popped into his hand, and Rocky watched Sela's eyebrows raise.

"You conquered his Territory in Toronto by yourself?" Her voice was somewhat impressed while still containing hints of something he couldn't place. The tone wasn't disappointment, but it wasn't a positive emotion. "Well, that might slow down future attacks, if nothing else."

He debated about adding it to Algonquin but in the end, he chose to let the council make that decision. He definitely didn't need to make these small choices anymore, and that was a realization that made him smile. He was no longer the leader of a single Territory. No, he was the leader of a large guild.

"Can you take me to see my family?" Rocky asked, as he leaped up to catch Sela's proffered hand. He likely could have just leaped out of the pit, but when someone offers help, you usually take it.

Sela, who had been frowning down into the hole at him, finally revealed a slight smile.

CHAPTER TEN

The Grotto itself had grown, and not only in numbers. The Guild Dome and Tower at the center of the space was less visible as buildings obscured much of the huge dome from view. Rocky felt a slight urge to get on Azoth's back and study the Grotto from the sky. He could tell that the southeastern quadrant was now full of numerous longhouses that appeared to be split between apartment and dorm styles. Rocky could even tell the new buildings from the original ones because the exteriors of the forty plus new constructions were treated wood, whereas the original ones were black dragon scale.

Right in front of him was the original barracks that housed the military, but two other extremely similar buildings sat on each side of the dragon scale one. Rocky glanced back at the stone wall and metal gate he just walked through to gain access to the Grotto.

"As you can see, our number one priority has remained housing, but after you captured your second Territory, the council made the choice to keep all housing to the southeastern quarter. Now, as you can see, we are building up instead of out," Sela explained with a casual wave of her hand at the residential buildings on their right.

Rocky could see that most of the buildings were currently being increased in height or already had been. Still, that clearly had a limit as well.

"Do we have housing for everyone we saved from New York?" Rocky asked, eyeing the quarter and its space limitations. The other quarters were nowhere near as full, but they still had some new buildings.

"We do have rooms for everyone, but the council used a great deal of the Territorial points to increase the floors below ground in the Guild Dome for that purpose. They also have juggled some of the population to other Territories," Sela responded with a half shrug. She pointed over her other shoulder. "On our left, you can see the manufacturing quarter." The area she indicated was the most barren of what he could see as they walked toward the central tower. Some buildings were constructed at the edges, but the center just seemed to be a large storage area of metal scraps.

Still, the way it was laid out made him blink.

"Is that going to be another battleship?" he asked when the shape came together in his spatial awareness. Sela nodded, but her stern expression and lack of response along with the direction they headed made him ask a follow up question, "Is my family staying in the Guild Dome?"

Sela nodded, but glanced toward the residential quarter. "I'm not sure if they will be in their rooms or in the mess hall. They were not on night duty, so they likely got to sleep in this morning despite the commotion."

"That wasn't the full force of the Grotto?" Rocky exclaimed, his voice a bit higher than he intended. A few people looked in his direction at his increased volume, but then just as quickly dismissed him. A few people nudged neighbors to point out Sela, but it seemed that many people didn't recognize him.

Sela waved at the people who pointed her out, and her lips almost turned up at the edges. As soon as she turned to him, that look became stoic again.

"That is not the most impressive part. Just wait 'til you see the training that Ragnar is putting groups through." Her voice, if nothing else, was animated.

Rocky felt a small smile tug at his lips from that news, but his excitement felt muted. Each step they drew nearer to the black dome of the guild, the more his stomach roiled. What would he say to his mom? His sister? To Benoit?

Sela seemed to take pity on him because instead of staying quiet, she filled the silence as they walked. "The northwest quarter is reserved for retail buildings, but the Aretrin

Bazaar is still the primary destination for shoppers. We do have four restaurants, and a few stores selling the gear that is crafted and sold to the guild, though.

"In the northeast, we have all the industrial buildings currently. A few groups have even commissioned office spaces for what they called entrepreneurial businesses. No idea what they are planning, but the council seems excited by the prospect. It is probably the busiest area between breakfast and dinner, with the manufacturing quarter being a close second."

Sela cut off as the titanic doors of the Guild Hall swung open and Rocky blinked at the pockets of humans heading out to the Territory and the equal number heading inward to the central kiosks. Sela and he walked right beside a well-geared group of five.

"Are you sure you want to do the puzzle dungeon again?" one of the five whined.

"It's been giving us the best loot and Etherience, so why wouldn't we?"

"I just hate the water level, and since our third clear, we seem to be getting it more and more…" The initial speaker continued to muse as Sela turned into one of the side doorways that Rocky knew led to residences within the dome of the building.

"Your family is down three floors in the northeastern stack."

"Stack?"

"It is what the residents have begun calling the rooms below ground." Sela motioned to stairs that went up and down but left her hand on the downward portion longer. Together, they began descending. After three flights, they exited the concrete staircase that reminded Rocky of an emergency exit in a high-rise and stepped out into a hallway that had all the personality of a slug.

It was only when Sela led them unerringly to the fifth door on the right that he realized she had clearly been here before. He felt his heart fall again, partially at what was about to happen after she knocked and partially because she had visited his family when he wasn't here.

"Sela, wait," he whispered as she raised a hand to tap the wooden door. His hands were clammy, and he was covered in goosebumps as well as a cold sweat. She looked back at him and must have seen something amiss because she lowered the hand and turned to look at him.

"Rockland, they have been waiting for you to come back for the last two months. They are probably one of the few people in the Territory that never wavered. I am not sure what has you so pale in the face, but I can assure you they want to see you…" Sela whispered as she turned back to the door. She raised her fist and knocked before Rocky could voice his fears.

The metal door swung inward, and Benoit exclaimed, "Sela! Have you come to join us for breakfast a—" That was when Benoit's eyes took in Rocky standing behind her. The widening of Ben's eyes made Rocky look down at the floor and he swallowed the lump in his throat.

"Hey, Ben," Rocky muttered to the ground. "Are my sister and mom home?"

A hand that wasn't Sela's rested on his shoulder, and he looked up to find Ben there. Ben smiled at him which sent a thrum of warmth through his chest.

"We were just getting ready to have some breakfast. At least this time, the plate of food we keep making for you isn't going to go cold." Ben squeezed his shoulder briefly and then he pulled Rocky into a hug.

After Rocky finally returned the embrace, Ben placed a hand on Rocky's back and steered him to the door. Sela must have gone inside already because she wasn't waiting in the entryway. The room was far better than the hallway as far as décor, but that was only because his family had hung paintings and even blankets from the walls to make it warmer.

That was when he realized he was avoiding looking at the two people that were in the room. It was also when they both crashed into him and wrapped their arms around him.

"You came back!" his mom, Nadine, cried into his side.

"Where did you even go?!" his sister, Lacy, shrieked. He could feel her mechanical arm as it tightened around him. He looked down to see his mother's single shoe and mechanical foot poking from her leather pants. He opened his mouth to apologize to them for the missing limbs, but found his sister's mechanical arm in his stomach.

"Oof," he managed, as he looked at her fist, which she was now shaking out.

"What are you made of?" she asked as she shook out the robotic hand that had just hit him. It took him a moment to realize that she must have pain receptors in the limb, and another second for him to realize she had done this exact same thing when he retired from basketball. The familiarity of the situation finally broke his maudlin and he smiled.

"Still the same genes that you have," he retorted, which produced a laugh from Nadine and Lacy. Benoit had left to set the table with an extra plate and dole out what appeared to be eggs and bacon.

Rocky pulled Lacy back into the group hug that his mom never ended and asked, "Why do you eat here, instead of the mess hall or the restaurants?"

"The mess hall is running on shifts lately because it cannot host everyone at once. We have three others in construction, but they are taking longer than normal due to the kitchens. We got kind of lucky when the first one was finished by that Territorial spell," Sela responded as she popped what appeared to be bacon into her mouth.

The last time Rocky had eaten 'bacon,' it had been rat meat, so he wasn't confident that this would be actual pork. "So, the people not on the schedule have to buy their own food?"

"No," Benoit responded this time. "If you live in the Guild Dome, you pick up a serving per household and warm it up in your rooms." He pointed to the kitchen that they had. It wasn't fancy by any means, but it contained an electric range, microwave, and small oven.

"Do the apartments and longhouses not have kitchens then?" Rocky asked, hearing the unsaid in Benoit's statement.

Sela made a 'kind of' gesture with her hand before clarifying. "The longhouses have a communal area with a single kitchen, and those are used to make a semi-communal eating area for the residents when it is not their turn to visit the mess hall. As for the apartments, that is entirely up to the occupants. They are equipped with the space for kitchens, but the appliances need to be purchased, and many groups are still saving to get them."

Rocky looked down at his mom and sister who still hadn't let go of him. "Guys, I'm not going anywhere. You can let go of me now…"

Lacy immediately released him and grew red in the face, but his mother, Nadine, just tightened her grip. The group hug became an individual one and Rocky felt his own tears, the ones he had held back with all his strength, finally release when he felt his mother shaking in his arms. The hug eventually ended, but throughout the morning breakfast and conversation many more bouts of joyful tears were shared. At some point, Sela radioed to the council that they would be late, and someone came to deliver lunch.

They talked about that first month after the wave. About what had happened to each of them. Rocky had to share the devastating news of what happened to their neighbors in Ottawa, and he watched Benoit react to the death of his friends. He explained the circumstances and the madness of Corsair. They toasted to the successful repelling of Frankie, who had been a constant threat that Rocky's family had been dealing with. Even Rocky, who hadn't been back long, could feel the monotony of that toast. It wasn't the first, and it wouldn't be the last one they gave to that effect, it seemed.

Throughout the time he spent with his family, Rocky felt a constant stream of happy emotions from Azoth. He considered sending his pet a questioning message about his morning, but the joyous, prideful feeling that spiked numerous times told Rocky that Azoth was spending time with his own family.

In the end, he only left because Sela informed him that they couldn't put the council meeting off any longer.

***

The town hall somehow stood out more because it was surrounded by longhouses. A fence had been placed around it, and a sign with a list of hours that petitions would be heard was displayed on the stylized metal. Rocky made note that there was one such gathering starting in three hours. No wonder Sela couldn't push back the council meeting any further.

Directly inside the outer door was a chamber like that of Fraser Valley. A long table was raised on the far side of the room, and a podium stood at the end of the middle walkway. Lining that walkway were hand-carved pews that would clearly accommodate people who were either there to make a petition or there to hear the decisions from the decision makers of the Grotto.

Sela walked through a doorway that led off the side of the chamber and made her way to the council meeting room. It was the same, but also different than before. A hand-drawn map of the Grotto's current structures hung from one of the walls, and Rocky felt his hand twitch with a desire to go study it. Blueprints also hung from the wall or were laying on the table. Rocky recognized some of them as buildings that were already constructed but then noticed others were from the world before Ether.

People were already sitting at the table, so he held off his curiosity and sat beside Sela, where she indicated a seat. Some gasps and a few excited conversations sparked up when he sat down.

"Thanks for showering," Derik sniped at Rocky as he sat down. Rocky looked down at himself and realized he hadn't cleaned up like he said. It had been more important to spend time with his family...

"This seat has been saved for you over the last two months." Sela placed a hand on his shoulder, interrupting any retort he might have thrown. She continued in a whisper when he looked up, "Some of the council members you will know, but there have been a few adjustments. Just ignore Derik..."

Rocky glanced around the room, avoiding looking at Derik for the time being. He recognized a few faces. It helped that the ones he did know waved in his direction. Astrid, the seamstress from Dorset, smiled at his appraisal. Gerard, a handsome man from Brent, nodded a blocky head when he passed over him, and Rocky recalled he was a tanking class. The dark-cloaked Jorge, of few words, practically sunk into his chair, and Yuri wore a blackened smithing apron. The members of the A-team were mostly absent, to Rocky's surprise. In fact, from that group only Derik and Smith, both currently glaring at him, were seated at the round table. He continued to avoid looking their way and instead studied the spots that had been Mr. Pip's, Bart's, and Amber's. They were filled with new faces.

Thinking of Amber soured the saliva in his mouth, and he looked away. He had thought long and hard about her over the last two months, and he thought he had a good plan to get her back, but that would wait. The council had twelve people on it and Rocky recognized one more. Carl, the Engineer who had shown him all the flaws in the crafter's hall, was also taking his seat.

"Today is a special council meeting," Smith stood and began. "Our second *leader* of the Territory is back and has joined us." Muttering both positive and negative was easily heard and understood by Rocky's Chimera Senses. He nodded along with both takes on his absence. "Since some discussions were tabled in his absence, I would like to ask the recorder of minutes to summarize those issues now."

"The largest issue that has been tabled at each meeting has been the inability to adjust the settings of the new Territories, due to missing permissions. The councils of North Dakota, Saskatchewan, Alberta, and probably British Columbia have sent lists of changes they have agreed upon." A woman Rocky didn't recognize spoke up as she shuffled papers. A quick Analyze told him her name was Mary. Rocky could tell she was a bookish woman before the turn when she tried to push up a non-existent pair of glasses on her nose. It was likely a habit from before the crash. Rocky had met many people who had issues with their eyes that were now totally healed thanks to the arrival of Ether.

I had a lazy eye myself…

"Additionally, the appointment of military ranks needs to be re-addressed, and Smith has a full report on possible changes there. Jobs and their growth slash inclusion is another topic that needs to be covered in the new Territories. Population dispersals, and Cardinal Dungeon negotiations slash acquisitions…" Mary continued to read from a list as she flipped pages. After the second page, Rocky felt his eyebrows rise. After the fifth, he buried his face in his hands.

This was going to be a long meeting.

CHAPTER ELEVEN

"Okay, Rockland has appointed people with permissions in each Territory and adjusted the current military hierarchy. We've also placed people in charge of job allocation and set the teleporter to allow individuals to use their personal Etherience to pay for transport between Territories. This point may be re-introduced at future meetings if this doesn't cause a population dispersal with the distribution the council hopes for.

"Rockland has also sent modified terms to the four other Territories to discuss with their dungeons and this will be covered once responses are given. The next point of discussion is what Territory boons we should accept from the three successful defense quests." Mary tapped her pen on the paper she was currently turned to and Rocky perked up.

The first few tabled discussions had been tedious to say the least. The fact that his military ranks now included up to General made Rocky think that all he needed to do was promote Smith and the man would do the rest, but Smith's promotion needed to be voted on, as did every appointment after that. The fact that the entire population of all his Territories could fit in the rank of Chief Warrant Officer didn't seem to 'warrant' putting everyone in that rank. According to the system, there were six billion spots in the Private rank, and he could only shake his head at that number. That was larger than the current population of the planet.

Especially after a near 95% mortality rate after the crash… Stop it. Be mindful…

So, of course, the completion of quests and boons was a welcome change. With Sela's help, they moved through the menus to find another quest log that Rocky had somewhat forgotten about. There were five completed quests on Rocky's and when he noticed the disparity, he hesitated to put up his hand, knowing that it would likely add some tedium to future proceedings, but after a moment he said, "I also have completed quests for North Dakota and Saskatchewan Territories to select."

Mary's face broke into a smile, and she pulled out two fresh pages to write on before adding to the bottom of the 'to be discussed in the future' piles.

Congratulations! You have completed a quest.
Protection Quest
Leader of Territory Algonquin Valley
Your people have successfully safeguarded the sanctum and even renewed a new timer for your Ether-assisted Protection.
Rewards:
250,000 Territorial Etherience (+62,500 Knight's Quest)
One minor Territorial Growth Boon from Aura List (See List)
10 Territorial Skill Points
Great job, Leader!
—

Minor Boon of Resources Level 1
This boon will increase the yield of all fields, resources, mobs and dungeons in the territory by 15%.
Lasts 1 cycle around Odin.
This spell cannot be stacked with any other Territorial or personal spells, and is only available to those with a Place of Power.

"Will that resource boost stack with my Land Baron resource boost, my Leadership Resource boost, and the Territorial skill resource boost?" Rocky asked after reading the description of the first choice the council wanted.

Sela read his title to the council and Mary made excited notes on another new sheet of paper. No one answered his question, though, and he assumed that was because no one knew. Sela did eventually volunteer her opinion. "I don't think so, because a title does not count as a spell, and I doubt that Leadership skills or Territorial skills do either. I think that particular notice is to stop people from picking multiple boon spells and trying to stack their effects."

Rocky nodded and the council voted, eventually confirming that as their first pick.

Minor Boon of Research and Development Level 1
This boon will increase the yield of all research and study by 10%, magically granting additional research points once every ten times.
Lasts 1 cycle around Odin.
This spell cannot be stacked with any other Territorial or personal spells, and is only available to those with a Place of Power.

—

Minor Boon of Crafting Level 1
This boon will increase the yield of all crafted goods by 5%, magically doubling bonuses on a piece of gear once every twenty times.
Lasts 1 cycle around Odin.
This spell cannot be stacked with any other Territorial or personal spells, and is only available to those with a Place of Power.

—

Territorial Skill Tree
Skill Points available: 85
All skills will affect any and all Territories owned by the same leaders. Skill points are awarded at 5 per level, in most cases. To discover more, level up and capture additional Territories.
<u>Skills</u>

Stat Boost

While individuals reside within the boundary of this Territory, all stats will be increased by X, where X is the number of skill points in this skill.

0 / 50

At fifty skill points, the skill will upgrade.

Resource Boost

Every resource that spawns within your Territory will give X% more when collected, where X is the number of skill points in this skill.

20 / 50

At fifty skill points, the skill will upgrade.

Etherience Boost

All individuals who gain Etherience within your Territory will be awarded X% more, where X is the number of skill points in this skill.

0 / 50

At fifty skill points, the skill will upgrade.

Growth Boost

All women will carry to full term faster by a factor of X%. All children will grow X% faster to maturity, where X is the number of skill points in this skill.

25<+85?> / 50

At fifty skill points, the skill will upgrade.

Mary took excited notes, but was forced to rip up several pages when Rocky refused to allow the council to vote on Territory skill point allocation. He had already promised women of the Territory where he was going to place those points, and nothing the council argued would change that. At least, not until that skill was maxed out, which Rocky assumed would happen around three hundred points. He placed the eighty-five points in Growth Boost and confirmed it. Then opened the upgraded skill summary.

Growth Boost Upgraded to
Growing Pains Upgraded to
Growing Up
All women will carry to full term faster by a factor of
110%. All children will grow 110% faster to maturity.
All women are 110% less likely to suffer pregnancy
complications.
All children will gain mental maturity at a rate 110%
faster.

—

Congratulations. You have completed a quest.
Hidden Quest
Personal Quest
Add to a Territory
Vanquish a leader, boss, or super spawn, convert it to
an orb and add it to a Territory you own.
Rewards:
Increased Territory Size Awarded
10,000,000 Etherience (+2,500,000 Knight's Quest)
Etherience has been increased since the owner already
has a Leader class.
Great job, Leader!

He dismissed the notice and frowned. "Did you add the orb to the Grotto, then?"

"Yes, the Etherience boost for the members of Meliora and the increased protection it should offer here is sorely needed," Derik responded in a clipped way that made Rocky feel slighted. Did the man think that was the end of that discussion?

"Hold on—"

"That brings us to the discussions about the excursion to Atlantis," Mary read from the next page and motioned to Sela. She looked at Rocky, and shrugged, which forced him to reconsider his frustration. Was he actually upset that the council added the orb to the Grotto? No. He was just upset with Derik's flippant attitude. He shrugged back at her, letting her know he would let the matter go.

Sela stood and smiled at the group. "Again, I must request that we put together a party that will be capable of going overland through this continent," —Sela pointed to the African landmass on a map hanging from the wall— "to reach Atlantis. If we have any chance of mustering a defense against the impending invasion of the Guild Collective, it will be in Atlantis."

Everyone looked to Rocky after that, and he realized she already had the council's support but she was expecting him to join this expedition. He sighed heavily. "Can this not wait, Sela? I just got back, and I can't just leave my family behind again to run off… Not to mention the ongoing threat of Frankie…"

"You left them behind for the last two months," Derik interjected. "What are another few weeks? It's not like we need the leaders here in the Territory to keep things running, or to defend against the zombies…"

"I knew this would come up," Rocky said as he stood and motioned to Derik. "I also knew who would be the first to broach the subject." Derik had the sense to blush at that offhanded dig at his character. "However, I think I should make you all aware as to the circumstances around why I was gone for two months…"

Rocky told them all the story of how he had been under the false belief that his family had died. How he had originally been trying to throw himself into life-or-death struggles to try to forget what happened. He even admitted that at one point he had wished for death from those same creatures. By the end of his admission, Sela looked somewhat stricken, and had retaken her seat.

If he was honest with himself, he may never be able to leave the Grotto again...

***

"We are still having numerous thefts from the warehouse shops, and even the ship building yard. Has there been any progress in discovering the thief?" Carl asked when Smith asked if there were any other problems that needed to be addressed. Rocky had been hoping that Smith's words were signaling the end of the meeting, but Carl's tone suggested that this was an ongoing issue.

Rocky tilted his head. "Has anyone checked the sales log of the shop to see if anyone is selling the stolen goods?"

Sela nodded her head. "I have provided the logs to the council on previous meetings, and we have not yet been able to find anything out of the ordinary. We will check again tomorrow. Carl, please provide the council with the report of the missing goods and we will pull the logs to bring to Mary."

"What about access to the warehouse? Didn't we only grant some people access?" Rocky asked, trying to understand how someone was managing to steal from a secure building.

"Early on, we removed all access to it but yours and mine, and the thievery still occurred. So, unless you have been sneaking into the Territory, and then leaving again with things from the warehouse, the thief is finding other ways inside..." Derik added, his voice holding a great deal of scorn but adding a bit of sarcasm to lighten the accusation he made. He must already know that Rocky wasn't sneaking back in.

In response, he just shrugged. "I've got enough junk in my bag of holding already. I don't need to go picking up more."

An hour later, Smith asked, "Are there any other problems that need to be addressed?"

Surprisingly, no one spoke up. Rocky sighed, and together with Sela, he left the meeting room. Sela headed for the stairs and he followed her after a moment's hesitation. While he didn't notice the weight of his bag of holding anymore, it might be nice to empty some of its contents into his room. That was when he recalled the shower that was up above, and he quickened his step. Sela veered off at the second level to head to her room and while he felt a slight pang at the distance between them, he shrugged it off, staying mindful of the sad thought.

For now, I will be happy with the shower!

***

That night, Rocky woke up to a door closing near his own. He blinked the sleep from his eyes, and checked the clock beside his bed. It was two-forty in the morning and about twenty minutes before the alarm he had set. Groaning, he turned off the alarm and slid out of the warmth his covers cocooned around him.

He checked the window and saw Sela disappearing in the direction of the mess hall, and wondered what she was doing awake this early. He shrugged it off as he got dressed in a fresh set of clothes and left the town hall in the opposite direction, toward the Guild Dome. The place was extremely quiet this late at night, but he did see some groups and individuals moving about either getting an early start to their days, or having a very late finish.

It was usually clear which were the late-night crowd as they stumbled from wall to wall looking drunk. The early risers, on the other hand, were geared up, and nodded at Rocky when they passed him. He wondered if the dungeon time slots the council discussed had anything to do with the several groups up at this 'early' hour. He had assumed that people would take a break at night, but now he wasn't certain.

He rode the elevator to the observation deck and found a few people manning stations. No one questioned his presence. Maybe because of the access restrictions, or perhaps because they knew him. Either way, when he approached the Altar of Michabo, which was also the place of power, he wasn't questioned.

He long ago had seen Amber's name fall off the list for possible resurrections, and never once had he seen the storage of enough Territorial Etherience needed to place her in the queue. That realization had made him spiral for a long while, until he remembered a Bottle of Gaia's Essence that he had received during the first few days of this apocalypse.

He placed a hand on the altar. <Michabo, can you hear me?>

<Welcome back, Barkclay. I've missed our little chats. What brings you to the altar today?> Michabo's voice sounded in Rocky's head like Azoth's did. Rocky rolled his eyes at the snark but was able to brush off the annoyance he felt with a slight effort.

<I would like to make a trade for Amber's resurrection,> he stated as plainly as he could.

<There is nothing you have that I could want, Barkclay. We're already sustained in this realm by the power diverted from your Territory, and Amber, unfortunately, was sent to the lowest realm to begin her climb through them all. It would take more power than we have to pull her out.>

Rocky placed the Bottle of Gaia's Essence on the altar but kept a hand on it. <Are you sure I have nothing you want?>

He knew that Michabo needed more Territorial Etherience, and Ether. He also knew that Essence was far more powerful than either of the two resources the bunnyman was hoarding. So, if this didn't work, he also knew that nothing would.

<I may have misspoken,> Michabo responded after a moment. <All you want in trade is your friend's resurrection?>

<I think this bottle is worth quite a bit more than that. What else can you do?> Rocky countered.

There was a long pause where Rocky could still feel Michabo's presence, but the Rabbit-man didn't speak. <I could grant you Territorial Etherience equal to five million points, in addition to resurrecting Amber.>

That gave Rocky pause. If Michabo had that much Territorial Etherience, then he likely had enough to resurrect Amber without the trade. Something was fishy and it was his turn to consider. <If you have that much stored Etherience, why can't you resurrect Amber without this Essence?>

<There are things that must be taken care of in the Spirit Realm with that Etherience. If you wish to make the trade, then we will use the Essence in place of the Etherience, but if not we cannot spare it.> Michabo's quick response conveyed a preparedness with that answer. Did that speak to it being made up, or a truthful fact?

It didn't really matter if it was truthful or false. Rocky needed to resurrect Amber, but perhaps he could get a bit more. <I want the allocation of Territorial Etherience to be adjusted to eighty-twenty from now on. Meaning—>

<I know what it means, dimwit. I cannot make that concession as the Spirit Realm needs at least thirty percent of what you currently make to sustain itself,> Michabo countered. Rocky felt a twinge of something in his head at that admission from Michabo. Why would the bunny-man be willing to take the bare minimum needed to sustain his realm?

He looked at the bottle of Essence, which had sat unused in his bag since the second day of the Apocalypse, and made the deal. Michabo had always been weird, and if he was lying and still taking extra Etherience, the adjustment was still good for Rocky and his Territories. This deal got Amber back using some random drop he had never found a use for. In his opinion, that trade was worth it and then some. A quick check after the bottle disappeared confirmed Michabo was holding up his side of the bargain.

Territorial Management Page
Click a tab to open the options within.
Spells | Buildings | Conversions | Resources |
<Rebirths>
Total Population: 147,012 Individuals within borders
Total Etherience per day: 1,470 Territorial Etherience
Current Etherience Total: 5,265,213 (17,265,213 –
12,000,000 for current Rebirth)

–

Rebirths
Thanks to your place of power, the Altar of Michabo, you have access to Rebirths. You can only use this option on spirits that reside in the Spirit Realm to place them in a physical body. Spirits need to have a constant stream of Territorial Etherience to be sustained in the Spirit Realm. If it runs out, they may either die a true death or be demoted to the 7th Layer.
Amber Dell
Journeyman Level 1
<Rebirth>
Cancel to refund 12,000,000 Territorial Etherience
Cancel?
23 hours, 59 minutes, and 30 seconds remaining until Rebirth.

Rocky looked at the twelve million Etherience it took to bring Amber back and felt his face blanch. Michabo felt the bottle of Essence was worth seventeen million in trade? He was tempted to try to question the bunny-man further about it but knew that Michabo wouldn't answer any question he didn't want to.

Maybe Rocky should not tell anyone about the trade?

CHAPTER TWELVE

"So, you saw the herds this morning?" Sela asked as she joined Rocky and his family in the Mess Hall. Rocky took a bite of bacon, that he now knew was actual bacon, and nodded as he made a delighted sound. Sela laughed then continued, "If you want to join Jason, Victoria, Gary, and me, we could go out hunting larger game, or take a turn through LFD?"

"I have to go meet Azoth's kits. He won't stop mentally sending me images of them…" Rocky responded as he took a mouthful of eggs. When he was finished chewing, he continued, "After seeing them, though, I would be up for something. Do you have a healer?"

"Yeah, we have a healer, he is the one who is being speed leveled to gain access to his regrowth skill." Sela popped bacon into her own mouth, and Rocky checked his plate to find a piece of his missing. He pulled his plate closer to himself and frowned at Sela in response.

"I would be happy to help. Should we bring Benoit too?" Rocky asked, trying to include his brother-in-law, the hunter, in the party. Sela actually smiled at Benoit.

"Sure. He needs to get better anyway," her voice was clearly playful, so Rocky laughed. Everything felt right in the world this morning, and he couldn't help but wonder if the mental weight of Amber's death that he lifted last night had been far heavier than he originally thought.

That and being back with my family.

After breakfast, the five of them made their way through the surrounding forest following rather spotty directions from Azoth. Luckily, Sela could check in with Black Beauty—Shiva— and confirm the directionally challenged manticore's instructions. They arrived at a small clearing with a large rock supported by smaller rocks. How the fifty-ton rock ended up balanced on top of ten-ton rocks was anyone's guess, but from inside the hollow it provided, Rocky heard small yowls and collisions.

"Azoth, you in there?" Rocky asked out loud for everyone's benefit. As if his words were a gunshot in the hundred-meter dash, Azoth exploded out of the cave holding a ball of black fur in his mouth. This was Nadine and Lacy's first time meeting the huge beast and they didn't hold in their gasps. Rocky wasn't surprised by the sudden explosion of fur and feathers because Azoth's appearance was heralded by a mental shout.

<Look, this son one!> Azoth exuberantly sent, before dropping the bundle of fur and feathers onto the ground near Rocky's feet. Before he could even respond, Azoth was into the cave and exploded back out again. <This son two! —daughter one —two —three...> The kits each had shut eyes, indicating just how young they were.

There were five male chimeras and eight females after Azoth was done with his parade. Each of the babies was black from head to toe. Nadine stayed somewhat hidden behind Benoit and Lacy as she eyed the kits warily. Lacy, and to a lesser degree Benoit, had no such reservation and were soon being swarmed over by the kittens. Sela had snuck inside at some point, likely to comfort Shiva as Azoth physically manhandled her children.

There was a wide range of shapes to the kits. Two of the sons and three of the daughters were clearly manticores like Azoth, but like his mother, the females had spiked tails. Another two of the males and one of the females looked to be just cats like their mother, Shiva. The rest were each unique in a way Rocky needed to categorize in his head.

One of the males and one of the females looked like gryphons, except the female version had a goat's head and the male had a lizard, almost draconic one. Two of the females were horse-like in body with wings and panther heads. The final female was some sort of goat-horse with snakes for tails. All the chimeras were stumbling around due to closed eyes and poor coordination. Their utter cuteness decided it for Rocky—they couldn't go by numbers like Azoth had just introduced them.

Shiva and Sela exited the cave, and the large panther with purple eyes moved to lean against Azoth. Since Azoth was standing next to Rocky, that brought the huge panther and Sela to his side. "Your kits are beautiful, Shiva."

"Shiva says thank you. She worries for them, and thanks you for letting them grow up in the Territory." Sela conveyed Shiva's response, and Rocky had to wonder if the panther was that good with the language or if Sela was adding to her message.

<Rocky, create more bonded!> Azoth crowed mentally. Rocky could tell that Sela and Shiva both also received his boisterous response because they flinched. He turned to his pet with a quizzical expression.

"Azoth, what do you mean?" he asked aloud so all parties could hear the response.

<Rocky Chimera Knight. Create other Chimera Knights, they bond kits. Kits grow big and strong like Azoth!>

"I don't think that's how it works, buddy," Rocky responded skeptically.

<Azoth know it is. Azoth feel it. Try!>

Sela's class had something like that in its description too… Was it possible his did as well?

Rocky looked at Sela, who, as far as he knew, had never searched for her ability to gift her class.

"Shiva says she is willing to let us try, as long as I confirm the process and only if we fully trust the person," Sela responded. Two pairs of human eyes and two pairs of cat eyes fixed on Benoit, Nadine, and Lacy.

"Would my family be acceptable?" Rocky asked Shiva and Azoth. Azoth began bouncing onto his back legs and landing heavily on his front paws. The action shook the ground and Rocky watched as Lacy and Benoit looked up in startled shock.

Their next action confirmed that they were good choices because they opened their arms and attempted to block the kits from moving in their excited father's direction.

    <Azoth, calm down. You could pancake one of your babies!> Rocky scolded and watched his pet fight with his own excitable nature. He stopped bouncing but his eyes were still wild.

    <Go hunting for now, buddy. Get that energy out. Okay?> he sent again, seeing the mood in the clearing. Perhaps if his family knew Azoth, they wouldn't have been so concerned, but the looks on Shiva and Sela's faces also bore a sense of nervousness. He knew Azoth would never hurt his own kids, but his pet was young, and it wasn't like accidents were impossible.

    Azoth did take off with a promise to bring back food for Shiva and the kittens. Shiva shook her graceful head and Sela conveyed, "She thinks he doesn't know how feeding works for the babies yet."

    Nadine was finally coaxed into playing with a rather cute pegasus with a panther head as it wouldn't stop following her around. While his family played, Shiva watched over the group, occasionally bringing a wandering baby back in her jaws. Sela and Rocky began searching through his screens, trying to find how he was supposed to impart the Chimera Apprentice class. Sela used her own screens and admitted, "I never looked into it myself."

    After searching his skills tree and status sheet, Rocky finally navigated through his pet tab. There at the very bottom of Azoth's information, he found a button he hadn't noticed before.

<u>**Chimera Order**</u>
King/Queen: 0
Prince/Princess: 0
Lords/Ladies: 0
Knights: 1

Squires: 0
Pages: 0

When he clicked the Knights tab his name was displayed, and his subclass of assassin was also shown. He blinked and clicked on Lords but found no additional information. Since he was relatively sure a Lord was above a Knight, he assumed it was something he may be able to promote himself to in the future. The same study of King and Prince tabs gave him no further information. He shrugged and clicked on Pages.

Pages
Each Knight can have a single Page under them. A Page can be raised to a Squire only if they bond with a Chimera. If someone becomes a Page and already has another class, they must reset their current progress to zero and begin again in the Apprentice ranks.
A Page can be anyone without age restrictions.
<Choose a Page> | Later

—

Squire
If a Chimera accepts the bond with a Page, they will be raised to the Squire rank. A Knight can have as many Squires as they have Chimeras to accept the bond. Squires cannot select Pages.

Rocky told Sela where he found his option, but since she didn't have a pet tab, at least not in the same place he did, she was forced to keep looking. Eventually, she found her option, but hers was slightly different than his. Her Apprentice Druid would reset progress as well, and she could only have one under each Journeyman Druid. After seeing her page, Rocky wondered if the Lord, Prince, and King ranks were just titles for his Master, Epic and Legendary class options.

The next question was who they should promote first among his family members.

"Benoit is the highest leveled at Journeyman, so would have the most to lose," Rocky began.

"I'm not sure I would want the class change, anyway," Benoit responded, scratching his beard. "It's probably better to give it to Lacy or Nadine. They are both Apprentice still, and only a few levels into 'the grind.'"

"I agree, especially if you can only do one at a time. Who knows how long it will take for them to bond one of the babies? What happens if the babies do not choose to bond with a Page?" Sela added, finishing with a pointed look at Rocky.

He shrugged but Sela's head turned to Shiva. "Shiva says that we should start with Nadine. The kitten following her around is very attached already."

Nadine was giving the horse-bird-panther vigorous scratches and something akin to a purring-whinny was audible in the silence that followed Shiva's insight. At Sela's conveyance of Shiva's words, Nadine had looked to Shiva. After a brief hesitation, Rocky's mother nodded, and looked to him.

"If you all think so, I am willing to reset my class, especially if I might get Cara as a pet," Nadine whispered over the thrum of 'Cara's' purring. Sela looked to Shiva and mouthed 'Cara' again. Shiva chuffed in response and Rocky smiled at the byplay.

His face almost hurt from the width of that smile, Rocky chose her as the first Page.

Congratulations! You have promoted your first Chimera Page. Chimeras often will bond with individuals based on their strength. Help your Page level up to help them create a bond.

As soon as the system confirmed the change, Rocky saw his mother slouch, almost falling in on herself. Nadine held a hand to her chest and sputtered, "That wasn't pleasant at all. I feel weak and sickly, almost like I've been laid up in a hospital bed recovering for a month…"

Cara, the panther-pegasus, instantly stopped purring as well, and stood up to circle Nadine. Rocky held his breath as Cara sniffed at his mother's neck, shoulders, and face. Then she lowered her head and headbutted Nadine in the chest before flopping on top of her again. The moment the purring resumed, Rocky got another notification.

Congratulations! Your Page has been bonded by a Chimera Kit. She has been upgraded to a Chimera Squire and will advance to Knight at the Journeyman ranks.

Nadine absently continued scratching Cara as her eyes tracked back and forth over something in front of her.

"Well, that was quick! What does it say, Mom?"

"Congratulations! You have been confirmed as a Chimera Squire—Pegasus, which is in brackets—by bonding a Chimera. Pegasus riders are granted the Outrider subclass of Chimera Knight. Outriders specialize in speed, support, and devastating long-range attacks. Best of luck, Squire," Nadine recited.

Rocky looked to Sela as he pointed at the other kittens.

"So, each of these will grant a different subclass based on species?" he asked and confirmed in more of a rhetorical way. When Sela shrugged he looked to Lacy. "Do you want to go next?"

Lacy looked at Nadine, who still looked sunken and sickly. However, their mother currently wore a large smile on her face as she played with the pegasus kitten. Eventually, Lacy sighed and nodded. He selected her as the next Page and watched her stats and levels drop. She looked even worse than Nadine had. Strangely, the kittens that had been swarming over her a moment ago all backed away once the change occurred. They continued to play with each other, Benoit, and some even joined Nadine and Cara but they would take a single sniff in Lacy's direction before turning to go another way.

Lacy was still able to catch up with them and pet them, since they really didn't have the coordination to avoid her, not to mention the sight to see her coming, but their playfulness with her was completely gone.

"Shiva says that Lacy should stay with the kits and her for the next week. The kits see her as something new now. Shiva can't explain it, but says that they need to sniff her out and get used to her new presence," Sela conveyed for the mother. "She also says that Lacy should gain a few levels to help."

Sela then looked to the three panther babies and back to Shiva. "It would appear that Shiva would like me to try to find Druids to bond with her non-chimera kittens."

Rocky looked at the three panthers and nodded to himself. He had been curious if Shiva was a chimera as well, but he thought this likely confirmed that she wasn't. All the strange combinations must come from Azoth. He wondered if his pet had recessive genes for horses somewhere in there, but eventually dismissed the old world's biological rules. It was unlikely they would still fit with the return of Ether and mythical creatures.

"Nadine, Lacy, do you want to join us on a dungeon run to help regain some of your levels?" Rocky asked his mother and sister. Nadine nodded but Lacy chose to stay with the chimera kits for now; Benoit also volunteered to stay behind.

<Azoth, one of your beautiful daughters has bonded with my mother,> Rocky sent his pet.

<Azoth bring back land lizard feast. We celebrate?>

Rocky laughed and asked everyone to wait for Azoth to return before they left.

***

The fifth wave of the Arena dungeon, Maximus, was a large alligator-snapping turtle and mutated fox called Toka and Razar. The experience inside of the dungeon this time was vastly different from Rocky, Sela, and Zippo's first clear of the place. This time, Rocky wasn't stupid enough to comment on the break between rounds, which activated hell mode in the past, and they also had an actual planned group to challenge each wave. Victoria was currently weaving and blocking blows from a swiftly moving fox and a powerful telescopic-headed turtle.

Gary the healer was the same man who had helped Rocky out of the darkest parts of his mind, and after their warm first greeting, Rocky had mostly avoided him. It was slightly awkward for Rocky, who had told this man things that he wouldn't have shared with anyone under normal circumstances. He worried that Gary viewed him as a monster, or at least something less than human. So far Gary occasionally eyed him worriedly, but otherwise hadn't brought up anything Rocky had shared with him.

He likely hasn't even told the people here anything about me… I wonder if that's because of his past life. Like doctor-client confidentiality.

Gary was just under six feet tall and had a mop of brown hair that clearly hadn't been styled in a while. He carried a walking stick, wore a robe, and seemed to be wearing far too much jewelry. Rocky assumed the accessories were all enchanted, but it still made the man look gaudy and vain, which he also knew wasn't the case.

Azoth had joined them on the sands of the arena, thanks to the overly large entrance. The manticore chased the nimble fox, attempting to clamp it in his jaws or pin it under a massive paw.

<Azoth, try attacking the turtle for now!> Rocky ordered, and watched Azoth slide to a stop.

Nadine and Cara stood with Sela and Zippo as they wove spells into the fray. Sela only had Blight, Moon Fire, Dark Vines, and Stalagmite available from range, but she was also acting as the last line of defense for his mother and Shiva's baby. Zippo had a great deal more firepower, but if a monster charged his mother, he only had his barrier skill and then his rather weak Stamina to act as a defense.

Nadine was already up to level twelve and Rocky sheepishly discovered that she could pick a skill that let her communicate with Cara on the first tier. This caused him to look at his ring and wonder if he had missed the chance to receive that skill since he only got the class at the Journeyman rank.

This wave ended quickly once Azoth switched targets and Sela locked down the fox with her vines. A countdown of sixty seconds began and Rocky Analyzed their loot from the fifth wave.

True Silver Bar
True Silver is one of the best conductors of Ether and Electricity. This metal is highly valued by most crafting professions.

Rocky held the bar up toward Sela and raised an eyebrow.

She saw the gesture and said, "We need a ton of that in the schematic for the battleship. So, we fed some to all our dungeons. The guild buys it from adventurers that are lucky enough to receive it as a drop. There are some other materials that could drop as well."

Fifteen waves later, they faced Monstar again, and this time Azoth didn't fly up to attack the spider. With all his party, other than Nadine, at a much higher level than before, they made quick work of the twentieth wave. Rocky looted the boss and was about to head to the exit when he noticed the timer was counting down for wave twenty-one.

"Since when does it have more than twenty waves?" Rocky asked the group.

"Since we fed it the ogre bosses…" Sela responded with a wicked smile. "It currently has thirty-five waves."

CHAPTER THIRTEEN

They faced five waves of escalating numbers of ogre minions until they reached the twenty-fifth wave. Rocky thought he knew what was about to appear when the door in the shale rock wall opened and he was right.

Out stepped Bam-Bam, wearing chainmail and wielding a large morningstar. As soon as his eyes hit Rocky, he reached into his pocket and threw four seeds onto the sand. They arched out and spread away from each other.

Instantly, the tree-vine totems began to grow, but this time Sela's Dark Vines reached up and began tangling with the quickly growing totems. Bam-Bam sneered at Sela and then began charging at her, Zippo, and Nadine. He only made it a step before Rocky's three stacks of Dark Blade collided with his side. Only two of the three connected, but Victoria somehow had predicted Rocky's attack and stood in the direct path of his third with her shield glowing. His final blade collided with her golden shield and ricocheted into Bam-Bam's back as he fought to stay standing.

Bam-Bam was now pinned between the three blades in an open-sided triangular pattern and the rest of the ranged fighters unloaded their skills into the boss as well. Zippo conjured his flame tornado, while Sela created a hollow sand-stalagmite with Bam-Bam and the tornado at its center. The sand quickly became fused together and instead of forming a wall around the ogre, it melted onto him.

Bam-Bam
Master-Yabba-Dabba
Level 23
Health Points 450 / 2450
Bloodlust
Boss

Rocky heard the drumbeat of Bam-Bam activating bloodlust, but it was like the first chords played on an old guitar, causing the strings to break. The tribal drums beat out only a few percussive notes before the boss died. Rocky smiled at the ease of this battle when compared to the struggle the Grotto had faced when Bam-Bam and Pebbles first attacked. If nothing else, this proved the group's increase in strength.

***

"What do you mean items from the Territorial inventory have gone missing?" Sela asked Smith after he delivered the bad news. "That should be impossible!"

Rocky, who had just dumped the loot from the dungeon into that same inventory, pulled it and more back out to keep in his bag for now. "I pulled out the stuff needed for battleship construction and have it in my bag of holding for now," he added, to make sure the two didn't think the withdrawal signaled more thievery.

"Our only guess is that the person is a high-level thief who can somehow access the warehouse and inventory without proper permissions." Smith pointed over to the warehouse which was attached to the gunmetal gray of the shop. Each of the components for a seed shop were made from a metal called arbuckle, and heavily enchanted to prevent thievery like this from happening. The warehouse currently had ten guards patrolling outside of it, which was supposedly a large increase from two.

Nadine, Zippo, Victoria, and Cara begged off shortly after to deal with other things around the Grotto, and the three leaders went to the shop. It was time for Rocky to check through the log of sales and purchases to see if anything was out of place. Not that he expected to find something that the council and Sela had missed, but he figured it was worth a try. They spent the next few hours checking through the listed items without finding anything.

"Do you think the thief is holding onto the items? Or selling them somewhere else?" Rocky asked, trying to figure out what they were clearly missing. He amended his first question. "What would be the point of stealing stuff if you're just going to hold onto it?"

Smith shrugged, but Sela tapped her foot as she considered. "What if they had found access to another shop in the area? How many teams leave the Territory to hunt?"

"No more than five, if that many…" Smith said as he opened notes on his screen. "Three teams choose to farm the larger beasts outside the Territory. Each team consists of twenty or more people, though."

"Unfortunately, the teleportation pad is going to complicate this problem, but my guess is that there is a second seed shop somewhere within a day's travel outside of the Territory," Sela surmised. "There's probably a detector for arbuckle in the shop. If we were to mount it on the battleship, we might get lucky."

Letoya, a good friend of Victoria's, came running and Smith held up a hand to help her find him in the crowd. She rushed over. "Amber just appeared up the altar in the middle of the operations room. She won't wake up, but doesn't Analyze as hurt. The shift lead has ordered for her to remain in place until we hear from you."

Sela and Smith both looked to Rocky who began scratching his neck. He attempted a nonchalant shrug, but clearly didn't convince anyone because Sela asked, "What did you do?" rather pointedly while scowling.

Smith, however, asked something that he probably should have recalled. "Didn't we all wake up naked?"

Letoya nodded emphatically. "The shift lead has asked everyone to exit the control room for now, because we're not sure if we can cover her in a blanket or move her before she fully wakes up."

Sela stared at Rocky with raised eyebrows. "You did not think to tell anyone? Or ask any questions, did you?"

Rocky just looked back at her, his eyes going slightly hard. "An omission is not a lie, Sela. Omission is something that a true leader must do…" he retorted in a whisper. Sela's face paled, and her head drooped to her chest after she couldn't hold eye contact anymore. He walked over and placed a hand on Sela's shoulder. "I was forced to live with the last omission, and I wasn't going to ask permission this time. Let's head to the control room and ask Michabo."

The walk to the Guild Dome and elevator ride up the Tower was dead silent. The only noise came from the whispering techs who hovered near the elevator entrance on the main floor. Rocky wasn't specifically happy to hear everyone talking about 'the naked woman who appeared out of nowhere' but he left Smith with the group to debrief them. As soon as the doors to the elevator had closed, he had expected Sela to begin questioning him, but she remained quiet. He risked a glance in her direction to find her studying the Territorial interface screen.

Just before the extremely fast elevator arrived at the top floor, she pointed at the Territorial Etherience number and asked, "Rockland, how did you end up with enough Etherience to resurrect Amber and still have five million?"

Rocky allowed the elevator doors to open, and he walked out before he answered.

"I traded the Bottle of Gaia's Essence for it."

He heard Sela stop walking behind him and he turned toward her. Their eyes met, and she blinked before she sheepishly raised her hand and scratched the back of her neck. The gesture was so akin to something he might normally do that he laughed. The laugh startled Sela, and she looked him in the eyes and her mouth cracked into a smile before she schooled it back to stoicism.

"I will not criticize you too much, but I hope you realize just how powerful that stuff was. Still, it will be nice to have Amber back, and as a leader I am also very happy to have five million Territorial Etherience to use for the good of our people." Sela held up her hand when she was done and a ball of nanoweave appeared a moment later. "Wait here for a moment, I'm going to give Amber some decency."

Rocky decided right then he would never tell anyone that he had received seventeen million Territorial Etherience and Amber's Rebirth had cost twelve of it. The fact that Sela, who had been rather stoic since his return, complimented the five million was a clear sign that Amber's Rebirth was extremely pricey. To Rocky it had been worth it, and the Bottle of Gaia's Essence had been his. So, that was all that mattered.

"She is awake," Sela called back. Rocky turned back around and found a smiling Amber regarding him in a skintight nanoweave suit. He coughed once and forced his eyes to meet hers. She was a good-looking woman, and he didn't want to ogle her.

"Amber," he greeted her warmly as he approached. "Sorry that it took us so long to get you back." He felt slightly awkward as he wanted to admit to her his hand in that, but couldn't.

"Thanks," Amber began as she stood up and looked down at herself. "What am I wearing?" she asked, and Rocky turned away as his cheeks flushed.

"It is a nanoweave suit of under armor. I think Rocky has some leather armor in the bag if you want something more?" Sela answered for him. He turned his back again as the girls got Amber dressed in some of the leather armor he had enchanted during the last two months. When he did turn back around, she was more appropriately dressed.

She met his eyes and then continued the conversation. "Don't worry about the delay. I spent most of my time with the Algonquin elders who taught me the ways around the Spirit Realm. Well, until about a day or so ago when everyone vanished…"

Sela's eyes narrowed but Rocky asked the clarifying question, "What do you mean vanished?"

"Well, Michabo kept preaching that the Algonquin Guild was biding its time and building their strength for some sort of conflict. In the last little bit, he continually held meetings with a lot of the powerful elders. I could tell that they were excited about something, but no one would talk to me. Then a few days ago—maybe less or maybe more; time was strange in there—they had a large gathering in the Grotto center, and I wasn't invited. I found it rather strange, because I was invited to almost everything else they did. They kind of saw me as the youngest member of the tribe. Still, when I woke up everyone was gone."

Rocky moved forward to touch the altar.

"Michabo, are you—" he began but as soon as he touched the Place of Power, he could tell that something was different. While it didn't feel hollow or empty, it did feel different. No cranky bunny-man responded either, and he looked worriedly at Sela. She stared back for a blink before she shrugged and patted Amber on the back.

"There are probably some people down below that would love to see you," Sela offered as she guided the Native American woman to the elevator. "Plus, we could likely power level you along with our healer Gary for a while," Sela offered.

After today, Rocky knew that Gary was one level away from the first point in Regrowth. While that meant quite a large amount of Etherience was needed because Gary was a Journeyman rank, it was still very much possible.

My family will be whole again, Amber is back, and we've even got some Territorial Etherience to spare for the war effort...

CHAPTER FOURTEEN

"Sela was right," Smith said as a morning greeting. "We found a seed shop at St. Matthew's Catholic Church in Madawaska. Only one group of adventurers that farms outside of the Territory has a member that was rescued from that town. We are waiting for them to return to arrest him."

Rocky was following along in the morning martial practice. Ragnar was easily identifiable on stage as he moved through stances. Rocky realized this was his first time seeing the massive man that they had saved from Apep's control, and he wondered if any of the twenty bosses they had just slain in defense of the Grotto would be turned as well. Smith began moving through the patterns with a practiced ease and Rocky couldn't help but be impressed.

"So, why is this my first time seeing Ragnar?" Rocky asked as he tried to match Smith's movements. It did help to have someone well practiced beside him. While Ragnar was certainly a good teacher, Rocky was separated from the stage by hundreds of bodies. A quick estimate put about ten thousand people currently working through forms.

"He teaches all day. We have approximately one hundred and fifty thousand in the Grotto and this field can only gather about ten thousand per hour. So, we broke practice into shifts to make sure everyone gets a turn. The Golem Knights, when they are in the Grotto, do the same in the mobilization yards."

"What if the Golem Knights aren't around?"

"Then someone from the A-team takes the lead. Or someone from the council. Usually, it's Derik because he has the highest Ether Channeling and Manipulation."

Rocky nodded and moved to the next sequence of forms as Ragnar shouted instructions from the stage. He seemed to be highlighting the importance of footwork in all aspects of combat.

The subtle differences between a step and an advance. Rocky wasn't going to pretend he fully comprehended the entirety of the lesson, but to him it was about closing off angles from the opponent while simultaneously opening your own.

Smith and he moved to the mobilization yard after their group of ten thousand were released. Most of the group stayed together and made their way there, but a few did leave for other tasks after the combat training. Today, Tao, seated in a cross-legged position, was clearly visible as they moved through the longhouses toward the entrance to the Grotto at the south. The three barracks were surrounded by hard-packed brown soil that had clearly seen the bottoms of many feet and backsides.

Rocky sat down near the back of the gathering and Smith lowered himself beside him. They watched perhaps half of the numbers from the combat training take their places on the hard earth.

"Is this always less popular than the training?" Rocky asked, with a head turn to address Smith.

"Unfortunately, yes. People all want to get stronger faster, and while some people know that Ether Manipulation and Channeling are important, many others either don't or have hit a plateau and given up."

Nodding, Rocky turned back to Tao. He himself hadn't seen as much improvement in the two skills over the last two months. He had tried numerous different circulation methods, even going as far as tracing out most of his circulatory system, but other than some rather fun patterns, he hadn't gained much. Still, because of the two skills, not only did he regenerate Ether faster, but he also spent less Ether when casting and was able to enchant gear at a slightly higher level. He couldn't point to a time they saved his life directly, but he kind of felt that they had done so numerous times.

Ether Channels

This skill allows you to increase the regeneration of Ether in your body.
Weak - Increases your Ether regeneration by 25%.
Moderate - Increases Ether Regeneration by 2% per level. Current: 68%.

—

Ether Manipulation.
This skill will allow you to form spells faster based on your skill level.
Weak - Increases casting speed by 12.5%.
Moderate - Increases casting speed by 1% per level. Current: 35%.

He had been hoping that Tao would be able to help him get past his current bottleneck, but that was slightly naive if what Smith said was true.

As the last people settled in, Rocky entered meditation and dove into his mind's view of the channels that circulated through his body. He had settled on a pattern that was similar to flower petals unfurling around the nucleus. Despite trying numerous, more complex patterns, Rocky had found this one easiest to maintain while sleeping.

"Today is a good day," Tao began. The golem wasn't really addressing the group but Rocky knew that the Golem Knight's method of instructing was often introspective speech. "When I look at a river, I know it will eventually find its way back to the ocean. The same can be said about lakes, creeks, and springs, but what of the rain?"

Rocky blinked, not sure he was understanding the lesson. The rain landed on the ground and made its way through the soil to the bodies of water or was absorbed by plant life before that. Right?

"When I look at a waterfall, do I not see some of the falling water mist away on the wind and not make it to the ocean? What of the snow that falls all around the Territory? Is it flawed because it can't make its way to the lakes?"

Tao was discussing the different states of water, when speaking on Ether. Was the golem just philosophizing? Or was he giving Rocky valuable information? He considered his current channels and the pattern they created. If the Ether pool was the ocean, and the channels were rivers—where was the rain, snow, and clouds?

Tao continued to talk but listening with half an ear, Rocky realized the next 'lesson' was pointing to the shapes that one's channels took and how each body was suited for a different pattern. Rocky, who had already traced his entire circulatory system and adjusted his channel patterns numerous times, wasn't in need of this advice. Instead, he focused on trying to find the states of Ether. He thought he knew where the ocean, rivers, and lakes were, but then, what was the rain?

Could the clouds be the ambient Ether floating in the air around him? He took that analogy a step further. Then the rain falling would be when the ambient Ether transmuted through his skin, and into his internal Ether. That energy traveled through his fat, muscles, and bones all the time to join his channels and then be carried to the ocean. Still, what then was snow, or what would evaporate the water to return it to the clouds?

He formed his Dark Blade skill onto his Soul Blade in the form of a dagger and watched the Ether from his pool activate and travel through his body to his right hand. Once there, it entered the Soul Blade and created a latticework of minute channels of Ether, but it didn't evaporate. He stabbed the soil in front of his crossed legs and watched some of the Ether disperse into the soil as it helped his dagger pierce through the earth. Still, the Ether flowed from the blade as if it was still liquid, it didn't disperse like evaporating water. Except, perhaps a tiny portion of Ether that just vanished from his mind's eye. If he had used ten points of his Ether pool in the action, he had felt nine of them flow away after the strike, but one point was gone entirely.

Growing excited, Rocky stabbed the ground again and tried to concentrate on all ten points of Ether. A twinge of pain in his forehead told him that he was straining his mind, but he persisted. The twinge turned into an ice-cold poker when the tenth point vanished. It might have been his imagination, but he thought he felt something gossamer float away. It reminded him of his connection with Azoth. A connection that he could feel but couldn't track with Ether.

That same feeling came from his bag of holding. Unlike other enchantments that he could trace in his mind's eye and replicate with his enchanting pen, the bag had something he couldn't quantify surrounding it.

Feeling around himself, he found that strange connection affixed to his aura and attempted to touch it with an Ether Channel. The channel seemed to pass through the strange phantasmal connection, and he didn't receive any new pieces of information. Shrugging, he returned to his earlier considerations and changed a few perspectives. If evaporation was what he saw happen to that single drop, then perhaps his Ether pool was a lake, and the ocean was the ambient Ether.

Then whatever had happened to that drop was just Ether changing states? That felt slightly wrong somehow, but he also felt it had some truth to it.

Alright, then you would just need to locate snow…

Feeling through his body, he found caches of Crystalized Ether throughout his muscles and bones. Perhaps it was because of the shape of the Crystalized Ether currency, but it wasn't hard for Rocky to interpret this form of Ether as snow. He could tell that the Crystalized Ether he found adhering to muscles, bones, and tissues in his body were reinforcing it, making it stronger. So, was the melting of this 'snow' what his mom and sister paid for their class changes?

They had lost their stats…

Once Tao finished his 'instructions' for the hour, Rocky excused himself from Smith. He really wanted to check out the crafters hall and look at enchantments with Tao's philosophy on Ether. He also wanted to see how the Territory was doing in that regard. When he had headed to New York to rescue his family, he had left instructions on all his findings, as well as the single enchanter's pen that he had at the time. Since then, he had purchased himself another pen, and had made a few additional breakthroughs. He wondered, though, if he would be teaching in the crafters hall or being taught.

***

"You see here," Erileth, a man Rocky had found after asking numerous people for the enchanting area, pointed to Rocky's Leather Jerkin of Protective Strength. He of course wasn't pointing to the object but the enchanting runes and the Ether flowing through them. "This jerkin could have sustained more Ether flow, which would have increased the enchanting levels.

"Yet, with this loop on the Strength rune you enter at a seventy-degree angle, loop around and exit on the level. So much of the pressure is used to climb here, and you don't return any of the potential energy. And you can see how slow the Ether is traveling after, which is why you returned so quickly to the pool of the item."

Rocky scratched his head and looked at Erileth. "There is only one way to write the Rune of Strength. So, I'm not sure how the entrance of that loop and exit are affecting the strength of the enchantment."

Erileth blinked at Rocky, and then guffawed, which caused Rocky's cheeks to heat up. He reminded himself that he had come here to learn, and it helped him calm his rising ire.

Still, it wasn't enjoyable to be laughed at. Luckily, Erileth beckoned him over to some sort of contraption made of what appeared to be clear PVC piping.

"Look here." Erileth pointed to a section of the clear plastic piping that rose straight up against gravity. "The top of this column is what provides the potential energy that the water then uses to travel all the way back down all of these snaking pathways to the bottom of this vertical tube, where it then climbs back up and starts again."

"Yes, but you are using a pump to have it gain that potential energy!" Rocky responded, feeling frustrated by an analogy that didn't fit with enchanting.

To his surprise, Erileth snapped his fingers and interrupted him. "Exactly! Yet, you didn't ask the fundamental question I was expecting. I am using this pump to counteract gravity. What is the force that is counteracting Ether?"

Rocky, who still had his mouth hanging open, felt it fall a little wider as his eyes also bulged. He had always just assumed it was gravity as well, but then turning the gear upside down would have changed the flow. He did that with the piece of gear but saw no difference. Erileth chuckled and made a gesture with his hands, like he was crumpling a massive piece of paper into a small ball. Rocky blinked and looked at the piece of gear, not understanding the gesture. "What does that mean?"

"What is all around us, all the time?"

"Ambient Ether," Rocky hurriedly responded. Having just come from Tao's practice session, it was the obvious answer.

"Good, picture our bodies like a low-pressure zone," Erileth said and pointed at the pump. "What happens in a high-pressure to low-pressure system?"

"Are you saying the ambient Ether is both the force the enchantment is fighting against and the pump in your analogy?"

Erileth smiled broadly and clapped his hands together. When Rocky didn't say anything more, he wheeled his hand in a gesture that seemed to say, 'And what else?'

"So, if we were to strategically apply that pressure, we can turn the force counteracting the enchantment's Ether into the force that is propelling it…?"

"Exactly," Erileth stated. "Let me show you."

For the next hour, they unenchanted Rocky's massive store of gear in his bag of holding and Erileth directed him on how he could create channels that used the pressure from outside to increase the flow of the enchantments instead of hindering them. It was a strange concept at first, as Erileth described the channel walls like cell walls in a human body. Eventually, Rocky understood the selectively permeable concept and was able to figure out that Ether was both entering and exiting the channels through micropores of the enchantments. All he needed to do was envision the entry ports as going in the direction of flow at about a forty-five-degree angle, and his flow inside of the enchantments increased. Then when he managed to make the exit ports also at forty-five degrees with the direction of flow, he watched the entire enchantment stabilize in a way he hadn't known it could.

He looked down at his new leather jerkin.

Leather Jerkin of Protective Strength
Quality: Great
Ether Pool: Moderate
Ether Pool: 80/80
Enchantments: Protection IV (40%), Strength IV (+4)

It had gone up approximately two whole enchanting levels. He would have continued the rest of the day if Sela, Zippo, Smith, Nadine, Amber, and Gary hadn't found him.

"We have an appointment to run Leesoo, the Realm dungeon, in thirty minutes," Sela said as she picked up and examined some of the gear. "This is better than some of our group's gear, I think. Did you make this or did Erileth?"

"Erileth helped show me the way, but since then, all of these sets were re-enchanted by me," Rocky said proudly.

"I do not want to know how many crystals you used for all this, but since it's already spent…" Sela responded and held some gear to Amber, experimentally 'trying it on.' Rocky laughed and nodded; it was the least he could do for the woman he had left in the Spirit Realm for months.

CHAPTER FIFTEEN

"Isn't this such an exciting opportunity? When it appears in front of people, they must just take it and think themselves the luckiest individual in the Grotto. I call it spontaneous entry!" Little Friendly Dungeon machine-gunned out at the group who stood staring at a small cave mouth that literally rose out of the ground when they exited the crafters hall.

Rocky initially thought the hole in the ground was a collapsed tunnel. Many tunnels used to run under the Territory to where the altar used to reside. However, when LFD's voice accompanied the sudden appearance, he couldn't help but facepalm. "LFD, we have a dungeon run scheduled for Leesoo soon…"

"Ahh, but Leesoo doesn't have the secret Hell Rabbit level that this entrance leads to. You, along with ninety other lucky Grottonian's, have won an opportunity to challenge the hordes of Demon Rabbits below. The Etherience is heightened! The loot, rare! You may never get the experience again!"

"LFD, we have talked about this!" Sela interjected. "You can't just create unorthodox new methods to try to have people run your dungeon. What book did you get this one from?"

"Don't worry, Sela. This isn't a way to get more people into my dungeon. Well, I guess it will get more people if I include the hundred… But that's not what the book was alluding to. It was a book for a popular game you humans used to love—all you have to do is combine a wooden leg and some sort of cube thing and bam! Secret level. Supposedly, this level offered hordes of creatures to fight, the best Etherience and gear drops. People used it to grind through the levels and get stronger. So, I created the homage and now will spontaneously open entrances for people every morning. According to Adventuring for Dummies, the stronger the populace, the stronger the dungeon. See, I thought this all out."

Rocky blinked at the onslaught and stopped Sela from responding heatedly. Instead, he looked at the group. "I think I actually played the game LFD took this from, and if it's what I think it is, we should go down there, right now!"

"See, and if you find a cube and a wooden leg in my dungeon, you can open access to this floor one time!"

"There it is," Sela said as she wheeled on the dungeon entrance. "I knew this had to be about getting better attendance than the other dungeons!"

"Seriously, Sela, let's go down there. If LFD did what I think he did, this is going to be a huge boon for the entire Territory, and we might even want to have people who find those items turn them in for Guild or Territory strategic use." Rocky didn't even bother waiting for a response and ducked into the cave that could only fit one person at a time. He considered calling for Azoth and pulling the big manticore away from his kits, but the size of the entrance made that impossible.

The light was dim inside, but he followed narrow stairs down and down, until he felt a breeze that shouldn't be this deep underground. His heightened smell picked up grass, water, and a scent that reminded him of sunlight. His ears perked up next when he heard the obvious noises of rustling trees, lapping water, and wildlife moving. Still, it was the yellow sun-like light reflecting up the staircase to his eyes that was the most shocking. Rocky estimated that he must have descended approximately ten levels worth of stairs if this was a high-rise.

When the floor leveled out and Rocky walked through an archway, he found himself in what appeared to be another world. It was clear that it was still underground but the foliage and light source, combined with the three-story-high vaulted ceiling made it appear to be an entirely different ecosystem.

Welcome to the "Long Forgotten Dungeon; Hell Rabbits."

You have entered in a group of 5, suggested group size 50-100
Good luck.
Level: ?
Age: 1 Day
Best time: N/A
Clears: 0
Ether Concentration: High
To exit the dungeon, reach the final boss.

He heard the scrapes of boots on the stone behind him change to the soft creak of the crabgrass as his party entered. Each person held their breath as they took in the change.

"LFD, how exactly did you manage this?" Rocky asked into that silence.

"Leesoo showed me how she created the realms and their ecosystems. While I couldn't create a different space entirely, like Leesoo, I could create a light source and I watched a movie called Bio-Dome, then I read a few books. Now I have a beautiful landscape that people will surely seek out, increasing—I mean, I did it for the beauty of the space."

Rocky shook his head, knowing that everything LFD did was for its own purpose, but this cavern had to stretch for kilometers because while he could see the light source and the sloping ceilings away from it into the distance, Rocky couldn't see the other wall.

"Are those bunnies walking on two feet, wearing armor?" Zippo asked and Rocky scanned the area to find a huge group of humanoid creatures milling around under the shade of the canopy. Closer examination of the trees they were standing under made his frown deepen.

"What type of trees are those?"

"I combined conifers and mushrooms—I call them conifooms. Aren't they beautiful?"

"This is really dangerous," Sela whispered beside him, and he turned to regard Victoria and her on his right side.

Smith stepped up to join them. "Why? Because of the new species of trees?"

"Look around us. Everything is a brand-new species. While the dungeon creatures themselves usually cannot survive outside of the dungeons, flora is a completely different situation. In fact, there was a time when some sort of spore escaped the dungeon and created a horde of mutated humans that ravaged a huge area trying to return to the power of the dungeon." Sela pointed around her at the grass, trees, plants, and flowers. At her pointing out each thing, Rocky realized that, while many of them did look familiar, they were in fact twisted and mutated.

"Don't worry, silly Druid. I read countless books 'for Dummies' and created my Dungeon Invasive Species act. All plants and lifeforms on this floor cannot survive without dungeon water, light, and soil. Some of the plants were combined to increase poisonous effects, while others were combined to increase healing," LFD shotgun answered, before mumbling, "Though I couldn't really test the plants, so…"

Rocky felt his eyebrows raise slowly, first from the worries Sela brought forward, then from LFD's forethought, and finally from the mention of new poisons.

Wouldn't that be something my class could use…?

Sela questioned LFD thoroughly about each species and eventually LFD stopped responding, either feeling annoyed with the questions or moving on to greet other groups that might have descended from other entrances.

Rocky raised a hand to get everyone's attention, "Let's not waste the opportunity. We will deal with problems that this might cause after we clear the floor!"

***

The groups of rabbit-men were not difficult to deal with for the party. They were, in essence, large groups of monsters that could be gathered up and mowed down by area of effect spells. It took longer to loot the small rock hearts that remained after the battles than it did to clear the mobs. LFD hadn't responded to their questions about the corpses, and from the flashes of blue that occurred when they killed the creatures, the group had surmised he must be reabsorbing them.

They were now directly at the center of the room, looking out over a large lake where they could see hordes of rabbit-men coming and going.

"Let's kill what we can, but see if we can find any other groups," Rocky somewhat ordered. He was extremely happy with his progress so far in his current level, but while the group had picked up numerous plants, no one knew if any of them would be poisonous, or beneficial. His roiling stomach did give him some idea, and he had wanted to try eating some of those plants to add them to his Poison Pool but, like the manticore poison, he couldn't know how potent the stuff was.

It took another hour for the group to clear the lake of any rabbit-men they could find, and to collect numerous plant samples from both inside the water and outside.

Sela pointed out over the water after they were done. "There is quite a large number of fish species in the lake. If we had brought fishing gear, we could probably catch a large amount of food for the territory."

Rocky nodded, but looked in the other direction of the lake, because his heightened senses were picking up the sounds of combat. He pointed into the copse of mushroom trees and said, "There is another group over there. Let's go see how they're doing."

Sela frowned at him, but followed when he began moving. He did have a fishing pole in his bag of holding, but he wanted to see if the other groups that came down were struggling against the mobs on this floor. When the group pulled up and saw another group of ten slaughtering a horde of mobs, he held up his hand. "Okay, it looks like we can leave the other groups to kill the mobs for themselves. Sela, do you want to try to fish in the lake then?"

She blinked at him and looked at the others who all shrugged.

"You know LFD cannot kill the others down here, right?" she asked after a moment.

"That's true, but shouldn't we create some sort of plan for groups that get lucky enough to come down here in the future?" Rocky asked, turning to her. "Like Maximus creating Ragnar who now trains our citizens, this place has given us a ton of Etherience, herbs, and possibly even food. How many people saw the entrances in front of them and didn't come down here because of fear? How many people are fighting alone instead of in groups? I think even non-power classes could utilize this space to help themselves level if they circle the edge of the chamber to find others. So, I just wanted to see the difficulty level for our average citizen."

Sela narrowed her eyes and then sucked her teeth. "It sounds like you are planning on staying in this Territory for a long time now. What about Atlantis?"

The group moved away as discreetly as they could as they heard the annoyance in Sela's words. All but Nadine, who stepped up to Rocky's side.

"Sela, do you really want to take him away now that he just got back?" Nadine asked.

Rocky looked at his mother and then Sela sheepishly. "Sela, I agree we have to travel to Atlantis, but if we strengthen the citizens, does it have to be us who ventures out there?"

Sela's eyes flew wide. "You are saying you do not want to go out and conquer more Territories, get stronger and save others?" Her voice was incredulous, and Rocky felt a sting in his heart. Was that what he was saying? "Were you only brave when you had a family to save?"

Rocky opened his mouth to respond, but Sela punched him in the arm. Hard. He snapped his mouth shut in surprise.

"I wasn't good enough to come back for?!" she mumbled in a voice he barely recognized. She wouldn't meet his eyes, and he opened his mouth again but she turned and stormed away. His mother's eyes were also wide, and her face was pale. He might have tried to chase after her, but it was not exactly the right time to have *that* conversation...

"Sorry, Mom," Rocky began but to his surprise she cut him off with a raised hand.

"She has a point, son. If you are the leader here and the strongest person, maybe you have a duty to help as many people as you can." Rocky felt his heart fall at Nadine's words, but a moment later she continued, "Not that I want you to go and put yourself in danger. I just can hear how much she needs you—just like we need you... just like everyone needs you..."

He grabbed hold of her then and held his mother in a tight hug. "Don't worry, Mom, I'll figure something out. Maybe I will have to go, but that doesn't mean I won't come back.

"Still, I don't have to leave right now, either."

CHAPTER SIXTEEN

"That's Thumper?" Rocky asked his group, which was more tightly packed around him, then the others. There were approximately fifty people gathered on the shore, staring at the monstrosity of a creature that stood in the lake. It was easily two stories tall if you only included the parts of it that were above the water. The 'cute' bunny had arms and legs wrapped for a martial arts tournament. Even the ears seemed to be pulled back and wrapped to imitate a topknot hairstyle. Rocky used Analyze.

Thumper
Master-Kick Boxer
Level 12
Health Points: 30,345 / 30,345
Active Skills: 5
Passive Skills: 13
Raid Boss

"Raid boss," Zippo said with a bit too much excitement beside him. Rocky turned to look at the group and then turned back to look at the cage of people that hovered on a dock in the water behind the creature. There were likely another forty people in there.

"You can choose not to challenge this boss and exit," LFD unhelpfully chimed in. It was easy to see the large elevator shaft that now resided about twenty feet from the group. Rocky looked at the prisoners and then his group of 'survivors.'

"What happens to the prisoners if we leave?" Rocky asked LFD.

"They stay here for one week, until you pay their death price, or until someone defeats Thumper."

"We've paid forward a great deal of deaths already, LFD," Sela countered rather sourly.

"That's for deaths in the dungeon. This is a new area entirely separate but still associated with me. We cannot accept payment for the deaths like previously—as this floor is a bonus level. To access the bonus there must be risk—see!"

Rocky began shaking his head, understanding LFD's logic but not liking that the dungeon was actually making sense. It would have been easier if it was being unreasonable. This area clearly cost the dungeon far more in terms of its power to create and repopulate, and honestly, it was worth it for the Territory.

Instead, he turned back to the group of people that had 'survived.' "Other than Victoria and Gary, do we have any tanks? Healers?"

Sela followed his gaze as only two other people put up hands. One was clearly a tank based on the large shield on his back, but the other one wore leather armor like everyone else. "Tank." Rocky pointed at the first. "And?"

The second individual stepped forward and called, "Apprentice level but healing skills."

"That's too bad—this encounter is going to need at least four tanks and far more healers to conquer…" LFD began gloating and Rocky turned to study the boss and the lake. This version of Thumper looked terrifying, but it was submerged up to about its waist in the water. Rocky squinted as he considered a way to safely take on this raid boss.

"It's only got five skills," he mumbled more to himself than to anyone as LFD continued to brag about how awesome the new Hell Rabbit level was.

Turning to Sela, Zippo, Smith, Nadine, Victoria, and Gary, he motioned for them to come closer and started explaining what he'd come up with so far. Once they heard the start of his plan, the group quickly filled in the rest.

***

A massive barrage of nearly fifteen different ranged spells and ballistics slammed into Thumper's face. The rabbit began chattering its teeth and a wave built in front of its abdomen as it began charging toward the opposite shore. Rocky crossed his fingers as two more barrages of spells crashed home before the creature reached a spot about fifty meters from the far side of the lake.

Then he dropped his hand and his side of the lake launched their spells. Thumper was hit full on in the back, shoulders, and neck by his group's attacks, but other than overbalancing slightly forward, it didn't react. It continued to close with the fighters on the far shore, and Rocky's group charged and released their skills again.

Twenty-five meters and five thousand health gone. A golden glint on the far shore told Rocky that Victoria was readying herself, just as the fourth wave of spells from his side cut open Thumper's back. With only about fifteen meters between it and the shore, it turned and clacked its teeth across the lake at Rocky's group. In response, Rocky's side released another wave of spells.

This time, Thumper took them to his front as he turned and rushed back toward the center of the lake. The plan was working. His side fired one more volley and then stopped, allowing Thumper to cross through the lake's center and out toward them.

The other side fired spells again after Thumper closed to within fifty meters. Unfortunately, it took approximately five new waves of spells to finally turn the raid boss which allowed him to close within ten meters. Still, the health was already down about eleven thousand points.

"That's not fair! Fight fairly!" LFD shouted as Thumper glowed and then karate chopped viciously into the water. It looked more like a giant toddler playing in a pool than a raid boss meant to kill people. Rocky smiled at the complaint as he saw Sela's Moon Fire spell wash down onto the beast near the lake's center.

When the boss crossed the halfway point in his health, he began a roundhouse kick that quickly turned into a whirlwind as he balanced on one foot and spun like a top. Rocky blinked as the ineffectual attack created waves and a small whirlpool around the boss.

"This isn't the way you're supposed to fight him! Thumper's attacks would have decimated all of your melee attackers. It said so in the dungeon guide!" LFD screeched into the room.

"It's called strategy, dummy," Victoria shouted from the far side of the lake.

"That's not fair. You're not even giving him a chance! It's bullying again!" LFD swore as Thumper turned the water around it into a frothy red mess.

"LFD, how is it unfair to use skills that Gaia gave us to our best advantage?" Rocky countered as his side launched their spells at Thumper.

"Clearly, those skills aren't meant to be used inside of *bonus dungeons*."

LFD continued to harangue their tactics right up until Thumper turned into a floating corpse about fifteen meters from Rocky's side. Rocky looted the bobbing samurai bunny.

Bunny Crown (Set Item)
Quality: Excellent
Ether Pool: Medium
Ether Effects: <Locked>

—

Thumper's Wraps of Pain (Set Item)
Quality: Excellent
Ether Pool: Large
Ether Effects: <Locked>

—

Chimera Knight's Leather Boots (Set Item)
Quality: Excellent
Ether Pool: Large
Ether effects: <Locked>

"Wait a minute! These are my boots that I was wearing inside of Apep's dungeon under Chalk River!" Rocky shouted, which effectively cut off LFD's sullen whining.

"That's right, now you will have to come farm my depths repeatedly in hopes of getting the full set! Good luck, noobs!

"In the meantime, I will come up with better skills for Thumper!" LFD continued to jeer somewhat rudely. Rocky didn't care about the entire set, but if he remembered correctly, the chest piece had a Stat Link enchantment that he was extremely interested in seeing now that he knew how to enchant.

He turned to Zippo, who had been on his side of the fight, pointed at the boots, and then at his chest piece, trying to let the kid in on the play. "The whole set? Dude! This is the best item I had. Why would I need anything else? These had that noise dampening enchantment, which would allow me to sneak around your dungeon poisoning all of your minions, and farming for that leg and box."

"Oh, good call, Rock," Zippo chimed in. "With your ability to enchant gear, you could probably reproduce that enchantment and all the groups of the Grotto could just stealth run the entire dungeon. Then LFD wouldn't have to repopulate its minions, only its bosses. I'm sure that would actually help everyone…"

"Only repopulate bosses—stealth runs?! No, no, that is not possible, you can't use gear I make that way! You would hinder my growth just to have people farm my bosses. That must be against the clauses in the Cardinal contract.

"This is why I need a dungeon wisp like that CAL character from the book Adam fed me. I guarantee that Dani wouldn't let people treat her dungeon core this way! I demand justice for dungeons, I will post rules at the entrance prohibiting these runs. Anyone who goes against it, would suffer legal penalties…"

Rocky blinked, not having planned to get the dungeon this worked up. Thanks to Zippo, he now had the eccentric dungeon where he wanted him. Who CAL and Dani were was anyone's guess, and he would have to ask Adam more, but all he needed now was the right push. "Well, that's all your fault for giving me such good gear… but maybe I'd trade it back to you…" He tried to scratch his chin thoughtfully, but from Smith and Zippo's laugh, he knew he was overplaying his hand.

Gary interrupted LFD's response as he came around with the other half of the group. "I reached level twenty-one and can use Regrowth! From my feeling of the skill, I need to use it daily for nearly a month to fully recreate a limb. It's also going to be very painful… I think the more points I put into the skill, the less time it will take in that procedure, but it will still be more than a single use."

Nadine blanched and looked at Sela and Rocky. "I'm not sure I am up for the pain… This leg works just as well if not better than my original one."

Sela stepped forward and folded his mother into a hug. "Nadine, I know it's scary to think of the pain, but I can assure you having your limb back will be infinitely better than a mechanical substitute."

Rocky, who had stepped forward to hug his mother, hesitated now that Sela was there. He wasn't sure if hugging his mother and including Sela in that embrace would be appropriate, especially after her earlier 'assault.' Her status as his 'girlfriend' was still very much up in the air. Sela saw his hesitation and stepped away, which told him the story. She probably wouldn't have appreciated being included in the hug.

He wrapped his mom in an embrace with a silent nod to his guide. Nadine was shaking, but she hugged him back fiercely. Cara, who had grown to the size of a small pony over the last two days, rubbed against them both as she purred.

Maybe Cara was already talking because Nadine looked at the horse-cat and nodded. "Cara is conveying that she can help with the pain. She also wants me to do it." Nadine let go of Rocky and kneeled to hug Cara, the panther-pegasus.

"Rocky! Stop ignoring me. Trade this gold chest for the boots back!" LFD screamed, vibrating the water. Everyone flinched, then glanced at the gold chest that had risen from the crabgrass while they looked away.

"What's in the chest, LFD?" he asked in exasperation. Dealing with the dungeon was always a chore.

"It's a gamble you will have to take. Spin the wheel. Chance. Is your luck high enough?!" LFD mimicked a game show host so well that Rocky couldn't help but smile. This dungeon was strangely current on human cultures before Ether.

"So, you're suggesting I trade the strongest item in the set for some unknown in the gold chest? No thanks, buddy... We'll be seeing you. Let's get my mother up to the surface—"

"Fine, fine, it's the other pieces of the set in there. The chest and leggings for the boots. Two for one. Buy one, get one free?"

Rocky pretended to hem and haw over the decision, but took the offered chest while hiding a smile. Now he just needed to get these pieces unlocked and he would be able to make gear with the Chimera Stat Link... he hoped.

—

Chimera Knight's Leather Chest Piece
Ether Pool Level: Large

Current Ether Pool Level: 0 / 250 (Refilling)
Ether Effects: Protection II (25%), Automatic Repair,
Stat Link I

Protection II

Ether Pool will be used to directly reduce melee damage to any area covered by this armor. Magical damage requires three times the amount of Ether from Ether Pool to reduce damage. Damage reduced up to 25%, depending on the strength of the blow. This effect can be increased by having an enchanter increase the rank of the enchantment.

Automatic Repair

Armor will mend itself as long as the Ether Pool is not empty. If the Ether Pool is empty and the armor is destroyed, it will forever be lost. Repairs are made at a speed of 1% per hour.

Stat Link I

Stat Link is a unique Ether Enchantment and creates a link between the owner of this armor and his Chimera. The owner's stats increase by 3% of Chimera's total stats. This link only works if the owner of this armor has a Chimera as a pet and if the pet is within range of the enchantment. This effect can be increased by having an enchanter increase the rank of the enchantment.

—

Chimera Knight's Leather Leggings
Ether Pool Level: Large
Current Ether Pool Level: 0 / 250 (Refilling)
Ether Effects: Protection II (20%), Automatic Repair,
Strength and Speed of Arms I

Strength and Speed of Arms I

The Ether in these leggings will bolster two of your stats as long as the armor has Ether from its pool to

**draw on. This effect can be increased by having an enchanter increase the rank of the enchantment.
+ 5 Strength and Agility**

Rocky just finished unlocking his gear in the automated portion of the shop and was now sitting cross-legged on the ground off to the side. He stared at the new enchantments that he hadn't ever seen with his Ether Manipulation sight. Automatic repair in and of itself was extremely unique. It wasn't so much of a rune, as a secondary pool of Ether and something else. He couldn't see what that something else was, but he could feel that whatever it was, was alive. The only reason he knew that something was alive in that pool was that when he touched the pool with an Ether Channel, he could feel things moving around, almost like those little fish that exfoliate your feet in a pond.

Studying the Strength and Speed of Arms enchantment was like knowing how words worked and then seeing a sentence. He could see shapes for the Rune of Strength he already knew and even Agility but what joined them together almost looked like directions. Instead of just two characters, this enchantment seemed to hint at complexities he found exciting. He returned to the chest piece after a moment and felt his face fall for the tenth time since he had unlocked the gear. Stat Link, which by its description was the most powerful enchantment for Chimera Knights like himself, seemed to be non-existent. Where the living pool and the Protection Rune 'ended,' nothing was there other than the most complex spiraling knot he had ever seen. He would compare it most to a tangle that somehow looped back on itself so many times that you couldn't find a beginning anymore. Or an end.

He put on the chest piece and felt the pulse along that phantasmal connection he had with Azoth but, just like the connection itself, he couldn't distinguish what it was coming from.

"Ether in a different state, huh?" he mumbled to himself as he pulled the chest piece back off.

"What was that?" Sela asked from beside him. She had also done some shopping and must have joined him when he was deep in thought. He turned to her with a smile and walked her through his discoveries from the day. Her eyes narrowed a few times throughout his description but by the end her mouth was hanging open. "That is what Tao was going on about in the training sessions? I just thought he was trying to help our minds fall into a deeper meditative state."

Rocky couldn't help but laugh a bit. It was kind of like a philosophical drunk friend at parties. They sounded deep in the moment but if you thought about their words when sober, they often lost all semblance of meaning. Tao's words could be construed as the deep thoughts of an introspective man, or the drunk ramblings of someone trying to fill the silence. Rocky assumed that to read deeper meanings into any of Tao's words, you needed to be ready to hear them.

"Regardless, I think we should go see if LFD knows what the living creatures in the repair pool are, and if he knows how this stat link enchantment was made..." Rocky considered broaching the subject of Sela's earlier comment then, but for the first time her face wasn't upset with him. So, instead of bringing down her mood, he let it drop.

Nadine was back in the chimera clearing, playing with the other kits and showing off Cara's growth to Azoth and Shiva. Lacy was supposedly really close to bonding with one of the gryphon babies, and Benoit had finally decided that he was willing to reset his class to have a bonded chimera of his own. Rocky was excited that the first Chimera Knights would be his family. He knew that they would need to expand the ranks with others to try to find riders for all the babies, but for the first four to be him and his family members just felt right.

"Rocky, since you left, I've made numerous changes to my monsters to protect against your cheating! Think impenetrable armor on every creature, you and your party won't stand a chance..."

A party leaving from the side exit of the dungeon looked at each other, looked at the speaking entrance and tried to hide laughter. LFD noticed it of course, and while Rocky didn't know why the party was laughing, LFD clearly did. "You lot got lucky; I hadn't perfected the thickness of the metal, so some of my creatures couldn't take the weight. Come on back tomorrow and we'll see who's laughing!"

One of the people in the group shrugged as they walked toward the bridge. "If you have more steel statues you'd like us to melt, just say the word, Forgotten."

Rocky looked at Sela who was also attempting to hold back a smile. The two of them looked away from each other so fast they could have given themselves whiplash, but they knew they couldn't laugh at LFD if they hoped for answers.

"Yeah, well now the gear is getting enchants and thinner slabs of metal. The Long Forgotten Dungeon won't be such an easy 'catwalk' next time," LFD shouted at the retreating party. Clearly, LFD had heard the incorrect term of 'catwalk' from the group or someone because his way of pronouncing it was beyond awkward.

Before LFD could continue ranting, Rocky cut in. "LFD, we were wondering if you by chance knew anything about what lives inside the self-repair enchant pools?" Rocky asked, beginning with the question that was less important to gauge how helpful LFD would be.

"The Ether-phages? What about them? I use them to clean my dungeon, as well. They are wonderful little workers."

"How do you create them? And how many are in one piece of gear?"

"Oh, they reproduce like—pardon my use of this idiom when I have Thumper—but like bunnies. I must reabsorb hundreds of thousands of the things a month. On any Self Repair enchant, I think I place maybe a thousand. Somehow the Ether Pool they are placed in stops them from reproducing like they do inside the dungeon."

"You don't know how the pool stops them?" Rocky asked, feeling his stomach knot when he realized LFD likely didn't know much about enchanting if he didn't understand that.

"No clue. I just copied the gear I absorbed, and they turned out the same. At some point, I will get back to experimenting, but last time I tried to adjust an enchantment, I kind of cooked Thumper…" Rocky bit his lip to avoid laughing, and after he was thoroughly in control, he asked about the Stat Link enchant. "That enchant uses second tier energy. Can't you see it?"

Rocky pretended he knew that already and excused himself and Sela shortly after. Clearly, LFD took certain things it could do for granted, but simultaneously wouldn't be able to go into much detail about it. "I think we can probably get something in the shop that will allow us to breed Ether-phages that we could in turn use to produce self-repairing gear," Rocky said as Sela and he moved toward the Town Hall.

"That would be extremely valuable to the hunters of the Grotto, and the adventurers. It also isn't common to find gear with that enchant in the shop, so we might even be able to find a market for it." Sela nodded toward the barracks buildings where large groups of individuals in military fatigues were either mobilizing, or watching something they couldn't make out.

"What do you suppose that is about?" Sela asked confusedly.

"Let's find out," Rocky said and began sprinting. The longer he watched, the surer he was that the military's stances were hostile.

"You can't arrest me!" someone was shouting from inside of the large circle of military men and women. "I did nothing wrong. What proof do you have of your thievery accusations?"

Rocky realized that the group containing the individual who was accused of stealing from the Grotto had returned. The rest of the hunters that had gone out with the dark-haired individual had edged away, leaving a gap beside him. Rocky stepped forward.

"We have the sales logs for the shop you have been visiting. We have the entries and the testimony of the foxkin inside that you were the person who has been selling the stolen goods." Rocky pulled out his sword and pointed it at the rather nondescript man. "You also have your class hidden from everyone. I can't see through the skill you're using, but I can tell that you have changed it. The last person I saw do what you're doing was Frankie Cocozza."

CHAPTER SEVENTEEN

Jeers and hisses erupted all around him as the military had a strong reaction to that rather evil name. The man, whose name was Lenny, tried to turn and flee, but the ring of the military members surrounding him was going to be very tough to escape—boosters ignited from the soles of Lenny's feet and Rocky swore.

"Shoot him down!" he ordered in a hurried shout.

Numerous laser rifles with hundreds of varied skills crashed into Lenny, which either stopped his leg thrusters from continuing, or destroyed the engines because he fell back to earth. Rocky was beside him in a heartbeat and when he re-Analyzed the man he immediately took his head off.

Lenny Desion
Journeyman-Mechanohybrid Thief
Level 44
Health Points: 1,000 / 2,100
Active Skills: 3
Passive Skills: 2

New gasps sprang up from everyone present and he turned to find everyone regarding him with ashen faces. Sela was looking around herself with a perplexed expression. Two others from Frank's group suddenly shot into the sky as well. The stunned military was too shocked to fire. Luckily, Sela hit them both with a Moon Fire skill and they crashed back down. They both had the Mechanohybrid classes as well, and Rocky hurried to decapitate them.

Smith walked through the encircled military to see the beginnings of the final executions and despite his shouting at Rocky to stop, he didn't. He wouldn't allow his enemies to live, not anymore. That was a lesson he already learned the hard way.

Warning! An army has crossed your Territory's Boundary!
Algonquin Valley has numerous sapient creatures and minions crossing the border! Push back these invaders or risk losing your Territory.
100 sapient beings, and 200,000 undead creatures have crossed the threshold.

The military remained stunned and frozen, and thanks to Smith's yelling, Rocky thought he understood why. They considered his actions as an execution without trial, which admittedly it was, but simultaneously not. He learned the hard way already that you don't leave enemies alive to strike at your back when you're vulnerable. This new world wouldn't allow that sort of softness.

"Form up!" Smith shouted, which broke the stunned silence and got the military around Rocky moving. Smith turned to Rocky after, and added in an angry whisper, "We will talk about this later!"

Rocky clenched his jaw; the man was still thinking about scolding him for the actions of killing enemies. The timing of this attack was far too coincidental to be anything but planned. Additionally, for him to have killed Mechanolords and be simultaneously assaulted by Frankie's undead spoke to a terrible alliance between their enemies.

<Rocky! They attacking kits!> Azoth sent, his mental voice screaming out a fear Rocky had never heard from him. Sela either heard Azoth or got her own message from Shiva because she turned to him, her face whiter than the snow.

"The kits!" she whispered and before even the military had fully cleared the square, Rocky was already turning and rushing out of the Grotto gates as they were closing. Not only the kits, but his sister had also been spending every waking moment in that clearing too.

Sela in her raven form cawed once as she took the most direct route over the sheer walls to the kit clearing. Rocky was forced to clear the entry path before he was able to leap into the trees and follow her. For the briefest of moments, he wondered how they knew the location of Shiva and the kits. Lenny's face flashed into his thoughts, and he wished he could kill the man repeatedly; painfully.

He arrived in the clearing to find Shiva and Azoth blocking access to the cave with the precariously balanced rock. Arrayed against them were twelve mechanoid humans and Apothis. In the deeper shadow of the cave, Benoit and Lacy kept the unaware kits from rushing out to their mother and father. From Benoit's constant glances out of the cave as he picked up and tossed another kitten back in, Rocky could tell that he wanted to help Shiva and Azoth.

Sela was likely circling above waiting for the real battle to start. Both Azoth and Shiva were heavily wounded already, but why the stoppage in the fighting had occurred, Rocky couldn't see from up in the tree.

"Give us just half of your kittens and we will leave," Apothis was saying as Rocky leaped to a tree just on the edge of the valley. "Or do you want them all to end up like this poor thing?" That was when Rocky saw a manticore with a barbed tail laying in the trampled grass between the two groups. Its body could have just been asleep if it wasn't for the blood leaking from its deep black fur near its chest.

Rocky felt his rage kindle, then burst. It was different now than it had been in the past. He could feel that magma core of rage by itself, and instead of losing himself to it, he felt his brain focus, then slow. He summoned his shadow clone before entering Stealth himself. A quick Analyze told Rocky that Apothis was a new version of himself but far lower in level.

Apothis
Journeyman-Necromonger
Level 22
Health Points: 1,100 / 1,100
Boss

He had been about to make his way to the backs of the Mechanolords and Apothis when the lower-ranked Apothis reminded him of his bottle of manticore venom. He pulled it out and applied a liberal amount to his Soul Blade. Two black daggers appeared in front of him and he emptied the remainder of the bottle onto them. Even if one of these enemies managed to escape, they wouldn't live long—he swore to it internally.

He felt Azoth's understanding of his resolve, and thanks to their months traveling, they didn't need to communicate the plan verbally. Azoth stepped back, seeming to be giving up. Shiva's eyes went wide and she growled deeply but refused to take her eyes off of the enemies in front of her.

"See, your mate understands," Apothis crooned. "You can always make—ahhkk!" Rocky cut off the disgusting creature's word by slashing his Soul Blade coated in a Dark Blade skill across the Necromonger's back. Due to Apothis' armor and inherent Ether, he didn't manage to cut him in half, but his blade did carve a huge gash through Apothis' papery skin. Black blood began to leak, as simultaneously his Dark Blade fought to spread the wound larger.

Rocky didn't stay still after the strike and moved to the closest Mechanolord as its boosters fired. His blade managed to clip the mechanical thigh of the converted human before it flew out of easy reach. Out of the corner of his eye, he saw eight other enemies fly into the sky, but a quick glance told him two others hadn't. One was melting and bubbling from around a black dagger Rocky recognized. Another had a large black-cat-Sela clamped down on the back of its skull.

Shiva leaped up and clamped jaws around a third, and Azoth flapped his wings once as he took to the sky as well. Distantly, Rocky's heightened smell picked up the same oil scent he had recognized, but was unable to categorize a few days ago when Frankie escaped. The Mechanolords in the air chose to fly away instead of returning to engage Rocky's party. Azoth gave chase as they fled. Rocky sneered at them as they shrank into the distance, but approached Apothis as he twitched on the ground.

"We'll just keep coming. You can't stop my soul from returning to Apep, not like that idiot Ragnar!" Apothis managed to show off a hideous smile, his teeth covered in blackening blood. "We'll keep you pinned here and unable to mount a defense against our new allies…"

"I noticed your Journeyman rank this time. Maybe if I kill you enough times, you'll end up back down in the Apprentice ranks," Rocky shot back, his time as a basketball player begging him to pull on that weakness from this fight. "Bet you can't even summon your precious champions this time…"

Apothis sneered at Rocky before forcing out a chuckle. "We can just spend more time leveling like we did in Chalk River. Instead of a few Master class bosses, perhaps we come back with hundreds of Epic leveled invaders—"

"Hmm." Rocky cut off Apothis' comeback. "Sounds to me like that will give us more time to level too, moron…"

Apothis opened and closed his mouth like a fish and Rocky shook his head at Apothis. He analyzed the shaking and stuttering half corpse at his feet. His health was falling fast, and he knew that Apothis' words were correct on some level. Apep, Frankie, and his allies wouldn't stop coming. He also knew that if he could remove this piece of garbage from the fights, they could remove Apep's queen from the board. He looked at his Soul

Blade ready to end the coughing mess Apothi—in theory, this blade could absorb souls…

He plunged it through Apothis' chest without a second thought and left it there, pinning the imbecile to the ground. Even if it didn't work, killing him was immensely satisfying.

Congratulations! Your Soul Blade "Dark Tidings" has consumed enough souls to gain a level!
Dark Tidings – Soul Blade
Level 10
220 / 220 Ether Pool
The Strength of Arms X
+20 Strength as long as the Blade has Ether from its pool to draw on. Unlock higher levels of your Soul Blade for more.
The Strength of Body X
+10 Stamina as long as the Blade has Ether from its pool to draw on. Unlock higher levels of your Soul Blade for more.
Dark Tidings refuses to absorb any more Golem Essence. Find it a new source of sustenance.
Dark Tidings has found its favorite sustenance. Sapient Essence will count double.

So, it did work!

CHAPTER EIGHTEEN

Once Rocky was sure that Shiva and the rest of the kits were okay, he left Sela, Benoit, and Lacy there before rushing back to the Territory. He needed to check on Nadine and the others. Now he stood frozen in the entrance, overlooking a scene so vastly different from his return to the Grotto a few days ago that he felt like he had somehow entered an alternate dimension. More than half of the buildings had huge holes in them, had fallen over, or were burning. None of the dragon scale buildings were affected, but that just meant more damage had been done to the others.

All around the Grotto, inside buildings, or on the grass, Rocky saw large abandoned drill machines. The mechanisms had clearly dug under the cliffs and gated entrance of the Grotto before surfacing and disgorging thousands of zombies. In fact, there weren't even any zombie corpses outside of the entrance. He pulled aside the first person in a military uniform he found and asked, "What happened here?"

"They came from below this time. We didn't know they could do that. Nearly half the military was ready on the wall, like usual. Luckily, the Golem Knights felt something was wrong and they managed to mobilize some of the others not on duty before it was too late, but still far too many non-power classes died."

Rocky dismissed the man with a salute before heading directly to the closest Golem Knight who was easily visible. It was Gamma, and Rocky almost turned around to head in the other direction. Gamma wasn't exactly the calmest of the Knights, but he froze when he saw what appeared to be tears on the ax-wielding golem's cheeks. "Gamma, are you okay?"

"We've failed you and your Territory, yet you ask if I'm okay?" Gamma knelt, a gesture Rocky had never expected out of the proud golem. "On whatever force animates my body—be it

Gaia or sheer circumstances—I pledge to never fail in the protection of your people again."

Gamma stayed kneeling and Rocky felt that a response from him was needed, but he couldn't form the words. It was like looking in a mirror in some ways. This was exactly how he felt, albeit now to a lesser degree. If he chose to look at the death around him instead of the life they had saved, then sure, it was impossible to completely ignore the people who had lost their lives this day, but each death had also saved countless others.

In this world, life is never guaranteed...

"Rocky, let me speak with him for a while," Gary's familiar voice said from behind him, and Rocky turned to see the healer who had started him on his journey approaching.

"Gamma, I cannot, will not, accept such an oath. All we can do is our very best and for you to swear on your life will only make a failure in the future cost us more. Talk with Gary, he has helped me in a way I can't put into words." Rocky turned to continue his survey of the damages to the Territory, but Gary put a hand on his bicep.

"The council is meeting right now and will need you there. May I say one thing to you as well, Rocky?" Rocky blinked and Gary continued without hearing an affirmative. "Like Gamma and the Knights, some people of this Territory must take on a greater responsibility. I'm very happy that you've gotten your family back, and while your family needs Rockland, the son, the brother, and the man... The world, this Territory, and even possibly other worlds need Rocky the hero."

Gary turned to the kneeling Gamma after his powerful words. "Gamma, let's go find your brothers. Perhaps some of them, and maybe even others, need to hear this outlook today."

Gamma rose to his feet and regarded the healer for a moment before he began leading the way to the nearest Knight, which appeared to be Omega.

Gary turned back to him one final time. "Rocky, I know you're feeling particularly awkward around me lately, but know I won't share anything you've told me, or are going through, with anyone and never have."

He smiled at Rocky before turning and following after Gamma. Rocky stood watching them go and thinking about what Gary just said.

***

"We can't have a leader summarily executing people without a trial!" Derik shouted into the clamor of the emergency council meeting. Rocky and Sela were sitting in their usual seats silently while the members discussed both the attack and Rocky's actions right before it. They were upset that the two of them had run off right before the attack as well, but there seemed to be an unspoken agreement to handle the 'transgressions' in chronological order.

"Some people need killing," Jorge whispered from deep in his shadowed cowl, but somehow his voice was easily heard.

"This goes back to the exile of Derik and the group of individuals who were being controlled by Frankie. Did they deserve death?" Astrid stood up to make her point as she motioned to Derik. "No, and if we had killed them because of one action, we would have lost a valuable ally and friend. For Rockland to just kill the three individuals for suspected ties to the Mechanolords and Allied Guilds sets a precedent that terrifies me and every human who hears it."

Smith raised a hand which managed to quiet everyone, at least for the moment, as he stood and addressed the assembly. "I think we are forgetting that the three individuals who were executed weren't innocent. They had been stealing from the Territory for the last few months. Not only stealing, but exclusively taking parts of the ship that are expensive and irreplaceable. Those thefts have put us months behind on completion of the second ship to help defend the world from enslavement. And now we've discovered what those parts were used for."

Smith finished by pointing at the mechanical diggers that were being piled near the ship building yard. Clamor broke out from those gathered at Smith's defense of Sela and Rocky. Smith raised his voice. "We may be able to recover from those thefts if the parts are in those machines, but I think it's safe to say that the executions should be lumped in with the attack that followed. Death on the battlefield."

Rocky tried to catch Smith's eye after that, but the man refused to meet his gaze. Reluctant support?

"This is the wrong approach. To equate three thieves to the fall of humankind on Earth makes them monsters. You dehumanize them, lessen their deaths. Rocky killed, before we can even question. They're not able defend themselves, so you say they guilty. What if they were not in control?" Yuri, the grizzled blacksmith, interjected in his commanding voice.

Sela stood up next and the room went silent in a way that spoke of fear or respect, but due to the current topic of discussion and people's wild eyes, Rocky leaned toward fear. "We found Mechanolord seeds and tech in the three thieves. This means that they were allied with our enemies, and their choice of items further suggests that they were targeting our ship construction, which you cannot spin in any other direction. Rockland killed three enemies in a war that has already begun.

"What is the purpose of us sitting here and discussing his actions before the invasion? What are you all hoping to gain? He is the leader—"

"No, I'm not!" Rocky interjected and slammed his fist on the table. "The system classifies me as a leader of this Territory, but I am not the leader, nor do I want to be. Let's not pretend we don't know what the council is wanting from us. Each person here wants to feel like they are more in control. They want to pretend that they can discuss the pros and cons before deciding, but all of you haven't been on the front lines. Smith has, and he sees the need for what I did. Sela has, and she stands beside me. Zippo has, and despite being younger than many here, he understands—he might not agree fully, but he understands. I'm not the leader of this Territory in the way that this council leads, but you will all turn to me the instant a threat appears that you can't handle... You will all attempt to blame me for the deaths of the innocent today, while taking credit for future achievements."

The silence that followed his rant spoke volumes as everyone on the council looked at each other to try to find fault in Rocky's logic. Before they could return to a semantic argument, Rocky continued, "As I said, I don't want to be the leader of the Territory, because that would be like saying this war is the Algonquin Territory versus the incoming fleet of the Guild Collective! No, I will be leader of Meliora, and this Territory answers to me, because Meliora is the power that will fight the war, but each Territory will have a council that can make all the decisions outside of that war. Make no mistake, though, today was a part of that war, and every action taken you have no say over."

Rocky sat back down and a potent silence continued for a time. The direction of the initial conversation was derailed, and watching the members of the council look at each other, Rocky felt his blood hum in his veins. These people wanted to somehow use his actions to claim that he and Sela were unfit leaders, while almost everyone in Algonquin owed them their lives... He could feel a deep anger and sadness down his bond with Azoth, and in a moment of panic he realized how much it was affecting him. He grabbed a firm hold of his current thoughts before they, and Azoth's mood, consumed him.

Mindfulness. The council is just doing what they think is right.

"I think, by the silence after that point, we can table that particular discussion," Smith began and flipped a page. "Amelia says she cannot obtain more arbuckle, but if we get her any that these diggers used, she can create more engine drives. Let's discuss how we are going to be able to prevent a disaster like this in the future." Again, he pointed to the diggers outside.

"Can I suggest using the Territorial Etherience to repair the buildings that were damaged during the attack?" Rocky suggested.

"How will that help?" Derik asked, his voice instantly confrontational since it was a suggestion from Rocky.

"If we use the right spell, it should convert all the buildings to dragon scale, which you can see from the destruction pattern has no—"

A runner bursting into the room cut off Rocky mid-sentence and the room turned to stare at him. "There is a huge line of people forming who want to use the teleporter to go to a safer Territory."

Rocky blinked and looked around at the stunned faces of the other council members. He couldn't help but wonder if this was a good thing. Frankie shouldn't know where the other Territories were yet, right?

418 people have left Meliora.
See full list?
<Yes> | No

Sela shot up and looked at Rocky. "Do you think that more people are allied with Dahrix, or are people leaving because of the attack?"

Rocky blinked at the notification and pulled up the list of people who left. If these four-hundred people were all Mechanolords, then the problem was far larger than he thought. For there to be that many enemy infiltrators inside his Guild...

"What's going on?" Derik asked, picking up on the question Sela asked, but not understanding the reason. Sela read the notice and the council's faces paled further.

Another runner crashed into the room, throwing the second door against the wall in his haste. "Smith, sir. There is a horde of people at the front of the town hall shouting about losing their loved ones, and demanding we go after them."

"I'm sure many people lost loved ones today." Derik sighed sadly as he stood up and moved to the window that overlooked the front of the building. "There's already three hundred people out there and we will likely get more as the day progresses."

"You misunderstand, sir. All of these people say that their loved ones left using the teleporter before the attack, without warning."

CHAPTER NINETEEN

"Let's go see what is going on," Rocky said as he stood up and moved to the doorway out of the council chambers. As he passed the runner he added, "We will see them in the petition hall."

"Wait! We haven't even gotten to the Mechanolord prisoners!" Derik shouted from his place at the round table. Rocky heard him but didn't bother turning around. He knew about the prisoner and still planned to talk with him later, with or without the permission of the council.

The rest of the council double timed it out of the chambers to catch up with Rocky. He hid a smile when they did. Maybe they were only following so he didn't kill everyone?

The big, bad Rocky, psychotic maniac...

Shaking his head, he felt someone grab his hand. Sela was beside him, and she gave his larger hand a quick squeeze. It was impossible for him to fully comprehend what her meaning might be, but the gesture said she would support him in whatever this mass exodus heralded.

***

"All four-hundred people that left before the assault were the same people that wouldn't wake up this morning?" Derik asked as he flipped through pages on the table in front of him. Many people in the crowd nodded along.

"So, they woke up and just walked to the teleportation circle in near unison, without talking to each other or anyone else?" Smith added. It had taken the council and present military nearly fifteen minutes to calm the crowd enough that they were able to get a good idea of the story. "Rocky, you said that four hundred people left the guild all at the same time, too?"

Nodding, Rocky put the list from his notification up onto the meeting board so everyone gathered could see it. Many of the people pointed at a name, or two names in some cases. This all felt odd to him. Of the people in the room currently, there were many that were wives, sons, daughters, or other extended family of the individuals who had left. Each of the people present seemed confused by that exodus. Had there been no signs of changes or talks of dissension? If the people who left were in control of themselves, they would have complained, right? They would have likely tried to convince their families to leave with them...

"Sela, does this seem odd to you, too?" he whispered. "Could everyone who left have been given a Mechanolord seed?"

Sela shook her head and whispered back, "That's impossible. It's just so random. Some of these people were crafters, others militia, and many more farmers, or businessmen who hadn't left the Territory. How would Dahrix have gotten to them all?" The room was relatively silent when she was finished, and everyone was looking at Rocky and Sela. "Sorry, I'm just wondering, how many of you all know each other?" When all hands raised, she clarified. "Point at the people you know."

That did emphasize her point, though. There were pockets of people that knew each other, but if the people who had gone missing somehow all ended up meeting, it would have been a statistical anomaly.

"What are you suggesting, Sela?" Derik leaned forward to look down the table at Rocky and her. They had taken seats at the front of the room instead of sitting up on the stage with the council. They were the guild leaders and not the Territory ones, and they needed to start drawing those lines a bit.

"Rocky pointed out how odd this all is, actually," she responded and motioned to him. He blinked and realized that he was now expected to quantify why this felt so odd.

"I was just trying to put into words why this felt strange. All your surprise that they just left without talking to you is disconcerting to me. Because of the attack, my mind first went to the Mechanolords and their ability to control people who have a seed in them, but why would they want their spies to leave before an assault? Why would they want their spies to leave the guild?" Rocky faded off as he saw Adam enter the room. He might not have noticed the young kid enter, but shadows that were clearly golems or Golem Knights fell over numerous windows of the petition hall. It was almost like Adam was the herald of death or bad omens. Others also noticed the change in ambient lighting and as a group everyone turned to the young man, who now stood silhouetted in the doorway.

"I got a really strange red quest from Gaia, and I was coming to talk to Rocky about it, but standing outside I realized it might be related." Adam's whisper carried over the hushed crowd like a dragonfly over a calm lake. A few ripples started where it fell and people around the noise hurriedly shushed their neighbors. Blinking, Rocky removed the list of individuals from the meeting projector screen, and motioned at it to Adam. The young man got the hint and made a motion in front of himself. Suddenly, they were all looking at a quest that tied into the current predicament.

Red Quest
Party Quest – Stone Bender
Rebirth of the Taken
418 people have gone missing from the Territory you reside in. Gaia has cataloged their absence as something that should not have happened and has offered you a quest to help right the balance. Find the heart of a Legendary Golem and place it on the Altar of Michabo to grant Rebirth to the souls trapped within.
Rewards:

Etherience
Crystallized Ether
Rebirth of the Citizens

Rocky instantly flipped to the Rebirth page in the Territory but found it empty despite the numerous deaths from the day. A few quick clicks gave no new information. Apparently Rebirth needed more than just the person to die on the Territory grounds. He scratched his head. He wished he had questioned Michabo more about how the altar worked...

He shook his head, trying to dispel the thoughts of the bunny-man and return to the issue at hand. The number four hundred and eighteen was just too coincidental to not be the same group that left the guild. How had the people teleported from the Grotto, left the guild, been cataloged as missing by Gaia, and also need rebirth?

"Michabo!" Sela exclaimed with all the subtlety of a freight train passing through a residential neighborhood in the early hours of the morning. Rocky flinched, but since he had just been thinking of the bunny-man, he instantly felt the connection form.

Amber had said that the people within the Spirit Realm had suddenly vanished.

"Did all of the missing people reside in the Guild Dome's residence?" he asked the assembly. The nods and affirmations of everyone present confirmed his worst nightmare. He had just traded Amber for four-hundred and eighteen people. He felt the dark thoughts pushing on his psyche then, but Sela placed a hand on his shoulder.

"Rocky, this isn't your fault. Michabo was always planning this. You just happened to give him the last of the energy he clearly needed to make it happen." He looked at her and saw the earnestness of her words conveyed in her eyes. He began nodding to himself and latching onto that thought.

Michabo began planning this the instant I took over Algonquin Valley…

Sela nodded at him, and he assumed that some of the color had returned to his face. He stood from his seat, and at the questioning looks from the council and the crowd said, "I need to go check on the Altar of Michabo. Adam, walk with me."

They were out the door just as people from the assembled group began standing up in their pews to try to stop him. Or maybe they just wanted to follow, but Rocky used his increased stats to practically flash across the intervening space. The golems outside were in fact Adam's puppets and the Golem Knights. Omega instantly opened his mouth to say something, but Rocky held up a hand as he guided Adam through the stone giants with his other hand on the kid's back.

"I think I know what the Golem Knights are thinking, but let me ask you. Do you have any idea why you were given this quest, and not Sela or I?" Rocky asked, as Sela jogged up beside him.

"The council is staying behind to help calm the people," she conveyed quickly before turning expectant eyes on Adam. Clearly, she also wanted to hear the answer to Rocky's question.

"I don't know, Rock. I woke up this morning to the quest and thought nothing of it. Other than that, there must have been a *tragedy* in the Territory. Then the attack happened, and I thought maybe that was the death toll, but how could it have predicted the attack? When I asked, I heard the deaths from the assault were far more than four hundred. So, I asked Epsilon about it, and he grew very excited. Still, I don't think he realizes how impossible it will be to find a legendary golem. Not to mention killing one to get its core…"

Rocky nodded and looked at Gamma, Epsilon, Omega, Tao, and Delta. "Guys, you do remember that Empire was still Epic-ranked, and that he could have squashed the entire Territory under one sabaton, right?"

"One must consider why a golem core of such power would be capable of giving your citizens Rebirth," Tao mused to the sky as he ran his fingers down his chin. Rocky shook his head at the golems because they all nodded at Tao's words.

Sela just shrugged. "We know that those massive mountain-sized golems are out there. Perhaps one of them is Legendary…"

"Yeah, great, and how do you expect us to defeat one of those?" Rocky retorted skeptically as they entered the Guild Dome. He felt his skin crawl once he was inside. Had this place really given Michabo access to take over citizens' bodies?

Soon they were on the elevator but without the Golem Knights who likely each weighed over ten tons. He doubted that they would ever get on the lift to test out its weight capacity. He sure wouldn't want them doing it while he was riding.

As soon as they entered the Control Room, Rocky rushed to the altar and placed a hand on it. He stood there mentally and verbally screaming Michabo's name for at least five minutes before Sela put a hand on his shoulder. She motioned to the room of techs who all wore expressions ranging from shock to fear. He grimaced and stepped back from the altar. "Sorry, I was hoping that the entity inside of the altar would respond."

Oh great, now they look like they think I'm more cracked…

The looks he got from that admission weren't much better than the fear, but it was the truth. Sela motioned for Adam to step forward and touch the black altar. The kid did so, and he exclaimed, "It asks for me to place the heart on the altar and confirm my sacrifice!"

Rocky could only conclude that the four hundred and eighteen people must be in the Spirit Realm.

They got back off the elevator on the ground floor.

"One of us could grind our way to the Legendary ranks and sacrifice ourselves to the altar!" Gamma shouted as the doors dinged open.

Sela rushed to the five gathered Knights, who were causing quite the scene, and somehow managed to stop their current conversation and get them to follow Rocky, Adam, and her outside.

"I think it is time we went and talked with that Mechanolord prisoner, Rockland," Sela said to him as soon as he walked up beside her. Rocky nodded along. They did need to speak with him. He assumed the prisoner was under Dahrix' control, but they needed to be certain.

Chapter Twenty

"So you have significant parts of your recent memories just missing, and you didn't think that was a problem?" Rocky sighed in exacerbation. The mechanoid was in a holding cell in the lower levels of the Guild Dome that Rocky hadn't known existed. Sela had led him here and he wasn't sure how to feel about the Territory's need for the things.

"Well, we talked about it amongst the leaders in our safe zone, and then more after we conquered the Territory, but we just assumed it was a side effect of the seed," the half woman said, her voice quiet and her expression one of disbelief.

"Is everyone in your Territory converted then?" Sela followed up, her voice hard.

"Yes, or waiting for their seed to come through the shop."

Rocky felt his blood chill at the Mechanolady's answer.

"How many are in your Territory?" Sela beat him to his question, and he held his breath.

"I still don't believe that we attacked you. What proof do you have?" the mechanoid-woman asked instead of answering.

Rocky turned to Smith who was standing at the edge of the cell. The man had joined them on their descent down to the stairs to the holding cells after the elevator ride from the top floor. Adam had left the Guild Dome with the Golem Knights.

"It has been like this from the start," Smith responded to Rocky's questioning look. "We had captured many more of them, but they initiated a self-destruct sequence. She did too, actually, but since it was so close to the Guild Dome, we pulled her inside and shoved her into an empty room. When nothing happened for a solid ten minutes, we opened the door to find her shaking on the floor."

"How you managed to initiate my self-destruct sequence is troublesome," they all heard the whisper from the half-human woman.

Rocky clenched his jaw. How was she still questioning this? How could she believe that they turned on her self-destruct sequence? Dahrix had attempted to blow her up like a cheap pawn piece, and she still believed that he wasn't the enemy.

Sela looked at him and they met eyes, then she motioned at the concrete that surrounded them.

"What are the chances that Dahrix's signal is blocked inside of the dragon scale buildings?" she asked Rocky and included Smith with a quick glance.

Rocky couldn't help but nod at that. It would fit best with the story they heard so far. Dahrix initiated the self-destruct and this woman deactivated it as soon as she had control. He hadn't yet analyzed her for a name because he didn't want to think of her as human yet, but he reluctantly turned to her and used his skill.

Heather Jamen
Master-Mechanoid
Level 33
Health Points: 4,078 / 10,080
Skills: 12

"Heather, did the person who gave your people these seeds get you to set up a beacon as well?" Rocky asked after his assessment. She nodded and he continued, "Do you know of any other Territories that were given seeds?" Another nod. "How many people are there in your Territory or the others that have been converted?"

"Hundreds of thousands," she whispered and gulped audibly.

"I assume we don't need to test the dragon scale blocking the signal hypothesis?" Rocky asked Smith, mostly as a courtesy since he was representing the council. Smith shrugged at him, and Rocky returned the gesture before turning back to Heather.

"Look," Rocky began and waited until she met his eyes. "We aren't going to do anything to hurt you, but we are going to keep you here for your safety and ours. Do you understand?" She nodded and if she didn't have a mechanism controlling blood in her veins, he was sure that her face would have paled.

He immediately turned and the three of them walked from the room. As soon as the door closed behind them, Sela grabbed Rocky's arm. "I think we need to talk about heading to Atlantis again."

"Why?" he asked as his eyebrows raised. He had been wanting to get outside and go check on Shiva, Azoth, the kittens, and his family. This subject wasn't even on his mind.

"There used to be an array that the city controlled, and it would not allow foreign signals onto the planet unless they used proper channels. I do not think we can destroy every beacon at this point, do you?" Sela scowled at him, and Smith nodded along.

Rocky looked at the man who had been somewhat indifferent toward him since his return, and then back to Sela. He could feel his anger wriggling in his chest but managed to slow down and think, thanks to his new mindfulness. He heard Gary's words from earlier repeated back to him and he nodded.

"Okay, I agree that we need a solution to Dahrix remoting into people, and this seems like a good option, but I still want to check on the chimera clearing." Sela nodded in response as her face paled. Rocky wondered if her mind had gone to the same image of a broken manticore kit lying on the ground. He shook the image away but felt some wetness on his cheek.

"I will go talk to the council," Smith said when they exited the dome and Rocky snapped around to him. Smith was being somewhat better toward him since he found out the reason for Rocky's two month hiatus, but he needed to make something clear.

"I need you to tell the council that they don't have a say in the decision that comes next. At this point, it's bigger than them, and whatever Sela and I decide is the final decision. Make sure they understand!" Smith blinked at Rocky but otherwise gave little indication on what he was thinking.

"Right now I need to go comfort Azoth, he lost a child today, and needs me!" Rocky finished before turning away and walking to the stairs.

***

<We kill them all?> Azoth growled into Rocky's mind. Azoth had brought back two Mechanolord corpses and a great deal of injuries to himself. The manticore was currently pacing in front of the cave. Rocky used a double-stacked Dark Mend on his pet, hoping that it would help him calm down.

"He won't let us leave or Nadine in," Benoit called out from inside the cave, his voice sad and concerned simultaneously. So far no one had approached the lone manticore corpse in the center of the valley, which immediately broke Rocky's heart. He choked back a sob; he could feel Azoth's anger. He could feel that same uncontrollable rage that he had felt after the battle of New York. Across their bond he sent his wordless support, and his own resolve.

He attempted a Dark Mend on the body of the baby manticore, but as he expected, it rebounded. Rocky sighed before slowly approaching Azoth.

<Yes, Azoth, we will ensure that we stop them from ever doing something like this again,> he mentally sent and watched Azoth stop pacing and approach the manticore kitten. He sniffed at it and the strength of his breath moved the tiny corpse.

<Azoth, look at me. You need to let Shiva come to grieve with you. You and I need to go for a flight, okay? Let the others in the valley see what they can do.> Rocky was sure that the kitten was beyond saving but he also could see Shiva's wide eyes and defensive stance at the entrance to the cave. While Rocky was sure that she was just as hurt as Azoth, if she was feeling his rage, she was also protecting her babies.

Rocky continued to slowly approach his best friend, and stalwart companion. He kept sending as much unspoken comfort over the bond as he could. When he reached him, he interposed himself between Azoth's massive lionhead and the kitten. He grabbed Azoth's jowl and hugged it fiercely as he slowly turned the huge manticore away.

<It's okay, buddy. Let's go fly. Let's just get away from it all for now. Like in New York...>

Azoth turned away and allowed Rocky to mount up before his powerful wingbeats took them through the canopy and into the sky. Usually, Rocky would have tried to find somewhere else to launch from, as this location made him feel like he was beaten with baseball bats, but also in this situation he barely felt them.

***

The next day was filled with funerals, and the dead bodies of the Grotto citizens were given to the chosen Dungeons of the surviving families. Somehow this had turned into a common occurrence, and while there were still families against this who wanted traditional burials, Sela made a single speech which reminded people of necromancy, and the number of dissenters drastically decreased.

Only one body was buried in the ground and that was the adolescent one of Shivath, a name given to her after her tragic death. They had chosen not to give the chimera corpse to any of the dungeons due to the potentially terrifying power that might be awarded. After the burial of Shivath, which had been a small ceremony containing only Rocky, his family, Sela, Azoth, and Shiva, Sela met his eyes, indicating she needed to talk with him.

Rocky sighed. He had spent the remainder of yesterday and this morning consoling Azoth. He assumed Sela had done the same for Shiva. He also knew what this talk was going to be about. It would be a call to arms. A call to leave his family, and even though he was prepared to do so, he still felt conflicted.

He looked at his feet as he followed Sela. She was leading them to a place away from listeners. A glance over his shoulder showed his family leaving with Shiva, Azoth, and the kits.

He took the time to resolve his inner turmoil over leaving his family, and the kits. In the long run, that would be better, right? Sela coughed to bring him back to the moment and he met her eyes.

"I think the only way to prevent Dahrix from remoting into all of his seeds on the Earth is going to be Atlantis. Are you finally ready to go?" Sela reiterated her earlier point.

Rocky looked to his family as they herded the playful chimera kits before nodding. The decision was made, and he only needed to tell them that he was leaving again. Azoth was already on board after the long conversation they had last night.

He took a deep breath and turned back to Sela again. He rubbed his arm where she had punched him. The somber mood reminded him of the hurt she showed him recently. "Sela, you know you were enough, right?"

Her cheeks flushed and she looked to the ground. "That was not the direction I thought this conversation would go in, Rockland."

"I know, but I never said it after you hit me. I should have said it. I should have come back, but honestly, I figured you would be better off without me…" She hit his arm again, and her blush turned into something else.

"Nothing could be further from the truth. Imagine losing one of them," Sela gestured over a shoulder at the shrinking members of his family. "Remember that hurt you felt when you thought they were gone. That is the only thing that your death would cause."

She chuckled then and punched him more lightly. "Idiot."

He smiled and transferred his gaze from her smile to his family, Azoth, Shiva, and the kits. "We should probably go tell them the bad news."

They walked back together, and caught up rather easily thanks to the rambunctious kits that didn't seem to want to all head in the same direction.

"We have to leave for a while…" Rocky choked out as soon as they drew within range. He needed to get it out, or he would likely not be able to say it.

"Gary talked to us all," Nadine said as she hugged Cara close to her. "He said you would eventually have to go out and save the world again…" She managed a weak smile to accompany her words.

"Do you think we should move Shiva and the kits into the Grotto?" Benoit asked, changing the topic bluntly. Rocky blinked. That was it? He saw everyone had plastered on smiles and were looking at him so he took the cue.

He began nodding, having considered that same thought earlier. With all of the destroyed buildings, the people fleeing to other, less developed territories and the Territorial repair spell, Rocky was hoping they could convert some buildings for Shiva and the kits.

Based on Shiva's size, it was really the entrance to a longhouse that would need to be enlarged. Lacy and Nadine were in the center of the kittens watching Rocky while absently playing with them. Rocky smiled at them and then Benoit. "We should move them, yes. And I promise I will be…"

"Don't you dare." Benoit punched him in the shoulder, right where Sela just had. Rocky rubbed the spot and looked between the two as Benoit continued, "We'll see you after you manage to capture Atlantis. You think they will have a penthouse nice enough for your famous brother-in-law? I think my fans are sick of me staying in a concrete box." Benoit winked at Rocky at the end and Rocky couldn't help the small smile. It probably would have been a full-blown laugh under any other circumstances.

"No, not that way, Thing One," Lacy shouted as she chased a panther into the trees.

"Thing One?" Rocky asked.

"Yeah, that one is Thing Two," Benoit said and pointed toward the second panther kit. "Watch. They are smart, and like to play off each other." Sure enough, Thing Two bolted in the exact opposite direction from its sibling. It startled a laugh out of Rocky, and a chase from Benoit.

"Do they all have names?" Rocky asked once the two managed to catch the kittens and carry them back.

"For now, the four manticores are named for their personalities. That one is Prickly," Benoit pointed to one of the living females with a spiked mace tail. "The other female is Lazy." This time he indicated the female currently dragging her tail on the soft forest floor. "That one is Pounce." He motioned to one of the male manticores with a scorpion tail, who aptly attempted to tackle Sela. "Doofus." The final manticore was headbutting a tree.

Rocky couldn't help a sustained chuckle as Ben continued to give him names that perfectly fit each baby's personality. Soon enough, he had to abandon the chat and help the others keep track of them all as they herded them through the huge trees of the Valley.

It took the entire group to finish corralling the kittens back to the Territory. Once there, they picked out the least damaged of the longhouses that had been abandoned and repaired it with modifications for one hundred thousand Territorial Etherience. A timer for an hour began as the phantom tentacles surrounded the structure.

Unfortunately, that hour gave the council members time to find them, and demand to talk to them about their plans to leave for Atlantis.

CHAPTER TWENTY-ONE

"We can't just let you all leave," Derik practically shouted before Rocky, Sela, Adam, Zippo, and the Golem Knights were at the campfire. Rocky knew that they were reacting to the power that the Territory would lose with their departure. He also didn't want to leave the Grotto defenseless, but simultaneously, what other choice was there?

"The first thing we need is a plan to capture a golem heart," Epsilon added the Golem Knight's 'plan' to the conversation.

"No, the first thing we need is to ensure the Grotto's continued safety," Zippo countered the Golem Knight.

"I think we need to calm the citizenry and move people out of the Guild Dome," Smith said calmly to everyone present. Rocky looked at Smith, but the man wouldn't meet his eyes.

"And here I was thinking we need to stop Dahrix's influence on the planet," Sela said with a shake of her head. Everyone looked to Rocky in the silence that followed, and he joined Sela in shaking his head. This was a problem and he agreed wholeheartedly with Sela. The real issue was that most of the groups in the Territory had differing agendas.

"Give Amelia the metal recovered from the diggers and ask her to remake the drives. I will reimburse her." Rocky pointed to Zippo who stood next to Smith. He moved his finger slightly to change his next address to the Native American man. "Allow people to move out of the dome and into the empty longhouses if they wish. We have plenty of empty ones and Territorial Ether to repair them."

Rocky adjusted his point again to encompass the line of people circling the dome building in the distance. That was the reason they had so many empty longhouses. There had been a relatively steady flow of non-power classes leaving the Grotto to join other 'safer' Territories. He returned his eyes to Smith.

"It might also help to let people know that Michabo can't use that 'trick' again. He is gone, and we kind of have a plan to get our people trapped in the Spirit Realm back." Rocky pointed to Adam.

"Do we have a plan?" Gamma asked his brother Golem Knights.

"No, Gamma, we don't yet, but we will try to come up with something. Regardless, we clearly do plan to find the Legendary Heart, but I think a plan that doesn't involve suicide, or sacrificing one of you, would be best. Don't you?" Rocky addressed the Knights. Ignoring Derik, he turned to Sela as he addressed her point instead, "Sela, I agree we need to stop Dahrix, but how sure are you that Atlantis is the answer?"

"Even if Atlantis can't stop the remote signal, which I highly expect it can, there could be thousands of already-built ships from the Gaian Military docked and just needing crews. Lastly, we could find out what dried up all the Ether in this quadrant of the EtherVerse before it happens again…"

The final point was not of immediate concern to Rocky, but her confidence in stopping the signal from Atlantis, plus the possible fleet, was powerful enough to silence the council members present. "Sela's point is by far the most pressing. Even if we ignore the ships and the 'mystery' of Ether. If we can stop Dahrix, we remove a rather powerful ally from Frankie, which will go a long way to ensuring the safety of this Territory. Just think how many times the *rotten tomato* got away."

Sela raised a single finger and smirked, mouthing 'that's one.' Rocky smirked back, despite the sadness of the day. He was just happy to see a small glimpse of his companion's original attitude toward him.

"We still need to vote on this with the full council present. We can't just let all of our strongest defenders leave at the same time!" Derik hissed at everyone present. Rocky expected this reaction from Derik. Since he hadn't responded to the man's first shouted point, Derik voiced it again.

Sela rolled her eyes and turned to walk away from the group. Rocky understood her annoyance at both the procedures and the possible delay that might cause. Still, they weren't beholden to the Territory, and he needed to make that clear. Smith gave him a small shrug, showing that either he hadn't conveyed Rocky's words or that Derik hadn't listened.

"I'm sorry, but this is now considered an edict from Meliora, and no longer the decision of the Grotto's council," Rocky stated as calmly as he could. "We need to stop Dahrix before he discovers the location of our other Territories."

Derik looked at him with wide eyes as he too prepared to leave. It would seem that Derik didn't understand. Everything in this valley belonged to Meliora, and if Rocky or the guild needed it, then they would take it..

Rocky turned to each person present and began giving orders. He didn't bother with Smith or Derik, figuring that they might prove more difficult than the delegation of tasks was worth. They could do what they wanted for all he cared, as long as they didn't get in his way.

Everyone left after their task was assigned. Rocky let his feet lead him and he ended up in the chimera longhouse. Azoth was allowing Cara, and most of the other babies, to play with him on one side of the house. The few remaining kittens sat with Benoit, Lacy, and Nadine as they watched Azoth play with his children. Each face held a smile, but also sadness.

Azoth noticed Rocky and bounded carefully to him, avoiding his children in the enclosed space. They both stood looking at each other, neither one mentally saying anything as they felt the connection to each other. Rocky had grown used to it over the two months away, but he could feel his friend's mood, and he could tell that his pet was trying to distract himself. Deep down, under the outer layer of playfulness, Azoth was seething.

He searched Rocky's eyes for how they were going to handle the revenge he desperately wanted.

<We're going to Atlantis, buddy. We're going to try to cut off Dahrix's influence on the Mechanoids across the entire planet.>

<Good. When leave?>

Cara crashed into Azoth's side and the large chimera turned to the kit just as the rest of the babies pounced on him. Rocky felt his pet's confusion, his oscillation between warm joy and terribly cold anger.

<Buddy, take the time to play with them for now. We will leave when everything is ready. Enjoy them when you can...>

<Rocky sound like Black Beauty. She say losing kits is common in the wild. We must cheer...ish—the ones alive.>

<She's not wrong, big guy, but it's okay to feel angry and hurt about Shivath too. Both emotions are right and everyone needs to find their way to handle that loss.>

<Kill them all—too violent?>

<I don't think anyone would fault you, buddy. Still, let's make sure we separate the controlled Mechanolords from the evil ones first. Okay?>

In response, Azoth chuffed and resumed his play time with his kittens. Rocky felt the tears he was holding back retreat slightly at the happy sight, and he turned to his family.

A woman's startled laugh made him tilt his head as he focused on Lacy, who had made the sound. Sela and Shiva looked over from a corner of the longhouse. Nadine and Benoit untangled the two kits that were on top of them. Lacy was gazing deeply into one of the gryphon's eyes with a huge smile on her face.

Rocky got a notification.

Congratulations! Your Page has been bonded by a Chimera Kit. She has been confirmed as a Chimera Squire and will advance to Knight at the Journeyman ranks.

Lacy squealed in further delight as the male gryphon began nuzzling lovingly into her with all the energy of a puppy. "It says I'm a ranger!" she squealed. "Wasn't that the name of that guy in that ring movie?"

She clearly was asking that as a rhetorical question as she instantly hugged the gryphon. It was entirely black, with a draconic-lizard head, lion's feet, and a lion's tail. The wings that were flapping excitedly were clearly avian.

"I think I will name you Onyx," she squealed delightedly.

Shiva walked over to Azoth as he rolled back to his feet from under the pile of babies, but she made practically no sound on the highly polished floor. Rocky watched her pass Lacy and give her kit and his sister a lick. Sela conveyed her sentiments. "She says that she is very happy another one of her kits has made a bond."

Shiva continued to Azoth and her remaining kits, likely needing to feed them. Azoth shook himself and mentally said, <Shiva says all babies find companion. This true?>

<If you think it best, then yes.>

<Rocky swear this?>

Rocky flooded their bond with how much he loved Azoth, and his fierce determination to never see another one of his kits hurt. Azoth chuffed in return.

<Azoth go hunt now. Rocky not need Azoth yet, kits need food.> He pumped his wings to fly away. Sela and Rocky both looked to Shiva as the powerful black panther shook her head in obvious exasperation.

Still doesn't know about mother's milk, it seems...

Rocky opened his mouth to apologize, and then to tell Sela about his orders as Meliora's head after she'd walked away. She must have seen his apology on his face because Sela shook her head. "No, you aren't the person I am upset with. I can't force you to be a leader. I'm just glad you're willing to go to Atlantis with me."

"Actually..." Rocky then did tell her of his orders after she left the council and he couldn't help smiling along with her. "We probably still need a bit of time to get everything in order, though. Maybe a day or two to get all the food, equipment, and people we might need?"

Sela nodded in turn, and Rocky shrugged before turning to Benoit. "Are you ready to become a page?"

"I didn't stop my leveling these last few days to say no now!" Benoit countered. "Just don't get upset when I'm stronger than you and Azoth."

Rocky hurriedly sent out the offer and Benoit fell to his knees. Rocky cheekily asked, "Sorry, what was that?"

As much as he used this opportunity to give Benoit a hard time, Rocky had been paying attention this time and watching with his Ether Manipulation skill. It was very hard to see specifics, but Ben's entire body had flashed a vibrant indigo before he had suddenly seemed to deflate. One second, Rocky could sense a large Ether gathering inside of Benoit and the next second, the man seemed to dull to his senses. It wasn't extremely helpful in his quest to find answers to his Ether Manipulation and Ether Channels, but it did confirm his earlier hypothesis—or at least he thought it did. Resetting Benoit, Lacy, and Nadine's class had cost them their stored Crystalized Ether.

Sela helped Benoit back to his feet and asked, "Do you want to level some first, or just stay in here for now, like Lacy and Nadine?" Benoit chose the first option and Sela left with him to create a party and find a dungeon they could tackle. Nadine and Lacy left with them, and Rocky was soon alone in the chimera longhouse. He had a lot to unpack after the events of the last few days, and instead of tackling them consciously, he chose to meditate while he did.

He glanced quickly at the kits and Shiva who was feeding them all. He was certain they would remain distracted for his session.

He pulled off his Chimera Knight gear so he could absently study the runes on them. He needed to be able to replicate this gear for his family and future Chimera Knights. As he traced the runes and tidied up his internal channels, he considered Sela's need to head for Atlantis. They definitely needed a 'Hail Mary' to stop the attacks on the Grotto and challenge the invasion when it arrived.

He considered Michabo and the bunny-man's recent actions. It felt like a betrayal. Still, Michabo had clearly set-up the entire thing long before Rocky had even been born. How could Rocky feel betrayed by something planned for so long? What was Michabo's plan now? He had said that the Algonquins were after an evil far greater than even Apep…

Absent-mindedly, he traced the runes and his internal channels as he tried to find back up plans for if Atlantis didn't solve the problem. He needed to have a plan B to ease his mind. As much as he wanted to finish this mission and stay here with his family, he also knew that they and the entire world needed protection from the upcoming invasion. Shouldn't that motivate him to continue fighting? To take any opportunity…

A headache started just behind his eyes as he mulled over options. He could capture more Territories, but in the next nine months they had no way of overcoming the Guild Collective's numerical advantage. He doubted that they could close the level gap either. So, if the powerful fighters from the invasion made it to the surface of the planet, they would likely never win. Was that why Sela was so adamant about Atlantis? Was she thinking that far ahead?

These 'what if' scenarios just hurt his head so much. He could literally feel himself sweating as his internal body temperature ratcheted up. He checked in on what rune he was tracing and realized he was tracing something that came after the complex knot on the leather chest piece. As soon as he tried to consciously trace whatever path he had been on, he lost it. It was from one beat of his heart to the next, suddenly he couldn't feel the tenuous shape anymore.

His headache also immediately dissipated, which might not have been because of the tracing at all—he had stopped thinking about his current decisions after all—but it also could have been. Somehow, he had been tracing whatever came after the complex knot!

He began at the Ether Pool for the chest piece and followed the line to where it entered the knot. Right at the 'top' of the complex pattern. He then felt it spiral in ever tightening circles until the weave was so dense, he could feel the pressure push out the strands around it. It wasn't a knot but a tightening spiral that seemed to be a—

He reached a point, and he felt the Ether from the pool change, just like he felt that single drop vanish when he stabbed the earth. However, this time the Ether that changed to mist or something else was still there. His headache started up again, and he confirmed that it was from sensing this new state of Etheric energy. Still, as he consciously felt along it, he kept slipping right off the 'invisible' path, and once he fell off, he couldn't find it again…

He chose to attack it from a different angle and dove into himself. What would happen if he created that knot in himself as his channels rejoined his pool? He traced each channel and before they returned to his pool, he began thinning the channel and spiraling the Ether it contained in tightening concentric patterns. He felt the pressure building, starting to push the outer spirals of his 'knot' outward.

He began to sweat as the pressure inside the channel began fighting against his mental control. It was like he was trying to hold onto a snake covered in grease. Just before that snake leaped from his hand, he connected the channel back into his pool. He had a metaphysical moment to tilt his proverbial head and watch something sink through his Ether pool. It looked like an air bubble moving through water, except instead of it moving up, it sank through. Then Rocky's brain chose to tell him it was finished working for the day.

Blackness swarmed in from the corners of his vision and he had time to think, '*Oh, I didn't think I could meditate myself into unconsciousness,*' before he fell to the floorboards.

Congratulations! You have learned a new skill, Essence Conversion.
Essence Conversion
You have made your body a better vessel for converting Ether to Essence. Your body's ability to act as a filter increased fractionally. Planetary Gods always need more Essence; since you stand out in this regard, you will be awarded 1% more Etherience per kill per level in this skill.
Current Rank: Weak level 8.

CHAPTER TWENTY-TWO

Rocky woke up to one of the panther kits nuzzling into his side. His head ached like he had a sinus infection, and even pressing his forehead into the cold wood wouldn't alleviate it. He cracked an eyelid to find a screen hovering in his interface and read the message. A new skill?

Not just a new skill but a skill that increased his Etherience gains… He had heard of Essence before, obviously, but hadn't really done the mental gymnastics to understand what the second tier of Etheric Energy was. As he woke up, he found more small blobs of heat pressed into his body and he realized all the remaining unbound kits were snuggling into him.

He entered his meditation without moving, trying not to disturb the babies that surrounded him and found that his tight spiraling knot had shrunk to half the size it was originally, but simultaneously was still producing that single air bubble that sank through his Ether pool every so often. He wanted to examine that drop of what he assumed was Essence, but the ringing in his head told him that was a bad idea at present.

Instead of trying to learn more right now, he slowly adjusted the kits around him and sat up. Shiva was wrapped around him protectively, and as he moved, her head rose from the wooden flooring to look into his eyes. After a heartbeat of examining him, she adjusted her sprawl to wrap around his back and give him something to lean into. He smiled and gave her some affectionate scratches as he did so.

He had been considering all his problems right before the 'discovery' of his new skill. Now he returned to a conversation Sela had with him and three young men what felt like years ago, but had only been a few months. She claimed that all life on the planet converted Ether to Essence, and that Essence was energy that Gaia used for growth. Right?

No, she never claimed that Essence helped Gaia grow. Just that the planetary gods stored and used Essence in some way…

So then, was Gaia awarding him with more Etherience because he had become a better filter for her? That seemed like the reasoning for the reward or something very similar to that direction of thinking. Rocky watched the blob of Essence sink through his Ether pool like it was a lava light and couldn't help but ask himself, "If I can see this energy, can I use it?"

"Can you use what energy?" Sela's voice floated to him from somewhere behind the curled-up Shiva. "Shiva told me that you collapsed but were alive—so I got Smith and Zippo to accompany the group into the Challenge dungeon while I came here to check on you."

She walked around Shiva's resting form and came into Rocky's view. As soon as she saw him, she blinked and stood stunned for a moment. "Wow. The whites of your eyes are filled with blood, and you look like some sort of demon. Should I get you a healer?"

Rocky glanced at his debuff bar and found that he was suffering under a negative effect.

Traumatized Mind
You have touched something with your spirit that almost melted your brain and has given you something far worse than a migraine.
You will experience jolts of pain for the duration of this effect.
Moving will increase this pain exponentially.
Duration: 25 Hours

Rocky read the effects to Sela, and as he finished, he felt a wave of cooling water wash over him. It felt similar to a healing spell but this time it was more akin to an ice-cold rag pressed directly onto his brain. The duration of Traumatized Mind decreased by an hour every few seconds and washed away a great deal of Rocky's discomfort.

"That's my Rejuvenation skill. Give me a moment, and I will recast it on you. While its effects keep working, can you tell me what happened?"

Rocky nodded, but then immediately grimaced as he heard and felt bells ringing. It wasn't an experience he wanted to go through again, so he said, "Can we wait 'til my head feels a bit better?"

Sela nodded and they sat in relative silence as she recast her Rejuvenation. Relative silence because Rocky was surrounded by lightly snoring chimera kits. While he waited, Rocky forced a question of his own out, "Are you going to recruit some druids to bond the panther kittens?"

Shiva raised her head and stared at Sela when he asked the question. Sela shook her head after a moment or two and swatted at Shiva. "Yes, yes!" she began, and turned her swats into affectionate scratches. "Yes, Rocky—I am told I have no choice in the matter…"

Rocky scratched Shiva along her ribs where he was resting and heard her begin purring in contentment. Likely from changing Sela's rather stubborn thought processes. Rocky had noticed that Sela was very much against sharing things that would give others power. This had not been a huge point of contention between them, but he had noticed her looks of discomfort whenever he chose to share what she deemed dangerous.

Thirty seconds later, his debuff fell away and he breathed a sigh of relief. Without the pain, the excitement of his discovery took hold of him, and he felt his heart trill as his temperature ratcheted up. "Sela, I may have discovered something that would explain why Ether Channels and Ether Manipulation were skills that weren't shared in your time."

Sela's eyebrows raised comically, and he couldn't help but smile more broadly. He pointed to his chest piece that still lay on the ground. It was half under the second gryphon kit, but if Sela used her Ether sight, that wouldn't matter.

"Trace this enchantment with me," Rocky said and felt her probing and shaky Ether Channel join his near the Ether Pool of the chest piece.

Together they circled over the repair pool, and the Strength and Speed rune before they reached the knot. To Rocky's amusement, Sela's Ether Channel kept slipping off the tightly woven knot, so he tried something. With his mind he wrapped a tendril of his external Channel around hers to guide it.

That was when he felt her. It was like having an identical copy of the willful and powerful woman suddenly appear in his head. He jerked away and his channel rebounded into himself with a snap like an elastic band. He could tell that Sela was surprised as well by the sensation because she also jolted. For just the briefest of moments Rocky had seen her thoughts...

Is she really trying to decide whether to kiss me or punch me?

"I'm sorry, I didn't know that would happen," Rocky stuttered out. Sela just stared back at him, her expression unreadable. Was she going to hit him? She moved forward and he closed his eyes, expecting a punch in the face. Instead, she somehow fell on top of him? He opened his eyes to find her arms pressed around his neck and her body in a strange position to avoid any of the kittens, but she was definitely hugging him.

Rocky smiled and opened his mouth to poke some fun at the woman's reaction, but her finger came to rest across his lips. Then she returned it and hugged him tighter. What exactly had she seen or heard in his head?

"Let us continue this lesson away from the children," Sela whispered into his ear. For a split second, he thought she just meant the discovery he had made, but she added, "And with a bit less chance of someone walking in."

Rocky stood up and gathered his gear, his cheeks feeling like they were on fire. It didn't help that Shiva was wearing a very noticeable cat grin. Or that Azoth chose to mentally ask, <Rocky need tip? Azoth try one time, has kids. Rocky and Sela try many time, no kids. Azoth help!>

He took off his ring and placed it into his bag of holding to stop Azoth from offering any more 'help.'

***

Rocky woke up the next morning in Sela's bed. The sound of the shower turning on had been the final stimulant his brain needed to crawl out of his shallow sleep. The night before had been wonderful. Almost like the three months, all the worries, and the stress he agonized over hadn't existed. There were still moments of awkwardness but thanks to his little trick of sharing consciousnesses with the woman, they had quickly gotten over it.

Sharing his inner thoughts wasn't pleasant, at times, for Rocky. In fact, it had taken more courage than he thought he had to open up with the wonderful woman, but once he had, it was like a weight lifted from his chest. It was one thing to tell her about all his internal struggles and another entirely to show her how badly New York had broken him. How severely damaged he was before it.

It had also been truly magnificent to see her feelings for him. To stop wondering if this was just a casual occurrence for her. It was also somewhat helpful to see himself through her eyes. It was surreal, terrifying, and humbling all in one.

Still, giving Sela lessons on Essence Conversion while we 'rested'…

He shook the delightful image out of his head and chose to trade it for the real thing as he got up and moved to join her in the shower.

***

"We cannot share this new skill with just anyone," Sela cautioned. "I understand that you want everyone to gain strength, and this will help that, but for humans to control Essence… It's just too much possible power to hand out. We need to discover the extent of power this could mean before we just dole it out like candy."

"Sela, if we allow everyone in the Territory to work on a problem with us, we will solve it that much faster!" Rocky countered. "Just think about how much it might help in repelling Frankie and the invasion in nine months."

"Please, just wait on this one," Sela began with a hand on Rocky's shoulder. "We at least need to talk to Tao and the Knights about it first. You said Tao was seeming to hint at this possibility to you?" Rocky nodded and she treated his nod like an agreement to her first point. Rocky shrugged internally; it wasn't like they wouldn't talk about it again. "Speaking of the invasion. Today should be the inaugural flight of our new ship—as long as Amelia finished the engine drives."

"That would explain the group of onlookers in the manufacturing quarter…" Rocky mused as his eyes peered through the window to take in the groups of people that were making their way in that direction. Sela and he also joined the slowly milling crowds once they moved downstairs, together everyone ambled toward the large, currently grounded, battleship.

A hum slowly grew in intensity as they made their way closer, and Rocky, with his increased senses, soon chose to stop.

"Sela, that hum is getting too loud for me, do you mind if we stop and watch from here?"

She nodded but looked at the ship worriedly. "I do not remember the Scourge ever being this loud. Do you?"

Rocky shrugged. "That's tough for me to say. I got a skill that increased my hearing, sight, touch, and even taste. So, honestly, everything is kind of new to me."

Thanks to that increased hearing, he might have been the first one to hear the rattle that joined the hum. His head jerked in the direction of the back engines as they turned toward the ground. When the Scourge battleship did this, it would lift the massive ship into the air. This time he watched the engines vibrate violently.

The crowd began shouting when they, too, heard and then saw the problem. Sela squeezed his arm hard when both engines caught fire.

"That's not good," Rocky said unhelpfully.

Sela's Dark Vines exploded out of the ground in numerous locations under the ship. Other skills joined hers and together the people of the Grotto who reacted fast enough managed to cushion the ship's crash back to earth. Rocky still grimaced when the center of the ship cracked and bent violently. He breathed out slowly and began massaging the bridge of his nose.

"Sela, let's get ahead of this and go see if we can meet with Amelia," Rocky said as he looked in the direction of the retail quarter. He sighed as he realized he was in for a ridiculously long morning of dealing with more problems on his final day in the Grotto.

***

"I was forced to use some True Silver in the build. There just wasn't enough recovered arbuckle in those machines you gave me. It sounds like True Silver just can't keep up with the Ether draw…" Amelia surmised after Rocky and Sela explained what had happened. "You are going to need to send the engine back and get another pound of arbuckle…"

"We, like every other individual in the EtherVerse, do not have an arbuckle mine," Sela said, sarcasm lacing her words. Rocky couldn't help but smile at her dry response to the situation, but before Amelia could quip back, he raised a hand.

"Wait, why can't we get our dungeons to produce arbuckle?" Rocky asked and heard two girls click their teeth, which definitely meant his question was stupid.

"Dungeons can't produce arbuckle," Amelia said dismissively.

"Okay… but then how did you get arbuckle for the original stolen engine drives, Amelia?" he asked, trying to steer this conversation away from his 'stupidity.'

"As your colleague seems to already know," Amelia snarked, while looking at Sela. "There aren't any mines of arbuckle. People can find small deposits that have either fallen to earth or are somehow being pushed up by the planet, but that's about it. So, to answer your question, I have nanobots searching through Helion Prime daily. Those first engine drives were from my personal stores, and you two managed to lose them."

The way she said the last made Rocky recall just how upset she was with him when she first ported into the meeting room. Clearly, she hadn't been happy with his absence from the meetings over the last few months. Even more clear was that her relationship with Sela had degraded even further over that time. Garnell, on the other hand, was very happy to see Rocky again and had even spent the short time waiting for Amelia's arrival conversing with him about his time away. Then again, Garnell's excitement might have been because of how much material Rocky had ordered for the Territory.

I even used my own savings, but we really need the buildings to be repaired as dragon scale...

"Please, like you did not get anything for those first engine drives. Our Territory has been selling you stores of monster meats and grown foods at one tenth of their actual market value. You managed to get Derik to sign a contract that grants you these prices for five years, too!" Sela snipped back, and Rocky realized just how much that would cost the Territory in the long run.

"Doesn't change the fact that you lost the arbuckle!" Amelia grouched. Rocky and Garnell looked at each other, both men seeming to ask for help in the current situation. They shrugged after smirking.

Rocky stood from the table. "We will try to find some arbuckle for you, Amelia, but it seems like our chance of building numerous ships to repel the invasion just went out the window. I'm sure the council wants to meet and beat this dead horse for a while, so we should probably go..."

Amelia pointed to Sela. "Didn't she say there might be a massive store of already-built ships somewhere on your planet? Even if the tech is obsolete, there would be arbuckle in each of the engines, and maybe even weapons if they are old enough."

Sela pointed at Amelia as she, too, stood up. "We are planning to head there soon, we just need to get our group and supplies together.."

Sela ported out while Rocky blinked and processed the two women agreeing on something. Amelia stood and stretched her skeletal black wings behind her. "If I were you, I'd probably listen to her more. She has a good head on her shoulders." Amelia ported out as well, which left Garnell and Rocky to stare with mouths hanging open.

"Do they hate each other, or not?" Rocky mumbled as he waved goodbye.

"Women are strange creatures," Garnell responded just as Rocky exited.

Outside the arbuckle dome of the shop, Rocky found Sela pacing while Zippo and Smith stood by. Smith turned to Rocky as soon as he exited the shop building and said, "The council sent us to find you, and request your presence immediately…" Sela rolled her eyes and shook her head as she made a motion with her hand in the direction of the town hall.

Rocky could barely hold back his chuckle. She was clearly impatient to be doing something and not heading to a council meeting to talk needlessly about it, but like Rocky, was resigned to that fate. He nodded and they began walking.

"Do you think we will be able to build any more ships before the Guild Collective's fleet arrives?" Zippo asked, his voice small, almost scared.

"I don't know, Zippo," Rocky responded and put a hand on the young man's shoulder. "I hope so, but I don't know where to start—" Sela gave him a look, and he hastily added, "—other than our trip to Atlantis."

The next few hours were filled with tedium that made Rocky's jaw hurt from clenching, and in the end did nothing to address the problem. The council was scared and looking for answers, which Rocky couldn't give. His and Sela's plan to travel to Atlantis was also met with skepticism, but luckily Rocky and her were no longer bound to follow the council's decisions, which she was far too happy to point out.

I wish she wouldn't rub their faces in it…

"We are leaving to go find Atlantis tomorrow morning. Either get behind that decision or do not. We do not need your permission," she shouted as she turned and stormed from the room. Rocky assumed having her request denied for so long had played a rather large role in her current outburst. Still, he agreed with her sentiment—while a council was great to handle day to day needs of the people in the Territory, it also failed miserably to handle crises like the ones they were currently facing.

Is it strange that it took Amelia telling me to realize that Sela is often right…?

CHAPTER TWENTY-THREE

Rocky might have been shocked at the speed the group was put together if it wasn't for the fact that he had gotten numerous runners for the remainder of the day yesterday with updates. The first runner had informed Sela and him that the excursion was 'approved.' Then that the date was set for today, even after they had clearly told the council they were leaving in the morning. Another runner informed Rocky and a laughing Sela that the excursion was deemed of utmost importance and that the council would be deciding on who would accompany them. Her laughter had cut off quickly when the party included people that Sela didn't know. She had dragged Rocky back to the council chamber and berated Derik and the others for their childishness.

Now they stood on the cargo deck of the Scourge with Smith, Zippo, Amber, Victoria, and an extremely reluctant Gaston as a healer. Rocky had begun pushing for Gary, until the man had informed him that he needed to stay in the Grotto to keep applying Regrowth to his sister and mother. Gaston worried the group because they all recalled that the man was a coward and a scammer. In fact, they had been forced to keep him under guard during the first Territorial invasion by the ogres.

Still, any healer was better than relying on Rocky's Dark Mend skill exclusively.

The council had also come up with a 'plan' of approach for the Scourge. The group had even floated the idea of an actual HALO jump by the party to land on the city, but thanks to Sela they dismissed it. According to his companion, the city had numerous defenses against aerial assault, and even if they weren't active, there was still the massive white creature they hadn't yet identified. Instead, the Scourge would come in above the African continent and drop them as close to the Mediterranean Sea as they safely could.

Rocky got the feeling that this plan had been decided on specifically for expediency of the party to and from Atlantis. If they were fast getting there, the council likely believed that they would be fast coming back. Rocky could only shake his head at the reasoning, even though he agreed with the process. Azoth was also reluctantly with them on the cargo deck as the spaceship slowly lifted back out of the Territory.

<Feel shake. Azoth no shake when fly.> Azoth mentally continued to commentate on all the strange noises, smells, and feelings the battleship underwent.

<Just wait, buddy. We are about to leave the planet,> Rocky responded, and pointed at a nearby window that showed the land mass under them shrinking away. Azoth moved to the window and attempted to crane his neck down or up to see more, but by his grumbling didn't get very much more from the 'tiny pinhole.'

The engines changed directions once they were high enough and a forward vector was added to their ascent, which Rocky felt thanks to a quick stumbling step backward. The blue of the sky was replaced by the black of space and any mental commentary from Azoth cut off.

Rocky walked over to his pet.

"Pretty crazy, right, buddy?" he asked as he patted just above Azoth's front knee. Azoth laid down to give him access to his shoulders and neck, which Rocky gave a healthy dose of scratches to.

Sela joined them as well and together they watched the endless blackness filled with tiny pin pricks out the window. Sela eventually said, "It's crazy to think that it's grown even bigger since I was last campaigning across its depths."

"While I simply think it's crazy that you have traveled to other planets…" Rocky mused, realizing that for him the novelty of being in space, period, was something that Sela had long since conquered.

She seemed to understand his sentiment, because she placed her hand in his and turned to enjoy the view.

<Stop holding hands and give more pets.> Azoth interrupted the moment.

Rocky managed to look away from Sela and his pet to see the rest of his group. Smith and Amber were standing with crossed arms on each side of Gaston, which made him worry again, but he still felt that having a healer and a tank would be a massive boon. Zippo and Victoria stood chatting near another window wearing looks of wonder that probably mirrored his own.

Within ten minutes, they were entering Gaia's atmosphere again and coming to rest over a very large landmass that Rocky assumed was Africa. Once the pilots deemed them low enough, the cargo doors opened, and a rather loud roar of wind drowned out any of the group's further conversation.

Except for Azoth's mental commentary. <This not that fast.>

The heat of the air was like a slap in the face. Especially coming from the Grotto and the north of the North American continent. He could feel the dry heat on that wind even though they were likely thousands of feet above the ground. He also smelled something on that wind that he couldn't quite place. Almost like dust, but simultaneously more sterile than dust.

The ship was clearly slowing down and in response Rocky, Victoria, and Zippo jumped aboard Azoth in preparation for departure. Azoth could only carry three people, and the plan was for him to drop them off on the ground before returning for Smith, Amber, and Gaston. Sela, of course, was going to use her raven form.

Almost as soon as the Scourge coasted to a stop, Azoth leaped from the doors and began descending in a heart stopping dive. Rocky, who was used to his pet's kamikaze flight style, didn't flinch, but the tightening grip of Victoria on his abdomen told him that Azoth effectively terrified her. Azoth touched down, and the group was just preparing to dismount when a raven caw made Rocky look back up.

The Scourge, which was probably a thousand feet above them, was firing all of its engines on one side of the craft. Of course, that caused the ship to list dangerously and Rocky couldn't understand the reason for the maneuver at first. Two missiles whooshed audibly as they ricocheted off the shielding and deflected down and away to splash into the ground.

Eight Mechanolords arrayed themselves in front of the Scourge and an exchange of missiles, lasers, and ballistics ensued.

"Victoria, dismount. Zippo and I are going to go help," Rocky said as Azoth turned under him.

<Sela say she no can turn back,> Azoth mentally growled into Rocky's head. Victoria slid from the saddle and Rocky squinted back up to where Sela was attempting to fly back to the ship. Instead, she seemed to be bouncing off of what appeared to be rippling air.

"What in the *Alvin and the Chipmunks*?" Rocky attempted to swear before grumbling and mentally telling Azoth not to fly up there yet. If this was a new skill from the Mechanolords having another fly bash into it wasn't going to help. "Zippo, do you think you can break that shielding with a spell?"

"I can try. Maybe warn Sela, though," Zippo said as he landed and began molding a bright red ball of undulating fire in his hands.

<Azoth tell her,> Azoth said as he growled and raised his hackles at the continued firefight he couldn't join yet. Sela flew away from that direction before banging into another section of air.

This field is massive, how did the Mechanolords manage it?

Zippo's Fireball, which was aimed at the backs of the engaged enemies, exploded prematurely as it also collided with a field that hadn't been visible a moment before. This time, the intensity of the collision and power behind it illuminated a dome of muted blue that arced toward the ground in the distance. Rocky tried his radio, but only heard static in response.

Sela landed beside them and transformed as the group blinked up at the fight they couldn't take part in.

"What should we do?" Rocky asked her as she morphed from avian to human.

"I am not sure. I think we are in some sort of defensive field that is emanating from the ground. There is no way that the Mechanolords fighting up there are projecting this... Blast!" Sela ended with the closest thing to a curse Rocky had ever heard from her.

The ship, which was the much larger target, was finally hit as a part of the shielding that had surrounded it collapsed. Zippo and Victoria swore comically as they watched on. Instead of continuing to engage, the Scourge fired its engines and retreated to a place that the enemy couldn't follow—space.

Unfortunately, they suffered a few more hits before they exited the stratosphere and Rocky worried what that meant for the crew of the Scourge. Those thoughts were driven from his head as the eight Mechanolords turned in eerie unison to stare at their group below.

There must be a reason they aren't coming down to try to kill us...

That was when a snake's head, easily double the size of the Scourge itself, seemed to blur into Rocky's vision from the right. Rocky felt his mouth fall open as he traced the body down, and down, and down the thousand plus feet back to an area outside of his line of sight. The white snake might have connected with its attack, but because of the sheer girth of the monster, it was hard to tell if the hovering machines were dead, or just behind the body. The thing literally blocked out the sun!

Sela's breathing began to intensify as her chest heaved, but she did manage to mumble, "That massive white snake is a legendary-ranked golem…"

She turned her Analyze window.

Jormungandr
Legendary-Golem Sea Serpent
Level 112
Health Points: Unknown
Active Skills: Unknown
Passive Skills: Unknown

"Scourge, this is Rock. Report?" Rocky tried. As soon as he depressed his button, the static abated for a moment, but once he finished it came back sounding louder thanks to the momentary absence. He tried flipping channels and trying again for about a minute, but even the channel that was supposed to connect to the control rooms in the Territorial towers wasn't working.

"What do we do now?" Rocky asked, about a million thoughts going through his head as Jormungandr disappeared under the horizon. Luckily, no Mechanolords were left in the sky, so either they retreated or, better yet, were inside the creature's belly!

"There are protocols in place for these sorts of situations, Rocky," Victoria said sternly. "Like Joe used to say, if the situation is FUBAR, compartmentalize and finish the task."

Sela nodded, seeming to shake herself out of the fear she had been showing. "Military mission protocol. Each individual has a mission to stay alive. Trust the people on the Scourge to accomplish that to the best of their ability, and they will trust us to accomplish ours."

"That sounds like an excuse to abandon others to fate," Rocky responded, his body tensing.

"I think that's the point," Zippo whispered. "My Fireball didn't even dent that shield. Should we just stay here banging our heads against it? I think Sela and Victoria are right, and the reason just needs to be a good enough one to not do something stupid."

That sounded so much like what Gary had taught Rocky that he paused for a moment and adjusted his thought process. *Mindfulness.* He just needed to believe in those on board the Scourge to take care of themselves.

He wrestled with those thoughts for the next few minutes, and it must have shown on his face because the others began looking around them as he did. He cataloged the environment himself absently as he came to grips with the situation. To the group's right, there was some greenery that seemed to surround a river of some sort. To their left, front, and back stretched sand as far as he could see.

It was extremely clear to Rocky that they should fly along the greenery. That thought made him turn to Azoth. Strangely, his pet had both of his wings open and up above his head. He was also turned away from the group. Rocky's scrutiny caused everyone to look to the giant manticore.

"What are you doing, Azoth?" Rocky asked, trying to tilt his head to understand the posture better.

<Sun, hot. Shade head. Azoth go break through barrier,> Azoth responded, and Rocky felt his eyebrow raise. He hadn't even considered how this extreme temperature would affect Azoth. Especially with Azoth having likely adjusted to the winter temperatures up in Canada.

The moment of confusion allowed his pet to take off. <Azoth, not even Zippo's Fireball could break through.>

<White nope tube smell like garbage, Azoth want closer look.>

The group watched in horror as Azoth climbed. Then, like a fly hitting a window, Azoth bounced back. A ripple of blue spiraled out from the impact and the group watched as Azoth repeatedly created more and more of the things.

<Nothing here. Azoth see nothing,> his pet mentally commented.

"I don't think he is going to give up anytime soon…" Rocky surmised after watching Azoth change directions and keep trying. "Maybe it's best we head to the shade of those trees for now? Does anyone know where exactly we are?"

"Sudan or Egypt," Victoria stated. "We are south of the Mediterranean and out the Scourge window, I'm pretty sure I could see the Red Sea in that direction…" She pointed past the greenery they were walking beside. "I don't know enough about geography to say for certain, but I'm leaning toward Egypt, because that greenery in a desert like this likely means a river, and I'm sure you've heard of the Nile."

Rocky blinked and tried to remember if he knew anything about Egypt other than the names Victoria had just used. He came up blank and shrugged. "So, we just travel north, and we'll eventually get to Atlantis?" Everyone shrugged, and he blinked at Sela. "You don't know?"

"No, I just do not have a better idea," she responded.

Azoth continued to bump into the barrier above them as they walked. He did send a few mental questions about possibly having tried a spot before, which admittedly made Rocky chuckle.

"What's that?" Zippo asked as he pointed to the group's left as they crossed the sand.

Rocky looked in that direction to find a strange distortion in the air. When he looked around, he saw the same in other directions as well. "I think that's just a mirage. You know when light passes through different temperatures of air?"

"Not that, dummy. Look at the sand," Zippo said, as he adjusted his hand to aim more down.

Rocky saw it then. The sand dune was undulating. It was difficult to see because of the mirage that sat above it. The mirage made it seem that the entire desert was moving but the largest sand dune, perhaps three dunes over, was shifting. Rocky hurriedly checked every other sand dune to find two others that might have also been 'alive.'

"Let's get to those trees. Now!" Rocky shouted, and the others, who had clearly come to the same conclusion, immediately broke into a run. <Azoth, can you see those moving sand mounds? Can you see what's causing it?>

<Massive black thing. Like ant, but big back and mouth creepies,> was Azoth's somewhat helpful response.

"Azoth made it sound like some sort of beetle," Rocky shouted as they continued to close with the nearest line of trees.

Somehow getting to the tree felt like an accomplishment, and Rocky's heart slowly began to decrease its tempo.

Right up until Azoth mentally asked, <Why you run to huge gray chimera?>

A massive roar shook the frond like leaves of the trees they now hid under. Rocky swallowed and turned toward the water to watch a towering hippo-esque creature pull itself free.

CHAPTER TWENTY-FOUR

Nile Protector
Master-Taweretan Chimera
Level 21
Health Points: 11,320 / 11,320
Active Skills: 10
Passive Skills: 10

The more of the hippopotamus that emerged, the more Rocky realized why it was classified by the system and Azoth as a chimera. Its head changed from gray to green as the ridges and scales of a crocodile began. The mohawk-like streak of green continued right down the massive creature's back, merging into a long lizard tail. The front feet that were on land looked like lion paws far larger than Azoth's. Rocky gulped seeing the level, health points, and skills his Analyze had revealed.

Looking at Victoria, he asked, "What do you think?"

She looked behind them at the desert and shook her head. "We can get back on Azoth and try to retreat, but…" She made a gesture back the way they had come just as Azoth collided with the barrier again. "The water it's guarding may be the only source for miles in any direction. I don't think we have a choice…"

A cool wave Rocky recognized hit him, and he watched a look of euphoria come over Victoria and Zippo's faces in unison as Sela's Rejuvenation hit them as well. "Rocky, you will have to somewhat act as our healer. So don't burn through your Ether!"

I guess Sela has already decided…

Rocky wished he had more than the single healing skill, but he assumed it was better than nothing. <Azoth, get down here, we are going to need you.>

<Chimera not friend?>

Unfortunately, Azoth had been traveling farther away from the group, and without his ability to fly higher and then dive to gain speed, it didn't look like he was going to arrive quickly. Victoria's golden armor glowed, and she stepped forward while simultaneously directing her shield at the Nile Protector. Rocky watched the sun spot her shield created begin to blister the skin on the hippo before it began to sizzle and blacken. The creature roared its frustration and tracked the searing light to the source.

That's one way to get the thing's attention, Rocky thought as he began clearing out of the way. The hippo-like creature charged forward, its back legs splashing out of the Nile to reveal two more lion paws. The claws on the front and the back dug into the sandy grass as it charged directly through the palm trees in its path. Some of the trees broke but many more just bent flat and then sprang back to standing after the beast ran past.

The gray skin continued to cook under Victoria's skill until the crocodile scales on the beast's back glowed green and shifted. The scaling pattern didn't move so much as grow. One moment the scales were isolated to the spine, and the next green hexagons grew to cover the place the light was burning. The blackened gray skin of the beast was pushed up and off from below the skin of the Taweretan as the scales replaced the thick hide from underneath.

Next the lion paws of the beast seemed to increase in tempo, and the ground under Rocky began to bounce. It reminded him of Yin-Yang's skill, especially when he could track the ripples in the sandy grass around him. Still, this wasn't dense soil, which became immediately apparent when his entire foot sank into the sand.

"It is making quicksand!" Sela shouted and reached down to place her hand on the ground. The waves diverted around them, which allowed Rocky and the others to pull their feet free. The cancellation of its skill caused the hippo to change tactics again and suddenly the sand and water rose behind it. By this point, it was about twenty feet from Victoria and maybe fifty feet from the water. The wave of sand and water hurriedly closed that gap, and suddenly the creature was riding the wave in an assisted charge right at Victoria. Victoria's shield began to glow, which Rocky thought meant she was preparing a Reflection skill.

The monster crashed into Victoria's tiny form like a human foot on an ant, but the bong of her skill kicking in rang strongly. Instead of Victoria moving, the Taweretan rebounded back the way it had come. Unfortunately, the sand tidal wave continued, and Rocky was suddenly being tossed around like a cat in a laundry machine.

The clumps of sand felt like fists punching him all over his body. He was sure the armor he wore mitigated some of the damage, but when he hit the ground and the tumult continued on, he could feel welts forming all along his front. He groaned as he levered himself to his knees and feet. Everything hurt and he desperately wanted to cast some Dark Mends. But he was the only healer and Victoria might need him. The hippo had closed back with Victoria in the few moments it had taken for the wave to regurgitate Rocky. She was weaving between stomps and swipes from the Taweretan, but was already showing signs of injury. He tossed Dark Mend on her and watched the ball of shadow fly to her and then congeal on her shield arm.

The group was now unloading spells into the beast, and Rocky could see many of its passive skills activating as the damage from searing red Fireballs and Moon Fire were mitigated by scales. More of the skin became green crocodile scales even as the health of the creature dropped. The speed of the dropping health bar gave Rocky hope until he realized that it was slowing down in its descent as more scales and defenses appeared on the Taweretan. Azoth crashed into the back of the beast, and the manticore's lizard claws dug into joints in the crocodile scales. His teeth then latched onto a spot just above the thick neck of the creature while his tail began bouncing repeatedly off both hide and scale.

The beast glowed gray and suddenly Azoth fell off the back of the creature when it bucked. Rocky could see both of Azoth's lizard talons still gripping the scales of the Taweretan in them as the manticore fell. It was hard to tell, but he was pretty sure that gray skin took the place of the scales on the back of the Chimera. The gray glow changed to yellow, and the beast let its legs fall out from under it as it tried to pancake Victoria under it. Rocky swore and began preparing a futile Dark Mend. If the bulk of that creature landed on top of a human, skill or no, that human would die.

Victoria glowed golden and seemed to vanish as the waves of fat enveloped her. Rocky cast his Dark Mend, knowing it was likely too late, but suddenly the hippo's head jerked up and a golden, twenty-foot-tall statuesque woman stood where Victoria had moments before. He blinked as he realized he'd seen her in this form during the Grotto battle, but had attributed it to party buffs.

To call her form awe inspiring didn't cover it. It was beyond impressive to watch her practically turn into a golem in front of his eyes. Still, even with her new size and obvious strength, her statue form struggled against the bulk of the hippo chimera.

Slowly, the statue's arms began moving and its punches rang the rib cage of the Nile Protector like a bongo. Rocky, who knew a powerful cooldown skill when he saw it, decided healing was no longer necessary. Instead, he loaded his blade with three stacks of his Dark Blade and Envenom before running into the fray. Azoth again leaped onto the back of the beast and bit into the much softer gray skin he had uncovered. Zippo and Sela continued pumping spells into the beast as well.

The creature was just getting its back feet back under it when Rocky slashed through some thick gray skin on its belly.

He watched the blackness of his Dark Blade begin spreading before that area of skin and flesh underneath was ejected by a forming scale. He cursed and struck again, and again, seeing his plan to poison the creature slowly slip away. When he reached twenty percent Ether in his pool, he thrust his sword into a crocodile scale and then backed away to assess the fight.

Azoth continued to tear skin and scales off the back of the creature, while Sela in her panther form joined him. Zippo was continuing to lob Fireballs, but simultaneously was directing a stream of magma at one of the back legs. The sand near that leg had long since turned to glass—which held the massive lion paw in place.

Victoria was the one that worried Rocky the most—her statue form was cracked in numerous places along its arms and body as she continued to take bites and swipes from the creature. The Nile Protector was down to two thousand health, but it seemed to be a race between its health and the duration or health of Victoria's penultimate skill. He cast some Dark Mends on the statue but felt them rebound and adhere to him instead. He sighed slightly when the pain of his bruises was lessened, but that had taken almost the remainder of his Ether. He pulled out a medium Ether Draught and looked around for options.

A glow of orange told him he didn't have time to get distracted, but as his head whipped around, he found Azoth glowing and not the Nile Protector. Azoth's muscles bulged and rippled across his body before he bit down again at the base of the hippo skull. This time an orange spiritual lion head made the action with his pet and instead of just clamping onto a large patch of skin, the jaws enveloped a third of the neck. Rocky heard scales creak and scrape against each other as the powerful skill forced them together.

Then the poisons that he had thought the creature effectively dispelled took hold, and muscle spasms began. The two thousand health that remained seemed to drain away in a breath, before the chimera hippo collapsed to the sand. The group stood panting as they alternated staring at the cracked statue form of Victoria and the still-glowing form of Azoth.

"What skills were those?" Rocky asked both.

Victoria's statue laid down before disintegrating into brick-like dust that looked like wet sand. Once she stood up out of the remains, she answered, "It's called Titan Form. I can use it once per day and it lasts until my health runs out. It can't be healed or repaired, though."

"Are you telling me you just canceled your form to answer my question?" Rocky asked, and Victoria looked between the darker patch of sand on the ground and Rocky before dropping her reddening cheeks. He shook his head and turned to Azoth.

<Gift of the Lion,> Azoth said. <Azoth eat beast?> he added, and Rocky could hear the mental drool.

"No, Azoth, you can't eat it yet. We are going to need to skin and butcher it first. Not to mention loot," Rocky said as he walked up and mentally commanded the latter.

Ankh
Quality: Excellent
Enchantments: None

"Okay?" Rocky blinked at the screen and turned the rather heavy ankh around in his hand. It appeared to be made of gold or something similar, but the fact that it had no enchants made the fight for it seem rather unimportant. Rocky scratched his head and showed the item to Sela.

"I partied with Adam a few times, and sometimes loot is locked to individuals for dealing the killing blow… Maybe you aren't getting all the loot?" Zippo stated, and he walked over to the corpse as well. A moment later he, too, was holding a golden ankh. "It did have another of them on it, but other than the material it's made out of, what good are these things?"

Everyone moved forward and looted the corpse but nothing other than more ankhs came out. Rocky even coached Azoth, who probably got the killing blow, to loot the body, but his pet didn't receive anything different. Shrugging, Rocky got to butchering the massive creature. Luckily, Azoth was patient enough to wait for him to finish skinning before he began eating half of the meat beneath.

Instead of waiting for the manticore to pick the bones clean, Rocky and the group began walking north along what Rocky would have called a lake. Was the Nile this wide? He had never visited this part of the world, so he couldn't be certain if this was the river he originally believed it to be. As they walked, they kept their eyes on the water on their right and the sand to their left, trying to see any predator before it saw them. The group wouldn't fare as well against another Taweretan without Victoria's single-use daily skill.

They did find numerous Journeyman-ranked jackals that roamed the area in packs. However, they were only about three times the size of Rocky, so not even a quarter the size of Azoth and were easy to deal with. The jackals dropped Crystallized Ether sporadically and nothing else. The group ended up going a bit more east to keep the water and its greenery on their right side, but occasionally had to veer back west and north to circle around places where the bank of the lake or river had eroded.

It was during one such course adjustment that Rocky saw buildings in the distance. "Are you all seeing that?"

"It looks like an entire town… I think I even see paved roads… and an airport!" Victoria pointed to things in turn. That was all the confirmation Rocky needed and he began jogging to close the distance faster.

Azoth was back to pinging against the invisible dome so Rocky sent, <Can you see any people in those buildings ahead?>

<Here. Nope. Here—coming,> Azoth's constant commentary cut off when Rocky sent a request, and the birdbrain gave up his fruitless task to come check out the town. <No smell. Something wrong...> was his response as he winged over to perform another pass.

The town was stunningly beautiful. The trees, while large, almost appeared trimmed and well-kept. The shore—which had consisted of weeds, rocks, and sand in equal parts—gave way to large gray rocks that created small inlets and coves that jutted toward the buildings. Most of those buildings were the same color as the sands, or lighter, and they reflected the sun that dappled the water. It was surreal to see a city that still stood fully intact. Rocky could tell which buildings were farms because the fields still had fences or shrubs separating them. The signs, written in a language he didn't understand, still hung on the sides of businesses.

Eventually his mind caught up with the eeriness of the situation and he slowed his jog. Zippo and Victoria continued for a bit before they, too, realized it was weird, or recognized that he had slowed down. He couldn't be sure which. Planes still sat on the runways, looking ready to take off, and even the bridges over the small inlets stood looking freshly cleaned and polished. Yet not a single person moved on the sidewalks, or inside of the buildings.

Rocky's Chimera Senses smelled what Azoth must have sniffed earlier from above.

"Do you smell antiseptic? Wait, maybe bleach?" he asked the group.

"Not sure what those are, but something is wrong here," Sela answered. "First, how did all these buildings that are not schools, hospitals or libraries survive? Second, why do they all look like they are brand new?"

Rocky saw movement at the same time as everyone else and all heads jerked to find a pack of jackals walking from behind one of the buildings. This particular building had a courtyard and a pool that he could see and looked to have been either a mansion or a hotel for guests of the town. The sight of the jackals made Rocky tense, not because of the threat they represented, but because if the canines were roaming the streets, it likely meant that no humans were living here.

Slowly the group moved toward the town and at some point, the pack of five jackals picked up their scent. They yipped happily and came at them, but were made quick work of by a flaming tornado sent from Zippo. Rocky added a single charge of his Dark Blade for good measure, but when the flames faded, he could tell that his additional attack was likely overkill. They spent the next couple of hours searching the sparkling town and killing overgrown insects and more jackals before Rocky gave up.

"There's no way there are any survivors here, but if these buildings didn't suddenly turn into golems and stomp the inhabitants, shouldn't they have been fine for those first few days?" Rocky asked Sela.

"Let's not get ahead of ourselves. Just 'cause the survivors aren't in the city doesn't mean they aren't alive. They might have migrated to a larger town to join up with a bigger group?" Sela responded. "Let's continue along the river for now—"

<Here. Ouch. Over water. Nope. Ouch. This way.>

Rocky looked up to find Azoth attempting to fly northeast but coming ever lower from his hundred feet as the dome angled down to ground.

Rocky pointed to his pet. "I think the dome is circular and goes all the way to the ground…"

Sela must have sent a request to Azoth because his pet followed the invisible barrier down in a slow bumping flight. When he reached the ground, he sent, <Who installs air? They leave no door?>

Rocky felt his brain stutter. They were trapped!

CHAPTER TWENTY-FIVE

<Azoth, can you try using one of your skills to break through?> Rocky sent, not willing to try to dissuade his pet from thinking of the 'barrier' as something breakable. It wasn't worth the explanation and would likely hinder what he wanted.

A ripple that Rocky could see flashed up into the sky and really highlighted the dome in the northern direction. <Stupid air absorbs Gift of Lion, Azoth try Gift of Ram.>

Another much larger flash of blue rose up into the sky fifty kilometers north of them.

Rocky watched it climb and noticed that the shape of the dome in that direction pointed somewhat back in this direction. He tried to recall Azoth's fly-like bouncing-flight against the dome and realized that the western edge was curved and pointing northeast, where the eastern side was curved and pointing northwest. "I'm thinking the center of this dome is just north of us. Does that make sense?" he asked as he pointed to a general area his rough estimate brought him to.

"I will try to convince Azoth to tell us what's there," Sela offered and then scoffed a moment after. "He says he tries Gift of Lizard. Azoth not lose to air." She shook her head and said, "I am out of charges right now. I suggest we find a place to rest in town for today and continue tomorrow after my and Victoria's cooldowns have reset. Maybe by then, Azoth will have given up."

The group agreed, and they moved to the building they had seen the jackals emerge from behind. From their quick tour of the town, this building seemed to be the largest. It had numerous white archways, surrounded by yellowing stones, stairs, and arched windows. The group agreed that it had been used in the past for guests to the town, and they all felt most comfortable with a courtyard to cook in.

They set up, and Rocky pulled out the Ether-powered camping stove he had been using on his trek west across Canada. Zippo frowned at the size of the contraption but got to work almost immediately. Rocky moved to the roof of the building and took another look over the town. He noticed something that he hadn't before. A large, carved sandstone rock jutted out of the sand directly to their north. He could see a walkway made of stone and wood that seemed to enter the mountain, and he thought he could see four humanoid shapes carved to look like they were sitting in thrones. Their carving was distinctly Egyptian thanks to tall, stylized hats and square, blocky beards.

"Sela," he shouted down and pointed at the cave-like structure. Victoria and Sela jogged up the stairs and joined him on the roof. Zippo looked like he desperately wanted to see what would make Rocky shout, but stayed with his cooking Taweretan meat. "What do you think that is?"

Sela squinted at the rock he was pointing toward. "I can barely make it out." She bent down and touched the ground, then gasped. "That feels exactly like Maximus did when we were traveling back to the Grotto. I think it is a dungeon," she stated excitedly.

Rocky nodded at her after she confirmed his suspicions. Victoria was still squinting at the structure. "I think it's an Egyptian temple. I visited the Abydos Temple once, and that kind of looks like the same carving patterns."

"That's exactly what I was thinking. This clearly isn't a pyramid, but it looks like it's Egyptian for sure—"

"Oh," Sela began and looked back to the structure. "Oh! If this is the Territories of the Egyptian guilds, then they built several protective buildings that none of the other guilds were ever able to fully figure out. The Mayans came the closest, but the Egyptians could erect a dome like protective barrier over their Territory. The thing was capable of stopping attacks from destroyer-class ships and even Epic-ranked fighters." Sela pointed at the blue flashes, which indicated Azoth still hadn't given up, to further her point.

"Do you have any idea how they did it?" Rocky asked and Sela shook her head. "Any idea how to turn them off?" he followed up and she shook her head again. "Do they originate inside structures like that one?"

"That was the consensus, but honestly, how could structures from so long ago still have survived?" Sela asked, unable to see the connection that both Victoria, based on her smirk, and he clearly could.

"Some of those structures have been a mystery to the world for a long time. Maybe they still had blueprints lying around or something?" Rocky concluded with a shrug. "Regardless, we couldn't figure out entirely why the ancient Egyptians built the pyramids the way they did. The consensus was that they were for burial chambers for the pharaohs, but I think I read something once that claimed they might have been some sort of electrical generator. Imagine those historians discovering that they were some sort of Ether construct…" Rocky finished with a nervous laugh.

Sela gave him an odd look and he cut his laugh short. "I don't see the humor. We are trapped in this dome unless we can figure out how to turn it off. My earlier suggestion stands. Let's sleep here and explore those ruins in the morning…"

After some coaching, Azoth did eventually give up on the barrier. He came to join them just as the sun began to dip below the horizon. He also pestered all of them until they cooked him a few Taweretan steaks.

<Bloody-rare!>

Rocky was going to stay inside the building with Sela until Azoth curled up in the courtyard, and asked him, <Rocky snuggle?> He might have even sent the same to Sela because she stopped heading toward a room on the second level of the building and they both turned back to the manticore in unison.

"It is not like we have a shower and a comfy bed up there," she said and added a wink. Then she tugged Rocky back the way they had come from.

***

"These are the golems I was used to seeing in my lifetime," Sela said, and indicated the four seated figures that looked like overly large human statues of ancient Egyptian pharaohs. "These will stay inactive unless the structure of this building is under threat or the owner of them commands otherwise…"

Rocky looked at the statues and then at Sela skeptically. "You're sure they aren't just going to get up and try to stomp us?"

Sela made a face and added a shrug that made it clear she wasn't sure in the slightest. Rocky summoned his shadow clone and immediately was reminded why he hadn't been using it as often. His shadow self-appeared with its arms crossed and shaking its head. "Dude, they might not even wake up. Just get close enough and see, please?"

<Azoth think shadow Rocky is coward…> his pet said from right beside him, and Rocky couldn't help but chuckle as he absently patted the manticore's leg.

Begging yourself to do something was not a fun experience—especially when the second you couldn't truly say no, and Rocky felt his mouth twist into a sneer. In the end, he forced it to his will. Still, before it moved, the clone pointed questioningly at the blue revolving portal that sat in the doorway between the four behemoth golem statues.

"I already explained it to Rocky. It is an instanced dungeon, meaning we could be entering the depth of this rock or an entirely different planet. There is no way of knowing which before we enter."

The clone shook its head more emphatically.

"I think it's saying it can't enter that portal," Zippo suggested and Rocky watched his mirror image indicate the kid and clap dramatically. "No need to be a dick about it…" Zippo mumbled at the overly dramatized response.

"I didn't tell you to enter the doorway," Rocky scolded the clone. "And insulting people isn't going to change the facts. Now get over there and stand between the four golems. That's an order!" The final bit made the clone walk forward even though it clearly didn't want to.

It waved its hands in protest as its feet continued to carry it ever closer. Rocky watched with held breath as his twitching and dancing puppet reached the feet of the golems. They didn't come to life, and he breathed out audibly and unsummoned the clone that was now giving him the dual birds. "Well, I don't think we have any other choice but to enter the temple. Especially if we have any hopes of getting out of this barrier."

Victoria led the way to the blue shimmering portal, and everyone else followed at a safe distance. Even though his clone had just tested the golems, there was always a chance that the clone wasn't considered a target by whatever was controlling the statues. Rocky Analyzed one of them again.

Guardian Golem
Master-Temple Protector
Level 45
Health Points: Unknown
Skills: Unknown

Victoria paused at the portal and looked back to wait for the others to catch up. "Sela, you said we most likely won't get separated by the transportation this thing puts us through?"

Sela shrugged. "Unless that's what the dungeon is intended for. There are solo dungeons but the challenges inside were always scaled to the individual and to the rank the person holds."

"Great," Zippo grumbled beside Rocky. In response, he ruffled the fifteen-year-old's hair. "Stop it, Rock!" Zippo shouted as he ducked out from under the assault. Rocky just smiled at him and after a moment the kid cracked a grin but quickly looked away to hide it.

"Let's see if we can't get out of here," Rocky cheered exuberantly, and began walking toward the portal.

<This dungeon make good entrance. Rocky share this with other stupid dungeons!> Azoth chimed in as Rocky walked into the large, blue, liquid-like opening.

His arm that hit the swirling pattern first felt like it sunk into ice, and he would have pulled back if the portal hadn't sucked him in. It felt like some terrible, unbeatable beast took hold of his forearm in freezing jaws and yanked him forward. The rest of his body took an ice bucket challenge to the face, and he found himself shivering in a dark black space for a split second before, between one blink and the next, a bright golden light was suddenly being reflected from all directions at him.

Welcome to "The Temple of Ramses II."
You have entered in a group of five, suggested group size 5-10.
Good luck.
Level: 55++
Age: 1,512,311,122 Years
Best time: 32 minutes, 50 seconds
Clears: 213,888
Ether Concentration: High
To exit the dungeon, you must defeat the final boss.

Rocky found himself inside of a room with four golden walls, carved with beautiful symbols. He rubbed his arms to remove what remained of the chill and looked up to find a flame hovering in mid-air above him, lighting the space.

The others popped into the space beside him and shivered as he was spinning to take it all in. The bottom and top of the walls had two parallel lines with numerous symbols carved into them, almost looking like writing, or decorative crown molding. The walls themselves had lines every four feet that broke the stone into panel-like sections. It reminded Rocky of sidewalks in some ways, because he could tell that the lines were carved there, and not individual pieces of the golden rock. Whoever made them was creating stress lines, and not putting up the panels individually.

"Well, at least we are all together," Zippo said just as Azoth popped into the space. "I spoke too soon!" Zippo added when everyone was forced to back up slightly to avoid being trampled by the excitable Azoth as he spun around.

"Azoth, stop!" Rocky shouted as the manticore's tail chipped a piece of the wall.

"Dungeon size deemed insufficient. Calculating response. Solution dispensed," a cultured and musical voice sounded through the room. A rattling of glass on stone rang out from behind Rocky and he turned to find a bottle roll out of a hole at the bottom of the wall. A moment after the bottle rolled out, the small hole closed and a symbol of a large cat next to a small cat became visible again. Rocky picked up the bottle and Analyzed it.

Elixir of Pet Size Reduction
This Egyptian Elixir is commonly used to adjust the size of their pure-bred hunting cats so that they can accompany the owners inside of dungeons.
Click here for instructions.

"Azoth, I've got a treat for you," Rocky said, cheerfully. He was fairly certain Azoth wouldn't be keen on shrinking, but simultaneously he wasn't sure. If this potion meant that he might be able to enter more dungeons in the future, perhaps he would be excited about it.

<What kind of treat? Better not be those jackal things— they taste like poop.>

Rocky blinked as he took in this information. They had skinned the jackals for leather but not taken any of the stringy-looking meat. It seemed that Azoth had chosen to eat at least one of them and regretted it. "No, buddy, it isn't jackal, and those weren't meant as treats for you…"

<Maybe next time you no leave out for Azoth!> Rocky chuckled and told his pet to lay down, close his eyes and tilt his head back. <Surprise treat. Azoth hopes for juicy steak.>

Rocky took the hint and pulled a piece of the hippo steak out from his inventory. Then he both poured in the bottle and dropped in the steak. Azoth chomped down on the meat and allowed the 'juices' to flow down his throat.

<Ick. Whatever sauce Zippo make taste like hair.> Rocky couldn't respond to that because before his eyes Azoth began shrinking. One moment his pet was fifteen feet high at the shoulders and the next he was fourteen, then ten. He continued to shrink until his back was a few feet off the ground and the hippo steak was protruding from his mouth. <Growing steak, Azoth's new favorite surprise!>

Rocky looked at Sela, who had her mouth hanging open. She shrugged at him and moved up to scratch the Doberman-sized manticore.

"It is like he is back to being a baby!" she exclaimed in a bit of squeal. The exclamation caused Azoth to open his eyes and jump back from Sela.

<Who made Sela giant!> he shouted mentally before he took in the rest of the group. <All you grow giant. Azoth can't fly

with you no more, Rocky,> Azoth said, his mental voice sounding a bit pitiful.

"Don't worry, buddy, it's just an elixir to make you capable of running the dungeon with us," Rocky began. "I should have told you about it first, but I wasn't sure how you would feel about getting smaller." Rocky hurried, clicked the bottle's instructions, and facepalmed. The effects would last for four hours, and he was supposed to have modulated the dose.

Azoth took the size change in stride once he realized how much easier petting him became. However, after about five minutes, Victoria coughed. "I get that Azoth is cute in this size and everything, but I think we may want to figure out why we couldn't leave this area…"

"Ahem… Temple of Ramses, can you tell us why we weren't able to leave the area surrounding your dungeon?" Rocky tried. He figured the most direct route to answering Victoria's question would be a conversation with the billion-year-old dungeon. If it could talk.

The silence was punctuated by Azoth's loud breathing and occasional sniffing of the walls and doors that surrounded them. Finally, Sela had enough.

"Dungeon! We heard you talk just a moment ago. Why can't we leave your surrounding area?"

"Our apologies. The entity known as Ramses the second no longer exists, and that's who you addressed," the same cultured and musical voice responded neutrally.

"Then who is speaking if it isn't the dungeon core of the dungeon we're in?" Zippo asked, genuine confusion in his question.

"We've been known by many names in our long lives. Great South, Southern Tower, The Third Quest, The Impossible One, and quite a few other unsavory names that cannot be repeated due to the laws."

Sela's mouth was hanging open, which effectively cut off the conversation from the entire group. Rocky was trying to place the voice of the entity. He knew he had heard it before, but he just couldn't put his finger on it. Still, the voice seemed to relax him while simultaneously keeping him demanding more story.

"You are telling me you are one of the four Atlantean Towers?" Sela finally whispered, and when the rest of the group looked to Rocky for answers, he could only shrug.

"That was another name we were included in, but not our name specifically. Long ago, when the Ether was vanishing from Gaia, and the people were fleeing—"

"Oh my God, you're using the voice of Mr. Freeman!" Rocky shouted, finally placing the voice when the 'story' started with a phrase that most humans on Earth had heard the actor say.

"Rocky—" Sela began when he interrupted the entity. She might have scolded him further, but the others in the group cut her off.

"That's why the voice is so familiar!" Zippo exclaimed.

"You can't just use someone else's voice. They can't do that, right?" Victoria questioned, her indignance clear to everyone. Sela looked at the three of them, her face twisted in horror.

Azoth trotted over and sniffed her. <Why Sela mad?>

Rocky didn't have time to respond because the dungeon began speaking again.

"We didn't realize the voice chosen upon our awakening was so well known," the entity said, chagrined. The voice had changed and while it was still cultured, the tones that sounded like that of Mr. Freeman were gone.

"As we were saying, long ago when the Ether was vanishing from this galaxy, the dungeons, Territories, and structures built using the energy were sentenced to a slow death by starvation. At that time, the city of Atlantis, the Prime Dungeon, and its four towers decided to protect as much as they could in hopes that Ether would one day return. We each took a cardinal direction and spread out our awareness, taking in dungeons and Territories that we could reach. For a long while, we were able to preserve the lives of the dungeons and, in some cases, keep the structures of Territories intact. However, the drought lasted too long, and eventually we needed to make a new decision. We needed to choose whether we would all die, and Atlantis too, or if we would let the younger dungeons we protected die instead.

"Atlantis has always been the most important Territory, so we chose to maintain it. That is how we've come to oversee the dungeons in the cardinal directions of Atlantis."

"That still doesn't explain why we're trapped inside of a dome shield that likely originates from this dungeon," Rocky responded, his interest not as piqued as Sela's, who currently looked torn between worship and anger with the rest of them.

"Ah yes, that. I was getting to that. After we consumed the dungeons we had saved, the drought continued. Eventually, another choice was needed. Kill ourselves to keep Atlantis whole, or to shut down its functions to preserve the Ether stores longer. We chose to preserve as much of it as we could and allowed the floating Territory to sink into the sea. And again it wasn't enough.

"The next choice was to shut down its Ether shielding, and then its other defenses. We were about to shut down the functionality servers for the Ethernet when Ether finally returned."

"So, why not just turn everything back on?" Zippo asked, logically.

"Unfortunately, we were never given the permission to shut down the functions that we cannibalized…"

"So, you damaged them and can't repair them?" Rocky responded, following the same logical chain as Zippo.

"Correct."

"Then the shields around this dungeon are you and the other—" Rocky started and looked to Sela, asking, "three towers?" She nodded so he continued his question. "Protecting Atlantis in place of the systems you cannibalized?"

"Correct, again. You sure are much easier to deal with when compared to the other groups that tried to infect the dungeons with their influence."

"Wait, the other groups are trying to corrupt you and the other dungeons? They are trying to get to Atlantis?" Rocky shouted. His heart was pounding in his chest as fear took over. If Apep took control of Atlantis, it would be a total disaster.

"Nothing can corrupt our cores that no longer reside in this realm. And, yes, they are attempting to conquer the dungeons to make their way to the city of Atlantis as well."

Sela finally asked a question. "How do we get to Atlantis then?"

"Two dungeons must be conquered in the cardinal direction of approach. That will give you partial ownership of the Territory and allow you to modulate the shielding of the structures. Finally, you must defeat the Prime Dungeon's champion to gain access to the sacred Territory."

"How many dungeons have the others conquered?" Sela followed up.

"They are attempting the second one now. However, I cannot give specifics of the dungeons they conquered. Each group must fail or succeed on their own merit. We have pledged to offer no help to any one group. Whoever earns the right to enter Atlantis will be able to choose the path. All we can offer you is this quest, and some explanation. In fact, I think we've gone over my allotted time for first contact. Good luck, champions."

"Wait, that's it?!" Rocky shouted as the entity stopped talking. When no response came, he clenched his jaw and pulled up the quest notification.

Atlantean Territory Quest
Territory Quest
Prove Your Worth
The God Dungeons of Atlantis have protected it for billions of years, keeping the Legendary Territory active, despite the Ether Drought. Unfortunately, they were forced to take out most functions and now protect it in the only way left to them, with Dungeons, Shields and Monsters. Conquer the defenses they've put in place to gain their approval, and access to Atlantis.
Rewards:
Etherience
Greater Atlantean Defense (Choice of 1)
Access to Atlantis
Accept the new Quest?
<Yes> | No | Later

CHAPTER TWENTY-SIX

The three others in the group nodded as they stood up off the floor and studied the room again. "Okay, so he will probably talk to us again if we defeat this dungeon. So, how do we leave this room?"

Rocky looked around and pointed to the four panel-doors with extremely large pictogram symbols on them.

Sela nodded at his gestures. "Rockland's right, those doors make me guess that this is a Challenge dungeon. So, we are supposed to pick which path to challenge to get to the end," she said.

"Right, but in the Grotto, we know what the symbols mean, and now even what the challenges behind them are. Here, we have no clue what the symbols mean. Maybe the dungeon could tell us!" Victoria shouted at the ceiling. When she received no answer, she spun to study each of the symbols. Two of the four were eyes. One of the eyes appeared to be a left eye with a raised eyebrow, large pupil, and makeup to create a tar and a cat whisker pattern. The second eye was a right eye with a lowered eyebrow, small pupil, and heavier makeup in a mirror pattern of the first.

The other two didn't appear to be related at all. One was three flowers. Two on each side with closed buds and a third in the middle open to the flame above them. It was blue in color where the two eyes were black. The final symbol was of a bird with a human face and an Egyptian long beard.

Rocky shook his head and shrugged, not making sense of any of the symbols and what they might mean. He looked to Sela, who was studying the symbols in more depth, and then Zippo, who was looking up at the flame. Azoth decided for them when he eagerly ran up and put both paws on the bird-man symbol. Before Rocky could say anything, Azoth's front paws pushed the swinging door open.

A screech like that of a female woman mixed with a bird of prey penetrated Rocky's enhanced hearing, and he covered his ears as his brain sent false signals to his body. He fell to a knee as his muscles spasmed beneath him. Strangely, he could see the rest of the group moving around and even felt someone's hand on his back.

"Mur ooo achey?" The competing sounds came from right behind him, and he assumed the person, which he confirmed with a half turn to be Sela, had spoken to him. Still, the shrieking continued to affect his body. A glance at the door showed Azoth in a twitching mess on the floor.

"Close the door!" Rocky shouted, wanting to be heard, but unable to hear his own words after they left his mouth. He tried again, and again, before finally the high-pitched caterwauling ceased. He collapsed to the ground and allowed his body to roll him onto his back.

"What in the hell was that?" Sela asked. "We opened the door and you two just collapsed, and then you started screaming for us to close the door..."

Rocky, now in control of his faculties, checked his debuff bar to find it empty, other than a Traumatized Mind status ailment. He hadn't been able to think straight once that door opened.

"I'm not sure what it was. I think Azoth and I got bombarded by some sort of sonic attack. I wasn't even able to think of looking at my debuff bar," Rocky whispered. "Do you think you could cast a few Rejuvenation spells on me and Azoth?"

A wave of cool hit him and took the edge off his skull-tearing headache. He closed his eyes and allowed Sela's skill to tick away his pain. After the second application, he sat up and looked over to find Azoth cowering on the floor.

<Are you doing okay, buddy?> he asked.

<Azoth no like dungeon. First shrink Azoth—next Azoth ears break. Dungeon no fun.>

Rocky had a decision to make. He knew that whatever had assaulted the two of them had truly terrified Azoth, and he didn't blame his pet for that. Still, if he allowed the stubborn manticore to use that to decide to never enter a dungeon again, he would lose a powerful ally for the group and himself.

"Azoth is scared of dungeons after the first door we opened," Rocky said, conversationally to Sela. She was near Azoth, so his voice was raised slightly to 'carry the distance.' "I don't know if he will be able to handle dungeons in the future, if this is all he can do…"

Sela must have caught on to his tactic because she shrugged and pet Azoth as he jerked his head up to look at Rocky. "It is okay, buddy. Dungeons can be challenging, and no one would blame you for staying out of them. Remember, most of this group pretty much died in Chalk River in a dungeon. Fearing death is natural…"

Azoth roared and Rocky needed to cover his ears again as the dog-sized manticore bellowed a challenge into space. Somehow his roar hadn't diminished even though his size had. <Azoth no scared. Azoth strong. Azoth kill stupid dungeon… after head no buzz.>

Rocky smiled and stood up pointing to the door with the left eye on it. "Let's try that one. Be ready to pull it shut again if me or Azoth collapses."

Zippo patted Azoth affectionately, clearly not being privy to the mental conversation.

"It's okay, big guy. You're still the strongest manticore I know…" Azoth's lion muzzle scrunched up and he growled slightly. Zippo blinked and looked to Sela and then Rocky in turn. "Did I say something wrong?" he asked them. They both hid a smile, so Zippo looked to Victoria who just shrugged.

"Don't ask me," she monotoned as she moved to the door and gave it a light push. The door groaned slightly as it creaked open. Victoria looked back to Rocky and Azoth before she pushed it open further.

When the door opened enough that they could see the room beyond, they all blinked at each other. Rocky squinted to make sure he was seeing what he thought he was. On a golden throne sat a woman with golden skin and black lines snaking in beautiful patterns along any exposed area of her body. She wore a white gown that was see-through in areas, but thicker and opaque around her bust and midsection. The golden hue to her skin made her look like part of a statue that included the throne, but the rise and fall of her chest countered that effect.

Caretaker of the Path of Horus
Journeyman-Priest
Level 34
Health Points: 700 / 700
Active Skills: 0
Passive Skills:12

Rocky looked around at the group, who all wore different expressions on their faces as they gazed into the room.

"Why is that bare-chested golden guy lounging on a throne?" Victoria asked, as she shoved the door the rest of the way open.

Bare-chested guy?

"I see a young girl…" Zippo stated, and Rocky thought he understood. Each of them was seeing a different entity on the throne. He turned to Sela, who was tilting her head back and forth before looking at the symbol on the door more closely.

"Let's enter the room together, and see what happens?" Rocky asked Sela. She pointed to the throne which wasn't facing directly at them. Instead, it was facing slightly away, and angled toward the door with the other eye on it.

"I've got a strange feeling about this. Notice that the Caretaker has no active skills?" Sela responded and Rocky shrugged, not understanding her point. "With the low health and only Passive skills, the creature likely has some very powerful effects that will target us if we enter..." she added.

"Okay, close the door and let's check a different one?" Rocky suggested. Victoria closed the door and moved to the other door with an eye. She opened it and they found a desecrated corpse with nearly identical markings all over its body, in a throne that looked like it was made of rusted metal. A green fog seemed to swarm around the creature like tiny insects flying in ever changing patterns.

This one's throne was facing through the wall back toward the other throne.

Caretaker of the Path of Ra
Journeyman-Scourge
Level 34
Health Points: 700 / 700
Active Skills: 0
Passive Skills: 12

The same problem existed in this room, albeit with a slightly more discernible outcome. "Is that some sort of disease swarming around it?" Rocky asked Sela. She nodded, and they moved onto the door with the three flowers in different stages of opening. When Victoria pressed on this door, it seemed to be locked, or so severely stuck that it made no difference.

Rocky looked at Sela, who pointed to the door with the left eye. "Our best bet to start is there. My guess is that the creature inside possesses extremely high Charisma, which is why we are all seeing a figure of desire."

<Azoth see strangely dressed Rocky,> his pet mentally sent. <Call this light Rocky?>

Azoth's comment made Rocky remember his clone and he used the Shadow Clone skill. "Azoth reminded me that we can send in a guinea pig first!" Rocky stated, with a sharp glare at his 'other self'. In response, 'Shadow Rocky,' as Azoth liked to call the clone, turned around, kissed a hand and slapped its ass. "Go open that door and enter the room," Rocky ordered and watched on with the rest of the group as his clone followed the order.

As soon as the clone crossed the threshold, it fell to its knees and crawled toward the seated figure. Rocky blinked. His clone normally would have just entered the room, turned around, and given him the finger. Instead, it was crawling on the ground? Its crawl wasn't one of pain but more of reverence. Once it reached the womanly figure, it began kissing the feet of the Horus Caretaker.

"Well, that doesn't look like fun," Zippo stated, and then made a gagging noise.

"Can we just blast the creature from the doorway?" Rocky asked.

"It could work because of the low health but, simultaneously, the dungeon could penalize us for the action," Sela answered plainly. That was when the clone chose to prostrate itself in a new position directly in front of the feet of the golden woman, instead of off to the side. The shadow clone shook itself, stood up and gave Rocky the finger.

That's more like it...

Rocky studied the situation as his clone chose to moon the group.

"Attack the Caretaker," Rocky ordered in annoyance when he found his own bare backside being presented to the group. The clone didn't respond, and Rocky tried to mentally send the order. Still nothing. He tried to dismiss the clone but found that it wouldn't work. Rocky conveyed his finding to the group, and they all looked back and forth from Rocky to the other Rocky in the room.

The clone escalated a moment after when it didn't receive the response it was looking for, or didn't think it received the response. It began backing the bare butt in the group's direction, but as soon as its feet left the area in front of the throne, it fell back to its knees and began kissing the golden figure's feet. Rocky tried dismissing the clone and it worked this time. "Well, that was strange..."

CHAPTER TWENTY-SEVEN

"Open that other door again," Sela said as she pointed to the right eye pictogram. Victoria opened the door, and Sela pointed at the two Caretakers' feet before moving her arm in a line from where their toes pointed. The two thrones were facing each other, Rocky thought. Sela continued though, "Look at the way the thrones are facing and then think about where your clone was when he stopped responding."

Everyone began nodding except for Azoth who was sniffing the air wafting out of the two rooms. <Bad poops. Flowery thing,> Azoth commentated mentally. Rocky looked at the Caretakers and decided on a different course.

"If spells and skills don't work in the room if you are in the path of the thrones, let's try the disease room first. With that room we could enter, get diseased, but then enter the area and likely be 'cleansed.' I feel like it's better than hoping we grovel our way into the path of that room." Rocky pointed to the golden woman sitting on her throne.

Sela and Zippo nodded, and that seemed to decide it for everyone, because they all gathered near the doorway with the right eye and the zombie-like woman. Victoria counted down from three and then they sprinted into the room. Rocky watched a debuff pop onto his bar and hurriedly read it as he followed behind the group.

Swarm of Diseased Flies
These flies will not only consume your skin but will also leave behind their saliva that melts your skin, muscles, and soft tissues.
50 damage per second.

Rocky felt stinging bites pepper his hands, face and any other exposed area of skin. The areas began to burn like an ember on his skin that was increasing in temperature. As soon as he crossed into the area in front of the throne, the burning ceased and the debuff fell away. Azoth growled and his head glowed red for a moment before his massive red lion's head chomped the undead corpse on the throne in half. Strangely, Rocky saw all of that happen but didn't hear anything. Sela's mouth was even moving as she looked at him, but he couldn't hear her at all. He also realized that the scent of decay he smelled briefly when they entered the room was gone.

He stepped back out from the front of the throne and both his hearing and smell returned. The latter smelling like raw sewage, thanks to the fetid green blood now oozing from the undead corpse Azoth had bitten in half. The debuff and stinging bites returned, and he hurried back to the front of the throne. Before anyone could copy his action, he tried to mime what had just happened to him. He failed to convey the message because each person stepped out and then back into the space one by one.

Rocky tried to cast Dark Mend on himself and couldn't. He held up a finger to the group and overexaggerated an excited pondering face. His acting likely needed a lot more work, because they just looked at him confused. Azoth was luckily trying to clean the yuck from his mouth and hadn't begun running around the room. Rocky moved to the front of the group and put both hands on the throne's armrests. Then he attempted to turn the metal throne slightly to his right, and back to the doorway they entered through. It moved minutely with no sound and Rocky looked back to the group.

They all nodded and Sela went as far as to move to Azoth's side to prod the manticore into looking up. Rocky tried to mentally chat with his pet but couldn't. After a countdown on his fingers, Rocky slowly began the process of turning the throne. After a few degrees, the screeching sound of metal grinding over stone returned and Rocky stopped his actions in panic. He checked his debuff bar to find it empty.

Simultaneously, Azoth began retching violently onto the floor. <Poop smell now taste in mouth,> he whined as he vomited the hippo steak breakfast from earlier.

"I think this throne silences skills and spells," Rocky surmised.

"Seems that way," Sela answered, and then pointed to the door. "Get it turned to the door so we can get out of here. Azoth is practically wanting to lick the walls in this room to remove the taste from his mouth."

Rocky returned to the task and soon had the throne facing the doorway they entered through. Zippo, who had been at the back of the group, was the first to file out, and then each person followed.

<Awful taste,> Azoth said as he began pawing at his own tongue. Rocky pulled out a water bowl and filled it for his pet before turning to the group.

He cast a stack of Dark Mend on each person as they stood to the side of the effects of the turned throne. He had tried while in line with the throne but clearly it didn't work. Even outside the room, the effects of the throne continued.

Pointing to the room with the golden figure on the throne, he said, "We likely have to turn the throne from that room—" He pointed at the disease room. "—toward the entrance of that room, so we can kill the person on that throne and negate their effects. Then I think that throne silences the screeching from that room." Rocky finished by pointing at the bird-man pictogram.

"So, this is a Puzzle dungeon then?" Zippo asked, looking around the room at the doors.

"Not sure yet," Sela began. "This is definitely a puzzle that needs to be solved, but theoretically you could just go into each room and kill the creature inside without solving anything… if your level were high enough."

Rocky volunteered to turn the disease throne, and rushed out of the room as fast as he could so he didn't suffer too much from the stings and bites of the disease debuff. He cast Dark Mend on himself once he was finished and then pointed to Zippo. "I think you should go in, stand only in the doorway and burn the gold figure inside. That should avoid a penalty."

Zippo frowned, but did as Rocky asked. Still, once he got into the doorway, he didn't form a fireball in his hand. After a few moments he turned back and came outside. "I'm sorry, I can't kill a young girl." Rocky blinked and tilted his head as he regarded Zippo. It was just a dungeon minion, after all.

Placing his hand on the kid's shoulder, he moved him to a corner of the main room. It wasn't exactly private but it was the best he could do. "What's up, man?"

"I know that everyone sees something different, but that little girl looks almost identical to a girl I used to know. Sure, she has golden makeup and black lines all over her body, but it would be wrong to just fry her…" Zippo started off heated but his voice faded as he continued.

Rocky tried to think back. Zippo had fought with him against the Mechanolords in Ottawa, and against the hordes of zombies in the Grotto. He had even fought in the battle of New York, but to date he hadn't had to kill a pure human before. Not to mention a human that looked like a childhood friend.

"Okay, Zip, I get it, but honestly what happens if a human is attacking you in the future?"

"I don't know, Rock. I think I'll be fine, but I can't say for sure, now can I…?" Rocky nodded along with the kid's words. At least he was thinking about it now.

"Sorry, I wasn't even thinking. I'll go do it," he responded overly loudly to hide some of the awkwardness. He then walked into the room without looking at Victoria, Azoth, or

Sela. He charged two stacks of Dark Blade and let fly in a thrust. The blow was more power than he needed, and the girl practically exploded on the throne. He let some of his disgust show on his face at the blood and gore that splattered the ground, but consoled himself with the fact that the figure was a dungeon creation, not a person.

He stepped into the room and moved to the back of this throne to avoid some of the carnage. He then turned the throne to face the doorway he entered through, which coincidentally made it face the doorway with the bird man on it. He watched as his friends, who had been standing in the middle of the previous room, chose to move out of his line of sight. He walked back to the main room and entered the path of the throne to exit. His hearing and smell vanished until he moved to the group, who were clustered to the right side of his doorway.

Victoria volunteered to open the bird-man's doorway again, but as soon as she cracked it, Rocky and Azoth collapsed again. Seeing this, Victoria shut the door, and luckily the duration of the pain lasted for such a short time that both he and Azoth were able to recover without Sela's Rejuvenation. The two of them entered the silenced strip in front of the door and this time Victoria could open it without hurting them.

Inside was a large owl-like bird in a cage. The thing had a human face but the ability of an owl to rotate its head one hundred and eighty degrees. Rocky shivered the first time the beast did it. The others in the group still didn't seem to be affected by whatever noise had crippled Azoth and him. Staring into the room with an eerie silence, he felt that something was off. Why would it affect the two in the group with sharpened senses and not the others?

BA
Master-Harbinger
Level 55

Health Points: 12,222 / 12,222
Active Skills: 12
Passive Skills: 14
Boss

He motioned to Victoria to close the door, but she didn't see it. He rushed to the door himself and pulled it shut before exiting the line of the sense stealing throne. "I'm worried that once we enter that room, the noise Azoth and I are hearing is going to affect everyone."

"So, what you're saying is we should all fight in a line from the doorway?" Victoria asked.

"Absolutely not!" Sela stated. "Think about it like standing in front of a high-powered Ether Tech tank. If we spread out, we have a chance to force the tank muzzle at one person at a time. That person can also move to avoid the strike, but if we cannot move to avoid the strike and all line up like wickets in throwball, we are going to be easy to pick off."

"Throwball?" Zippo asked while looking at Rocky, who shrugged and pointed to the other room.

"The boss is in a cage so, in theory, could we silence it with the other throne?" Rocky asked.

Sela nodded. "That would make standing in a line possible, but it's not like the boss is obligated to stay in its cage."

"Hold on, I want to open the door and take a look around the room," Rocky concluded and mentally told Azoth to lay down in the effects of the silencing throne. He walked over and opened the door before peering every which direction he could. To his surprise, he found an empty throne in one corner of the room. This throne was facing at a forty-five-degree angle, bisecting the corner it sat in. Which meant it was facing a corner nearest the door that Rocky couldn't see without sticking his head into the room.

He began to lean forward but Sela grabbed him and pulled him back, and then pointed at the door, before miming for him to close it. They both stepped out of the doorway after, and she explained. "That door is spring loaded so it's likely going to slam shut after you enter. So, if you activate the boss fight by leaning in, we might not be able to activate it again. I think we should go with your earlier plan of turning the spell silence throne to the boss and standing in a line."

They followed that logic and got everything set up before Victoria gave the final orders. "Okay, everyone needs to put a hand on the shoulder of the person in front of them. When I rush in, everyone stays right on each other's heels to avoid the door locking anyone out. We are going to have line of sight issues if we can't leave the thin pathway. Zippo, you stay as far left as you can. Sela, you shift to cat form and try to get behind the cage and the boss. Rocky and Azoth, same goes for you. I will try to stay right and out of your way, Zippo. Got it?"

The group nodded and after a deep breath, they got into position in order; Victoria, Sela, Rocky, Azoth, and finally Zippo. Azoth couldn't hold Rocky, but his head was firmly pressed to Rocky's butt. So much so that Rocky could feel the ever-growing goat horns that were often hidden in the manticore's lion mane. Zippo held Azoth's scorpion tail.

Once Rocky checked the two behind him, he tapped Sela's shoulder, who then tapped Victoria's. In a train, they flowed into the room. Rocky watched Victoria step to the front of the boss on the nearest side of the cage and whack it with her sword as Sela changed to her panther form and jumped over the ten-foot-high cage. Rocky followed her lead, but was forced to latch onto the golden bars and climb the last foot before turning and sliding over the rounded top. He slid down the other side and saw Azoth easily clear the cage. So easily, in fact, that his wings clipped the ceiling.

The collision caused him to dip a wing and he veered heavily left. As soon as he left the pathway, his wings folded tight to his body and he fell like a rock, bouncing off the cage and colliding with the floor. The lack of sound made the scene surreal, but Rocky could tell Azoth was twitching more violently than he had in the outer chamber. Sela pointed to the boss and spun her hand in a 'hurry up' motion.

As Rocky looked back, he found a look of terrified worry on Victoria's face as she slashed repeatedly at the boss with her executioner's sword. It took him a moment to realize what the problem was. She couldn't use her skills either from that side of the cage. He wanted to convey that to Zippo, but it was too late. Zippo threw his first red Fireball, which splashed through the cage and onto the bird-man. Some of the fire came through and almost hit Rocky and Sela before sparking just in front of them.

BA began attacking Victoria, who used her shield to fend off the claws and beak but another problem was quickly apparent when BA moved to the front side of the cage. Sela and he at the backside of the cage couldn't reach it without going inside. They could slide through the bars and attack, but without Victoria using her tanking skills, they were likely going to pull aggro. Not to mention the inside of the cage was likely silenced as well. Rocky didn't even consider using his ranged spells because those would endanger Victoria and Zippo.

Glancing at Azoth, who looked like he was dying, Rocky charged his blade with five stacks and triggered his Envenom. Using a mental command, he forced his Soul Blade into the longest form he had ever used before. Then, careful to stay outside the cage while also staying on the 'line of silence' to avoid the screeches that were hurting his pet, he slashed. He watched as the tip of his sword tore into the owl's wing, but the spreading darkness never took hold. He closed his eyes as he realized the boss wouldn't be affected by his poisons or spreading Dark Blade since they had it silenced both in the magical and non-magical spectrum.

Dammit, why didn't we think of this?

Sela was inside the cage and tearing into BA from directly behind it. Rocky continued to slash and hack, imbuing his Dark Blade into every strike for the extra penetration power, but he stayed at the edge of the cage. Sela didn't really have spells she could use in cat form, so her being unable to cast didn't affect her damage, hopefully.

After his eighth strike, he swore internally as the boss turned its hideous head in his direction. Thinking fast, he backpedaled away from the cage while ensuring he didn't leave the line from the silencing throne.

BA crashed into the bars and its sharp teeth, in its too-human mouth, closed a hand-width away from Rocky's nose. The owl-man beat against the two bars, attempting to get to Rocky as Sela and Victoria were forced to fight against the wings and body of the owl-man to rearrange themselves. Once they managed to get behind the boss again, they crowded close together to stay inside of the silence effects.

This brought up a different dilemma. Zippo, who stood at the closed door, was forced to stop casting, or risk hitting the two women. Rocky couldn't do much from this position, but he continued to attack with his elongated blade as the claws of the owl attempted to snatch him through the bars.

He stopped imbuing his strikes with any of his skills, hoping that Victoria or maybe Sela would be able to pull aggro, but BA didn't seem interested in anyone but him. It kept fanning its wings out behind it, which caused Victoria and Sela some trouble as they had to dodge the flapping and powerful appendages. A quick check told Rocky they weren't going fast enough. BA still had eight thousand health points and Azoth's twitching was growing worse.

Rocky pulled away from the boss and pulled out a length of rope he had gotten into the habit of keeping on him. He looked from the rope to the dog-sized manticore and prayed to any god that might exist. Hurriedly, he tied the rope into a slip knot, allowing one side of the rope to form a closable circle. He wasn't a cowboy with experience trying to lasso something, but his increased stats must have helped him, because he managed to get the loop around Azoth's back leg.

Dragging Azoth into the line wasn't as easy as it should have been based on his pet's new size, and Rocky had to assume that the weight of his pet had somehow remained the same. When Azoth did enter the safe zone, his twitching stopped but Rocky could tell that he was unconscious. He tried a Dark Mend, but it bounced off. A quick Analyze told him that Azoth was suffering a Traumatized Mind debuff.

Maybe Sela could come use her Rejuvenation spell?

Of course, the boss chose that moment to turn and target Sela's panther form, and she leaped out of the cage. Rocky jumped back into battle as Victoria dove under the extended wings of BA and resumed her chopping attacks with the executioner's blade. Zippo also was able to resume his spell casting, which helped the health points vanish from the owl-man chimera faster.

The fight was frustrating because they had no way to communicate changes to each other. No use of skills to help them have BA target who they wanted. Rocky wondered why Victoria hadn't exited the zone and used a taunt type of skill that he knew she possessed, but then hurriedly recalled that she needed to say something mean or insulting for the skill to take effect. Would that count as a somatic portion of a spell?

Rocky and Sela bounced aggro back and forth and whenever his Ether ticked up enough that he could use his spells from outside of the cage. After about thirty minutes, he was breathing hard, which felt all kinds of wrong when you couldn't hear anything. His body was liberally coated in sweat, and the owl creature was finally down under a thousand health. It took another few minutes of this hacking and slashing for the creature to finally fall to the ground dead.

Rocky pointed to Sela and then at the still unconscious Azoth, which was probably unnecessary, but definitely got the point across as she transformed back to human and rushed over. He looked to the throne next and then at BA's corpse. Was the screeching from the boss or from the throne?

Unfortunately, due to Azoth's immense weight, the group was forced to wait for him to wake up, which didn't happen right away. They could drag him, but the cage made it impossible to get the manticore out of the room that way. Rocky, Victoria, Sela, and Zippo stepped out of the room to be able to converse again. As soon as Rocky exited the room, he collapsed as the wailing he had heard earlier assaulted his ears. He slunk back into the silenced zone before crawling to the doorway and closing it for the time being. He made sure to glance at Azoth before closing the door.

"Is he going to be okay?" was Rocky's first question once he closed the door and stepped out of the sensory deprivation line. Sela glanced back at the door before nodding.

"I think so. I cleared the debuff he had, but he was out there for a long time…" Rocky heard an accusation in that statement, and felt his blood suffuse his face as his anger attempted to claw its way up and out of his throat. When he realized he was likely about to spit vitriol, he managed to clamp his jaw shut and take a deep breath through his nose.

She isn't saying it's your fault, and he is going to be fine…

Rocky opened his eyes once he felt he was back in control and found the group looking at him. "Sorry, I am just upset he got hurt at all. I'm really trying to work on being conscious of what emotion I'm actually feeling. I should probably just apologize ahead of time for an explosion in the future…"

Sela smirked at him and came over to give him a short hug. Zippo turned away and made a disgusted sound before he walked over to the fourth doorway. He gave a light shove to it before turning back to the group. "This door is still locked."

"Of course it is…" Rocky retorted with as much sarcasm as he could.

CHAPTER TWENTY-EIGHT

The locked door was an issue that was easy to see a solution to, but infinitely more difficult to enact. The assumption was that all three thrones needed to face the final door for it to unlock. Simple and easy enough to test. Rocky rushed into the disease throne room and got in front of the throne before turning it strategically to the northern door with three lotuses.

"The third lotus is lighting up," Zippo shouted from outside and Rocky quickly rushed back out of the room before casting a double stack of Dark Mend.

"So, we need to wait for Azoth to wake up before we can turn the sensory throne that direction," Rocky stated, as he looked around at the group.

"How are we going to turn the third throne, though?" Sela asked and pointed to the room that Azoth was still asleep within. Rocky blinked and felt his head fall as he came to the realization Sela had clearly already reached.

He walked to the center of the room and looked at Azoth before turning to stare at the throne causing the disturbing lack of his senses. Moving to the doorway, he tilted his head and pulled out some chalk from his bag of holding. He marked the centerline of the doorway and then exited the silenced zone. "First, we need to make sure that the sound attack is still affecting that room. I think it's best if someone else does it, as my senses have been increased."

Zippo volunteered and they both entered the room. Rocky gripped Zippo's hand as the kid slowly shuffled away from the safe area they had used to attack BA. Rocky felt Zippo's hand clench in pain the instant he crossed an invisible line about five feet from the center Rocky had drawn. He heaved Zippo back and they exited the room again.

"*Holy nut cheerios*, that was not fun at all. Tell me that at least helped formulate a plan?" Zippo complained.

Rocky moved to the room with the throne and made a chalk mark starting at the center of the throne, on the line it currently was on. Then he marked a new one at about five degrees of rotation from the center. He then continued this line to the doorway where he ran into the wall. He measured the distance from the door to be his hand width and then began the mark on the other side of the golden bricks before adding a few more inches and drawing it across the room. By the time he reached the other wall, he was pretty sure that the five degrees was almost enough to reach the throne. Likely another half degree or one full degree would accomplish it.

"I see what you're thinking, but that's going to be near impossible to coordinate. The person in the room won't be able to hear the person turning the throne," Sela said as she pointed down his current line and back toward the throne in the room with the left eye.

Rocky looked up and made a back-and-forth gesture with his hand still holding the chalk. "It will probably have to be done on a timer. And in one-degree increments, from the looks of it. We might even be able to have someone stand at the door to each room while one of us changes the angle. The real issue is that both Azoth and I can't be outside of the zone…"

***

<Azoth head hurt!> Azoth mentally screamed into Rocky's mind. Rocky had just tried to explain to him what he needed to do, but clearly the manticore was out of sorts from the mental assault he had just undergone.

<Just stay in front of the throne as Victoria turns it. Right in front, or it will hurt you again.>

Azoth whimpered at the reminder of the pain he must have gone through. The mewling sound caused Rocky, Sela, Zippo, and Victoria to bend down and give him plenty of scratches. He had only woken up about ten minutes ago after being unconscious for a few hours. Azoth's entire body spoke of continued pain and reminded Rocky of a kicked dog. His and the rest of the group's hearts went out to the poor manticore, but they need to get the final door open. After another five minutes, Azoth understood and positioned himself in front of the throne as Victoria stood behind it.

Rocky stood in the room and looted BA's corpse to ensure they didn't forget.

Ankh
Quality: Excellent
Enchantments: None

He stored this one, too, and wondered why these things were dropping from dungeons and monsters in this area. They didn't seem to be anything special, at least not to his Analyze. He exited the silenced zone and reminded everyone to collect their ankhs as well. Then he got back into position and began psyching himself up for what came next.

Once he was ready, he signaled Zippo toward the doorway he gestured to, then Sela in the other doorway. Zippo held up five fingers and counted down. Rocky moved to the edge of the chalk line that demarcated five feet and moved in unison another five feet as soon as Zippo's hand hit zero. Then he held up a hand to stop the next countdown and readjusted the rope that was tied around his waist.

Once he built up his resolve, he moved just far enough until he felt the screeching. Inside the room, it was at a much higher decibel level than outside. He would have collapsed and likely fallen further into the room if Zippo hadn't tugged on the rope. Shivering and shaking off the pain in his head, Rocky marked the spot on the floor and measured about five feet back before assessing where the next area would cover on the throne change.

He signaled Zippo and they managed to move through each of the changes, which allowed Rocky to turn the throne to the doorway. The way back was much easier thanks to the markings he had made on the floor. He still rushed from the room and closed the door behind him as soon as he could. Then the group turned the final throne toward the doorway and saw the central lotus light up. A loud click resonated over the room and the door vanished to be replaced with a swirling blue portal.

Congratulations!
You have completed "The Temple of Ramses II" in 2 hours, 45 minutes, and 16 seconds.
Bonus:
Due to dungeon level, you have been awarded 0 Etherience as a clearing bonus.
The dungeon has been re-classified as a Level 66 zone. This dungeon is a partial holder of a Territory; since you are the first to clear the dungeon since its revival, you are rewarded a quest.

—

Territorial Quest
Leader Quest
Take Temporary Ownership of the Holding.
This Territory was left in a holding state by its previous owner. To remove the holding state and become the temporary owner, you must conquer one more Cardinal Dungeon and become a majority stakeholder. To take full ownership of the holding, conquer at least four Cardinal Dungeons. Since you are now a quarter owner of this Territory, you can move around freely through its defenses.
Rewards:

Etherience
Crystallized Ether
Territory
Accept the new Quest?
<Yes> | No | Later
—

Rocky blinked at the zero Etherience and showed Sela. She shrugged and together they conveyed the quest to the others.

"Does that mean our radios might work again?" Zippo shouted and rushed through the portal. Sela opened her mouth and held up a hand, clearly trying to stop the kid, but he was through the swirling blue portal before she could make a sound.

"We better go after him," she said flatly, with a head shake. "That portal might not lead back outside…" She looked to Rocky, and he started immediately moving to the 'exit' which prompted everyone to join. His body immediately began to feel cold when the swirling light sucked him in. Then, as if he was being beamed into a star ship, he watched as his hand turned into motes of light. His heart wanted to burst when the 'dissolving' of his body continued, but once it reached his head, he was instead watching the back half of himself form in a new location. It was surreal as his brain tried to compute the flip. It was almost like clicking the mirror button on a phone camera but so much more brain twisty.

Welcome to "The Tomb of the Deceased."
You have entered in a group of five, suggested group size 5-10.
Good luck.
Level: 25++
Age: 1,512,311,122 Years
Best time: 1 hour, 10 minutes, 50 seconds
Clears: 1,000,888

Ether Concentration: High

"I don't think it took us outside," Zippo murmured as he tried clicking the button on his earpiece radio. Rocky stepped up to him and looked around this new space. It was an oasis in the middle of a dessert?

The notification said it was a new dungeon...

"Are you there?" Rocky asked the air as he looked around.

"Just a moment, we are watching an attempt on the Prime dungeon," the cultured voice responded. Its accent and enunciation had changed again. Rocky raised an eyebrow before looking at Victoria and Zippo.

"That was Mr. Clooney for sure," Victoria said a little huffily.

"Oh right! I couldn't put my finger on it until you said it," Zippo confirmed. Rocky shook his head and instead looked around the space.

"Let's look around while we wait on the dungeon," Rocky said as he placed a hand on Zippo's shoulder.

Sela was already scanning the area and Rocky joined her. Outside of the oasis was a large stretch of sand in all directions. However, the sand was wrong, somehow off.

"Why is the sand so flat?" Victoria asked, and Rocky squinted at the sand in the direction he was staring. That was it. There weren't any sand dunes. Well, that was not quite true; there was one single sand dune that was one hundred meters away from them and encircled the oasis in what looked like a perfectly round enclosure. However, the dune came down and then flattened into perfectly still sand, before some green weeds and trees began pockmarking the area and merging it into the oasis.

"That structure seems to be at the very center of the circle." Rocky pointed at the rickety-looking bamboo or palm tree logs that were lashed together with woven leaves. The bottom of the structure wasn't visible from here, so Rocky added, "Let's go check it out?"

        <Azoth not like. Smell like cave. Look like world...>

        Azoth took off and flew toward the round sand dune. The bamboo structure now forgotten, everyone watched as he winged toward the dune. <Do you see anything, buddy?>

        <No. Ground gone, sky continue?> Azoth flew over the 'dune' and vanished.

        "Azoth!?" Rocky mentally and verbally shouted.

        <Azoth here.> The manticore sent along a mental image of looking at the oasis from the other direction. Rocky spun and saw the dark black form of his pet speeding toward him from behind. He turned back and forth and scratched his head. So, they were inside some type of never-ending-black-hole-circle-thing...?

        Azoth landed at the top of the rickety tower before Rocky could stop him and, to everyone's surprise, the structure didn't collapse. Everyone followed Rocky toward the rickety tower, and they discovered a pond of water about fifteen feet across at its base. The bamboo structure had eight posts made of what Rocky could now tell were palm trees that had been lashed into groups of four before climbing up to the pinnacle which resembled a large ship's crow's nest, open to the sky. Each of the eight legs had a rope with interspersed knots running down the slanted wood and was clearly for the purposes of climbing up.

        <Azoth see red button. Push button?>

        <No!> Rocky shouted, but clearly his pet had been a bit too eager. The sky, which had been a vibrant blue, flashed red before returning to blue, but with a large red sixty hovering somewhere near the center. The sixty changed to fifty-nine and Rocky cursed under his breath before scurrying up the closest rope. The platform at the top was probably just large enough to hold Azoth if he was at full size.

As it was, he stood in the center where there was a bamboo stick pedestal with a red button on it, and a few barrels filled with bows and arrows as well as one with a screen inlaid on the top. The platform flexed under Rocky's feet whenever he stepped between supports. The wood clearly was not as solid as cedar or other pressure-treated woods, and Rocky asked Azoth to take to the skies again as everyone else also joined him on the terrifying tower top. They all looked at the bows and arrows in the barrels dubiously.

"Azoth got overeager again?" Sela asked, and Rocky could only nod as he continued to blink at the bows.

"Are we supposed to use the bows and arrows to fight something?" Zippo asked while attempting to pull a bow from the barrel. It didn't move at all, and he looked at it more seriously before trying to heave it out with more strength.

"It won't let you. You have to buy upgrades for the tower here," Sela said as she stood over the second barrel with the screen and navigated through its pages. "It seems that there will be monster waves that will attempt to consume the water beneath us. We get points as we kill the monsters and can add defenses to help us protect the Oasis."

Rocky glanced at the sky; twenty seconds. "Do we have to attack from range and stay up here?"

"Not specifically, no, but the cost for upgrading to a level two tower is one thousand points. So my guess is that there are going to be a lot of monsters coming. It will likely scale challenges up as we continue, like an Arena dungeon. With so many monsters below, you could get swarmed and killed. Additionally, a Challenge dungeon like this usually protects the participants. So, if the monsters capture the water source, we will lose and be allowed to leave. Or at least that's usually the case," Sela finished as she looked around her at the circular world.

<Black hands from sand?!> Azoth mentally shouted to Rocky, and from Sela's flinch, her as well. The countdown timer

reached zero and suddenly the yellowing sand was filled with a carpet of brown and white that began moving toward them. Rocky blinked as he performed a slow spin. They were coming from all directions. He also noticed a strange glow from below him and peeked between the palm tree planks to the water. On the surface a green '1,000' was displayed.

"Looks like we can't let a thousand of them into the water," Rocky inferred. "How many are coming, though?"

"Quite a few. Everyone take a side and wait 'til we've analyzed the monsters before—"

Azoth dive-bombed into the carpet, and as if he had dove into a ball pit at Dave and Busters, black dots exploded from the impact point. Sela shook her head, but the group watched as Azoth slaughtered hundreds of the creatures only using his jaws, claws, and tail to pulp them.

Rocky waited until they got in range and Analyzed one of the foot-long black necrotic hands as they inched their way toward the pool.

Crawling Hand
Apprentice-Fingers
Level 5
Health Points: 25 / 25
Active Skills: 0
Passive Skills: 0

"Fight from the ground except for Zippo," Sela shouted, clearly having noticed the same thing Rocky just had. These mobs weren't a huge threat. "Don't let them swarm you!"

Rocky jumped down and began rushing to the edge of the oasis. The hands were about halfway from the dune to the trees and he prepared a single stack of his Dark Blade skill on the run. Once the hands wormed into range, he released it out in a horizontal slash near the ground. It decimated the ones it hit as it spread out and kept grinding the hands into meat and bone dust. He noticed what the problem was going to be once he saw the edges of the hands just keep inching toward the oasis.

Rocky stood on the edge of the oasis and looked at his Ether pool. It was already down ten percent and, while he could slaughter these creatures with relative ease, he wasn't sure if they would be given opportunities to recharge Ether between waves. His first blade probably killed five hundred or more, but he needed to be more efficient.

The hands began to form a bit of wedge shape as they targeted him, and Rocky allowed them to close to within a few feet before he released his next attack. This time his blade swept out and expanded, leaving a few stragglers near him, but killing hundreds at a time as it continued. Rocky entered his Seraphim Sword form and swept his Soul Blade through the stragglers he'd missed as they attempted to claw at his feet and ankles. He did his best to use this strategy and slowly released a mass attack every fifteen seconds or so to give his Ether a respite while he cleaned up the ones his blade missed.

Still, by the end, his Ether was down to sixty percent. When he couldn't find any more hands in his direction, he chose to check on the others. Zippo had long since cleared his side and moved on to help Victoria. Sela, still in her human form, was using a strategy similar to his but with her Moon Fire spell. He loped over and helped her clear up her remaining hands without using any more Ether.

"I see you wanted to make my day more interesting by giving me two entertaining fights! Well done," the Atlantean South Tower said.

Rocky vowed on the spot to start calling him South from now on. "Sure, that's why we did it… Can you answer some more of our questions now?" he asked.

"Sorry, the other group is still fighting the Prime, but I'll come check on you after they're done!" South exclaimed.

Rocky groaned as the sky flashed red again, and this time a hundred and twenty second timer began.

Sela and he climbed back up and hurried to the screen. They had received four thousand, nine hundred and thirty points and Rocky wondered why it wasn't a round number. A gut feeling made him glance at the pool. The green number now displayed eight-hundred and sixty points. Somehow, they had let one hundred and forty black necrotic hands through to the water?

The water now had some black murky spots near the edges and the water looked fetid in those areas. There was a small current that seemed to wash the black water into the larger pool in small stringy pathways. By the math of the pool, combined with the points they received, they had just faced ten thousand crawling hands and received half a point per kill.

"So much for consuming the water. It's more like they are going to pollute it. Should we upgrade the tower to level two? It says it will create a wooden wall around the water on the next level." Rocky pointed to the water to make sure everyone else saw why they might want a wall.

Sela nodded at him while Zippo and Victoria tilted their heads. Rocky clicked the button and watched as a blue glow surrounded the wood all around them and the pond below. To his surprise, the first upgrade didn't reduce the points on the screen. A quick message scrolled across the electronic pad, telling Rocky that his single upgrade credit had been consumed. He shrugged and looked down to watch the blue light form into a shape.

The 'wall' was more decorative than it was protective. It consisted of driven posts and two parallel pieces of wood laid between them. It reminded him of an old farmer's fence, and he hurriedly hit the upgrade button again for another thousand points. This upgrade added one strung piece of chicken wire between the lower cross guard and the sand. Groaning, he clicked it one more time to see another piece of the wire flash into place between the two parallel pieces of petrified wood.

The tower he stood on also changed and now the cracks in the floor had become almost non-existent, along with the wood firming and flattening into slightly hardened planks. The railing that surrounded the platform also filled in in the same pattern as the wall below. He could consume the remainder of their points and bring the tower up two more times to level five, but seeing the small changes made him extremely skeptical that two more upgrades would provide much increased protection for the pond. Instead, he clicked over to a defender's tab and purchased two level one archers for two hundred and fifty points each.

Two humanoid blue shapes phased in beside the terminal and in between blinks took on color. Each figure was identical with darkly tanned skin covering rippling muscles. Both wore a white sheet-like skirt that covered them from waist to knee while having bare chests. However, the most shocking part of their appearance was the cat heads that sat atop the human bodies. Each black cat head regarded Rocky and the others with yellow slitted eyes before turning and easily pulling a bow out of the barrel.

"I thought those were stuck in there?" Zippo asked, his voice sounding chagrined. Rocky shrugged as he analyzed the defenders.

Bes' Defender
Level 1

"They don't have any arrows?" Victoria offered. Rocky nodded and looked to Sela who shrugged in response. Well, they would just have to hope they would do something, it seemed. A quick glance up to the sky told Rocky they were out of time between waves. When the countdown hit zero, the group watched as the horizon turned blue with summoned enemies.

"We have two thousand, four hundred points remaining. Should I do anything else?" Rocky asked hurriedly.

"Probably save some for now and see what's more effective, defenders or the tower." Sela responded as she hopped over the new wall surrounding the tower top.

Okay then...

<Azoth, what are you seeing this time?> Rocky sent his pet.

<Ugly flesh blob...>

CHAPTER TWENTY-NINE

The next wave came into view, and it made Rocky's stomach flip. A flesh blob was one description and he now saw why Azoth had made that comment. Still, the creature was much closer to a human torso that ended at the hips. Instead of leg bones, the skin and muscle of the lower half of the creature had formed a disgusting skirt that undulated and creased as it moved. The upper body also had sagging flesh and malformed bones. Some arms were long and muscular while others looked like they were stolen from children. And many others even looked like they had the muscle and flesh needed for the muscular style appendage but the bones inside weren't large enough. It was the head that sat directly on top of the shoulders, without a neck, that made Rocky feel the sickest. The sagging, pinkish-black face seemed frozen in an expression of absolute horror, like all the malformations were causing it constant pain.

Lemure
Level 10
Health Points: 100 / 100
Skills: 0

The one benefit of such terrible creatures was the relative lack of emotion Rocky felt as he moved in to begin slaughtering them. It felt like he was putting them out of their misery. The group took up the same positions they had in the first wave and began cutting into the approaching horde of undead as they waddled over the sand. Rocky sent out a Dark Blade on a rotation that bisected the blobs of flesh while using his sword to clear out stragglers in between.

After one such Dark Blade, he turned around to try to check on the others. Each party member was easily keeping this wave at bay but some of the flesh blobs were sneaking in from the corners of the rough square they had set up. The two defenders shot arrows into the blobs, but it took approximately four of the arrows to down one of the creatures.

Rocky couldn't leave his position, so instead he took a rough count and estimated that about two hundred had already made it through before resuming his slaughter. It wasn't long before his side was clear of new minions, and he spun hurriedly to help clear out the ones that made it through their rough encircling. He found one hundred and twenty dead with arrows sprouting from their bodies and another eighty or so stuck within the chicken wire on the poorly constructed fence. However, the oasis pond now read eight hundred and four which was an improvement, but if they continued like they were now, the black decay would spread, and they would fail. It took another fifteen minutes before the sweating and heavily breathing party regrouped atop the tower.

"We should probably fight from the edges of the oasis and decrease the radius of the circle we're trying to form," Rocky panted into the sounds of ragged breathing from Victoria, Sela, and himself. Zippo, unlike the other three, hadn't needed to run around and instead used smaller Fireballs to pick off stragglers on his side. It seemed like this dungeon was made for ranged damage dealers as they could just take a side and strike from the safety that the tower and wall offered.

A quick glance told Rocky that the time in between fights was also increasing as the waves progressed. It currently sat at one hundred and forty seconds, but probably added a full minute of rest.

Zippo pointed to the defenders. "They weren't very effective…"

Rocky nodded as he, too, had noticed their lackluster performance. It had taken four strikes from the bowmen to take down one creature with only one hundred hit points. If the mobs continued to grow in strength, then they would become nothing more than nuisances to the beasts. The issue was trying to make the 'best' strategic decision in the limited time they had between waves.

"They are upgradeable, and we have more than double the number of points from the last wave," Sela interjected from the barrel with the interfaceable screen. Rocky looked at the points total over her shoulder to find twelve thousand, four hundred and ninety-four points, which meant they had gained ten thousand and sixty-four points from this wave. That number didn't make any sense, because the water was indicating they had missed fifty-six creatures, and the wave had only consisted of ten thousand. The first wave had been relatively simple math of a half point per hand. This wave seemed like it was a single point per lemure but with a tiny decimal addition?

That doesn't make much sense, unless something is giving us additional points. But we didn't add any bonus options... only the defenders.

Sela noticed his attention wandering and nudged him before pointing to the upgrade option on the guards that cost an additional two-hundred and fifty points. A quick glance at the group didn't give Rocky a definitive answer about the strange points number, but it wasn't like the group lost points, so he put it aside.

"Upgrade one of them," he stated with as much conviction as he could. Sela pressed the button and one of the two glowed briefly before continuing to walk around the deck. Sela shrugged and hovered her hand over the upgrade option again. Rocky shook his head and pointed at the tower first. "See if upgrading the tower will repair the wall, first."

It turned out that it did repair the wall and added a small stack of stones around each driven wooden post, almost like a poor attempt from a farmer to MacGyver a solution. The tower also upgraded, gaining what looked like concrete or an extremely flat rock at the bottom of each of the tower supports. There were other tabs that they could click over to as well, and Rocky took over hurriedly from Sela. He needed to read them all and form a strategy. This dungeon was reminding him of base defender games and he knew that those ramped up in difficulty quickly, while requiring good strategy to stay ahead.

There was an option to add defensive mines, and even an option to add a variety of water filtration filters that escalated in point costs based on the speed displayed in the corner. There were further tabs that seemed to add priests who would mummify bodies, or personal healers, and with each tab, Rocky grew more anxious because of the complexity of this dungeon. Why would they need NPCs to collect bodies? However, it was the final tab that made him squint the most.

It had options that were all grayed out. The most expensive option on the first section said it cost ten thousand points and would cast a spell called Ra's Cleansing Sun. But the group had ten thousand points…

He glanced at the symbol that preceded the points needed and then looked up to the total summary of their points on the top of the screen. One had a golden ball beside it, and the other a black ball. He clicked on the symbols and found that one was called death points and the other holy points. Currently they had only gained death points.

"I'm going to take over the strategy, but if anyone has suggestions, let me know," Rocky said quickly as he flipped back to the priest tab. "I think this is a tower defense strategy, and I have a few ideas from playing video games."

For a hundred points each, he added priests, and the group soon had ten smoky blue figures engulfing corpses of crawling hands and lemures. The blue glow from the smoky, almost ghost-like creatures increased slowly and the flesh of the undead slowly seemed to shrink in on itself. Once it was shrunken enough, blue wraps sprang out and wrapped the flesh, turning the creatures into mummies. The holy points ticked up by one and Rocky smiled.

He returned to the previous tower and defenders tabs. Based on the time, the other tabs would need to be explored on another break. He hit the tower upgrade button again and this time a much more noticeable change occurred.

The supporting bamboo of the tower legs morphed into rough cut stone bricks with old and dry-looking mortar. Simultaneously, the outer edge of the tower's crow's nest became a rough brick-like square as well. The crisscrossing bamboo firmed further under Rocky's feet, but probably most disturbingly, the price to upgrade increased to two thousand points. The wall below them also had its wooden posts replaced by stone supports. The dead trees and chicken wire stayed the same though.

The counter was dropping from twenty, so Rocky rushed back to the defender tab.

"I'm going to try getting the defenders to level five as well." Thinking that perhaps they would have a similar increase if they were upgraded past that threshold, he clicked the button of the one defender three more times, and they watched as he glowed in three steady blinks.

Once the third one finished, he walked to the barrels and changed the arrows and bow he was using from a brown wooden bow to something that looked more like a composite hunting bow. The arrows also became a quiver of black-shafted broadheads that looked far more deadly than the steel-capped wooden ones he traded in. Rocky raised an eyebrow and checked the point total that remained. Eight thousand, four hundred and ninety-four. The level five defender now cost five-hundred points per level, which meant they couldn't upgrade it to level ten without spending two thousand five hundred additional points.

Ten seconds…

The tab that used holy points flashed once on the screen and Rocky clicked on it, wondering what had just happened. A new option was at the top of the page. Elemental Defender infusion for one holy point. He clicked it and a list popped up.

Level 1 Elemental Defender
Fire
Water
Earth
Air

The timer was going to run out, so he clicked Fire. Some quick math told him he could create five more level five defenders and increase the other original defender to that level as well. That would be most of the points they had, but he was gambling on those bonus points from before. He had a suspicion that the party wasn't meant to be killing in this dungeon…

He clicked the defender button and chose one of each of the elements before doubling up on fire, water, and earth. He looked up as the horizon turned blue, but his eyes were drawn to the defenders with their composite bows and glowing eyes. There were now two with red, brown, and blue eyes. The final one had swirling white eyes. Rocky nodded to himself and asked Azoth what was coming.

<No skins?> Azoth mentally screamed, startling Rocky as he reached the brick wall of the tower.

"Why are you not going down there?" Sela asked as she placed a hand on the wall, looking like she was preparing to vault it.

Rocky placed a hand on her shoulder. "I think we are supposed to defeat this dungeon by controlling this tower, and only adding our aide to the defenders here as a last resort." He shrugged when she narrowed her eyes at his response, but she did step back from the wall as she did it.

"That could mean that this is a Strategic dungeon…" Sela surmised as her eyes went wide. Then she turned to the rest of the group. "You heard Rockland, let us try to avoid killing the monsters unless we have to."

Azoth, of course, chose that moment to dive bomb into a huge portion of the skeletons. Rocky felt his hand on his face but at everyone's look he just shook his head. That was an argument that would be fruitless. Instead, he watched the manticore begin shredding the skeletons, making sure they didn't turn on his pet. They didn't, and the mobs' lack of interest in Azoth gave Rocky more confidence that he was on the right track.

The archer with glowing white eyes pulled back his bow and loosed an arrow to the north at the approaching horde. The skeletons were perhaps halfway between the edge of the dungeon and the oasis when the archer loosed. The whole team turned as one to watch it arc through the sky. It seemed to whistle like a nerf football before it crashed into the sand in front of the charging wave of skeletons, missing all targets. Rocky was ready to curse when, like a held breath of a god, the impact site exploded in a blast of air—similar to that of his Dark Blade but harder to follow. The only way to track the wave was to watch the sand itself.

The wave collided with the leading skeletons and Rocky watched pieces of bones blast off the monsters, but possibly more important than that was that they were pushed backward and collided with the skeletons behind them, pushing them back as well. The air defender was already firing another shot and Rocky couldn't help but smile. It seemed that this defender had the longest range but soon after, the defenders with red and blue glowing eyes loosed in the southern and eastern directions. Azoth engaging the skeletons on the west side seemed to have slowed the approach.

The water arrow also missed the target of the lead skeleton but where it hit, a different explosion occurred. A ten-foot-tall tsunami rose from both impact sites of the water archers that fired south. The waves rushed out and skeletons hit by them seemed to be unaffected by the impact. However, the monsters were in range to be Analyzed, and that told a different story.

Skeleton
Level 15
Health Points: 150 / 200
Skills: 0

An additional effect was apparent when those southern skeletons attempted to move forward. Their feet sunk into the sand, causing them to have to fight to continue forward over the now wet sand.

Slowing effects…

The fire arrows landed east and Rocky, who had expected a massive explosion or a wave of fire, watched that impact site with narrowing eyes. Zippo gasped beside him, and he turned, wondering if the fire mage was looking in the same direction. Zippo must have read the question Rocky wanted to ask because he just nodded and pointed back to the west. The first skeleton stepped forward and its leg caught fire.

"Those arrows are creating a super-heated zone around them. The sand is heating up to levels that are—ahh, see, glass!" Zippo explained as a circle around the impact site blackened before becoming a glowing orange. The skeletons continued to advance as more arrows flew in each direction and instead of watching anymore, Rocky hurried back to the tablet.

Whether it was because of Azoth, or the archers, his remaining twelve hundred and forty-four points had turned into two thousand and twenty-three. So, he purchased another air defender and then studied the tab that used holy points. It was rising in points, but it was only four hundred points total. He purchased seven more priests and added an eighth when his points total jumped up by another seventeen points. That bottomed out the points of the group, and he looked back up.

The earth defenders were now firing as well. They had taken the side Azoth was on, and their arrows landed inside of the oasis as the skeletons began dodging the foliage to make their way to the water. Yet the foliage wasn't exactly letting them through. Instead, vines spiraled out from the arrow impact sites and began wrapping around skeletons, pulling them back to the edges of the oasis, tripping them, or crushing them like a boa constrictor.

"Uhhh? Should we attack now?" Zippo asked from behind Rocky. He turned to see that monsters were entering the oasis on all sides. Many were dying but they didn't have enough defenders yet.

"Wait one second," he responded and glanced back down at the tablet before switching to the holy points page. He had over five hundred of these points now and seemed to get them for each corpse the priests mummified. He clicked the first option on this page.

Taweret's Stampede (Spell)
500 Holy Points

From the pond of water, a rumbling honk began, and the tower shook in resonance from the deep bellow. Something like the hippo-chimera exploded out in all four directions. In the wake of the semi-translucent gray creatures was some sort of phantom wall. It might have been sand or brick, but it moved so fast that Rocky couldn't quite tell. The wall passed through the foliage of the Oasis, as did the ghostly hippos, but where the hippos struck skeletons, the creatures died instantly. Where the wall hit skeletons, the creatures were pulled back as if an invisible hand was grabbing them all and sending them flying. The Taweretan spell ended halfway between the edge of the area and the oasis, and the skeletons, now released from the huge pushback effect, returned to rushing back in an even larger grouped-up version.

One of the hippo ghosts actually passed through Azoth, and Rocky was told about it. <Why ugly gray chimera ghost haunt Azoth?>

"Well, just do that a few more times and we won't need to…" Zippo said with a whistle.

"Can't, it has a cooldown of fifteen minutes, plus the points aren't that fast to fill," Rocky responded, then checked his points total. It had shot up a large amount from the spell, and the archers' efforts. "If any more get too close, start killing them," Rocky said as he went back to exploring more tabs. He started by watching the death points closely.

There were three sources coming in, but it was somewhat difficult to differentiate. At different times, the total jumped up by three points, two points, or one point. He looked to Azoth and tried to time a large crushing downward paw before glancing back to the total. It increased by one. He then glanced to the glass circles of the west and watched a skeleton crumbling from flames. A glance down told him that it was worth three points. It took him a bit longer to find the two points, but he did. Two points were awarded every second kill from Azoth. So, his pet was getting them one and a half points per kill, while the defenders and spells awarded them three!

He needed more defenders—or more powerful ones. His points total was over seven thousand. So, he started by upgrading one of the air defenders to level ten. To his horror, the defender stopped firing and walked slowly back to the barrel, exchanging the recurve bow for a long bow. The northern skeletons surged forward in the absence of the second archer, while the holy points tab flashed again.

Level 2 Elemental Defender
Lightning

Hurricane
Sandstorm
Tornado

CHAPTER THIRTY

Rocky wanted to consider the options, but the battle was still going on, and if he left the upgraded archer standing at the barrel in a daze, his group would be forced to fight. That, of course, wasn't a bad thing, but it wasn't ideal. He went with the hurricane talent hoping that it was a combination of air's knockback effect and water's slowing.

He glanced up to find that the earth side was the next worse off, only worse than the air side of the tower. It wasn't that desperate yet, but having watched the results before the holy point spell, he knew that even with Azoth's help, it would soon be overwhelmed. He chose that one to upgrade next. He spent another twenty-five hundred points.

Level 2 Elemental Defender
Magma
Geyser
Pit
Shockwave

This time he went with magma, at complete random, to try to get the defender back to the wall more quickly. He registered that the base of the defender gave different options in its combination with similar elements but left that alone for now. He could check that later.

He had enough points for another upgrade and chose the water defender. This time it was again due to experience from the last approach of the skeletons; while the water slowed them, it didn't seem to damage them as much as fire.

Level 2 Elemental Defender
Blizzard
Tsunami

Mud
Water Bullet

Blizzard became the choice, and he finally looked back up to discover that the first two level two defenders were being stared at by his entire team. Not only were their eyes glowing new colors but they also wore a suit of armor colored in a similar style. The blizzard defender traded out its bow for a longbow and its eyes also changed from the deep blue of the sea to the faintly translucent blue of ice. Rocky marveled at them and Analyzed the blizzard defender.

Bes' Blizzard Defender
Level 10
Health Points: 1,000 / 1,000

The part that really stood out to him was the increase in health. If the NPCs of this dungeon increased in health, it likely meant that the tower would be attacked by creatures at some point. After he made that discovery, he checked on the progress the second level elemental defenders were making.

He couldn't help but smile. The hurricane defender fired an arrow that seemed to sail over the heads of the approaching skeletons, but in the wake of that arrow, small, sharp bullets of water tore skeletons apart. The width of the strike was only ten feet, but each arrow was clearing rows in the approaching mobs. The only weakness seemed to be that the firing rate, when compared to the level one air defender, was slow. Yet the second defender on that side knocking back enemies was keeping them from making it to the oasis.

The magma defender was landing arrows that created a bubbling circle that seemed to melt skeletons as soon as they stepped on it. At first, Rocky squinted, worried that the skeletons would just go around, but they didn't. He then worried that the radius of the area of effect was too little, but the effects seemed to last long enough that there were already five such circles just outside of the oasis zone. That paired with Azoth scything down skeletons in the field meant that side was starting to clear.

He turned and watched the first blizzard arrow launch toward the skeletons. He smiled when it seemed to burst in the sky over the mobs, and it didn't rain down fluffy snow. No, shards of sharp ice and hail blasted down in a circle far larger than the magma arrows. The randomness of the ice strikes left some of the skeletons affected by the arrow alive, but the area turned into a slush soon after and slowed those that survived.

"Well, I think that confirms that this is a Strategy dungeon," Sela said while pointing out at the mobs. "Rockland, are you confident enough to continue to take the lead?"

"Yes, I'm just frustrated that I can't choose what cardinal direction a defender takes."

"Oh, that's on the home page. There is a summary screen, and it shows a layout of the tower top. I bet you can move things around there." Sela pointed to a tab Rocky hadn't explored because it was only a home screen button. He hadn't been the first one to the terminal and just hadn't seen it. He smiled when he clicked over and saw the colored dots on the square. He could now see that each side had eight spots for defenders. He could probably move them by dragging the dots but chose to let them finish their current cleanup.

"Sela, can you try to get Azoth to stop attacking mobs out there? It gives half the points if he takes the kills. I don't have the time to argue with him." Rocky made a sour face and winked at Sela, who smiled and raised her eyebrows.

"You think it's going to be an argument?"

"I think he's as stubborn as I am..."

<Buddy, listen to Sela. I need you to stop attacking the mobs and come rest on the tower top.>

<What? Why? Even Rocky kill with ease… Oh! Sela talks now.>

Rocky shook his head and went back to the terminal. His first goal should be to get as many level one defenders as he could and upgrade a single defender on the fire side to the second level. He started there.

Level 2 Elemental Defender
Inferno
Steam
Fire Pillar
Firestorm

He double stacked its fire element, and it rejoined the fight. The effect wasn't totally recognizable at first. It took him comparing it to the regular fire archer for him to finally see. It was the speed and intensity of the flames in the area of effect. Where the first level took about five skeleton steps to drop an attacking mob, the inferno archer took one and a half. Quite the improvement in overall damage.

From that point on, whenever the points ticked up over twelve hundred and fifty, he purchased an additional level one elemental defender. At the end of the round, he was able to get eight more of the level one elemental defenders. Meaning he added two more to each direction. He placed a water and an air defender in each direction, wanting to stack the slow and knockback effects. In directions where there was already an air or water defender, he chose earth as a final line of defense.

His current strategy was to push a single defender on each side up and increase the damage output, while using the level one defenders' effects to give the high damage dealers more time. It wasn't a terribly inventive strategy, but he would test it out in the next round. The timer above him counted down from two hundred and forty seconds, and Azoth finally came back to the tower top.

"Told you he would argue," Rocky teased Sela before turning on his pet. "Buddy, stay here. This dungeon is a Strategy dungeon and we need to maximize points."

<Okay, but I charge in if they make it past grabby trees, yes?>

"Sure, buddy. But only after I use the spell that pushes them back," Rocky began before remembering the cooldown. "Or a different one," he amended.

"You know it's easier for me to just lob a fireball, right Azoth?" Zippo came over and gave the shrunken black manticore some head scratches.

<Tell Zippo he no fly.> Rocky chose not to share that particular insult for now. Zippo really loved flying, and had a fascination with the Scourge, and future spaceships. The fact that Azoth picked up on Zippo's sensitive spot was slightly disturbing to Rocky. It showed his pet's rise in intelligence, but also a lack of morality at the moment. In essence, it felt like a low blow and Rocky chose to explain that difference to Azoth when he had a moment.

"It seems like you've got a pretty sound strategy, but I'm guessing the levels will get harder soon. I wish the dungeon would come back so we can ask how many levels we have to complete."

"Sorry, we're still watching the raid on the Prime dungeon," the voice of Mr. Clooney answered.

"Stop using other people's voices!" Victoria and Rocky shouted in unison. The dungeon didn't respond but Rocky hoped that it wouldn't come back with another borrowed voice.

"Why does it matter?" Sela asked, her voice confused.

"I'm not sure, but it feels like the dungeon is stealing something precious from our world," Victoria said. "Like it's not giving proper credit to the men who worked hard to establish their voices as something all of humanity would recognize. Instead, the dungeon is just using it in an attempt to put us at ease or make itself more familiar."

Rocky was a bit surprised by the depth of the response and could only nod. There wasn't anything to add to that. She had captured his feeling pretty near perfectly. After his nod of agreement, he glanced up to the timer and licked his lips. One hundred and twenty seconds until the next wave.

"Do you think they will capture Atlantis first?" Rocky asked, looking at Sela for the answer. She was the only one in the group that might know what the difficulty of a Prime dungeon might be.

"No clue. Remember, dungeons were mostly shunned during my time. They had been turned into things that were a perversion of Gaia. It is strange that I never thought of the Atlantean Towers as the enemy, but I can tell you that those that knew of Prime dungeons when I lived kept them fairly secret."

Rocky felt a knot build in his stomach. For the Mechanolords and Apep's forces to be ahead of them wasn't a good feeling. For them to be ahead of them and still threatening the Territory was causing him to feel helpless.

"I don't like just hoping they will fail," Rocky admitted. "It feels too much like we are relying on prayer or luck."

Sela's jaw tightened before she shrugged. "I get it, but trying to rush could make it worse…"

The silence that followed her statement lasted until the timer reached zero.

Azoth took to the sky with the promise to return and not fight the creatures he went to scout.

<Walking rot corpse. They attack Grotto before,> Azoth reported, and Rocky took it to mean zombies. The ten thousand mobs being zombies also fit the shambling gait of the front lines—it almost seemed to be stumbling or wavering even to his improved eyesight.

The first arrow flew a moment later from the air defenders and the battle began. Rocky watched as the front line began to stagger as pockets of enemies were pushed back on each side. Finally, the mobs came close enough for him to see more clearly. While they were zombies, and similar to the ones that attacked his Territory, they were also different.

Where the zombies created by Apep's dungeons were pale-skinned, these were blackened and clearly rotting. They also seemed to have a multitude of different clothing and 'hair styles.' Each zombie was also not whole, missing anywhere from an entire muscle grouping to dragging its intestines behind it over the sand. Rocky swallowed the bile that rose in his throat at the sight and instead watched the points begin rising from the seven thousand, six hundred and ninety-four he had been left with after the last wave.

This wave seemed to be bringing in four per zombie, and if they could get the full forty thousand points that would award, he could fill all the defender spots.

CHAPTER THIRTY-ONE

Rocky watched the zombies attempt to push into the oasis and fail at every turn. Every so often, he would look down to the summary page on the tablet and smile, both Holy and death points were rising steadily. They were now out ahead of the mobs in current strength, which left him wondering what the best option forward would be.

"Okay, so the option at this point of the competition seems to be to upgrade defenders to higher levels, increase the number of defenders, or increase the tower level. What do you guys think?" Rocky asked the group, not wanting to just plow ahead and miss something they might have noticed.

"The level two defenders are doing the majority of the DPS," Zippo pointed out.

"The other tabs have to be valuable as well," Sela suggested.

Victoria and Azoth just widened their eyes. Of course, Azoth added his unhelpful two cents, <I vote I fight!>

"I agree… Not with you, Azoth. With Sela. I feel like we might be missing something." Rocky looked through the tabs. Traps, Purification, Priests, Defenders, and Tower. After scanning all the options on each page, he was left in the same predicament. It felt like taking those options may water down the points, instead of solidifying an advantage.

Zombies continued to die, and their points kept climbing. The summary screen looked like a winning slot machine at a casino. The windfall of points made Rocky's stress level increase. It felt like a warning tale of winning a lottery only to overspend and go into such deep debt that he could end up poorer than he started.

Thirty-nine thousand points and climbing. He looked out over the field of dying zombies. There were less than two thousand remaining, and not a single corpse had made it to the line of trees that demarcated the oasis.

"Why change what's working, I guess?" Rocky responded to the questioning looks of his team. They all nodded after his statement, agreeing for the most part. He interpreted the straight faces as the same feeling he was getting. An apocalypse wasn't exactly great for stress levels—he always felt like he was waiting for the other shoe to drop.

The timer of three hundred seconds flashing into the sky made him stop stalling. The level ended with forty-seven thousand, six hundred and ninety-four death points and nearly ten thousand holy points. He briefly considered banking all of the points, but inevitably chose to keep the holy points as back up and spend half of the death points.

In theory, he could fill out all the remaining spots with level one defenders or upgrade the four level two defenders to level three. Just remembering how devastating the increase from level one to two had been, he chose that option.

To his surprise, the defenders only had two options for upgrades each except for the purely fire defender.

Level 3 Elemental Defender
(Hurricane)
Water-Blade Storm
<Storm Wall>
(Magma)
Molten
<Meteor>
(Blizzard)
<Absolute Zero>
Dry Ice
(Inferno)
<Flame Tunnel>
Confirm selections?

<Yes> | No

The defenders switched out their longbows for weapons that materialized in their hands. Rocky blinked as each one now handled a crossbow that seemed to have taken on the aspect of the defender. The armor which had already glowed now became flowing robes and capes that radiated power. Each member of the group stepped out of the way as the defenders moved back to their original positions. All but Azoth, who whined piteously as he attempted to sniff the Storm Wall defender and ended up with a zap on the nose.

<Why it scold Azoth? Azoth no hurt it.>

"I don't think it was intentional, bud. Like when I give you a static shock. Still, I would expect it to only hurt if you approach those things again."

Incoming Boss

The message began flashing in the sky between countdown seconds once the timer crossed under ten seconds. Rocky swore internally, a habit he had been forced to pick up when he was around Sela.

"Good thing I saved half of the points. Do you think it will be one mob or multiple? Should we join the attack—" Sela and Victoria were looking away from him, without response. He followed their gazes. "*Poodle paddles*," Rocky swore outwardly this time.

All the corpses that hadn't been changed by the priests were coagulating into a single, large, roiling ball of skin, muscle, and bones. This scene was terrifyingly familiar, and Rocky had to wonder if Apothis was somehow in control of this dungeon despite what it had said earlier.

"Rock," Zippo said from behind him as he simultaneously poked Rocky's shoulder. "If that thing is the boss, then what is that?"

Rocky spun and locked eyes with a blue glow in the north. The blue glowing outline looked like a massive dog mixed with a gorilla. The creature was phasing in on two legs, but the front appendages were long and nearly touching the sand as well. The back feet had five human-like digits that seemed to flex into the sand as the creature became solid. Its entire body was made from thick muscle, and not just dad-bod muscle but tight, iron-wire, super-tensile muscle. It looked like it had spent every waking day in a pre-Ether gym.

"Great, a green gorilla-hound on the juice!" Rocky exclaimed as he noted the hideous face. While its entire body was green, its face was flesh-colored, with two holes as nostrils, black hungry eyes, and terribly vicious canine teeth. The only aspect of the beast that seemed slightly less terrifying were its ears. They seemed like overlarge bat wings that drooped and flopped as it began charging toward the oasis.

Giant Dretch
Level 15
Journeyman-Demon Fiend
Health Points: 10,000 / 10,000
Active Skills: 5
Passive Skills: 3
Boss

Spinning again, Rocky felt his mouth drop open. The good news was that the blob of flesh hadn't become an abomination. Still, Rocky wasn't sure what it had become was any better. A massive ball covered in millions of tiny, blackened eyeballs was jiggling on the dune where it had formed. It was a huge ball of decaying skin, muscles, bone, and flesh. Rocky wanted to puke just looking at it. Instead, he Analyzed the blob.

Unholy Slime
Level 45
Journeyman-Skinner
Health Points: 29,050 / 40,000
Active Skills: 14
Passive Skills: 0

All the priests had circled the unholy slime but were moving with the creature as it undulated over the sand. Rocky's pulse pounded in his ears. Did this mean they should abandon the tower and fight one or both bosses? Or continue to let the defenders handle them? He couldn't decide.

"The dretch is coming way faster, and the archers are already firing!" Zippo poked Rocky, which forced him to turn in the direction he was indicating. Nodding, Rocky moved the four level three defenders to that side. The slime was plodding at its speed, and Rocky could tell that it would take another few minutes before it even got to the halfway point between the dune and the oasis.

After a moment's consideration, he moved all the defenders that could fit to that side as well. Each defender that he slid across turned and marched across the tower top as the group dodged out of their way. Azoth took to the air, hovering over the tower with powerful wingbeats as soon as he saw the level three defenders coming. His black manticore eyes tracked them suspiciously as they strode to their new posts.

The dretch placed its claws and bat-eared head into the first trees of the oasis just as a wave of eight arrows left bows. The level one air archers struck fastest, and the buffets of air nudged the simian-like rear feet a few meters back. That was when a wall of black cloud filled with lightning collided with the dretch. The group inhaled sharply as they heard and felt the air force itself out of the dretch's lungs. Then the bolts of electricity in the wall lashed out and the expelling air turned into a roar.

Next came an expanding arrowhead that turned into a glowing rock, five feet in diameter. The meteor was surrounded by flames and left an orange trail in its wake. When it struck, it drowned out the dretch's roar with the percussive note of a god cracking a mountain in half.

The black cloud and plume of fiery sand flash froze in place as the air itself literally crystallized in a sphere, encapsulating the area like a festive snow globe. It only lasted a split second though before a rod of orange spun into the area, shattering the scene with the roar of a jet engine. A smoking body was flung out of the area, and Rocky Analyzed it.

Giant Dretch
Level 15
Journeyman-Demon Fiend
Health Points: 9,000 / 10,000
Active Skills: 5
Passive Skills: 3
Boss

The distance it rolled away before regaining its feet increased slowly as more and more of the air defenders fired. Rocky watched as the four elemental defenders placed their crossbows down and began using a stirrup to reload a bolt. The action meant the firing rate between blasts increased further with the upgrade to level three. Still watching the terrifying, monstrous gorilla-hound slowly pick itself up and resume its charge, Rocky was giddy with the increase in firepower.

He glanced back to check the Unholy Slime's progress and blinked.

"Is that a flesh baseball?" Rocky asked stupidly as a massive projectile crashed into the tower, rocking him and all the occupants atop it. Rocky fell to his knees and watched the grout turn to powder under his hands as he braced himself. He swallowed hard and pushed himself to his feet hard.

The Unholy Slime had set up halfway between the oasis and the dune and was launching pieces of itself at the tower like it was a catapult.

The next ball hit, and a crack in the stones gave him a view of the pool under his feet. The first massive flesh ball was dripping into the water, and the number on the pool was dropping before Rocky's eyes.

"Abyssal Hells! I knew upgrading defenders only felt like too easy an answer!"

CHAPTER THIRTY-TWO

Rocky rushed back to the screen and upgraded the tower to level six for two thousand points. The cracks the flesh projectiles were making quickly repaired themselves, but the globs of blood, chipped bones and flesh didn't clean themselves up. Rocky's eyes followed the oozing blood and saw it dripping into the pool of water under them. Each piece of flesh continued to drop the total.

"We need to attack that thing ourselves," Rocky decided. "It might not give us as many points, but the pool can't keep up with the bombardment." Rocky clicked over and spent ten thousand more points on water filtration from the purification tab. It was the most expensive option and he just hoped it would be enough.

"I'll stay and fire from long range," Zippo suggested and motioned at the controls Rocky stood at. "I can upgrade the tower if it gets too damaged."

Rocky nodded and followed the others in the group off the tower.

<Super headbutt!> Azoth sent and Rocky watched as the top of an ephemeral ram's head formed above the sparse trees. The head glowed a blueish-black for a moment before a boom shook the air.

"He moved it back off its spot!" Sela exclaimed as she was the first to clear the trees. Rocky smiled as he joined her on the sandy expanse and saw what she meant. The flesh slime had been backed up perhaps ten feet and was now undulating back over the sand to re-establish its position before firing more balls of flesh at the tower.

<Azoth, does that skill have a cooldown?> Rocky asked, hoping to keep the unholy slime from launching more projectiles.

<Sixty weeks!> Azoth responded unhelpfully, but Rocky knew his pet was mistaken. Rocky had seen him use the skill

outside the dungeon on the dome. Azoth wasn't exactly good with time. It wasn't that he didn't understand its passage, but that he mixed up terms assuming they meant similar things.

<How many 'weeks' left on that cooldown now, Azoth?> Rocky asked, already having learned the best way to deal with his pets' confusion.

<Fifty-eight days, now!> Azoth responded.

Rocky estimated it had been about two seconds and that his pet had been trying to say that the cooldown on the ram skill was a minute. <As soon as it comes back up, Azoth, use it! Okay?>

<In fifty-six years, Azoth use again.>

Rocky rolled his eyes and assessed the fight. It took another six seconds for the unholy slime to begin firing again, which meant they would only get about a ten second reprieve once a minute. It was better than nothing. His team began unloading Sunday skills, or their penultimate skills, into the unholy slime before it got set up, but none of the skills had the power to knock back the massive ball of flesh.

Massive didn't really describe the creature from this close. It was easily as wide and tall as a five-story building. And the smell! The stench was reminiscent of opening a septic tank that had gone bad. The odor also continued to get worse every time a skill landed and damaged the monster. Each skill would knock loose flesh, blood, bone, and hair from the sides of the disgusting semi-gelatinous slime, and they would splash down onto the sand, adding to the horrible aroma.

However, the issue was that some of that liquid disgustingness would return to the boss creature before the priests could seal it. Using Analyze, Rocky confirmed that each time some of the 'substance' of this creature returned, it would gain back the health it had lost.

"Shoot, slow down on the attacks for a moment!" Rocky shouted both over the radio and to his team. "Zippo, we need more priests!" Rocky added over the radio to the fire mage. Holding his breath, Rocky then closed the distance and began laying into the boss from close range, not using any skills.

"Kept ten thousand points for tower upgrades, the rest I spent on getting fifty six more priests. The gorilla boss is close to death. Pool is dropping below five hundred!" Zippo reported over the radio.

Rocky clenched his jaw. While fifty-six more priests increased their current total from ten to sixty-six, he knew they were fighting from a deficit. They still probably couldn't just burn down this boss without more priests stopping it from healing, but simultaneously they were starting to run low on points. They needed to balance tower upgrades with priests.

In the end, the group could win or lose this, and it all depended on the defenders against the undead gorilla-like boss.

Rocky stepped back and assessed the situation. He found about thirty of the new priests standing idle, and shouted, "Increase damage."

The group began using skills sparingly and the priests that had been without work began wrapping up and sealing the disgusting flesh blobs as they splashed onto the sand. Rocky radioed for twenty more priests, and they increased damage further.

A glowing ram's head emerged, and Azoth collided with the boss creature, pushing it back again. The knockback effect reminded Rocky of the spells that the tower had used holy points for.

"Zippo, is the knockback spell under holy points off cooldown?" Rocky asked over the radio.

"Thirty seconds," Zippo responded and Rocky smiled. That should help. It might even knock the slime back farther than Azoth's skill. He debated again about using one of the other spells, but with the strange names associated with them, they wouldn't know the effects.

"Alright, keep us updated on the dretch," Sela ordered over the radio, seeing what Rocky's plan was and adding to it. Rocky nodded to her as he stepped back in and began carving pieces off the unholy slime as it returned to its original position. Rocky still saw pieces of the slime reattaching itself as the priests worked overtime to try to kill it.

"Forty percent. Tower was upgraded to stop crumbling," Zippo reported.

The unholy slime began launching projectiles again, and Rocky felt his stomach twist. Should he order Zippo to attack the dretch? The group would likely lose points, but each projectile brought the group closer to failing the dungeon. His teeth tightly clenched as he breathed through them, Rocky chose to wait until after the Holy spell.

"Spell's off cooldown! Tower upgraded," Zippo said and he must have pushed the button because the very air seemed to vibrate with power. Rocky's eyes widened as he turned to see the charging hippo chimeras rushing toward the unholy slime and his group. He only had time to close his eyes and hope that he hadn't just made a huge mistake.

The hippos lowered their heads and collided with the unholy slime. Luckily, they passed over Rocky, Victoria, Azoth, and Sela. He exhaled as the slime was pushed backward to the bottom of the sand dune that bordered this dungeon. He gave chase and continued to carve pieces off of the slime as it rumbled back toward its original position.

"Thirty percent left on the dretch, and the water is recovering slowly," Zippo reported.

Rocky used Analyze on the slime.

Unholy Slime
Level 45
Journeyman-Skinner
Health Points: 19,250 / 40,000

Active Skills: 14
Passive Skills: 0
Boss

Its health fell steadily as it rolled back into position. Before it returned, Azoth's Ram skill was used again, knocking it back.

"Twenty percent."

The slime returned to its position and resumed firing flesh balls at the tower.

"Upgrading tower!" Zippo called.

"Try another spell!" Rocky shouted in desperation. With two thousand points left, they could only hope to get lucky.

"Babi's Hunger!" Zippo reported and the sun seemed to grow dark in the sky above them. Rocky blinked and looked around to find a huge ghostly baboon standing over the slime. Instead of attacking, it was sucking up the flesh that fell from the creature and consuming it instantly.

"Unload with max damage!" Sela said, noticing this spell's effect before Rocky.

Rocky charged his Dark Blade with ten stacks and loaded his blade with all his poisons. Raising the blade above his head, he swung down and released the skill from point blank range. Ten circular saw blades began rotating into the side of the unholy slime and created a stench so horrific that Rocky felt the need to step back from it. The Dark Blades dripped poisons as they continued to penetrate.

The next moment, a wave of heat gave Rocky enough warning to dive away from the slime. Zippo's fireballs began crashing into the creature as Sela's Moon Fire skill also began cooking it from above. Victoria lobbed fusion grenades as well, and Azoth glowed with an orange lion head, followed by a brown scorpion, and finally a large lizard. Each blow rocked the slime and the huge amount of flesh that peeled back off of it entered the vortex of the massive baboon's mouth.

In a blink, the health of the slime dropped below ten thousand points.

"Five percent. The baboon on the dretch is laying into it with fists and teeth!" Zippo called, and in the next breath adjusted his report further. "Giant dretch down!"

"How many points?" Sela and Victoria asked in unison as they chugged Ether Draughts.

"Fifty-two thousand!"

The baboon above the slime boss vanished as Rocky chugged his Ether potion. "More priests!" Rocky decided.

"Two-hundred and fifty priests purchased!" Zippo reported. Rocky nodded to himself and did the math. That was half of the points they just earned. He was proud of Zippo. That amount more than tripled the amount of priests, allowing Rocky's group to expend Ether skills and burn down the unholy slime.

"Grab another filter," Sela suggested, and Rocky nodded to her.

"Purchased."

They were now in a race with the boss's health, and Rocky hoped they had done enough.

The unholy slime which had started as a five story building continued to shrink, now looking more like a small house. Finally, it became a pickup truck before Rocky's blade sliced it in two, and the priests swarmed over it.

Rocky breathed a sigh of relief and looked back to the tower just as Zippo upgraded it to level ten. He nodded to himself as his screen exploded in notifications.

Chapter Thirty-Three

Congratulations!
You have completed the first boss in "The Tomb of the Deceased" in 22 minutes, and 16 seconds.
Bonus:
Due to dungeon level, you have been awarded 0 Etherience as a clearing bonus.
The first stage of the dungeon has been reclassified as a Level 29 zone. This dungeon is a partial holder of a Territory; since you are the first to clear the dungeon since its revival, you are rewarded an additional quest.

–

Territorial Quest
Leader Quest
Take Further Ownership of the Holding
This Territory was left in a holding state by its previous owner. To remove the holding state and become the full owner, you must conquer two more Cardinal dungeons, or the Prime dungeon. Since you are now a half owner of this Territory, you have access to most Territorial features and can move around freely through its defenses or even challenge the Prime dungeon.
Rewards:
0 Etherience
500 Crystallized Ether
Partial owner of Territory
Cash out rewards now?
Yes | <No>
Continue quest for additional rewards

–

"Alright, alright, alright! Well done with the first boss!" the dungeon said in another Hollywood actor's voice. It even used the catchphrase of the person in question.

"Stop it!" Rocky and Victoria said together. "This time it's McConaughey," Rocky continued. "Can you please just use your own voice!"

"Sure. But it isn't as endearing to the humans of this era," a deep baritone responded. "Are you planning to continue in this dungeon or try another?"

"Well, this dungeon gave us zero Etherience again, can you explain that?" Sela asked, cutting off Rocky who had been about to ask a different question. He shrugged, as that was also a question that was on his list.

"Again, do you think the rewards of Crystals and a Territory aren't appropriate for the challenge?" the dungeon responded. "If you feel cheated, you can always move on to the sixth level."

Rocky shook his head, conveying to Sela that he didn't want to chase that line of questioning. They might have a time limit again, which needed to be used wisely. "Okay, since this counts as a completed dungeon, can we challenge the Prime dungeon now?"

"Yes, you have full access to the Prime dungeon and can join the other group in attempting it."

"They're still going?" Sela asked and Rocky felt his eyes go wide. He looked at Victoria, Azoth, and Zippo, who wore expressions he assumed looked like his and Sela's.

"It's getting rather repetitive in there, but yes, they're still attempting it," South said. Rocky thought he could hear boredom in the voice but shrugged it off.

"Do we teleport from here directly?" Rocky asked.

"No. The dungeons are connected, but teleportation of people from the exterior holding dungeons is impossible."

Rocky looked around to see if anyone else had any questions and saw that everyone was returning the same look to him. So, he volunteered, "Please let us exit the dungeon then."

A portal opened on top of the tower and Rocky rushed through it right behind Zippo and Azoth. The same chill and stretching feeling returned to his body and the moment stretched out. Then he was watching the back half of his body reform as a shadow from a building behind him blocked the sun. He turned slowly to look up at a shining pyramid that tapered up into a point above him.

To his left was another pyramid, and he could see a third one to his right. In front of him, there were large stones that had clearly been ruins of ancient buildings, which at one time might have served the Egyptians as temples. There were some modern buildings directly in front of him as well as a parking lot filled with numerous empty cars. He scratched his head and looked up. Here, unlike before the dungeons, he could see the blue dome that had been invisible around the Temple of Ramses. Strangely, this blue dome of protection ended at the pyramid they stood in front of and stretched into the distance.

Maybe because I am a partial owner now?

Rocky continued to walk away from the dome until he reached an edge of the pyramid and could look behind it. A rather impressive city stood there. There was sand and roads that covered a good kilometer or two before the city began, but the collection of structures looked like a completely normal, highly populated metropolis from Canada or the States before the crash.

The protective dome came down and ended right on the far corner of the pyramid they just exited. The dome seemed to separate this pyramid from the town and on the other side of the dome, Rocky could see numerous people fighting with creatures on the sand outside the city. He scratched his head again, and called over his shoulder, "We probably should have asked what direction the Prime dungeon is." Sela came and joined him at the corner, noticing the city and the people as well.

"That is a large collection of buildings. What is their purpose?" she asked him, and he shrugged helplessly in response.

"That's most of the city of Cairo," Victoria said as she joined him and Sela. "It seems to cut off right at the edge of that blue dome, see." She pointed to where golems were patrolling outside the dome in the far distance, and Rocky noticed it for the first time.

"Hey, the radios are working!" Zippo called over as he pointed at his ear.

"Did you get in touch with the Scourge?" Rocky asked, cutting off the current conversation due to the new information. Zippo nodded and Rocky asked the obvious follow up. "Are they okay?"

"Yeah, they've returned to the Grotto. They can't come anywhere near this area without the Mechanolords attacking them. There also hasn't been a fresh assault on Algonquin. They say they have to stay put and wait for the next assault."

"That might be because all of the opposing forces are taking on the Prime dungeon," Sela suggested, reminding everyone of the urgency. Rocky nodded and turned to Azoth.

"See which way leads toward Atlantis from the sky?" Rocky asked out loud. While he wanted to go check in with the people in the adjacent dome containing Cairo, they had lived this long. And if they wasted time with them as the Mechanolords conquered Atlantis, he knew they would regret it.

<That way,> Azoth said unhelpfully while flying in a circle above the pyramid, going into and out of the dome. Rocky watched as the people that were currently between battles noticed Azoth entering and exiting a dome of protection.

<Azoth, fly in the direction of Atlantis for a second,> Rocky retorted as more and more people looked in his pet's direction.

Dammit, he's probably terrifying them because they think he is a foreign monster. At least he's still small.

Azoth flew in a direction and Rocky asked him to return once he figured out the bearing the group needed.

"Okay, everyone, let's get going in that direction," Rocky said, pointing to what he assumed was north. It didn't take long before they crossed not one but two domes in quick succession. When they did that, people began pointing at Rocky's group and Azoth as he flew back to them.

Rocky felt torn. These people had likely been trapped in these domes since day one of the Ether crash. While they could have some outside visitors, those people would also become trapped inside shortly after. Seeing the people begin gesticulating wildly and pointing at his group, he wanted to immediately stop and inform them of the reason why they could now leave the dome. He even wanted to hear their stories, but knew that stopping could cause disaster for all of humanity.

Still, when the gesticulation turned into arm waving in a crossing motion and physical chase being given, he began to slow down slightly.

"Is it just me, or does it look like they are trying to warn us away from the direction we're going?" Rocky asked the others. They were all looking at the approaching people like he was. Sela was the first to come to a stop, and Azoth was the last to notice they stopped running. He continued on for another hundred meters before he looked around and halted his run by sliding over the sand.

<Race over then?> Azoth asked, not understanding why the group had been running in the direction they had been traveling.

The nearest group came within shouting distance of Rocky's and began shouting something in a language Rocky assumed wasn't English.

"Sorry, I only speak English!" Rocky responded in a yell of his own.

"That way is death!" the person yelled back in accented English. Rocky nodded and looked at his group with a meaningful expression. He couldn't speak for everyone, but he was certainly willing to wait a few moments longer if that was the warning.

The other group rushed over but stopped approximately ten feet away with their hands raised and open to show they weren't holding weapons. In the present day, this wasn't exactly a perfect way to show no hostility, because people like Zippo or Sela could just cast a spell, but it still held the meaning of the old world for Rocky, at least.

"Please explain," Rocky said in way of greeting, still not wanting to get into a lengthy introduction if he could help it.

"Everyone who enters archway never come back. Those that go around archway killed by Jormungandr snake. No reason go that way…"

"We have to go that way because people are trying to kill the snake and get access to the city it guards," Sela pointed out. The man looked at her and then made a sound of disgust in his throat. Rocky checked the man's group for the first time and noticed it had no females in it. Sela was about to say something again when Rocky raised a hand to forestall her.

"Thank you for the warning, but we must continue on this path," Rocky said and turned away. The man actually growled at Rocky's response, and he might have even chosen to attack Rocky, but Azoth growled back. When the man growled, it could have been misconstrued as someone clearing their throat. When Azoth did it, he still seemed to possess the size of a small house. The sand under Rocky's feet literally trembled.

<Thanks, buddy,> Rocky said as he patted his pet's head and resumed his jog. The others joined him and Sela pulled up beside him in an easy lope.

"What in the Silver Spires was that?" she asked as she glanced back at the other group. Rocky glanced back as well to see them trailing at a respectful distance behind them.

"I'm not one hundred percent sure, but I think he is one of those fools that believe women need the protection of men. I got the feeling that he thought answering you would be beneath him." Rocky turned back to Sela and saw Victoria press her lips tightly together as she chanced a glance back as well.

Sela just blinked at Rocky, and he shrugged helplessly. He didn't know enough about Egypt to say if that was a common reaction here before the collapse, or if that was just one idiot's viewpoint after the apocalypse. He didn't feel like sorting it out at the moment, either.

An archway made of glowing yellow stone quickly rose in front of the group and a single line of glowing yellow stones spread out from it in both directions as well. Each stone was only about a foot high, but it clearly delineated a line that shouldn't be crossed. The archway itself grew larger until the group stood in front of it. The bottom of the arch was probably ten feet high and the air inside of it seemed to hum and glow with a golden hue. It was almost like the sun was shining through a mist that hung heavily only inside of the arch.

"Well, I assume this is the entrance," Rocky said, and motioned at the strange doorway.

"You sure we shouldn't wait for more people from our group?" Zippo asked and looked back at the group that had stopped more than a hundred meters back. As Rocky turned, he discovered other groups joining the original in a steady stream. Rocky sighed, and looked to Sela, Victoria, and then Azoth.

"If the Mechanolords are already in there, I don't think we have a choice," Rocky whispered.

Sela nodded, her eyes bright. Victoria nodded, but in a resigned way, like she was preparing herself to die. Azoth just wagged his scorpion tail, and Zippo turned back before nodding as well. The kid's face paled before Rocky's eyes.

"Why don't you stay out here for now, man? If we don't come back, someone needs to tell the Grotto." Rocky put a hand on Zippo's shoulder. He truly meant that statement, and wasn't just trying to comfort him.

Sela nodded, and also joined Rocky by placing a hand on Zippo's shoulder. "That is actually a really good point. We need someone to stay outside, and by their reactions," Sela made a gesture at the people slowly arriving in the distance, "it cannot be one of us women. They might try to attack us. It has to be you, or Azoth. And let us be honest, he cannot ever get a message right."

Zippo chuckled and wiped a tear from his eye. Rocky nodded at him before turning back to the archway. "Alright. Shall we, ladies?"

<And gentle manticores!> Azoth added.

The four of them stepped through the portal.

CHAPTER THIRTY-FOUR

Rocky stood in a space that was perfectly black. It was difficult to describe the darkness that surrounded him. The lack of light was so complete that he couldn't see his own body. He couldn't distinguish between a blink or open eyes. He could feel that his body was still there, and that his feet were on something solid that he tentatively called ground, but other than his heart beating in his own ears, it was silent.

He turned on his Dark Cloak ability, felt it trigger, but the Dark Vision that it added did nothing to illuminate the space.

"Is everyone okay?" he tried, his voice fleetingly small in the strange space. While he heard his own words, it was like they were sucked instantly from him and fled, rushing away.

The lack of a response from nearby told him that he was probably alone. Despite the strangeness of the situation, he just shrugged and pulled a flashlight from his bag of holding. He had ended up in a few dungeon dives like this when he was adventuring on his own after New York and learned to be prepared. When he turned on the light, the beam didn't illuminate anything. Instead, it felt like those times camping as a kid when he would inevitably turn the flashlight up toward the night sky. He still saw the edges of the beam as it left, but the circle of illumination that would have appeared if he was in a room never materialized.

He pointed the light at his feet and found a black fog that merged with his own Dark Cloak and covered up to his knees. Shrugging again, he spun in a slow circle looking for something to mark his position. Unsurprisingly, he didn't find anything.

"Welcome to the preparation zone of the South Tower," South said. This time his voice was feminine and in the clear tones of Nancy Cartwright. Rocky shook his head, and before he got the chance to tell the dungeon off, the voice changed back to the deep natural tones they'd heard in the Tomb. "Fine, I will use my normal voice. You should have more respect for an ancient dungeon, though. Like the lady druid…"

"Listen, we rushed here so we could try to stop the Mechanolords and Apep from taking Atlantis, so where exactly am I?" Rocky asked. He gave up on finding a landmark after he finished what felt like a full three-hundred-and-sixty-degree spin. Still, with nothing to orient himself with, that was tough to be sure of.

"As we said, this was the preparation area before people challenged the Southern Tower of Atlantis. If people entered here without the proper accomplishments, they would be deemed unworthy and sent back. While the function of this area has changed, it still has a purpose. Entering through this zone, you will be given the opportunity to challenge the Prime dungeon raid boss with proper parameters."

Two suns lit up and blinded Rocky as South explained. Rocky covered his eyes with his arm, and flinched back from the sudden explosion of light into the perfect darkness. He turned off his Dark Cloak as he rubbed the spots from his eyes with a hand. It still took several blinks before he could see what the suns actually were.

Two golden doors emanated light from not even five feet away. Where had they come from? Each door shone with a metallic glean that made him suspect that the doors were actual gold. In the center of each door, there was an ankh symbol sunken into the center. In the middle of the ankh, a stylized one glowed. After a few blinks, a golden figure of the hippo-crocodile also grew and shone beside the doors. A third ankh with the number one came into existence on its chest. Rocky raised his eyebrows and waited, figuring that the ancient dungeon would explain.

Instead of an explanation, more doors began popping into existence around him. These doors were dark and didn't have the illumination of the first three figures. They still had a small glow to them and an ankh with a zero in black smoke. He began counting the doors as they appeared, still waiting for South to give him something more. When his count crossed thirty new doors, he swallowed but kept counting. He finally gave up when he reached sixty doors.

"What are these doors and how many are there?" Rocky asked, looking up at the darkness above him.

"There are one hundred and thirty-five doors in total. These doors are all the dungeons that have passed into our stewardship. The illuminated doorways are the ones you've completed. That is all the information we are allowed to provide."

Rocky tried to wait patiently as the rest of the doors appeared around him but eventually gave up. "I can tell you that my group only completed two dungeons. Why do you need to check them all? Also, why is the chimera we killed here?"

"We have finished calculating your total ankhs. You may choose to leave, or enter other dungeons or attack the boss. Here is the doorway to the Prime dungeon if you are ready."

A portal opened with a clear picture onto the other side. Rocky noticed the very clear avoidance of his question, but the scene playing out on the other side of the portal captured his attention.

The huge figure of Jormungandr's body and head dwarfed a floating city made from white stone. The city itself sat atop a piece of ground that tapered to a triangle's point of stone hovering just over the water. If the snake wasn't in the scene, Rocky was sure the city would have easily been the size of what remained of Cairo. Yet with the absurd size of Jormungandr's head alone, the triangle shape could have been a toothpick.

The head and body of Jormungandr up close made Rocky squint to try to understand what he was seeing. Azoth's description of 'hot garbage' suddenly began to make more sense.

The white body of the snake wasn't a living creature's scales. It was made up of garbage, plastic, sunken ships, and other debris that humanity had clearly lost or discarded in the ocean over the years. He even thought he saw a submarine outline buried inside the slightly clear plastic farther back, embedded in the body of the beast. At places throughout the body, massive bones that reminded Rocky of dinosaur museums were sometimes visible.

From the portal-window, Rocky couldn't see the head all the time, but the body kept coiling back and striking forward, bringing the massive head into view in varying positions. What the creature was attacking also wasn't clear, but he assumed it was the Mechanolords.

"We're supposed to fight that thing?" Rocky whispered.

"That is the raid boss of the Prime dungeon, yes?"

"That's suic—" Explosions bloomed all over the creature's body as missiles from some unseen attacker collided into the snake. "Can I speak to my party?"

"They have all been assessed as well. You may now all occupy the same space." Three figures popped into existence around Rocky. Each figure was staring through the same portal he was. Even the usual exuberance of Azoth was missing, his black eyes wide and tail down near the smoke floor.

"Are we sure we should go in there?" Rocky immediately asked.

"Can we come back if we try?" Sela asked, looking up and clearly speaking to the dungeon.

"You can attempt to escape, but you will need to flee from the raid boss and exit the area or it could still attack you."

Rocky's eyes narrowed, and so did everyone else's.

"Wait, so we can flee back to behind the low stone wall?" Victoria concluded, and the dungeon confirmed with a single word affirmative.

"If the Mechanolords are distracting it, we have a chance," Sela offered. She ruined any confidence that was added by swallowing audibly.

"Let's wait for the size debuff on Azoth to drop off," Rocky suggested as he looked at his shrunken pet.

Victoria and Sela both nodded, and together they waited and watched the scene of Jormungandr attacking the unseen enemy. They also saw numerous explosions and projectiles launched in the other direction, but that didn't tell them much other than that the fight was still going on.

"So, what exactly do the ankhs do, South?" Rocky asked while watching the combat. "Do they increase our damage against the boss?"

"They can do that, yes," South monotoned.

"So, if we flee we can gather more to help us. That's something, at least …"

Azoth had taken a nap during his wait and didn't wake up even as his body suddenly enlarged again. So Rocky woke him up with a light mental nudge.

<Azoth, buddy, don't attack the boss no matter what! Okay?> Rocky sent as the group stood in front of the portal. They really were counting on the manticore as an escape vehicle this time, and they couldn't have him ruin the plan by suddenly attacking.

"Let's do it," Sela said, and joined hands with Rocky on one side. The four of them stepped through the portal and onto the cliff overlooking the ocean together.

The picture morphed in front of Rocky's eyes and he immediately glanced to the northeast, having determined that to be the direction the attacks were coming from. Seeing Jormungandr attack through the portal hadn't done the snake's size and speed justice. Each time the head whipped forward, the jaws clamped down on a fleeing robot or a figure standing on the distant shore.

Rocky followed the monstrous body of the white snake back past the majestic floating city and felt his jaw drop as he saw it enter the ocean before rising and falling out of the waves far into the distance. In the scale of everything going on, Rocky took a moment to even remember to Analyze the massive boss creature.

Jormungandr
Legendary-Golem Sea Serpent
Level 112
Health Points: 955,501,312 / 1,000,000,000
Active Skills: Unknown
Passive Skills: Unknown
Boss

Rocky's jaw fell as he watched numerous Mechanolords die to the creature. How much life was Dahrix throwing away? As he watched, an orange steel Mechanolord attempted to dodge a strike using his boosters and was swallowed by the creature. He was one of maybe a thousand of the metal humanoid shapes in the sky bombarding the beast, but he was the only orange-steeled one Rocky could see.

The health was falling slowly, but it was dropping. Rocky looked at his group. "Are they just planning to zerg it to death?"

"That seems like it would take quite a while," Sela said and she pulled fingers through her hair. She wore a look of confusion and had tilted her head. Suddenly, a barrage of missiles exploded in the air directly in front of Rocky, causing him to jump. A wave of heated air and the sound of the explosion reached him at the same time, but other than a dry, hot feeling washing over his skin, Rocky didn't feel any damage.

As the explosions dissipated, a blue shield became visible and a voice boomed over the area. "All actions against living creatures are disabled in this area. This is the first and only warning. Friendly fire will not be tolerated."

"I think they are using the term friend a bit too loosely," Victoria muttered as she lowered her shield. Rocky couldn't help but nod as he returned his gaze to Jormungandr. Based on the rate of health dropping, the other group had been at this strategy for about thirty minutes.

"Do you think they can keep this up?" Rocky asked as he made note of the numerous turrets and self-firing mechanical missile launchers that lined the cliff face most of the robots were flying above. Suddenly, something bright orange seemed to step out of thin air.

Rocky squinted as an orange robot joined the other Mechanolord creations attacking the boss. If Rocky hadn't seen the other one be consumed, he would have said they were identical, but he highly doubted that Jormungandr was just letting people out of his massively long, snaking body.

"Should we join the attack?" Sela asked, and Rocky shook his head.

"I don't even think Victoria in her statue form can survive a single attack from that boss. We need to retreat and come up with a plan," Rocky responded, and looked at his pet. Azoth nodded in response and knelt to give them an easier time to mount up.

Sela nodded but didn't immediately move to Azoth. Instead, she stared at the current situation.

"At this speed, it will run out of hit points in about ten hours!" Sela commented and rushed to Azoth after her quick estimation. Everyone held tight as Azoth took off and fled away from the battle.

Azoth crossed from the clear stone of the cliff and onto the green of the grass that slowly turned into sand in the distance and emitted a strange whine. Rocky had never heard his pet make that noise before and he immediately sent a wordless inquiry.

<Snake no let prey escape,> Azoth whined back.

That was when Rocky felt it. Like a hand grabbing his soul and shaking it violently. He glanced back just as a few buildings of Cairo came into view in the distance. What he saw couldn't have been more terrifying. An open mouth lined with literal rows of teeth took up his entire vision and was growing faster in a way his eyes could barely track.

Then the teeth snapped shut all around him, Azoth, Sela, and Victoria, and the sunlight vanished.

CHAPTER THIRTY-FIVE

"Am I dead?" Rocky asked. His words echoed away into the darkness in a way that was eerily familiar.

"If you're dead, I'm right there with you," Victoria said from nearby.

<Azoth is eaten. This where food goes?>

"I think we're back in the preparation zone of the dungeon," Sela pointed out, which was starting to become more obvious.

Rocky pulled his flashlight back out and checked the floor. He saw the black smoke hovering near his knees and blinked.

"Was that a virtual reality or something?" Rocky asked the others.

"No, that was the real world, but not your real bodies," South answered.

"Is that why the Mechanolords are able to continually attack the boss? They're just coming back into the dungeon once they die?" Rocky asked a follow up, but was forced to cover his eyes again when two bright suns burst into the darkness. He recovered much more quickly from the light this time and blinked away the spots. He saw the others beside him when he glanced around. Suddenly, the time between the orange robot's death and return made a bit more sense.

<Did archway also eat group then?> Azoth asked Rocky, and from Sela's silent chuckle beside him, her as well.

"No, buddy. Nothing actually ate us. Just some sort of surrogate bodies."

<Tower feeding boss Azoth and Rocky treats?>

Rocky tilted his head and looked at Sela, but she just held up a hand as she fought to control a fit of giggles. In between a round, she responded, "Actually, that is exactly what is happening, Azoth."

Victoria looked between Sela and Rocky, her expression begging for someone to explain. Rocky began chuckling and told her what Azoth had said. Perhaps it was because they had just survived death, but they all began laughing.

A difference in the scene made Rocky stop chuckling. The ghostly hippo-alligator didn't appear this time, and the other doors with dark zeroes had already started appearing all around them. He waited and the round gateway showing the ongoing battle with Jormungandr appeared again, but the chimera-hippo was definitely gone.

"Can we still choose to leave again?" Rocky asked.

The foggy archway appeared behind them, but the South Tower didn't respond. Rocky took the appearance as an answer and pointed it out to the others.

"I think each time we lose in that dungeon, it uses one of our ankhs." Rocky pointed at the space the chimera had been the last time. "South Tower, what happens if we run out of ankhs?" he asked, hoping the ancient dungeon would answer this time.

"Death."

That one word answer sent chills and goosebumps over his shoulders. The laughter of the others had cut off when he pointed out the loss of an ankh, and South's one word answer seemed to stop even their breathing. Rocky swallowed and could hear his Adam's apple click in his esophagus.

"Okay, well, let's go outside and tell the others what we've discovered." Rocky pointed to the archway and started walking. His gait was hurried by the fight he knew he would see if he looked back to the dome behind them.

***

Rocky was greeted by a similar sight to when they had entered the archway. Zippo had a hand on his ear and was clearly communicating with the Grotto, and while a few of the Egyptians had inched closer, they were still over fifty meters away. When a full-sized Azoth materialized out of the shining fog, the brave souls who had come closer instantly retreated to the others. Zippo turned to look at them and his mouth turned up to a smile as tears leaked down his cheeks.

"You guys are back!" he exclaimed with a type of pure joy that made Rocky's heart stutter.

Sela smiled back and Rocky made a motion at his own ear to tell Zippo he needed to talk to the Grotto. Zippo nodded eagerly and removed his hand from his radio. Victoria took Azoth over to Zippo, and Rocky took his own radio back out of his bag of holding.

Sela placed a hand on Rocky's shoulder. "What is the plan?"

"Honestly, no matter the situation, we're going to need reinforcements," Rocky said with a shrug. He added a motion to indicate the locals that were standing at a safe distance but seeming to be fighting amongst themselves, now. "Plus, we are going to need a lot more people with ankhs if we hope to be the ones to get the killing blow on Jormungandr, no?"

Rocky added the final bit, still not sure if the Mechanolords and their zerg were the correct choice, but knowing that it might be the only one available on the timeline they were currently under.

"Well, we might be able to recruit these locals as well," Sela followed Rocky's gesture, but made a sour face when she noticed that they were currently fighting amongst themselves. "If we had more time, I would say let's go gather some people from nearby, but in ten hours, we might only be able to get the immediate forces to run through the strategy dungeon."

Rocky nodded. "I'm currently wondering if getting to the second boss would award a second ankh. It seems like the best way to farm for additional ankhs in the shortest time."

Sela nodded at Rocky, before turning back and shaking her head in the direction of the locals. "I will get the Territory to send people over. We're going to need them. You should probably go see if you can talk to those idiots," she said, pointing into the distance.

"Thanks for giving me the easy task," Rocky responded with a sigh, and handed his radio to Sela.

When he walked by Zippo, Victoria, and Azoth, he held up a hand, not wanting any of them to come with him yet. After the first group's reaction to the women, he thought Sela might be right in sending only him over. Mentally, he tried to prepare himself for any direction this might go.

"Hand over all your gear, and surrender to Amir's Sun Tribe," a man said as Rocky approached. The largest group of men that were nearby nodded along as if they all agreed. Rocky immediately scanned the crowd, looking for someone who might feel differently. He found a smaller group of men, that contained a woman, who were rolling their eyes.

"Hello, my name is Rockland, what's your name?" Rocky asked as he moved in their direction. Sure, he could have Analyzed the man but he felt that might be a rude way to start the conversation. Considering that he also wanted to ask these people to help kill a massive sea serpent in the next ten hours, he felt it was best to start on the right foot.

"I am Adom," the man said, and extended his hand. Rocky took it and shook, hoping that the greeting was what was expected. He then Analyzed the man.

Adom Hassan
Level 21
Apprentice-Infantry
Active Skills: 3
Passive Skills: 1

"Great to meet you," Rocky began. "We have come here to try to capture the city of Atlantis. Do all of the locals think like this man?"

Adom followed his motion to the first man who spoke and shook his head. "There are many factions in Giza, and his is but one. May I ask how you crossed the boundary, from there, to here?"

It was Rocky's turn to follow Adom's motion, and he realized he was indicating the protection bubbles. He nodded and turned back. "Has no one conquered one of the dungeons since the waves of Ether?"

"Dungeon?" Adom asked, but immediately forgot the question as the first man and his group of idiots came and surrounded the entire conversation.

"Adom, you will surrender the foreigners to us, or it will be considered an act of war."

Rocky Analyzed this man.

Osaze Amari
Level 23
Apprentice-God Priest
Active Skills: 2
Passive Skills: 3

After getting the man's name, he turned to Adom, who was looking at his group of four others and then the surrounding group that supported Osaze. Rocky watched Adom make the choice not to challenge the superior group at this time, and when he looked down at the ground, his entire group did the same.

"Okay, *Osaze*," Rocky tried to pronounce the name he had never heard before, but likely butchered it. "I'm going to give you a count of ten to move your group away from here. I tried to ignore you and give you the chance to make the smart decision and Analyze me or my group, but you're clearly not getting the hint."

<Azoth, come halfway to me and roar,> Rocky added mentally to his pet.

<Azoth doing imitation! Azoth comes.>

Rocky held Osaze's gaze and tried not to react to Azoth's word choice. A moment later Osaze and his group jumped as a massive roar reverberated over them. Rocky punctuated the roar with, "I'm counting," and crossed his arms.

Osaze's face grew dark and Rocky became certain the man was about to attack. However, one of the men beside him placed a hand on his shoulder and pointed to Azoth. Beside Azoth, Zippo stood under three huge red Fireballs. Sela hadn't joined him, as she was likely still contacting the Grotto. Still, Victoria stood with her shield and executioner's sword ready.

Rocky couldn't help the small smile that came onto his face when he saw Osaze's face reverse colors. Of course a man like this still needed to say something,

"We will be seeing you again, Rockland!" Osaze retorted and made a motion which the circle of men responded to by moving away. Rocky just shook his head and turned back to Adom.

"I would suggest we leave this area immediately," Adom said with urgency in his voice. "Osaze will return with many more men."

"Great, that type of *butt itch*," Rocky deadpanned, then felt the urge to groan at the word switch. Instead, he made a motion to his group. When he turned back, he saw the lady in Adom's group smiling nervously. He nodded at her and the other three. "Lead the way."

Chapter Thirty-Six

"Our leader, Maat, is up above." Adom gestured up at a white building covered in deeply recessed windows. Rocky looked up and saw that Adom was actually gesturing to a small observatory-like structure that sat atop the building. He couldn't think of another word to call the brown stone structure with a white dome-like top to it.

"What building was this?" Rocky asked as they wound through streets and passed by a giant lion statue in front of a bridge that miraculously still stood. The streets weren't clear exactly, but the immediate area around his group cleared quickly when people saw Azoth. A few groups seemed to form up and get ready to attack the giant black manticore, but Adom motioned them off.

"It was the American embassy in Cairo," Adom explained and signaled another group to not attack Azoth as he rushed from building to building sniffing the area. "There are a few different factions in Cairo itself, and Maat managed to take the consulate as a defensible home base early on."

They arrived at the front gates for the compound, and Rocky studied the large brick walls and cast-iron gates. Rocky placed a hand on the brick and wondered if it was strengthened at all by Ether. With as much subtlety as he could, he dragged his fingernail down the side, and felt the brick crumble away under the pressure. He felt like if he gave the wall or gates a good punch, that they would come down easily.

<Azoth, be gentle with everything here. If you bump into something, you might surprise the people with how weak their defenses are.> Rocky turned to Sela to see her finally off the radio. She had been going back and forth with someone on the other end, and Rocky caught snippets of the conversation. It sounded like the Grotto was going to send people over right

away and then a larger group after. At his look, she nodded and quickened her pace to catch up with him and Adom.

"The council is going to arrive on 'Ziggurat I' immediately. They will then determine if they can wait for the construction of the Guild Dome and Tower here to send the rest of the reinforcements. They say that they can't risk the Scourge in this area." Sela saw Rocky open his mouth and held up a hand. "From what I can tell, the Ziggurats are dropships or fighter ships that have been purchased from Amelia. I'm guessing the Mechanolords attacking in the sky like that has made people think about how to keep the Scourge safe."

"They think we can construct a Guild Dome and Tower here?" Rocky asked, scratching his head and looking around.

"It's already being constructed somewhere." Sela made a gesture that told Rocky she didn't know where the structure was but encapsulated everything.

"Yeah, every time you set up a new Territory, the observation deck in the Grotto tower would get a new panel," Zippo pointed out from nearby where he had been walking beside the dark-skinned woman Rocky had noted from near the archway. He could only raise an eyebrow in response. He had not known that.

Victoria suddenly raised her shield and unsheathed her sword which made Rocky's entire group jump into defensive stances. It also caused the guards on the gates and Adom's group to do the same. Rocky followed Victoria's gaze and found a Mechano*lady* pointing its open palm at the group while bracing the outstretched mechanical arm with her second one.

"Are you allied with the Mechanolords?" Rocky asked Adom, who was oscillating between raising his weapon at Rocky's group or at his own forces guarding the gate.

"Wait, this is Anya, she is one of eight of the robotic people who entered our Territory. At first we were suspicious as well, but they have all helped immensely in solidifying our defenses against the monsters in the domes." Adom chose to step between Victoria and Anya before raising both of his hands. Azoth, of course, rushed through the gate and escalated the situation again by growling menacingly.

<Azoth, stop. We need to hear them out> Rocky sent.

<But that Dahrix! You say Dahrix try kill you and family?>

<Just hold back and let Adom explain, okay. Go to Sela or Zippo, buddy.>

"Look, from our experience, anyone who has taken the seed of the Mechanolords can be controlled remotely by Dahrix, the leader of their forces." Rocky pointed to Anya. "She and the other seven robots here could be spies or double agents."

Anya frowned and raised her mechanical arm to study it. She looked to be questioning herself, which Rocky had seen before with the Floridians. "Let me guess, you have holes in your memory that you can't explain?"

"I was in London, and then, suddenly, I was inside of these inescapable domes in Egypt. Me and the others have no idea how we got here, and are from multiple different places all over Europe," Anya whispered. She still had a human face and her eyes narrowed as she looked from her own arms, to the sky above her. "Since being here in Egypt, I remember everything with no strange gaps…"

Rocky looked to Sela who nodded her head upward. He tilted his head and then looked up and saw the blue sky with the extra blue tinge on the clouds. The domes were interrupting the beacon symbol!

"Holy *beetlejuice!*" Rocky swore, and then shook his head when Sela's lip quivered into a grin. "So these domes actually stop the transmissions from outside. Do you have any shops in here?" Rocky followed up his exclamation with a question directed back to Adom.

"Shops? Do you mean like our markets?" Adom responded quickly.

Rocky shook his head. "No, they should be domes of metal that have a strange sheen on them. The metal is called arbuckle, and if you enter them, they transport your consciousness somewhere else."

"Ahhh, we have these domes but entering them only provides safety. Many people used them to escape monsters or enemies. We call them safe stations," the woman beside Zippo responded this time, and Rocky nodded at her. So, these domes also stopped the arbuckle enchantments from sending the consciousness outside.

The hum of engines interrupted further conversation and Rocky looked up to see a small dot growing in the sky. It continued to enlarge as it dropped straight atop of the group. When it passed through the dome above, Rocky was able to make it out as a much smaller and sleeker spaceship. Where the Scourge looked like a tub, with huge engines, this much smaller ship looked like a Mercedes with its engines hidden by style. Rocky could see four small blue ports on the bottom that were likely the thrusters controlling the descent, but in comparison to the Scourge, this ship was dropping far faster and simultaneously seeming to be more controlled.

For the third time in minutes, the guards entered defensive stances, but this time Rocky and his group raised their hands.

"That's our council, don't attack. We called them here." Rocky looked at Anya over everyone else. She likely had the most firepower in this group, since she was a broken Master class. Everyone else was still an Apprentice, after all.

They lowered their weapons and everyone watched as the dark black spaceship continued to grow. Up in the sky, Rocky had estimated it to be the size of a car, but it quickly overcame that assessment and grew to something closer to a school bus. Rocky looked to Sela and when she noticed his attention, she said, "It's a corsair style. Much smaller and more maneuverable while still being a size bigger than a fighter or dropship."

The Ziggurat touched down and a door opened into the sky, reminding Rocky more of an extremely fancy car than a ship capable of making it to space. The first person to step out was Derik and Rocky cursed under his breath.

***

"So, you're the leader of this area now?" Maat asked, his voice stern. Rocky could tell that he wasn't thrilled with that news.

"This is the reaction I had when I first met him," Derik said to Smith beside him. Smith rolled his eyes but luckily it didn't seem that anyone other than Rocky heard their side conversation. While his Chimera Senses could be a blessing, they also were giving him access to things like this far too often.

"I was given partial leadership for conquering two dungeons with my team. Are there no dungeons, or sorry, pyramids, nearby that your group has challenged?"

"No one has returned from inside the Great Pyramid of Giza. Adom tells me that he believes you conquered the Pyramid of Khafre, before exiting that dome and entering ours? No?"

Rocky could only shrug. "It was called the Tomb of the Deceased. So, I'm not sure which pyramid we came out of. Still, we did cross the domes to try to get to the Prime dungeon."

Rocky motioned to the massive snake head that was weaving to the north. Maat followed his gaze and nodded a few times.

"You're the first person to return from the archway. It brought you in to attack that thing?"

"That's right, and we need to be the ones to defeat it. If the robotic humans conquer it first, the world will likely fall to foreign powers." Sela stepped forward. Rocky could feel her anxiety as the ten-hour timer continued to count down. Rocky knew she wanted to rush this conversation forward and begin finding people to farm ankhs, but the lack of interest Maat, Adom, and the others were showing at this news made Rocky interested.

"So you race the metal men?" Maat asked simply.

"Yes, and they cannot win!" Sela responded with clear exasperation.

Maat held up a hand and motioned to someone nearby. The man brought a telescope over and handed it to Sela. When Sela received the device, she looked at it, and then back to Maat.

"Watch. Very soon, the battle will change," Maat said simply and picked up a golden telescope, motioning at Rocky this time with what appeared to be his personal device. Rocky raised an eyebrow but accepted. Pretty soon the members of the council and Rocky's group all had a looking glass pointed at the battle.

Sela was the first to grow impatient. "Yes, they are sending endless troops at the boss, using something like the ankhs to create surrogate bodies. We saw this in person."

Rocky lowered his looking glass and half turned. This was what they had seen in person. Whatever Maat was wanting them to see wasn't apparent to him either.

"Look toward the cliff they occupy."

Rocky again focused in and saw multiple turrets, missile launchers, and other automated turrets scattered all over the space. "Okay, why do you want us to see the defensive turrets?"

"See how they aren't firing," Maat continued. "In a while, they will begin firing. These automated turrets are the new addition to this attempt."

"This attempt?" Sela asked, her voice incredulous.

"Yes, this is at least the tenth try for those robotic humans. Every time they have failed at what comes next." Maat motioned at the window behind Rocky and he turned back, bringing the telescope up to his eye.

Smith moved beside Zippo. "Do you know what they are talking about?" he asked the kid.

Zippo lowered the telescope and shook his head. At Victoria's gasp, everyone who hadn't been watching the fight anymore turned back to it.

"What?" Zippo asked a moment later. Rocky also hadn't seen a difference in the fight.

"Jormungandr's body is covered in something!" Victoria responded and Rocky suddenly saw it. It looked like a cocoon of water surrounded the white garbage snake. The next instant, everyone in the room went silent. All the turrets and Mechanolords began firing. It was like the Mechanolords, before this instant, had been holding back. The body of Jormungandr became a kaleidoscope of orange as explosions rocked it from its head to where its body submerged into the Mediterranean sea.

"They weren't going all out!" Sela exclaimed. "We need to get back in there right away!"

"Just wait." Maat's voice was so calm that Rocky couldn't help but listen. He did hold his breath though, as he continued trying to find Jormungandr through the black smoke.

His telescope crossed over an orange Mechanolord, and he stopped his panning, watching the same robot he saw die earlier that day firing missile after missile at something inside the smoke. Then the robot was gone. In its place was water that seemed to be raining sideways toward the smoke. A quick scan showed the same phenomenon happening all over the sky above the Mechanolords' cliff.

When Rocky returned his looking glass to the smoke and explosions, he could tell clearly that the bombardment was slowing down exponentially. Even the smoke began to clear, revealing Jormungandr with a thicker sheen of water surrounding it. Were the raindrops adding themselves to the monster and shielding it further?

"We never saw it use any skills," Rocky whispered, coming to a realization. "What is the water shield?"

"We have no idea," Maat answered calmly again. "But we do know that the robots have tried numerous times to beat it. This attempt will end soon, and they will wait a few more weeks before making another."

Rocky lowered the telescope again and looked at Maat. The Egyptian man shrugged in response, still sitting in his chair. So much for attempting to zerg the creature.

CHAPTER THIRTY-SEVEN

"Wait, Derik, you guys were up all night, and the best plan is our original plan on steroids?" Rocky asked. He looked over at Sela, who had spent the night and the morning with him. She was frowning in what he assumed was disappointment in the suggestion, but she also was nodding her head like she agreed.

"Despite your incredulous tone, Rocky, I'm waiting to hear *your* suggestion," Derik retorted. Rocky glanced at the other members of the council and saw the bags under their eyes. Jorge and Yuri shrugged shoulders at his look, clearly conveying that despite the long night, they truly hadn't been able to think of another solution. Smith was frowning at Rocky, clearly still disappointed in his original absence from the Territory and his current attitude.

Mindfulness. Don't get angry. They probably did think about this from every angle.

"Sorry, Derik, I *shouldn't* have used that tone. I was just hoping for something more, and took my frustration out inappropriately."

Derik blinked and took a deep breath. He narrowed his eyes at Rocky as if expecting a trap before continuing. "We went in circles most of the night, and Maat even helped us understand what he thinks the Mechanolords have tried already. We concluded one of three possibilities.

"First, the Mechanolords aren't strong enough. We dismissed this option because, while they are broken Master classes, we assume that over a thousand of them is still quite a force. Second, the boss is too strong and is never going to be overcome. We avoided this conclusion at this time because of how important Sela made conquering Atlantis. So, we were left with the third conclusion. The size of the attack force needs to be larger."

Rocky nodded along and felt his roiling stomach grow more unsettled the more Derik spoke. It sounded reasonable, but why would Gaia, or the Atlantean dungeons, or whoever was currently guarding Atlantis, want to keep humans out of it? Wasn't it a city created by humans?

"Rocky," Astrid began, her voice small and tired. "In truth, we concluded that our best option is to begin collecting ankhs and reassess later. The second question we believe is about gathering more allies. The dome and tower should be finished today, but what about looking for other survivors and Territories nearby?"

"I think we need to step back, and take another look at why we are focused so much on Atlantis when there are people all over the world that probably need our help?" Derik cut in again. Rocky felt his jaw clench and he had to remind himself that the man wasn't saying it to be derisive. It was the equivalent of Rocky's initial outburst after hearing the council's strategy this morning. He took a deep breath.

"Has there been another assault on the Grotto since the last one?" Rocky asked. Derik looked confused by the question, but Smith, Jorge, Astrid, and Yuri shook their heads. "I think the concentration of Mechanolords here, when they are clearly allies of Frankie and could likely overrun the Grotto, is worth thinking about."

"How long did Maat say they have been fighting against Jormungandr?" Sela asked. Rocky could tell by her tone that she hadn't considered that issue the previous day. Likely she had assumed they had found Atlantis around the same time she had.

"Over two months," Smith answered and looked over to Adom, since Maat had taken his leave to sleep. "Are you suggesting that Atlantis is somehow more important to Dahrix than defeating the Grotto?"

"I'm not suggesting, Smith. I think their actions make it crystal clear. There might have been a time that Dahrix and the

Guild Collective believed that defeating strong enemies on the planet was the most important strategy, but something has changed. You all saw how much weaponry and forces were there to attack Jormungandr."

Everyone took the news in different ways. Smith became introspective, while Derik's jaw dropped. Astrid and Sela both nodded, and the former started scribbling notes hurriedly. Jorge and Yuri seemed to be relatively indifferent while they continued to regard Rocky. After a few more moments of varied silence, Rocky shrugged.

"I agree with the plan to farm ankhs and recruit allies. Still, let's reassess before we try what the Mechanolords are doing. It clearly isn't working. Agreed?" Rocky said as he stood up. Derik looked like he was going to try to respond but Smith put a hand on his shoulder and whispered something. Derik nodded, and then coughed to gain the room's attention.

"We all need sleep anyway. Let's call it a night for the council members and we will reconvene in the guild dome and tower once it's located. Can we count on your group to find the new guild headquarters, Rocky?"

Rocky raised an eyebrow and quirked up a corner of his mouth. "That was cleverly asked, Derik. Still, we'll find it before you wake back up."

***

"Do you really think that the Guild Collective has discovered how important Atlantis is?" Sela asked as soon as they were outside the building and in the square surrounded by the embassy walls.

"I find it strange that they haven't attacked the Grotto with Frankie. It seems almost like they have been using Frankie to keep us distracted while they worked on something else. For all we know, it could just be the high level of Jormungandr that has them excited, but I think it is more than that."

Victoria and Zippo were standing beside Azoth as people from Maat's Marauders, the name of this force, came and gave the massive manticore pats. Sometime between last night and now, the fear of Azoth had dissipated, and now Rocky's pet was a kind of celebrity, it seemed. Rocky stepped in beside Zippo and patted Azoth's hind lizard leg. "Azoth, how did you manage to convince them all that you weren't going to eat them?"

<Oh, they pet Azoth after he roll over. Also like when Azoth purr, more pets. No treats, yet.>

Sela guffawed, and so did Rocky.

"Well, I'm sorry to disappoint everyone and deprive you of your pets, Azoth, but we need to go and locate the guild dome and tower that is building somewhere under all these domes."

<No disappoint. No one give Azoth treat, need food.>

"We should likely also try some other dungeons to see if they all give ankhs," Sela suggested, and Rocky nodded.

"It would be good to have a strategy for each dungeon and a map if there are really over a hundred spread out throughout this place. The real issue is that they don't award Etherience when conquered..."

"Yeah, that is a bummer. Still, maybe all the Etherience awarded is for defeating Jormungandr," Victoria said as she got into Azoth's saddle before even Rocky. He jumped up in front of her and Zippo joined behind her.

"He can carry four if you don't want to waste a transformation." Rocky held a hand for Sela, and after a moment, she took it. He pulled her up and got her situated in front of him before Azoth launched himself into the sky.

Azoth soon crossed out of the dome above the city of Cairo, and now that Rocky knew what to look for, he could see the minute blue gleam of numerous protection domes leaving the sand and returning to them in a half sphere. He could even see the pyramid that sat somewhere under each protective structure.

"Dive, Azoth!" Zippo shouted from behind Rocky, and he turned to find what looked like multiple fighter plane jet streams in the distance. At the head of the ten to fifteen air wakes were Mechanolords, and from the shape of the streams, Rocky knew they had turned around and were coming straight for Azoth.

"Azoth, just outrun them," Rocky shouted to Azoth. He had learned in Ottawa that Azoth was far faster than any of the Mechanolords, if he chose to be. Azoth folded his wings in response and suddenly the wind in Rocky's ears was louder than anything else. If the others were talking now, he wouldn't be able to hear them, even with his enhanced senses.

Azoth's speed continued to climb, and Rocky glanced back to see that they were no longer in any danger from pursuit, but he did also realize that both Zippo and Victoria didn't look comfortable. In fact, they looked like they were barely holding onto consciousness. Rocky hurriedly scanned the landscape from their vantage and saw what he thought might have been ghostly tentacles in the distance.

<Azoth, I don't think they can handle your top speed. Slow down and drop into the domes below. Head in this direction.>

Rocky sent a mental picture of what he had seen and after a few more seconds, Azoth cracked his wings as wide as they would go and started flapping them. After the speed dump, he dropped into the domes, but was unable to keep flying because Sela shouted, "I'm going to be sick, get Azoth to land!"

Rocky grimaced but didn't relay the order because clearly Azoth had heard it. They coasted to the sand and the three riders all hurriedly slid from the saddle. They all got sick after and Rocky grimaced. He had forgotten that he had gotten used to Azoth's top flight speed for over two months. He scratched his head from atop Azoth's back. "I'm sorry, guys…"

Sela glared at him and changed into her raven form in way of answer. Rocky pulled on his armored collar and pointed in the direction he thought he saw the guild dome. She flew off as Victoria and Zippo continued to collect themselves.

"Probably would have been smarter to just enter the domes right away, Rock," Zippo complained from all fours.

"Agreed. Won't do it again." Rocky held back a giggle and patted Azoth affectionately. He was almost proud of the manticore for going fast enough to cause this reaction in others. Almost.

***

Rocky stood outside of the pyramid they had just cleared with his eyes closed and facing up at the sky. This was the second dungeon in the area they had cleared, and each one was unique with complicated, puzzle-like choices. Even this one that seemed to be a Delving dungeon had complicated strategies to unlock doors to boss rooms or to reduce the damage the boss could do to the group.

"Are all of the dungeons going to be like this?" Zippo asked Sela nearby.

"Make sure no one mentions these dungeons to LFD," Victoria responded as Sela shrugged helplessly. Rocky pulled a water bottle from his bag and shared it around, even squirting some water in Azoth's mouth. The manticore was small again, the dungeon having provided another shrinking potion.

"We should get moving toward another dungeon. We still have about eight hours before the guild dome completes," Rocky commented as he stared back into the sky. At everyone's groans, he nodded and sat down instead. "Okay, a short break won't hurt."

"So far, the fastest was definitely that Strategy dungeon," Zippo commented on how the last two dungeons had taken well over two hours each.

Rocky felt his eyes widen. "Do you think we can get more ankhs if we keep going?"

"Probably." Sela made the wishy-washy sign with her hand. "Still, we should keep getting other dungeons cleared. Other than needing a healer, our group is the most likely to be able to handle any situation that might arise."

"There are definitely some people in the Grotto that run dungeons much more frequently than we do," Victoria pointed out. "Just because we have the levels doesn't make us the best choice."

Rocky leaned back on the hot sand and took a deep breath. "Do you think dungeons that don't award Etherience or loot other than the ankhs will actually be a draw for those groups, though?

"Either way, I suggest we head to the tower Strategy dungeon right now; we can take a break physically and let the defenders take care of the mobs."

The group all looked at their own sweat-glistening arms and, with smiles on their faces, they nodded in agreement.

CHAPTER THIRTY-EIGHT

As the group had hoped, and Rocky had guessed, the tower dungeon was cumulative. So, when they returned to challenge it again, they started on the sixth level with what they had purchased before.

Unfortunately, the plan to let the defenders handle everything and rest on the tower didn't work as well as Rocky hoped. From the sixth level to their current ninth level, they began facing enemies that all had some sort of projectile. While the mobs were still defeated and the group hadn't needed to join the battle, they had been forced to dodge out of the way or be hit by flaming seeds the size of softballs.

So far, the theme of these levels had been plant monsters. Starting with twig treants for the sixth level, before moving to needle blights for the seventh, and mushroom warriors for the eighth. Now Rocky was fending off ten thousand dryads.

Perhaps unsurprisingly, fire-attributed defenders were significantly more effective against the plant-based attackers, while earth- and water-based archers seemed to be less effective. Still, he was hesitant to create new defenders only in the air and fire direction. If these waves were weak to fire, the next waves might be strong against it. So, he kept upgrading defenders along all the paths available.

For each phase, he had received five points per mob, equaling one hundred and fifty thousand for waves six to eight, but he had been spending those points as fast as he could bring them in. To increase the level three defenders to level four would require five more levels at ten thousand points per level. So instead, he worked on increasing his twelve original level one defenders to level three and increasing the tower to level fifteen. This had left him with about forty-five thousand points remaining at the beginning of the ninth stage of this dungeon.

The two top tier filters had been behind in keeping up with the purification of the oasis water with the numerous projectiles, so Rocky decided to purchase two more, which kept the filtration ahead of the flaming, corrupted seeds. Still, at the beginning of the dryad round, he had twenty five thousand points, and so he filled out the remaining sixteen defender spaces with more level one elemental archers.

Rocky's planning worked, and the dryads weren't reaching the edge of the oasis. He was about to congratulate himself and start assessing which of the level three elemental combinations were most effective when Zippo said, "What was that?"

In the direction the boy was looking, it seemed like a change occurred, something similar in look to wind ruffling the grass. Rocky tilted his head. The dryads, which were five-foot-tall leafy green humanoids, suddenly became medieval knights. However, in place of metal armor, they seemed to be wearing tree bark, shaped into the knightly helmets, breastplates, vambraces, cuisses, and sabatons. He waited, expecting the projectiles to change as well, but the dryad knights continued to lob the corrupted seeds at the tower.

"The same change is occurring everywhere now," Sela called as she dodged a softball seed that splashed onto the stone of the tower and disgorged its horrendous black oil. "Is it just me, or have none of the dryads fallen since they armored up?"

"It's not just you!" Victoria called. "They are almost to the edge of the oasis."

Rocky panicked. He now had thirty-thousand death points but adding more defense for the tower or upgrading defenders wasn't going to help. Not if none of the defenders were damaging the dryads. Rocky hurriedly Analyzed one of the creatures.

Dryad Knight

Level 15
Journeyman-Plant Terror
Health Points: 4,000 / 9,000
Heavy Armor

He estimated about half of the dryads were already dead, but that was likely what triggered the armor. As he continued to watch, the dryad knight's health only fell by another hundred points. At this rate, five thousand of the creatures would get to the water.

Am I missing something, like the priests?

He checked the corpses of the dryads, and they weren't being absorbed by the other mobs to create the armor. There also weren't many corpses left on the sand, because the three hundred and ninety priests were effectively mummifying everything that died.

"Knock them back?" Sela suggested.

"Right, the holy points," Rocky whispered to himself and flipped tabs. He had nearly eighty thousand holy points, and he hovered his hand above the Taweretan knockback ability before choosing to scroll down and see if there was a better option. As he scrolled, the spells got more expensive, and he was about to choose Ra's Heatwave for five thousand points when his eyes saw that the next spell actually decreased in cost.

Holy Point Spells
Ra's Heatwave (5,000)
Taweretan's Stunning Bellow (3,000)

He scrolled down further and noticed that the spells were organized into levels. Each Egyptian deity had a spell represented on each grouping, and the further down he traveled, the more expensive those spells.

"Umm, Rocky?" Zippo prompted, reminding him that he wasn't free to keep studying the options. He jumped back up to Ra's Heatwave and clicked the button before confirming his selection.

The sun in the sky began increasing in lumens like a lightbulb that was getting ready to burst, and Rocky hid his eyes under his hand. He caught the rest of the group doing the same, and Azoth flattened himself atop the tower before placing both paws over his eyes.

The intense light brought a wave of heat, and Rocky first worried about sunburn before realizing he was likely going to catch fire first, if this continued. Just as he saw the others begin to huddle in on themselves, a blue wave was produced by the tower and the heat was subdued back to manageable levels. He tried to watch the effects the spell had on the dryads, but the plants of the oasis also lit up in blue contrast, further confusing the scene. The intense brightness dimmed down again almost as fast as it came, and Rocky blinked away the sunspots from the reflected illumination.

The dryads' armor was laying all over the sand and oasis floor, and it was on fire. The dryads themselves had returned to the regular mob as well and were dying in droves again. Sela moved over and asked, "What spell was that?"

He pointed it out and she continued. "So, you have to counter the skills of the mobs then? Why did you pick Ra?"

"Ra was the sun god in legend, and I hoped that fire would somehow be more effective against the armored dryads because of the theme of this current stage." Rocky shrugged and Sela tilted her head.

"Well, isn't that interesting? Ra was a very powerful fire mage in my time. Kind of like Zippo actually…" Sela responded with a gesture in the kid's direction. He blushed as red as his fireballs, which caused Rocky to laugh.

The stage finished, and Rocky looked back to the screen to prepare for the tenth stage, and what he assumed would be another boss. A quick Analyze told him that the defenders which had lost health in the attacks were returned to full again at the completion of the stage. With fifty-five thousand points, it was time to decide a direction to take. The countdown timer above gave him five minutes, but he didn't actually need that long. He wanted to see the fourth level of the elemental archers.

"Think I should upgrade one of the defenders to the fourth level?" Rocky asked the group as they sat back down hoping to get that promised rest in.

"Oh, which one were you thinking of upgrading?" Sela asked and motioned at the multiple combinations of defenders with crossbows around them. Rocky pointed to one of the original four and she followed his finger. "The flame-attributed one? Yeah, that makes the most sense, really."

Rocky smiled and clicked five upgrades on that defender.

Elemental Defender Level 4
Phoenix Wash

Since he had only chosen the fire element the previous three upgrades, it seemed like he had lost the ability to add a different element now. Still, this defender had been the most effective against the last four waves by a large margin. The Bes' Defender switched his crossbow for a small hand cannon. Rocky raised his eyebrow and pointed at it.

"It seriously looks like a miniature, handheld cannon, or an oversized musket," Victoria commented with a bit of a chuckle.

Rocky nodded. The weapon looked far out of place in a universe where laser weaponry existed, but he assumed that, because this was a dungeon, the physics weren't exactly important.

"Ahh, you've made it to another boss battle," South stated.

Rocky jumped, having almost forgotten about the entity. They tried to contact it during the last two dungeon runs and again in their current dungeon, but it had seemed to ignore them.

"We thought you would be more talkative since the Mechanolords failed at the Prime dungeon," Sela retorted as she shot to her feet. Rocky knew that Sela wasn't a fan of dungeons, so he held up a hand and interrupted her.

"It's nice to hear from you, South. We've had some questions to ask you for a while."

"Well, you have one hundred and twenty three seconds of my attention."

Rocky looked up to the timer and shook his head. Sela's face began darkening and when he saw that, he hurried to ask the first question. "We saw the strategy of the Mechanolords against Jormungandr, and it seemed to be working. Is that what we should be doing, too, gathering a large number of attackers and collecting ankhs?"

"Your strategy is your choice. Still, theirs grows rather boring, doesn't it?" South responded, and seemed to almost yawn, like it had just woken from a nap.

"Well, if you gave us a hint, I'm sure we could make our attempts more interesting," Zippo suggested helpfully and Rocky nodded to the young man.

"That isn't allowed. Still, the other Towers and myself did discuss if the first skill of Jormungandr is too difficult. Yet Prime vetoed the suggestion when we sent it in. We must watch and wait, it seems."

"Can you tell us what the skill was?" Rocky asked. "It seemed to turn the attackers into water and suck them in."

"You may study the skill in more detail in the dungeon."

"So, you really can't tell us anything?" Sela growled.

"I think I've said far too much already. Let's see how you handle the shambling mound boss…" Rocky heard his voice fade away as if he was leaving.

"Come on, we know you're still there and that was just an effect of your voice!" Rocky shouted up into the sky.

"Was it?" South said and echoed his voice over the sands in all directions. "If you only have stupid questions, I'm sorry to say that I will only provide stupid responses."

There were only twenty seconds left until the boss. "Well, now that we are full owners of the Territory here, can you tell us if we should find dungeon cores to take over these pyramids?" Victoria asked. That question wasn't even percolating in Rocky's mind but seemed like a good one.

"Unfortunately, you cannot do so yet. The Prime dungeon must be conquered before I or the other towers can relinquish our holdership state. However, we would greatly appreciate the help when that time comes."

The timer began flashing and Rocky blinked in time with it. He felt like that information gave him something. He couldn't place his finger on what, but he was sure that it meant something. The Towers couldn't release the dungeons yet…

A blue light began swirling and coalescing on the dune in the east, and Rocky moved all of the defenders with fire attributes in their combinations as well as the Phoenix Wash defender to that side with a slide of his finger.

"What made you think of that question?" Rocky asked Victoria as the blue monstrous shape continued to form.

"I've been thinking that the dungeons provide the ankhs we need, and thus they must be important to the defeat of the Prime dungeon. I wanted to test the South tower and figured he wouldn't answer a direct question."

Rocky nodded along but didn't respond as an overly large green creature fell atop the sand dune. It looked like a giant lizard covered in growing plants until it raised itself onto two legs and began waving its arms in the direction of the oasis. Its arms were composed of intermingling green vines with leaves, flowers, and moss growing atop them. Its entire body was the same, and the only reason Rocky's eye now made the distinction was because the waving vines were spreading out toward the oasis.

The vines slithered over the sands like green snakes, coming ever closer. Still, as soon as they entered into range, the eight level three archers began attacking. Arrows that froze, burned, steamed, and exploded all flew, and when they landed amongst the slithering vines, the appendages were destroyed. Rocky managed an Analyze just before the thickest vine was obliterated.

Shambling Mound
Level 22
Journeyman-Elderwood Guardian
Health Points: 19,450 / 20,000
Boss

At first, Rocky thought that the vines were burning and spreading blackness onto the sand, but a second look at the vine struck by the Phoenix Wash defender told a different story. It was bleeding green blood onto and into the sand. The massive, flaming, bird-shaped projectile continued to burn, but the sand wasn't blackening, it was turning green.

"Should we be worried?" Rocky asked and pointed out the phenomenon as best he could.

"None of the vines are getting any closer at the moment," Sela responded with a shrug. So, the group continued to watch.

<Azoth, can you go take a look from a different angle?>

<No sun spell when Azoth fly. Azoth no cooked chicken.> With that admonishment, Azoth took off and lumbered toward the darkening green sands.

<Azoth just see blood soaking into sand,> his pet concluded.

Rocky watched the health of the boss drop using Analyze, and when it reached fifteen thousand, the vines stopped. Instead of coming forward, they retreated and rejoined the undiminished shambling mound.

"Here it comes," Sela said as it dropped back to all fours and pushed off with its back vine trunks. Shambling was a good description of the way it moved. Each step, vines pulled up sand from the desert, raining it back down in a shower as it lumbered forward. The creature only ever pulled one leg off the ground as it came on, and Rocky held his breath waiting for the archers to begin firing again.

Its front leg hit the green sand and all of the defenders released in unison. If the green sand was a puddle, Rocky could have described what came next as evaporation. The edges of the area began shrinking in toward the boss. It moved its other three feet into the area as well just before the wave of eight powerful skills crashed into it.

The resulting wave of ice, fire, and explosions caused Rocky to lose sight of the boss, but not the edges of the green sand. They continued to shrink in, only now at an increased rate.

"*Newman?*" Rocky swore, and for once wasn't too disappointed in the swearing substitute.

CHAPTER THIRTY-NINE

When the boss came back into Rocky's view, the shambling mound was back on two legs and extending vines toward the oasis again. This time, the boss was much closer and standing midway between the dune and the first trees of the oasis. He narrowed his eyes. Something else had changed, but what?

The defenders were launching every arrow at the main body of the boss instead of the slithering snake-like vines. Rocky frowned at them. In the absence of defender's attacks, the vines were creeping toward the oasis unchecked.

Shambling Mound
Level 22
Journeyman-Elderwood Guardian
Health Points: 19,132 / 20,000
Boss

Rocky's frown deepened as he took in the information. The green blood had clearly healed the boss, and even as he watched, the health dropped and climbed. Each attack by a defender wounded the boss, but the blood would fall to the ground around it and be sucked right back into its body. At the current rate, the vines would reach the water long before the defenders dropped the boss back below fifteen thousand.

In desperation, Rocky flipped the defenders from their current spots using the pad on top of the barrel. As soon as they walked off the spot, he hurriedly replaced them, and when they retook their current positions, they targeted the vines instead of the main body. This wasn't a solution, and he knew it, but this should buy him some more time. He flipped to the holy points page and began scanning.

There had to be something on this page that could counter the healing of the boss.

"The boss is back to fifteen thousand health, and has pulled its vines back. It's moving forward again, but this time it's sucking up the blood as it moves!" Sela notified Rocky. "Incoming!"

Rocky glanced up to find basketball-sized seeds arcing down toward the tower. They landed with a light snick, and he blinked at them. That was rather anticlimactic, when compared to the seeds that popped and produced black sludge. Then the first seed exploded with a small audible puff and Rocky's face was peppered with beads that bounced harmlessly off his skin.

These seeds found the cracks of the tower top and fell through. When the small beads struck the water, it was like watching sped up Sea Monkeys. They sucked in the water, reducing the number on the surface. It grew worse when the filters sucked in the enlarged seeds, because they clogged the intake.

"Should I burn them out?" Zippo asked. Rocky looked at the rate of the seeds being launched by the boss and shook his head.

"For now, let me see if there is a spell here that can stop the boss," Rocky responded, and began scanning the spells again. Taweret, Babi, Nekhbet, Khonsu, Bes, Anubis, Serqet, Sobek. Bast, Horus, Nephthys, Set, Isis, Osiris, Shu, Geb, Nut, and Ra. Rocky read over it twice but the problem he now saw was not understanding what many of these names would indicate, and without a description of the spell he was in trouble.

"Sela, I need your help. Do you recognize any of these names?" Rocky asked, his voice urgent. His tone caused her to rush over and read the first level of spells beside him. She pointed to Set after completing the list.

"If I remember correctly, he was a very powerful geomancer or something of the like. Set was rumored to be able to control sand with his power. At least, those were the rumors I heard."

Rocky shrugged and clicked the first level spell. The spell cost two thousand points and was titled Set's Betrayal. His eyes flew to the shambling mound as it closed in on the first trees of the oasis. A quick Analyze showed the boss's health below twelve thousand. Further assessment showed why. The defenders were able to continue to bombard the boss as it moved, unlike when it lumbered from the dune to the last location.

Unfortunately, it was still healing at each step by sucking in the green blood. Rocky couldn't find any sign of Set's Betrayal spell and he looked down at the screen again to confirm he had used it. The two thousand points were missing.

"Is the sand changing colors?" Victoria said from behind Rocky, and when he turned, he was peppered with more beads from an exploding seed. He shook off the annoyance and focused on the sand that wasn't immediately surrounding the shambling mound. He could tell that the sand was, in fact, changing colors. When he looked back to the boss, he noticed that the green sand covered in blood was turning purple.

Unfortunately, the change in color wasn't stopping the boss from sucking its blood back up to heal itself. Rocky estimated he had about thirty seconds before it reached the largest pool of the purpling blood and began sending its vines out again.

"Is there another spell you can think of?" Rocky asked Sela beside him.

"I don't think we need one," Sela said as she pointed at the purple lines that were appearing on the boss. Rocky tilted his head. The consumption of the purple sand was clearly healing the creature, but there was a new addition to the Analyze.

Shambling Mound
Level 22

Journeyman-Elderwood Guardian
Health Points: 11,232 / 20,000
Boss
Set's Poisonous Betrayal

Rocky felt his eyebrows raise as the damage to the boss began to entirely offset the healing factors. The boss's health fell under ten thousand, then nine, and then it began to look like a payout from a slot machine as the numbers literally started flying off.

It hit one thousand points of health remaining just as its feet touched down on the large blood pool and the start of the oasis. The tower shook, and Rocky grabbed the sides of the barrel to stabilize himself. Sela grabbed onto him and nearly dragged him down. "What was that?"

<Water balloons seeds fly to boss,> Azoth reported from the skies. Rocky got his feet under him and looked down. The shaking of the tower dislodged more of the beads which fell into the water and began transforming. The wall, which was ten feet high and surrounding the pool, was filled with massive holes. Those holes were from the ballooned beads breaking through, and that was also what had shaken the tower.

The pool was down to five-hundred points and Rocky watched in horror as more beads began falling into it.

"Zippo, start destroying those expanding beads," Rocky ordered and looked back to the boss hoping to see a corpse. What he saw instead was a layer of water beginning to surround the boss. The shambling mound's health stabilized at five hundred remaining points, and the attacking defenders attacks were splashing harmlessly against the water shield.

"When I pop them, they turn into a green water that is being filtered," Zippo reported. Rocky was glad the kid thought to tell him, because he couldn't take his eyes off the boss. The water shield reminded Rocky of the scene through the looking glass. The water shield was almost identical to that which surrounded Jormungandr.

The shambling mound began extending vines toward the pool again and Rocky swore. They only needed five hundred health points…

In desperation, he chose the second level spell called Set's Storm Strike. This cost four thousand holy points, and Rocky crossed his fingers. He was hoping that Storm Strike meant lightning, because if it meant water, well that wouldn't be helpful against a water shield.

A sharp boom, almost a crack of a whip sounded, and something whited out Rocky's vision. He heard the rumble of thunder a moment after he lost his sight and he held his breath.

<Rocky promised!> Azoth screeched in his mind.

<Just hover if you can, buddy,> Rocky responded. <Like when we used the dragon fire.>

Eventually the shadows of the world resolved themselves into priests mummifying the remains of the shambling mound and Rocky breathed a sigh of relief.

"That was more fun to watch than the Jormungandr fight," South whispered into the dungeon. "Next time I will invite the others to watch."

"Can you help us understand why a boss of this dungeon used a skill similar to Jormungandr?" Rocky asked hurriedly. He didn't want the South tower to become unresponsive.

He received no answer. So instead, he turned to Sela and pointed to the spells. "Do you think these are training us how to deal with the Prime dungeon?"

"Like to use lightning spells or items against the boss when it uses its shield?" Sela asked.

Rocky shrugged. "I mean, it's more than what we had before."

"Let's stay here in this dungeon until the dome and tower complete," Sela stated plainly. "Maybe there is more to learn."

Rocky smiled and motioned everyone to follow him to collect the ankh.

***

They were flying to the dome and tower atop Azoth, having completed up to the thirtieth level of the Strategy dungeon. Currently, he had sixteen level four elemental defenders, and sixteen more level three. He had also managed to increase the tower level to twenty-five, which had added a second higher level defender platform that opened up sixteen additional spots, with an increased range.

Rocky left the dungeon with the level four defenders stationed atop the tower with increased range and a mix of sixteen level one and three defenders on the bottom layer. The boss fights had grown progressively more dependent on using the proper spell to defeat and with Sela, Victoria, and Zippo's help, they had managed to respond to each change. Of course, Azoth had tried to be helpful, but for the most part, his suggestions were anything but.

They also received four more ankhs in that time, which brought their current total to eight. Rocky was relatively confident that the tower dungeon was the fastest way to collect more ankhs, and he also guessed that it was somehow teaching them proper responses for Jormungandr's skills. That part wasn't tested at all, and the South tower was mostly ignoring their questions about it.

Regardless, it was time for people to start arriving from the Grotto and they needed to release the notes on the four dungeons they had faced so far. Rocky arrived to find the council in the shade of the corsair ship waiting for completion as well.

"How has your day gone?" Rocky asked the group.

"Maat has petitioned for us to allow his group to exit the protective shield and live in the guild dome," Derik said. "I told him it likely had just slipped your mind and you hadn't intended to leave all the people in Cairo trapped."

Rocky swallowed. He looked to Sela, and she saw his plea for help. Shaking her head, she opened some screens and navigated through them with ease. "Do you want everyone to be able to move freely, or…?"

"I didn't much care for that other group that tried to capture us," Victoria mentioned. Rocky nodded and scratched his beard.

"What if we say anyone who is a part of Meliora has free access?" Rocky suggested. The council looked at each other meaningfully after his suggestion and Rocky just rolled his eyes. "You know you guys are also part of the guild, right?"

"We just don't think it's appropriate to put one person in charge of so many," Derik sniped back.

Rocky shook his head and smiled. "When have I ever forced a guild member to do something?"

"You're forcing members of the guild to come here and risk their lives!" Derik shouted back.

"Weird, I was pretty sure we asked for volunteers," Sela retorted quickly. "Upset that people are leaving the Grotto for other Territories, or coming here to help us, Derik?"

Smith coughed. "Derik has never really conveyed his feelings properly, but I think we all worry about the safety of people back home as more people move away, or as our fighters come here. I'm your military leader, Rocky, and I can see the ranks growing frustrated. Many of them would come here, or take opportunities elsewhere, but they're forced to stay at the Grotto and defend it. We fought hard to make the Grotto safe, we worked even harder to make it livable, and then after everything, people can just get up and leave. Or worse, they somehow get possessed…"

Derik's argument was easy to dismiss, but Smith was right. The way Derik made his point trivialized the feelings that Smith just accentuated. Rocky looked at the council for a long time before nodding his head. He probably would have been flippant or angry with Derik if Smith hadn't stepped in. Yet after hearing the worry explained rationally, he needed to think of a solution. His family lived in the Grotto, too.

The sound of shifting sand made everyone forget about the current topic and glance to the dome and tower. The spiritual tentacles fell into the sand and right in front of them was a guild dome.

"I'm assuming you didn't bring an Ether converter?" Derik asked with a sneer.

Rocky pointed at the man. "Don't push it. You know we didn't."

CHAPTER FORTY

"That's correct, the guild will pay the teleportation cost for anyone who wishes to come through at this time," Rocky confirmed over the radio. "Make sure to tell people that the opportunity to gain loot and levels is strangely disabled here. There may be a massive payout in Etherience and loot when we defeat the legendary boss, but I can't guarantee that."

Rocky was about to turn around and leave the radio for the council members when he caught Derik's frown. "Make sure everyone knows that this is a request for aid, and not an order."

Derik rolled his eyes and Rocky smiled at the man. He knew that Derik meant well—at least, he thought the man did—still, his attitude was rather annoying, and Rocky felt that a few jabs back at the man wouldn't hurt. He even went as far as to stick his tongue out as he passed by to rejoin Sela and Smith near the elevator.

He arrived mid conversation.

"—marked on the map. Those are the dungeons we have run so far. According to the Prime dungeon, there are over a hundred controlled by the South Tower. Each one should reward ankhs, which we will need to resurrect against Jormungandr."

"Since teams will be coming through in a spread out manner, how many ankhs should each group try to collect?" Smith asked.

"Are we still going to try the zerg method?" Rocky asked. He would be the first to admit that he didn't have a better plan, but that plan also felt like insanity. If the Mechanolords had tried ten times already, and were using the ankhs to resurrect and return to the fight like Sela just insinuated, why hadn't they already defeated the Prime dungeon?

"I think if we choose to assault Jormungandr at the same time as the Mechanolords, we should be able to break through the water shield and continue to damage the boss." Sela looked at Rocky and tilted her head. "Especially if we can bring some individuals that use lightning, or bring some weapons from the shop that can channel electricity."

"For now, tell the groups to collect as many ankhs as they can. We will continue to attempt new dungeons and report our findings. Still, right now, the fastest collection method we've discovered is the tower dungeon here. The group will need to fend off a few waves early on, but once—"

"I've already explained it to him," Sela cut in with a smile.

Rocky nodded and turned back to Smith. "Well, you have all the same information we do then. If groups try other dungeons that we haven't, make sure they bring back detailed notes."

Smith frowned at Rocky, but when he tried to walk by the man to the elevator, Smith grabbed his shoulder. "Just be careful out there."

Rocky smiled at his friend and patted the man's shoulder in return. "Same to the council. Do you still plan to try to recruit local groups of survivors?"

Smith nodded and Rocky glanced over his shoulder at the others. "Just be careful. If you see even one Mechanolord with the group you're trying to recruit, move on," Rocky cautioned.

Smith patted his shoulder back, as if to say, 'We've got this.' Rocky moved to the elevator feeling at a loss for words. There was just too much to do and not enough time, it seemed.

Sela joined him inside after the door opened and she had said her farewell. "Do you want to return to the Strategy dungeon or keep testing new dungeons?"

Rocky sighed. "Let's try some new dungeons. I'd prefer to keep collecting ankhs as fast as possible, but I also agree that our group should be gathering good information for people that come after us."

The elevator opened onto the kiosk on the main floor. Rocky saw that people were already coming through, and noticed Gary was standing with Zippo and Victoria.

"Well, that should make dungeons go a bit faster," Sela exclaimed, also noticing the healer.

***

"Is it just me, or are these dungeons just a repeat of the one that we first entered?" Zippo stated more than asked. It had been four more hours and the sun sat on the horizon, ushering the desert into night with ample hues of red. They managed to defeat four other dungeons in that time, and Zippo was right. The increase in their speed of clearing was mostly because the dungeons were extremely similar. Almost eerily so.

"One more before dinner?" Rocky asked, but nodded at the fire mage. Everyone else nodded, and the five of them turned toward the next visible pyramid. They were currently attempting the numerous dungeons that sat just outside of Cairo, but so far had avoided the one inside its dome. Mostly to avoid the group that had threatened them. While Rocky was sure they could deal with the imbeciles, he also wasn't eager for confrontation.

It took fifteen minutes of walking over the cooling sand for them to reach it. Rocky would have liked to be able to fly on Azoth, but most of the dungeons they ran needed him to take the shrinking potion to be included. Still, if the current trend of repeating themed dungeons was all they found, they could return to the Strategy dungeon tomorrow, and he could likely stay large.

The group talked of small things as they walked, but Rocky could feel the tension of the looming fight with Jormungandr. Everyone, other than Gary, was talking jovially, but it was in their eyes. A kind of glazed look that spoke of their attention being elsewhere.

They arrived at the portal at the pyramid entrance, and Rocky didn't even hesitate before walking straight through it. He still wasn't a fan of the strange cold and stretching feeling, but he had also grown used to it.

On the other side of the portal, he found himself in a strangely familiar oasis, with a bamboo tower at its heart. "What in the world?"

"Are there really only two types of dungeons, then?" Sela asked as she too looked at the tower.

"Have you all been in a dungeon similar to this one already?" Gary looked at everyone and took in their nods.

"It's like the South Tower just repeated the layouts and strategies over a hundred plus dungeons," Victoria said while looking up at the sky. South didn't hear or chose not to respond to her obvious provocation. She shrugged, and gave the group a look that said 'it was worth a try.'

"Let's get through the first few levels and then Zippo can cook dinner as the defenders handle the waves." Rocky began jogging toward the tower. Azoth took that as a race and leaped into the sky.

<Azoth beat Rocky to red button!>

<Wait! Don't push it!>

A familiar timer flashed into the sky and Rocky gave quick orders to the others as he changed directions. Under his breath, he muttered, "I really can't take that birdbrain anywhere. I swear."

***

They only stayed for fifteen levels in this dungeon before returning to the guild dome. Smith and Derik were now cataloging people as they came through a white shimmering portal that hovered on the opposite side of the elevator column.

"Seems like a lot of people are coming through," Rocky commented as they approached the two men.

"This is nothing. Most people plan to come early tomorrow morning so they can get a full day's work in. Right now, we are just taking down their classes and if they have elemental spells. So far we have about ten with a lightning spell." Derik looked at his tablet and made a new entry as Smith asked the next person a question. Rocky was somewhat surprised the announcement didn't come with Derik's typical sass, but he assumed the man was tired.

"Alright, well, we discovered something about the dungeons that we wanted to report. So far, we have found only two types of dungeons with nearly identical mechanics. We believe that any dungeon entered will be the same and can be used to collect ankhs. However, we can't be entirely certain." At Rocky's report, Smith and Derik made a motion at some nearby military men and then traded positions with them. After a moment, they turned to Rocky and his group.

"Thanks for the report. We have one as well." Smith scratched his head and pointed to the military behind him. "I sent a squad in the corsair to try to recruit nearby survivors, and other than the ones currently under the domes here in Egypt, every survivor group has at least one Mechanolord with them."

"*Snaggletooth,*" Rocky swore. He didn't even look at Sela this time because he didn't care. This news was terrible. "Why haven't they converted them all already?"

"How would we know?" Derik returned with his usual sass. Smith placed a hand on the other man's shoulder.

"We have a theory, but only that. We think they don't have enough conversion seeds, or that humans aren't willing to become robots. Still, we didn't tell the military to approach further. Unfortunately, that's not the end of the bad news…"

"Spit it out, man!" Victoria stated.

"Another one of the Territories was filled with undead, and we think Frankie was there."

"When you choose to use the word undead instead of zombies, is there a reason?" Rocky asked as his stomach clenched.

Smith nodded. "We think it's some sort of undead that specializes in long range attacks, and not zombies."

CHAPTER FORTY-ONE

Everyone got a room assignment after they received the horrible news, and most people retired for the night. Sela stayed behind to work on logistics with Smith and Derik, and Rocky was glad she had. His mind was abuzz with inaction. He half debated about returning to the Strategy dungeon and continuing on his own for now.

Instead, he went outside and sat with Azoth as the enlarged chimera lay down in the sand.

<Azoth miss kits. Maybe we go back soon?>

Rocky blinked and asked the manticore if he wanted to go back for the night. He hadn't even considered it despite seeing numerous others come through in the other direction.

Azoth looked at him, and the sand he was laying in, before getting up and shaking himself. <Yes, Azoth want cuddle Shiva.>

Rocky could only smile as he returned to his feet and walked back in through the door. He considered if he should use the portal as well, but chose not to in the end. He wouldn't get any meaningful time with his family and while the people here didn't need him, per se, he needed to be present.

Azoth went through the portal after Rocky reminded him to come back early the next day. He also notified the nearest military personnel to convey that message to the other side, to keep Azoth honest. He figured someone might try to stop a dump-truck-sized manticore from just walking into the guild dome. However, they might not.

Rocky looked back to the exit of the Egypt guild dome and chose to head to his assigned room instead. The rooms here were all above ground, and Rocky's was vastly different than his family's had been back in the Grotto. He wouldn't say better except in a single place; the walls were a cream white, and came automatically styled complimentary to the interior side of dragon scale. The bed was just a frame, with no mattress, and empty spots existed in the kitchen area that clearly were meant for appliances. Because of the black counters, cupboards, and bed frame, the studio style apartment felt more posh than his family's rooms, but simultaneously less like a home.

He threw his sleeping bag onto the bed frame and went to clean himself off. The shower was tepid at best, and he assumed that all the people currently arriving were using loads of the hot water at the same time, as they got settled in.

Congratulations! Your Page has been bonded by a Chimera Kit. He has been confirmed as a Chimera Squire and will advance to Knight at the Journeyman ranks.

That cut his shower short, and he returned to the foot of the bed in a pair of boxers. The news of Ben becoming a Chimera Squire was excellent, and he wondered which kit had bonded him. He was sure Azoth would tell him. Even more now, his brain was telling him it wasn't ready for sleep while simultaneously feeling filled with unworkable static.

The feeling made him think of meditation, which, of course, led him full circle to enchanting. Rocky still needed to see if he could create the knots and other parts of the enchantments that allowed for stat links or bags of holding. With everything going on, he hadn't thought about it since his original discovery.

Rocky began by cleaning up his own internal channels and watched a few bubbles of what he assumed was Essence fall through his Ether Pool. It felt like watching a lava lamp when he was a kid, and some of his anxious energy faded as he watched the soothing motion. When he finally felt the last of his worry fade, he pulled a blank piece of leather from his bag of holding and then took out the enchanter's pen.

He sensed that it was still more than half full of Crystallized Ether dust, and so he pulled an Ether channel from his pool and touched it to the crystal stylus. He traced the patterns he could recall from his chest piece's Stat Link, and soon arrived at the complex knot. Using his internal channels as a guide, he moved his hand in a strange three-dimensional loop. He drew upon his sword practice as well, feathering the motion in a way that used his wrist and intention to reduce the line weight. When he finished that shape, he realized he didn't have a place to go and his pen came to a stop hovering in the air.

He took a deep breath and began moving it again, not in the shape of any rune but just allowing the channel on the leather to loop back and return to the pool. When he reached it, he cut off his flow of Ether and regarded the leather using his Ether sight. The small pool of Ether he created flowed along the path of his first enchantment before reaching the knot and increasing its flow. However, on the other side of the knot, the channel he created appeared to be empty.

His heartbeat continued steadily for about two more thumps before he saw a small bubble float down through the dwindling Ether Pool. He tilted his head and wondered. Then it happened again, and he was certain. The Ether Channel from his enchanting was able to direct the invisible energy back to the pool, but the pool couldn't contain it. After a short period of functionality, the pool of Ether ran relatively dry and the bubbles that mimicked Rocky's internal Ether Pool were no longer there, or were no longer visible.

Rocky studied the phenomenon. The pool wasn't refilling as fast as it did on enchantments that he created before this. He pulled out one of his basic pieces of enchanted gear and it was flowing and refilling normally. He then pulled his chest piece off the armor rack nearby and studied it. Both it and the basic piece of gear were maintaining full Ether Pools from ambient recharge rates. The chimera chest piece didn't have an

Ether channel after the knot, but that was the only difference he could find.

He kept studying his gear and trying new configurations, even dropping the channel after the knot. However, wherever he created the conversion knot, the pool drained. There was some sort of connection or piece of information he clearly was missing. It felt so close to what was happening here with the Prime dungeon that it almost brought back his earlier anxiety.

Well, if I was in the Grotto, I could ask LFD about the knot... Wait! What if there is something we are missing in the entry to the Prime dungeon? Why does it need to count our ankhs and show a link to all the dungeons we conquered?

He stood up and began pacing with nervous energy. Should he rush off to the Prime dungeon right now? Without Azoth, it would take a few hours of walking. Luckily, Sela came in and told him she was going to take a shower, which effectively put his mind on other things.

***

"South, why are you putting the doors that link to the dungeons we've conquered here?" Rocky asked as soon as he stepped into the preparation area of the dungeon. The space was still dark, and Rocky didn't bother pulling out his flashlight. In fact, he just closed his eyes against what he knew came next.

"That is a good question," South responded, his deep voice quiet. Rocky might have imagined the excitement he thought he heard or perhaps he didn't.

Through his eyelids, he saw the arrival of multiple blazing lights in the darkness which stopped his response. Once he thought his eyes had adjusted, he opened them, and asked, "Why is this area called the preparation area?"

"So you can prepare for Jormungandr," South said, but this time Rocky definitely heard something in the tone.

"Where can I find the options that will help me and my group prepare?" Rocky asked despite being inside the space by himself.

"Approach a door, and pay an ankh to unlock the options available," South responded.

Rocky rushed to the door which currently had a six on its front, and reached out a hand. A quick notification asked him to confirm the price of an ankh and he gladly clicked yes. The next screen made him nod, and with each line that bobbing of his head grew faster.

"Okay. Alright! So, all we need to do is get more ankhs!" Rocky shouted.

Tomb of the Deceased Options
Transport Tower Level 25 to Prime Dungeon (5 Ankhs)
Transport Defenders to Prime Dungeon (5 Ankhs)
Transport Control Kiosk to Prime Dungeon (10 Ankhs)

Not only could they transport the tower that they had been upgrading, but the elemental defenders as well. Still, it was the last option that made Rocky smile. The fact that it was more expensive was what gave him confidence in his belief. They could use the Holy Spells from the tower as well.

"Do I need to pay an ankh every time I open the options?" Rocky asked, his body buzzing with energy.

"It is unlocked in perpetuity for you and your group now," South said.

"Can you tell me anything more about what will happen when I bring the tower into the dungeon?" Rocky asked, hoping for an answer but was unsurprised when South refused to give one. "Alright, I will be back in a few days!"

Rocky quickly checked the other doors and found that they could link the thrones to the dungeon. After spending two ankhs, he hurried back out the archway to his group waiting outside. "Guys, I've figured it out. We need to get back to the dome and let everyone know, immediately."

***

"The portal to the tower dungeons closes after how many groups are inside?" Rocky asked, trying to make sense of the problem.

"Not just the tower dungeons, but all of the dungeons close after twenty-five people have entered," Sela said, as the group returned from farming the first tower dungeon they had finished. Currently they were at the eighty-first wave and Rocky looked down at his handwritten list of the tower's current levels.

Tower Level 55
64 Defenders
-32 Level 4
-32 Level 3
390 Priests
4 Filters

"Well, there are other dungeons out there that must be Tower dungeons, right?" Zippo chimed in from Azoth's back as they flew.

"They found eight others so far, but groups had to wait for the corsair to locate pyramids today. So, many people ended up farming the other dungeons," Sela called back over the sound of the wind.

"Still, forty-five groups growing their towers for an assault on the Prime dungeon on the first day, sounds like a great accomplishment," Gary said optimistically. Rocky, whose stomach had begun roiling, nodded along with the positive point. That was right!

Mindfulness…

"True, and maybe once Azoth drops you all back at the dome, he and I can go for a flight around the domes to find the others," Sela pointed out.

They arrived back at the tower a few minutes later and Sela told Azoth to wait for a moment while she went inside to check an updated map.

<You wait, Rocky. Soon all kits be bonded and big. Ben names his Medusa, cause of snake tails. Oh look, it kit Cara,> Azoth said with child-like excitement. Rocky turned in the direction Azoth was looking.

"Mom?!" Rocky asked, his voice coming out a little hoarse as his brain seemed to fry itself. "What are you doing here?"

"Well, they needed more people who could fly, and Cara has become quite agile in that department." Rocky looked around after her answer, fearing he would find his sister too. "She isn't here, Rocky. Her little one can't fly yet."

Rocky sighed deeply and looked at the panther-pegasus standing beside his mother. He had to admit that she had grown and was easily the size of a horse now. Considering that she was half horse to begin with, Rocky wondered if this was her size limit.

"Have you already been scouting?" he asked with an awkward scratch of his neck.

"All day, and we've found a total of one hundred and thirty-five dungeons. We were just waiting for your group to confirm how many are out there," Nadine responded.

"I think that's all of them actually," Rocky said while scratching his neck. "You don't plan to join dungeon teams or the large assault on Jormungandr, right?"

"I might, what's it to you?" she instantly responded. Sela's hand on Rocky's shoulder reminded him that they were in the middle of the guild dome. It also reminded him that he was out of line.

"Sorry," Rocky started. "Old habits, I guess. If you've found everything, have groups already gone out to each one?"

Derik popped out from behind Cara, and Rocky's eye twitched. It was probably this moron's idea to ask Nadine for help. "We have a group exploring each pyramid, yes. So, we're also just waiting to hear back as to how many Tower dungeons they find."

Rocky swallowed a lump in his throat and instead of responding to Derik, which he was sure would become angry as well, he turned back to his mother. "Would you like to have dinner with my group?"

"I'd love that," she responded happily before turning to Derik. "I'm assuming you don't need me anymore?"

Mindfulness… She's fine. She probably helped a lot…

"All done. Thank you again, Nadine, for volunteering. The Grotto will pay for your teleportation back when you're ready."

Rocky walked away before he could respond with something along the lines of, 'don't worry, the guild will pay for her!' He knew in his heart that was a gut reaction to Derik's offer, and him saying that the Grotto would pay for the transport. It didn't matter, and he knew it.

Zippo was wearing an amused grin on his face that Rocky chose to ignore but the kid clearly had other ideas.

"So, are you going to ask me to cook something?" Zippo asked, too innocently.

Rocky clenched his jaw and mumbled, "Could you please cook something for our group tonight?"

"What was that, Rock?"

"Zippo, would you please make a special dinner for my mother and our group?" Rocky shouted back a little too loudly, which got the entire atrium's attention. Victoria, Sela, Gary, and Zippo began laughing, which seemed to break the moment of tension that followed. The others in the room went about their business after that, a few with amused chuckles.

"Do we still have some of that alligator hippo?" Victoria asked hopefully.

"I think we do, but is it fancy enough?" Zippo asked, still chuckling.

"Zippo, anything you cook is good enough for me." Nadine came to Rocky's rescue and linked her arm through the young man's. It was Zippo's turn to blush as the group went back outside to join Azoth.

Azoth jumped up and down when they got outside. He circled Cara a few times and shouted happily into Rocky's head. <Look, she so big and strong now. Such beautiful fur, like Shiva!>

Soon, the two chimeras took flight and began playing in the air. Rocky watched nervously for a bit, until he was sure Azoth wasn't going to accidentally crash into Cara and knock her from the sky. Then he watched the aerial acrobatics with a contented smile.

My mom's here, and she's alive. She has a chimera like Azoth... My whole family does. Why was I angry again?

CHAPTER FORTY-TWO

Yeti
Level 43
Journeyman-Abominable
Health Points: 0 / 100,000
Final Boss

Rocky stared at the corpse of the boss he hadn't been expecting to appear. His group was in the Strategy dungeon, and they had all been surprised by the appearance of a boss on a stage that wasn't divisible by five.

"Wasn't that the ninety-eighth stage?" Zippo asked as he moved around to melt the yellow-tinged snow with a hovering fireball. The yeti had been tossing the yellow snow right from when it appeared on top of the dune, surprising everyone.

"Yeah, it was, and the next button says, 'Start Level 99,'" Rocky explained and motioned at the pad. Rocky glanced to the sky and found it devoid of a timer. Azoth wheeled around, and started coming back to the too-small tower top.

<Azoth! No, we can't push this red button yet!> Rocky scolded. <Plus, this third level of the tower is far too small for you at that size!>

<Rocky call Azoth fat?>

<No, we just don't have room for everyone on this shrinking tower top.> Rocky felt Azoth turn around and return to his earlier play, which was flying out one side of the dungeon space to appear on the other. Somehow, Azoth had discovered that flying into the edges of the circles at strange angles would have him exit, and on the other side, only to immediately fly out of that side again. Rocky watched for a moment as his pet seemed to pop in and out of sight from all directions. Shaking his head, Rocky turned back to his group.

"I've got a feeling that this next level is going to be the hardest one yet," Rocky said. "We only have one hundred thousand points saved now. I'll upgrade one of the level four defenders to level five."

The group just smiled. Since the beginning, the decisions had been left with Rocky, and it seemed it would stay that way. From stage eighty-one until now, he had focused on raising as many of the level three elemental defenders to level four as he could, but the approach of a new stage made him want to upgrade one to level five.

He surveyed the tower top, trying to pick a favorite elemental defender. He arrived at the asteroid defender, which was a combination of two fire choices and two earth. When it fired its miniature hand cannon, the ballistic missile grew and caught fire. By the time it landed amongst the incoming waves of mobs, it was at least forty feet in diameter and would not only flatten the mobs it hit, but also knock down the rest of the approaching monsters on that side.

If the ninety-ninth level is more minions, this is the strongest upgrade. Still, if it's a single boss...

His eyes found the lightning laser elemental defender. This defender was a combination of air, two fire, and a water choice. When it fired the miniature hand cannon, the projectile morphed into a beam of white lightning that cracked out with the sound of a thunderbolt. Wherever it struck, the monsters would be electrified, usually killing anywhere from ten to twenty minions. Yet its true strength was against boss monsters, as it carved out chunks of health points, and would stop them in their tracks for half a second.

In ninety-eight levels they had cleared so far, a boss monster had never been followed by another boss. So, he decided on the former and clicked the upgrade button for the Bes' Defender from level twenty to twenty-five, which opened the option on the holy screen for a level five elemental defender.

Elemental Defender Level 5
Comet
Meteor

There were only two options and Rocky had learned that the top option usually meant fire attribute, followed by water, earth, and then air. In this case, it only gave him a fire and an earth choice. Meteor would add a third earth component to the defender, and comet would add a third fire. As usual, the options didn't give him much insight into what the new skill would do, but Rocky felt that a meteor was the right choice. While comets were pretty things that passed by in the night sky, a meteor was what killed the dinosaurs, or at least that was what his brain was telling him.

The elemental defender placed his hand cannon into the barrel and pulled out a long-barreled musket. While it appeared to be less destructive in appearance, Rocky couldn't believe that upgrading a defender would provide less damage.

Once that was done, he was left with fifteen thousand death points and a huge store of five-hundred and ten thousand holy points. Rocky assumed the stockpile of holy points was meant to be used in the fight against Jormungandr, and thus tried to use them as sparingly as possible. However, his group did need to try each spell to have an idea of what it could do.

"The snow's all melted, Rock, and the filters are cleaning the pee out of the water," Zippo reported. Rocky nodded and shivered simultaneously.

So, everyone is considering the yellow on the snow the same way?

"Okay, then. Here we go!" Rocky pushed the button and held his breath. The blue lights from all directions made him believe he made the right choice. Level ninety-nine was going to be filled with mobs. The first creatures materialized and began rushing toward the oasis. Ten thousand monsters, but this time they weren't uniform.

Instead, Rocky could see crawling hands, lemures, skeletons, zombies, dryads, both blights, mushroom warriors, troglodytes, gorgons, and every other mob they had fought to date. He turned to the new defender as soon as the first mob hit the bottom of the dune, the current range of the defenders on the third tier of the tower. It fired its musket and Rocky waited to see an expanding musket ball. It wasn't there. In fact, the ballistic, which could have been a ball or a bullet, flew fast and struck the lead creature, a troglodyte, though the head before vanishing. The troglodyte fell and Rocky blinked—that was it?

A shadow over the corpse of the troglodyte made Rocky glance up, and what he saw made his jaw drop. A flaming ball of earth hurdled toward the sand, growing at a pace Rocky's mind was having trouble comprehending. By the time it landed, it covered over a hundred feet in diameter, and plumed sand up in a small mushroom cloud. Rocky grabbed the barrel in front of him as the tower shook but also smiled with satisfaction.

"Uhh, Rocky this side is still spawning mobs…" Sela called, and Rocky's smile fell from his face as he turned.

"What?" Rocky asked, not really wanting an answer, but responding with his gut reaction to the information. Sure enough, Sela looked in what he had been calling east, and even as the front wave of mobs died, more were forming and running down the dune. What had been ten thousand mobs doubled to twenty thousand, and then tripled to thirty. Rocky took a deep breath and then let it out loudly.

"I've got a feeling they aren't going to stop," Victoria said and pointed at the portal that appeared on the bottom tier of the tower. Rocky looked at it, too, and it seemed to click. This level was going to be a never-ending stream of monsters. He looked down at the tablet and found that the meteor defender no longer had an upgrade option. That confirmed Victoria's thought. This level was a point mining level to upgrade the defenders and tower.

A quick check of the death points total showed it jumping up by five per kill, just like previous levels that didn't have a boss.

"Uhhh, Rocky!" Zippo shouted, and Rocky jerked his head to the south. A massive blue light had replaced the huge number of smaller lights on the horizon. Suddenly, a boss dretch appeared and began charging at the tower.

"*Cumberbatch*," Rocky swore and felt his heart rate go from fast to belligerent in his chest. Of course, that was when the mobs which had projectiles began launching them. Softballs of flesh, oil, mucus, and even a few seeds shot into the sky.

It wasn't all negative. Now that the mobs had reached the midway point between the tower and the dunes, almost all the defenders were firing. Creatures began dying faster, and Rocky's death points started to climb in leaps, flipping so fast that only the number in the hundred thousand positions wasn't changing, at an almost unreadable rate.

Rocky started upgrading things as fast as he could. Starting with an elemental defender in each of the cardinal directions. After the dretch boss spawned, that direction had returned to producing mobs, so Rocky chose defenders with as much area of effect as he could.

He upgraded a comet defender, a dragon breath from phoenix path, and finally a deep freeze from a cone of cold defender. The landscape changed again in an instant.

"Rocky!" Victoria shouted, and he looked up. The corpses that littered the ground were turning into liquid and flying to the place where the dretch had just died.

"Not this again!" Rocky shouted as more and more monsters died, and the corpses that didn't have a priest nearby instantly turned to liquid. He had never added to the three hundred and ninety priests because they had been sufficient to clear ten thousand corpses before a boss was summoned. Now, it seemed that the death of a boss spawn was the cue for a fresh flesh slime.

He instantly dropped the thought of upgrading the defenders. This was caused because the defenders were killing monsters faster than the priests could work. He needed more priests. He flipped screens and began spamming the priest button while looking at the slime.

"Everyone, attack that slime from range!" Rocky shouted, notifying his group that it was time to step in.

"I don't have ranged damage spells," Gary said from the center of the tower where he was dodging projectiles.

"Healing spells will likely hurt that thing!" Sela shouted as she raised her hands and called down Moon Fire.

Rocky went from three hundred and ninety to a thousand priests, and just kept summoning. He would stop when they caught up to the death rate. The fact that blobs of flesh were still flowing to the massive flesh slime, and healing it, told him he wasn't there yet.

The tower shook as a ball of flesh the size of a meteoroid collided into its side. Rocky had the wherewithal to glance at the pool. Seeds were clogging some of the intakes to the filters and the number on its surface was falling fast.

"Zippo, those seeds!" Rocky shouted, and then flipped screens. He also hadn't purchased more than four filters. The breaks after boss fights had given the current filters more than enough time to clean the water below.

"A shambling mound just appeared, and monsters are entering the oasis," Sela shouted. Things were happening faster than Rocky could monitor. After adding four more filters he flipped to the holy spell page and hit the Taweretan Charge spell. He heard the trumpet call of the hippo-alligators but didn't look up. He would need to rely on his team to report as he acted.

He returned hurriedly to the filters and added eight more, doubling his current total again. Then flipped pages again to the priests, spamming the button as the number rose over two thousand.

"The wall and the tower are cracking!" Victoria shouted and he flipped screens again, clicking the upgrade button on the tower.

The next ten minutes became an absolute blur as his team shouted changes in the current fight, and Rocky reacted.

Priests climbed over five thousand in total, and Azoth mentally reported, <Plant thing put on armor again.>

"Close your eyes, everyone!" Rocky shouted to his group and sent mentally to Azoth, then clicked the Ra holy spell. Rocky couldn't close his eyes and instead shaded them as he flipped—

"More filters! It's at two hundred points!" Zippo shouted.

Rocky changed his page from priests to filters and doubled it again, to thirty-two. He tried to double the number again but found the limit for the filters was fifty. He crossed his fingers, hoping that was enough and returned to the priests, spamming the button again.

The sun flared and vanished, and Rocky just kept spamming more priests. "Werebear is already halfway to the oasis. Mobs amongst the trees!"

Rocky hit the second level of the Taweretan spell and a tidal wave of alligators with a hippo's girth flew from the tower and pushed all the mobs back to the start of the dune. Or at least, that was what had happened in the past—Rocky was already back on the priest page clicking the button over seventy-five hundred.

"Flesh slime down! Tower needs upgrade! Werebear started his ax whirlwind."

Rocky didn't even have time to think who called that out and upgraded the tower to level fifty-nine. He didn't remember upgrading it to level fifty-seven and eight, but he was also currently wiping nervous sweat from his eyes as he clicked the Geb's Embrace spell which, in the past, had grabbed the Werebear and stopped its spinning.

"Dung beetle and its massive ball of poop has spawned. Wait on Set's Cleaning Storm." This time he could distinguish Sela's voice. Was the situation improving?

"Pool is climbing, but still in the two hundreds," Zippo called.

"No flesh slime formed after werebear fell!"

The priests reached ninety-five hundred. Rocky rounded them up to ten thousand just to be safe. Finally, he glanced up from the screen. To his surprise, Victoria was right beside him, and she was covered in every shade of filth. As he watched, she moved and batted yellow snow out of the sky. It clearly would have hit him, and he realized that he hadn't been dodging projectiles this whole time.

Rocky swallowed a lump in his throat and looked at the dirty tank in a whole new light. She had literally been stopping all projectiles from hitting him. She glowed yellow for an instant, and Rocky transferred his admiration to Gary and Victoria. He would need to get Victoria a spa day or something after this, and make sure he got Gary something to thank him as well.

The healer had clearly been sending his spells to defenders that were low on hit points as well, because he was sweating profusely and chugged an Ether Draught as Rocky watched.

"Set's Cleaning Storm!" Sela shouted, and Rocky looked back.

That was right, they weren't out of the woods yet.

CHAPTER FORTY-THREE

Several hours after hitting the start on level ninety-nine, the group finally was able to go back to resting atop the tower. Everyone but Rocky sat down on the small fifth tier of the tower top and took a deep breath.

Rocky scanned the summary screen.

Oasis Summary
Tower Level 100
88 Level 5 Elemental Defenders
10,000 Priests
50 Filters

At this point, increasing the level of the tower cost one hundred and eighty-thousand points, which took about thirty minutes to gather, as far as Rocky could tell. The group had also been here for almost ten hours already and needed to leave to report their findings to other groups.

That, of course, brought up a problem.

"South, if we leave through the portal, is this level going to continue spawning bosses and mobs?" Rocky asked. He wasn't worried about the mobs, because with the tower's current firepower, nothing was making it into the oasis. However, the random boss spawns with their shielding abilities would destroy the tower or the pool under it as soon as no one was here to choose a holy spell.

"The level will pause as long as everyone leaves the dungeon," South answered curtly. "Does this mean you will be attempting the Prime dungeon?"

"Not yet," Rocky mumbled in response. Clearly, South was a bit eager for them to give him a show.

"Rockland." Sela pointed over her shoulder while still sitting. A vampire queen had her blood umbrella up. The umbrella covered thousands of mobs that marched around the small woman, and Rocky returned to the holy screen, selecting Babi's Bloody Martini.

The massive ephemeral baboon appeared and picked up the human-sized vampire queen before drinking the blood umbrella like it was a delicious cocktail. After Babi finished, it threw the creature down to the ground and vanished. The defenders made quick work of the mobs and the boss after that.

Rocky pointed to the stairs that now led into the center of the tower, where the portal had been moved. "Let's go before another boss spawns!"

The group groaned as they stood up, but rushed down the stairs and through the portal. Even Azoth with his crazy energy had long since landed and squeezed down the large staircase and into the portal.

***

"So, we want as many groups as we can to reach the point you and your group did?" Derik asked.

"I don't think other groups will have the firepower needed to keep up in those early stages of the ninety-ninth level," Smith pointed out.

Rocky blinked and looked around at the current state of his group. Everyone was covered in blood, oil, seed spores, and other accumulated filth. Each member also had a sheen of sweat or grease still lingering on their skin. It was only now that he realized that not everyone would be able to accomplish what they had.

He smiled broadly and nodded to all of them.

"We did good," he said, before looking back at Smith and Derik. "I think we've all earned the night off. I'll leave it up to you to spread the news and decide which groups should attempt the ninety-ninth floor.

"Let's get a shower, and then meet outside for a Zippo feast!" Rocky exclaimed.

***

"Do you have any way to recruit the people from the other factions of Cairo?" Rocky asked Maat and Adom.

The two looked at each other, before Maat raised a closed fist. "Ra's Power is mostly kids, and I think they will gladly come." Maat opened a finger on his hand.

Adom spoke next. "The Priestesses of the Sand will join. They don't like being persecuted by Amir's Sun Tribe." Maat raised another finger. They both paused for a time then Adom coughed and said, "Maybe the Magic Returns group will be willing to speak on it."

"They would need to get something out of the deal, I think," Maat responded.

"Something more than leaving the dome?" Rocky asked, and Maat made a 'maybe' gesture with his second hand not currently counting the groups.

"Honestly, the more people that we have the better," Sela interjected. "So if you can talk to even Amir's Sun Tribe, it might be worth it."

It was the day after Rocky's group had solidified the tower on the ninety-ninth stage, and they were currently letting other groups push their progress as far as they were able. Still, as it stood right now, the adventuring groups from the Grotto would be finished reaching the ninety-eighth stage in the next two days. Rocky had discussed their options with the council last night at Zippo's feast, and while the council was reaching out to the other Canadian territories, Rocky was given the task of speaking with the locals. They would only have a single opportunity to beat Jormungandr before the Mechanolords got wind of the tactic and copied it.

So they needed to go in with overwhelming force, if they could manage it.

"Would the newly arrived Golem Knights, and that child with golems as pets, be able to accompany us?" Maat asked, his voice sounding nervous. "We can speak with Anubis' Shroud and Amir's Sun Tribe, but both of those meetings could turn ugly."

Rocky looked at Sela and she shook her head slightly. Rocky got the meaning. "You can probably take the Golem Knights, and maybe even the puppet golems, but I don't think the Knights will allow you to take Adam in there if it's dangerous."

Adom and Maat looked at each other again before nodding vigorously.

Rocky and Sela moved back toward the doors to enter the dome, and as they went Sela asked, "Should one of us go with them?"

"I'm no expert on diplomacy, but I think having foreigners there may hinder the meetings. And from what we saw, a female foreigner might be even worse."

Sela nodded and they entered the dome before strolling down the hallway to the atrium in contemplation. The atrium looked abnormally full thanks to the massive bodies of Gamma, Omega, Epsilon, Tao, and Delta. Near Epsilon's feet was Adam and his group of teenagers, which Rocky thought were called Adam's Elites, but simultaneously, wasn't sure if that was a nickname given by others. So, he never used it publicly.

Rocky walked up to hear an argument between the Golem Knights and Adam. "I will enter the dungeons with my team and there is nothing that you can do to stop me."

Gamma rumbled a growl from somewhere in his chest, but Tao put a hand on his shoulder.

"Saplings must be allowed to grow," Tao whispered, but was overridden by Epsilon's cool voice.

"Liege, we cannot have you risk your life when you're this close. You've been given the red quest from Gaia, and all we, your knights, must do is defeat this creature for you!"

Liege? Well, that's a new development.

"I told you to stop calling me that!" Adam shouted back.

Rocky made a face by pulling his lips away from his teeth and turning to Sela. She was wide-eyed and looking back at him with her head pulled away, also expressing the awkwardness of the situation.

"Sooo!" Rocky loudly entered the conversation and got everyone's attention. "We actually need all of the Golem Knights outside right now."

"Did Zippo make pizza?" Omega asked in his surfer drawl.

"No, but if you accomplish the task I have for you, I will ask him," Rocky tried, and before he finished, Omega was already heading to the door while listing ingredients on his fingers.

"Mushrooms—and pepperoni—some cured monster meat—maybe some onions—could he make barbecue sauce?" His words became incoherent as he continued down the hallway. Tao and Gamma were just a step behind as they, too, left. Delta gave Rocky a shrug before he followed.

Pretty soon it was just Epsilon, Adam, his elites, Rocky, and Sela left in this portion of the now rather empty atrium.

"I will have to decline, on behalf of the Knights—"

"They are already outside ready to go. So, I think at this point you just need to decide if you are going with them, or staying where you are not wanted." Sela pointed at Adam who was glaring at Epsilon. The big leader of the Ottawa Knights looked at Sela, and then back to Adam, and then at the backs of his departing brothers.

"I'll keep Adam safe, Epsilon. Go now!" Rocky said, emphasizing the last words but in a polite way. The Knight's shoulders slumped, and he, too, turned and followed after his brothers.

"If you're—" Adam began, but Rocky held up a hand in the kids direction.

"Sela, can you go ensure that the Knights understand the task?" Rocky suggested before turning back to Adam. "Tell half of your golem puppets that they should follow Sela and her orders for the time being."

Adam tilted his head, but did begin gesturing in the empty air in front of him. Rocky assumed he was fiddling with his screens.

Once the Knights exited the doors, and Sela was halfway down the hall, Rocky finally lowered his upraised hand, which had stayed pointing at the teenager.

"If you're going to tell me that I can't—"

"I think this is a great opportunity for you and your group to break into smaller groups and go challenge some Tower dungeons, don't you?" Rocky interrupted again, his voice filled with an abundance of enthusiasm he didn't necessarily feel.

Adam's serious expression gradually gave way to a growing smile. "You mean it?"

"Well, I would wait 'til the Knights depart on their mission in Cairo, but then I don't see why not," Rocky suggested. "However, I'm sending Azoth with you, and I'm going to test you right now on the strategy. All of you!" Rocky included the rest of the group with a sweeping gesture of his arms.

***

"So, only two other groups were able to complete the ninety-ninth level to where your group is." Mary looked up from her stack of sheets. It had been about a week and Rocky's team had farmed many dungeons for more ankhs in the meantime, but had spent most of their time in the operations room receiving reports.

Unfortunately, two of the local groups hadn't received Maat and Adom for negotiations. Still, the other two groups joined Meliora and were now also farming for ankhs.

"And how many groups have completed the tower to the ninety-eighth stage?" Rocky asked. Astrid scanned pages, then ruffled through some before she looked back up.

"One-thousand and five groups have entered the Strategy dungeon. Of those groups, two hundred and twelve couldn't pass by stage five. The other eight hundred and five have since reached and completed the ninety-eighth stage." Rocky opened his mouth, but Astrid held up her hand.

"Of those eight hundred and five, only three hundred and sixty-two attempted level ninety-nine. Those that failed were forced to restart their progress from level one. Based on our estimates, they will all have returned to the ninety-eighth stage by tomorrow morning.

"So, in total, we have seven hundred and ninety-one towers ready for the attack tomorrow," Astrid finished.

"Okay, and each individual will have five ankhs on their person, while the remaining excess are transferred to the group leaders?" Rocky summarized an earlier conversation.

"Correct, we took the liberty, and have asked the two hundred and twelve groups that couldn't pass the fifth stage to transfer all excess ankhs to other groups."

"Another issue," Jorge spoke from deep in his robe. "What shall people with little to no ranged skills do?" Rocky pulled a high end laser rifle from his bag of holding.

"Everything we can!"

CHAPTER FORTY-FOUR

It turned out not everyone just carried a laser rifle with them. Probably because very few people had a dungeon bag of holding. So, a good deal of the deep hours of the night were used to send thousands of the weapons across the teleportation portal. Rocky could have gone back and put them all in his bag of holding, but he took the opportunity to sleep instead.

Sela looked as anxious as Rocky felt, and the two fell asleep playing a 'what if' game that he wished they hadn't, but simultaneously appreciated. Meliora was going to get one shot at this with their current advantage. After that, the superior ranks and firepower of the Mechanolords would figure out the strategy, and Rocky wasn't sure they could keep up after that.

Due to that foreboding feeling, Rocky found trouble falling asleep. He tossed and turned and couldn't remember how long he took to find it. He also was up before the sun was even peaking over the horizon. He and Sela didn't speak as they got into their armor and moved through the dome.

Maybe we talked enough last night?

Rocky and Sela arrived at the cooking fires as some of the first in line. The people in front of him were all council members, or cooks that were grabbing a plate before the morning rush. Rocky looked around, and once he was facing away from the fires, he was caught up by the fading starlight. Like a great deal of the Earth nowadays, the stars seemed to be close enough to grab. The destruction of the Earth's infrastructure removed light pollution, and Rocky always felt the change most strongly in the deep of the night.

No wonder ancient civilizations worshiped and took portents from the stars...

After collecting a plate of enormous eggs, monster bacon, and some sort of potato hash, Sela and he moved around the side of the dome before finding Azoth. They sat away from the manticore, not wanting to wake him up but still wanting to enjoy his company.

"Do you think we're ready?" Sela whispered before taking her first bite.

"I don't think we have a choice. Our strongest groups are already here and only the A-team, Adam's Elites, and our group were able to challenge the ninety-ninth. We can't farm for levels here in Egypt, and the longer we wait, the higher the chance Dahrix figures out the mechanics that the Tower dungeons put in place." Sela coughed a bit as she tried to chew her food and laugh simultaneously.

"I just realized that the Tower dungeons of Atlantis placed a tower strategy to defeat the Prime dungeon's boss. How conceited is that?" Rocky smiled and chuckled a few times.

"What are you two laughing about?" Victoria asked as she joined them.

"To defeat Jormungandr, the Atlantean Towers have offered us upgradable Towers." Rocky explained, and Victoria gave him a funny look. "Guess you had to be here…"

Zippo and Gary joined them about halfway through breakfast and the group seemed to make a collective agreement to talk about everything other than Jormungandr. Luckily, Gary had some good stories from just after the first wave that he seemed to pull out whenever the conversation hit a lull. It turned out that everyone had stories, and it was an easy thing to remember those moments with a certain vivacity.

The group was all lounging in the sand by the end, feeling a bit more comfortable when Smith walked over. He had a bottle of something in his hands and a stack of cuppa macht leaves as well. He motioned at Zippo, and the young teenager jumped up to help him. Everyone took a cup in silence before turning back to look at the Native American man.

"I'm not one for speeches, but I think today needs a toast," Smith began. Rocky could feel his resolve firming as he said those first words to break the silence. "Today, we're here in a foreign place, surrounded by old and new friends to take up a fight that is larger than us.

"When I took an offer from a strange man in the middle of a forest, all those months ago, I thought I would just use it to find my feet in this new world. Take a moment to gain strength before I went out on my own. I still remember the crippling fear from those first days. The thoughts I berated myself with when I sat and did nothing for weeks because that first step seemed too large." Smith's words started out comical before morphing to a morose emotional tone that drew Rocky in. Then the man surprised him with a hearty chuckle and a motion that indicated Sela.

"Then I was dragged by a beautiful *maiden* into the harsh reality of our new world, and today, I'm reminded of that same feeling. This doesn't need to be my fight, and many of our people have reminded me of that." Somehow his tone and slight chuckle told Rocky that Smith was meaning Derik and others like him. "And yet, if we chose to sit in the safety we created, to think we should just bide our time gaining strength and our feet, this world will swallow us whole.

"So, I came over here to toast the people who dragged us up. The people who demand that we take up a fight that is bigger than us, because in the doing is where we find strength. To Sela and Rocky for seeing the larger picture, when we see small borders!" Smith finished and raised his glass. The others in the group had stood up at some point, and Rocky realized that only he and Sela hadn't done so. They were all smiling down at them and holding their glasses high. Then they all drank, and Rocky found that his hand was shaking.

His cheeks were wet. He tried to smile, but the lump in his throat seemed to pull the corners of his mouth down every time he got them up. He looked to Sela and saw tears there as well. He raised his shaky hand in her direction, and somehow, she must have felt it, because she turned to him. She raised her glass to him, and they both drank.

It was orange juice, and Rocky sputtered, spilling a great deal of it because of his shaky hand and the surprise he felt in the choice of drink.

"What, did you think I would bring alcohol before a fight?" Smith laughed.

<What all coughing and tears for?> Azoth sent in a groggy mental voice as the lump behind the group began to stir.

Everyone laughed, and hugs were passed around after that. Azoth demanded to get hugs from everyone as well, still not understanding the situation. Still, between Rocky and Sela directing people, he got his hugs.

***

Rocky, Sela, Zippo, Gary, Victoria, and Azoth were the first ones to enter the Prime dungeon. Rocky held in his hand a water bottle made from carved bamboo and looked at it with skepticism. This had been what he purchased for twenty ankhs when he selected import tower, defenders, and screen. He panned his vision up from the bottle and swallowed.

Jormungandr and his immense white plastic bulk was resting his massive head atop the floating city of Atlantis. Rocky guessed that the city was two times the size of the Grotto, maybe three, and the massive monster's head hung off all four sides of it. Rocky let out his held breath slowly when the snake didn't immediately move to start attacking the six of them.

"Okay, so it doesn't attack immediately and even gives us some time to set up?" Rocky whispered. The others turned wide eyes on him for breaking the silence, and he swallowed again.

<Azoth attack now?>

<Noooo!> Rocky mentally screamed and heard a chuff from his pet, telling him that the birdbrain had been joking. It didn't seem that funny to Rocky, mostly because his heart was thumping against the prison of his rib cage after the inappropriately timed joke.

Rocky walked to the edge of the cliff and poured out the water from the carved bamboo bottle. The bottle might have been the size of a soda can and Rocky expected about three hundred and seventy-five milliliters of substance to pour from it. Instead, a torrent of water exited the bottle as it began evaporating in his hands. In an instant, Rocky was ankle deep in a pool of water, and it was still growing.

He hurriedly waded out of the pool, and saw the shape of the tower supports forming, as well as the staircases that spiraled around the huge stone legs. This staircase, while unused except on re-entry to the Strategy dungeon, had added itself at the twentieth tower upgrade. Now it looked like the stairs for a battlement of a castle during a siege. Each stone of the tower was as large, if not larger, than Azoth. The tower continued to materialize out of thin air, and Rocky craned his neck up and up.

From the ground, the tower was at least twenty meters tall by the time it finished forming, but the import item wasn't done yet. The walls that had surrounded the pool began forming on only the front side of the tower. Instead of ringing the water here, they stacked themselves in front of the tower facing Jormungandr and merged into a huge, quadruple-thick structure that seemed unbreakable, until you took in the monstrosity of a creature behind it.

Other groups had been phasing into the dungeon as Rocky's group watched their tower form and they all seemed to be watching the first tower materialize. Once it was truly finished, the group climbed to the top and noticed a difference right away. In the dungeon stages, the tower had four sides that had spaces for defenders. Now, the backside of the tower was flat stone with no walkways. Instead, the walkways that faced Jormungandr were twice as wide, and the two walkways on the sides were shortened.

Rocky nodded to himself and checked the screen on the barrel. It had no options for buying more components of the Strategy dungeon, but he could still place a list of defenders on spaces of the new configuration of the tower. Just as it seemed. All the spots that would have been on the back side of the tower facing away from Jormungandr had been moved to the front side. One other surprise awaited him, and that was a layout map of the cliff the tower was on.

"There is a limited number of spots for towers!" Rocky stated. This possibility had come up in the strategy meetings, and the other groups below were waiting to get orders, in case of that possibility.

"How many?" Sela asked, as she motioned to the radio in her hand.

"Five hundred spots," Rocky responded. Sela immediately conveyed that number, and Adam's Elites, easily distinguishable by the huge group of golems and Golem Knights that stood nearby, stepped forward to place their tower. Simultaneously, the A-team moved and placed theirs. After that, it became a free for all, somewhat controlled by Smith over the radio. Soon, the layout map below showed Rocky a full cliffside, or at least a full map of the portion of the space that they occupied.

Rocky placed his defenders on his tower, every one of them a level five elemental defender. He then turned and looked both ways down the line of towers. It was slightly strange as each tower was of differing heights, and Rocky assumed that each defender composition would also differ widely. The quadruple-thick walls were also varied, going from the siege stones in front of the three central towers, to ancient brown brick in places, then to places where Rocky could still see the palm tree wood. He looked at his group and they all were taking in the sight as well.

There had been a red button on the home screen, and Rocky sucked in a breath before returning to that tab. He motioned to Azoth. "Did you want to do the honors, buddy?"

His pet was all too happy to slap his paw down on the tiny screen.

A volley of bows, crossbows, hand-cannons, and muskets launched in unison. Skills like Lightning Laser, Meteor, Tornado Drill and so much more blasted into Jormungandr's side. The skills struck its nose, head, neck, and all the visible parts of its body before it disappeared into the water. A startled roar bellowed from the beast and Rocky felt his heart, already hammering, grow frantic. It had begun.

Before Rocky could react, something slammed into a wall to his tower's right. He managed to look over to see the tower crumbling to the ground. Jormungandr's head was rearing back up toward the city at the center of the sea. Rocky Analyzed the creature out of habit as he held his breath.

Jormungandr
Legendary-Golem Sea Serpent
Level 112
Health Points: 975,501,312 / 1,000,000,000
Active Skills: Unknown
Passive Skills: Unknown
Boss

That first wave had taken the boss down nearly two and a half percent. He felt a surge of hope as another tower crumbled under Jormungandr's blow. The hope was because another wave of attacks was already dropping the creature's health further, while simultaneously a new tower was replacing the first fallen one.

That was right, Meliora had backups!

Five percent down, and it had only been seconds since the start of battle. Meliora was even holding back. They had taken a page out of the Mechanolords playbook and were waiting to unleash their full damage. They might need to burn through a water shield, if the holy spells didn't work.

"Uhh, Rock, why is our tower getting cracks already when it hasn't been attacked?" Zippo asked as he looked down at his feet. Rocky looked to see what Zippo meant, and sure enough, there were cracks forming. A flashing light also got Rocky's attention and he looked through the murder hole down to the oasis. There was a decreasing number for the pool, and he swore.

"*Poodle tails!* The tower must exist in both places at the same time!" Despite numerous meetings they hadn't even considered this. Rocky's brain whirred as he looked at the mounting damage. "We need to get members of our group, Adam's group, and the A-team back to the Tower dungeon. They will need transport once they exit too."

"We can't just exit," Sela pointed out.

"Get me two volunteers from the other groups, now, Sela! Victoria, and Gary, mount up on Azoth," Rocky ordered and heard another tower crumble. Sela jumped on the radio and conveyed Rocky's first order as well. "Azoth, I need you to go pick up volunteers from the other two towers too."

<Azoth no attack snake?> Azoth asked in a voice Rocky recognized as his pet's belligerent bloodlust. He wouldn't get through to Azoth now, and it was everything his pet could do not to launch himself at the massive snake.

"Okay, buddy, I'll make you a deal. After you pick up everyone, you can attack the snake. *But* if you die and end up in the black room, you need to exit and get all those people to the dungeons they want. Deal?" Rocky shouted over the noise of

One beam fell from the sky like it was sent from a satellite in orbit in a James Bond film and then several others joined in. The concentrated sunfire swept down the scales, igniting five before vanishing. Even with five hundred towers all using the skill, many scales remained untouched. Jormungandr was just massive. Still, its health that had been stuck at eighty percent began falling again.

The A-team's tower took another blow, and Rocky looked over at the members atop it. They were firing laser rifles and Mr. Pips was even infusing skills into most shots. Rocky pulled Dark Tidings and released nine stacks of Dark Blade, finding his Ether Pool refilled from his last attack. He wished he had a more consistent ranged attack that he could throw, but he switched back to the laser rifle and continued the assault. By the time the Dark Blades hit Jormungandr, they were extremely widespread, and they reciprocated over green scales, and the blackened and burned ones as well. The blades that found the green armor didn't penetrate, but the others broke away black carbon and sunk into the plastic flesh beneath, adding damage.

A boom shook his eardrums simultaneously with the tower rumbling under his feet. Their wall had been struck again. Rocky looked at the pool and found it at two-hundred points. This was now a race between Jormungandr and the monsters in the Tower dungeon for who would destroy the tower first.

The next strikes of the massive snake dropped more of Meliora's towers, and Rocky heard Sela mumble, "We've only got fifty backups left."

Adam's tower took, and withstood its first strike. Rocky looked that way and found the Knights atop the tower top, making it look crowded. Almost as if Adam had been waiting on Rocky, two golem puppets launched off the top of the tower. Rocky expected them to plummet like the stone they were made of, but a massive black tar paraglider snapped open as it caught the wind.

The sight was amusing enough to make Rocky forget about the pressure on his chest. At least until the paragliding golem was struck from the sky in an attack on a tower.

Rocky kept firing, but clicked Ra's Burning Sunboat, a fifth level skill costing one hundred thousand holy points, hoping it would help take out more of the scales and increase damage on the beast. At this rate, they were going to run out of towers before they beat the boss.

A flaming boat easily the size of Atlantis appeared in the air and sped straight at Jormungandr. When it hit, it turned into a wash of light and flames that ate all the scales on the snake's head, neck and partially down the creature's body. Rocky saw the numbers for the boss's health begin falling faster, and he smiled.

"Everyone save your holy points!" Sela shouted and glared at Rocky. "Only three towers have the ability to get more!"

"Our pool has fifty points remaining. Saving Holy—" The number of holy points dropped without Rocky touching it. Then the wall in front of their tower suddenly reformed, as well as all the cracks under their feet.

Victoria and Gary made it!

Adam's tower wall and tower also reformed, and Rocky turned to the A-team on his right. It took another blow from Jormungandr. It, too, was now one strike away from disaster. He kept firing his rifle without looking and held his breath.

"Rockland, the pool is still falling!" Sela shouted and he remembered to breathe as he looked down the murderhole.

25 / 1,000

He stood back up and watched Jormungandr dive into the water as he Analyzed it.

Jormungandr
Legendary-Golem Sea Serpent
Level 112
Health Points: 699,492,773 / 1,000,000,000
Active Skills: Unknown
Passive Skills: Unknown
Boss

Rocky recalled they had used Geb's Thrust when a beetle boss did this in the tower, but this was water and not sand. He scanned down and found Nephthys Floating Freeze.

"Sela, what was Nephthys known for again?" he asked hurriedly.

"Water magic!"

"Nephthys Floating Freeze!" Rocky called as he pushed the second level spell. The holy points were still falling, and he knew that Victoria was fighting off the bosses that were attacking the pool on the far side. At first, Rocky thought nothing happened, but the water of the Mediterranean sea began to grow more violent. Either Jormungandr was doing something or all of the tower's spells were. Rocky caught a glimpse of a white scale and analyzed it.

The boss's health was over seventy three percent now. It was healing!

He looked down through the murderhole again, his lungs shuddering in their breathing.

33 / 1,000

Victoria and Gary did it. The crumbling sound of a tower surprised Rocky, and he flung his head in the direction of the noise. The A-team's tower fell in on itself, as if some demolition team placed charges on key structural supports.

"Rock, Jormungandr is being pushed out of the water now!" Zippo notified him, and he looked away from the tragedy beside him. Massive blocks of ice were forcing the snake to the surface, and as soon as he was visible again, the defenders on the towers began striking. His health had climbed to seventy-eight percent, and they now had to redo what they had already done.

The Mechanolords began attacking as well, and blue light indicated their first tower materializing on their cliffside. To Rocky's surprise, a massive tower with layered perches, constructed of huge trees, and sporting leather walls and a leather roof materialized. The wall in front of it was made of driven logs that looked to be of a similar diameter to their siege stone ones.

No other tower immediately appeared, and Rocky looked to Sela.

"I think the Mechanolords have to be killed first before they can go back out."

The boss's health fell back below seventy percent, and it didn't dive back into the water. A quick glance told the story why. The surface of the water was covered in huge floating islands of ice, almost icebergs.

"We are out of backup towers," Sela stated as the health of the boss neared sixty percent. Rocky glanced over to the Mechanolords' shore and found their tower total climbing. He formed Dark Tidings again and unleashed his fourth nine-stacked Dark Blade. At this point, they were fully committed.

At sixty percent health, blood from the cliffs, water, tower defenders, and fallen Meliora members formed a shield between Jormungandr and the towers in both directions.

Rocky didn't even need to tell Sela the skill as he used Babi's Bloody Martini. Even as hundreds of ghostly baboons appeared on Jormungandr, something else changed and a debuff flashed to the top of Rocky's view.

Jormungandr's Primordial Roar
In thirty seconds, Jormungandr will release its rage
and call forth the Shock of Ragnarok.
The Shock of Ragnarok will stun all who hear it for five
minutes.

"We never faced anything like that in the tower?!"
Rocky exclaimed, complaining to everyone on the tower top,
and the Atlantean dungeons watching. He motioned Sela over
and they both began scrolling down the list of holy spells.

"Wait—Maybe we did?" Zippo muttered.

"What do you mean?" Rocky shouted and turned on the
teenager, eyes wide.

"Well, I was thinking of that owl hybrid monster that we
couldn't be in the same room with," Zippo mentioned, and
Rocky licked his lips. Was that the answer?

He looked at the screen and saw an arrow at the end of
the tabs. He clicked it and found images of golden doors along
with an ankh total displayed. Luckily he had paid to open each of
the options while in the preparation zone.

"That's it! We need to get the Throne of Silence from
the Temple of Ramses, or something similar," Rocky reported to
Sela and began tapping each door. Most dungeons had an effect
like this but not all of them. There were ten seconds remaining
when he happened across the Temple of Ramses I, which had
been almost an exact copy of the first one they entered. He paid
the single ankh and then spent another ten ankhs to import the
Throne of Silence.

All the sounds of battle vanished when the throne ported
itself atop a raised dais at the center of the fifth tower level. The
debuff continued to count down and Rocky looked around
hoping people were finding the right option on other towers.
Adam's group had an urn on a dais, so he knew that tower was

good, but the new tower on the right didn't seem to have one and they were motioning at each other, possibly shouting.

The countdown reached zero and Jormungandr raised his head skyward. Rocky thought he could feel waves of something in the air, and as he continued firing his rifle, he watched Mechanolords fall out of the sky like stunned flies. A part of him was happy to see them fall, but another part knew that their damage had been helping bring Jormungandr's health down. In addition to the falling flyers, all towers on the Mechanolords' side stopped attacking.

Rocky scanned down their own line and found at least sixty of Meliora's towers had stopped attacking as well. Just as Jormungandr lowered his head, Rocky heard breaking glass, which shouldn't have been possible, and he turned to the throne. It was heavily cracked and getting worse. In a blink of his eyes, it shattered and the sound of defenders' skills going off returned.

He launched another Dark Blade as damage from those who managed to avoid the stun resumed. To Rocky's surprise, the towers on the Mechanolords' side of the cliff began appearing far faster than before and he realized that all of those who fell from the sky must have died and re-entered.

Damage increased as the Mechanolords' defenders also joined the fray. From this distance, the defenders of the huge tree towers looked like archers from the Hun dynasty. Yet even with his enhanced senses, he couldn't see them too clearly. Something else came out on the side of the Mechanolords, and that was numerous skeletal mages and zombie spitters. Rocky chose the names after seeing the way they attacked. The skeletal mages fired numerous types of elemental bolts that, when compared to Zippo's in size, looked like ice cubes to the icebergs below.

"It is about to cross fifty percent!" Sela shouted, and Rocky flipped back to the holy spell options. Jormungandr shimmered as if moving faster than Rocky could see. Then the snake split into two, then four, then eight, and before long, over a hundred smaller versions of itself. Damage continued to pile on, but all of the snakes raised their heads and started spewing a green fog.

"Osiris' Revival!" Sela reminded Rocky as she shouted into the radio. He clicked the spell and a massive magical force began compressing around all the bodies of the snakes. The magic did nothing about the green fog, and Rocky flipped back to the door that represented the Temple of Ramses.

"I'm taking the Throne of Disease and its Poison Immunity," Rocky called to Sela and she relayed that through the radio as well. This time the throne was slightly different than the one the group first encountered, where the one in Ramses the Second temple silenced all skills and spells, this throne only removed diseases. Rocky was gambling slightly by not taking the more powerful option, but if he did then the damage of the defenders would stop.

The squeezing magical cylinder began constricting the snakes enough that they flashed out of sight for a moment before becoming a larger body. Soon all of the bodies would join together again.

This time Rocky could hear the responses over the radio.

"We never were in a dungeon with that—We're out of ankhs unless we use our personal ones—Our group has skills for poison immunity…" They kept coming and Sela tried her best to answer people where she could, but soon it was too late and the fog fell over the towers in all directions.

CHAPTER FORTY-SIX

"We are under three hundred towers remaining and forty of those towers have no defenders because of the poison," Sela reported. "But all the stuns have worn off!" Sela added a piece of good news at Rocky's frown.

He assessed the situation. Jormungandr's health was closing in on the twenty percent mark, and the Mechanolords were still raising new towers. As much as he hated to admit it, together they could do this.

"After this skill, get the fallen to come back and get in other people's towers. Grab the strongest range damage dealers in ours and Adam's. It's time to zerg," Rocky ordered. The other towers still fell with a single strike from Jormungandr, but the numerous flying robots and undead had also become targets. So, their side was holding up for now.

Jormungandr
Legendary-Golem Sea Serpent
Level 112
Health Points: 209,133,007 / 1,000,000,000
Active Skills: Unknown
Passive Skills: Unknown
Boss

Water flowed over the snake from the sea below. Rocky hovered his hand over the Storm Strike skill but suddenly the water began to crystallize as it turned to ice. The icebergs in the Mediterranean had long since melted, but this time the entire surface, and the snake, became a sheet of hardening clear glass.

Rocky looked down. This was a new one and he didn't know what to choose.

"Rock!" Zippo shouted and he looked back up. Skills of the defenders were reflecting back and so was a fireball from Zippo.

Rocky flipped to the home screen first and removed all the defenders before pointing at the incoming barrage. "Can you shield us from that?"

Zippo shook his head and pointed behind the skills to an open maw. The jaws of Jormungandr were spread wide and in its throat a white light was growing. Rocky flipped to the ankh screen and purchased the spell Silencing Throne. It would hinder the damage of the defenders when he returned them, but he couldn't think of another option. He also thought this would stop the reflected skills.

It flashed into existence on the dais, and Rocky sucked in air as he prepared for impact. Sela communicated Rocky's Hail Mary over the radio, and then ducked into the staircase she was near, pulling Zippo in as well. The reflected skills vanished when they drew within forty feet of the wall and Rocky breathed out finally. That was one problem, now for the iced-glass skin.

Sela exited the staircase and joined Rocky. She pointed to Isis' Betrayal on the fifth tier of magic. It cost eighty thousand, which was half of their remaining points. Rocky looked back and tilted his head before shrugging and going with it. There was no point confirming the choice, as they hadn't seen this skill before. They knew what Isis' betrayal spells usually did, and if Sela thought it would work, he would try it.

The cliffside was whited out as Jormungandr unleashed his breath skill, and the entire area that Meliora occupied was washed in an energy that had a physical substance. Towers that didn't have the silencing throne up were blown away. Those with the spell silence items had an effect occur in the thin air forty feet from their walls. Like water hitting a bulwark, the energy broke and flowed out around the walls and towers.

Strangely, the light didn't return to normal but instead became a rainbow of colors as seen through stained glass. Rocky followed the shimmering pattern and found a beautiful woman with wings falling from the sky, as Jormungandr prepared its breath attack on the Mechanolords. The lady landed on the top of Jormungandr's head, and where she touched, a sickly yellowing-green color spread. Rocky watched in horror-filled fascination as Jormungandr didn't react, and the woman Rocky assumed was Isis flew away again.

The boss unleashed its breath on the Mechanolords and decimated almost everything that stood there. Only five towers remained, and Rocky blinked away the spots, trying to make out anything else. There wasn't anything, and he felt his heartbeat stutter. If Isis didn't break that reflection shield soon, they were going to lose.

The silencing throne shattered atop the dais, and the yellowing-green color reached the ice-covered water below. That was when Jormungandr finally reacted. Instead of returning to his attacks, he began to thrash around, almost spasming. The ice on his body cracked against the ice on the water, and its health dropped to nineteen percent.

Meliora's fallen began arriving back inside the dungeon and Rocky, hoping the cracks meant the spell reflect wouldn't work anymore, replaced his Bes' Defenders to their previous positions. Amber, Mr. Pips, Smith, Derik, Jessica, from British Columbia, and many others began climbing the steps to Rocky's tower. He tuned it out, and kept watching the boss thrash and break both its armor and the sea's ice-covered surface.

A lightning bolt skill struck, from one of his defenders, and it didn't reflect.

"Replace your defenders!" Rocky shouted with excitement and then realized Sela would need to repeat it over the radio. The boss's health dropped to eighteen percent and

Rocky jumped up and down. Now he was certain that it had some type of poison effect from Isis helping them damage it.

The zerg began, and projectiles, spells, skills, and laser bolts began flying from the cliffside. Rocky added a Dark Blade and kept watching Jormungandr's health plummet.

At this rate, they would be at the ten percent mark soon.

At eleven percent, the rest of the ice shattered and the spasms finished. Jormungandr returned to his usual white color and Rocky clenched his jaw. He had a hundred thousand holy points left and hoped that would be enough. Rocky's perspective changed and he raised an eyebrow. Had they just gotten higher?

He looked down and noticed that the tower now had six tiers. Victoria must have upgraded the tower past one hundred and twenty-five levels. Eight more defenders became available, and Rocky shuffled his existing elemental defenders to place the newest level one and climbing defenders down low and keep the highest-level defenders up top.

Ten percent.

Balls of light appeared all over the boss's scales and Rocky recognized the final skill as something he had seen already. It had been a boss called the powerful hag in the Strategy dungeon. She had created a never-ending barrage of magic and Rocky flipped to Nut's tier one spell on the holy list. Nut's Protective Sky had the same name across all five tiers, but each spell was just longer in duration. Tier five lasted one minute, and each tier below that lasted ten seconds less.

"We need to coordinate Nut's Protective Sky and keep a shield up until the boss drops!" Rocky shouted. Sela nodded, and in the communication said they would go first.

"Rocky, what's that?" Derik asked from down below and pointed at the sea. At first, Rocky didn't see what he meant. Then the rock at the edge with green veins vanished under the surface and he realized that the water level was climbing.

"What do you think?" Rocky turned to Zippo, who got on the radio and conveyed the same question to Adam. Adam was hands down the most game-savvy individual they all knew, and so they waited as they continued to attack Jormungandr and prepare for the first ball of magic to fly.

"Enrage timer?" Adam said over the radio, and Rocky swore. Of course, Jormungandr's whole body would be at play if the water kept rising.

"Everyone consume Ether potions!" Rocky shouted. He realized he would have made the same order regardless of the rising water, but the timer did add urgency. Rocky popped his first Ether Draught and unleashed Dark Blade. The first ball of magic took off from Jormungandr and Rocky also clicked the first tier of Protective Sky. "Twenty-seconds."

Jormungandr crashed his head into the protective shield and Rocky felt the air itself begin to crack like a window hit with a hammer. "Never mind the timer. Next!"

Six percent.

Mechanolord towers began popping into existence again, but Rocky ignored them. At this point, any increased damage was helpful, right?

Sky shield after sky shield was shattered, and damage kept mounting. Rocky clicked his thirty second tier two version. At this point, he didn't care if skills overlapped. Jormungandr was breaking shields far faster than they lasted anyway.

Three percent.

Rocky consumed his eighth Ether Draught in as many seconds and managed to fire off his third Dark Blade. His heart started to pound with hope. They were doing—

One percent. Rocky's Dark Blade collided with the interior of their sky shield and he blinked.

What?

All the skills of Meliora, its summoned defenders, and projectiles hit a shield in front of them. Instead of the light blue color that he knew was Nut's spell, the spell that blocked their attacks was shaped and colored like a mountain. Rocky Analyzed it.

Adaghan's Stand
Turkish Holy Spell

Rocky looked at the Mechanolords with wide eyes as Jormungandr's health dropped to zero.

"Noooo!"

CHAPTER FORTY-SEVEN

Rocky fell to his knees, and his hands hit the stone floor a moment after. Somehow, in the insanity of the battle, he had labeled the Mechanolords and Frankie's undead as helpful. Sure, he knew that the temporary ceasefire was only because of the Prime dungeon mechanics, but he never would have thought that they would have a method to stop Meliora's damage and take the final killing blow.

His whole body ached, and he could still taste the souring Ether Draughts' exotic flavors on his tongue. He wanted to try to be positive, to be mindful, but he felt it unraveling. He sucked in a deep breath and prepared a frustrated incoherent shout.

A wave of pleasure washed over him, and for a moment he thought Sela had used her Rejuvenation spell, but when he clamped his mouth shut to stop his scream and looked up, she was also collapsed to the ground. Yet instead of the anguished look he expected, she wore a look of excitement. That was when he recognized the feeling more clearly. The slight stretching pain as muscles and organs in his body changed. He had leveled and not just once.

A screen popped up in the corner of his interface, and he maximized it to fill his teary-eyed vision.

Congratulations!
You have completed "The Trial of Atlantis" in 8 hours,
10 minutes, and 16 seconds.
Calculating rewards...
Five distinct groups found...
Dahrix's Minions
Frankie's Corruption
BattleNet Robotics
Meliora

Unassigned

Damage and bonuses assigned...

Dahrix's Minions – 15% Damage + Final Kill Bonus = 40%

Frankie's Corruption – 5%

BattleNet Robotics Guild – 12%

Meliora Guild – 73%

Unassigned – 1%

Rewards calculated...

Dahrix's Minions – 400 million Etherience + Leader awarded with 'Dirty Kill Stealer' title.

Frankie's Corruption – 50 million Etherience + Title of 'The Strongest Solo Necromancer.'

BattleNet Robotics – 120 million Etherience.

Meliora – 730 million Etherience + Leader awarded with 'Champion of Humanity' Title + Permanent Atlantean Council Seat + Dungeon Rewards

Unassigned – 10 million Etherience

–

Atlantean Territory Quest

Territory Quest

Prove Your Worth

Meliora Leader

The legendary Pentaclimbs designed a test for humanity and anyone else who wished to take control of the city of Atlantis. This test required ingenuity, power, teamwork, and perseverance. The Godly Prime Tower has awarded the preliminary rewards for defeating the image of his champion. More rewards from the Godly Cardinal Towers will follow.

Rewards:

Dungeon Rewards

730 million Etherience (+80,300 Essence Conversion Skill) (+182,500,000 Knight's Quest)

7300 Crystallized Ether
One choice of Atlantean Perk
Permanent Council Seat for Meliora

—

Rocky blinked at the screen and saw Sela looking at her own screen. Since he could see her screens, he could tell hers wasn't in the same overall design as his.

"Sela, come read this!" he exclaimed, staring at her. The pain and hurt vanished from Rocky, making it clear to him it was in his mind after the illusion of defeat more than it was an actual physical ailment. He easily jumped back to his feet, and found his body to be light, and overflowing with excited energy.

He bounced from foot to foot as Sela rushed over.

"This is—oh my God! Rockland, this means…" She faded off at his excited nodding. She reached out and selected the Atlantean Perk.

The screen changed.

Choose one of the three following Atlantean Perks
Jormungandr's Planetary Defense
Jormungandr's body will be converted to numerous defenses both in space and on the planet. These defenses will be in the control of Meliora and can help defend against any enemy they deem.

—

Jormungandr's Atlantean Repair
Jormungandr's body will be converted to Ether and materials to help repair the city of Atlantis and all of its functions.

—

Jormungandr's Planetary Ring

**Jormungandr's body will create a ring around the
planet that will be habitable, upgradeable, and will
block any unapproved transmissions, including shops.
<Current Selection>
Confirm selection?
<Yes> | No**

Sela's eyebrows climbed higher with each option. Rocky read the options as well. Once finished, he looked between Sela and the list waiting for her to make the decision.

"Would Atlantis fully restored be able to provide a fleet? No—the fleet was probably used in evacuations, right?" she mumbled, and Rocky didn't bother answering her. Her eyes had taken on a distant look that he knew meant she was deep in internal thought.

<Azoth thought Rocky kill garbage snake?> his pet asked.

Rocky blinked and looked at the corpse of Jormungandr in front of him. It was floating on the water. <What do you mean, buddy, it's floating right there?>

<No, snake thing moving around, rest head on white stones of flying rock.>

<Are you outside of the dungeon still?>

<Azoth at archway, all people out here say that smelly snake almost die. Some say ugly thing did die, but now fight over, the floating snake disappear—snake return to rest on flying rock.>

<Okay, hang on, buddy,> Rocky sent mentally and then switched to ask Sela, "Azoth is saying Jormungandr is still alive from his point of view. What's going on?"

Sela stopped mumbling to herself. She had moved the selected option on his screen approximately twenty times in his brief conversation with Azoth. She blinked at him, and then looked at the corpse floating on the water. "Don't be silly. Help me pick."

Rocky pointed to the Planetary Ring option. "That was my first choice when I saw them."

"Why?" Sela asked and squinted at the screen.

"It's the only option that says it's upgradeable, and it may even solve two of our largest problems." Rocky shrugged and motioned at the Mechanolords cliffside. Every so often a missile or laser blast fizzled in front of Rocky's group, and he knew that they were testing the Prime dungeon's anti-killing measures.

"I can definitely see Dahrix losing control of his minions, but you think Apep, too?" Sela asked, and then pointed to Atlantean Repair. "This option may include those as well, though."

"Two thoughts on that," Rocky countered. "If the city of Atlantis could stop Apep, why did you still know about it in your previous life, and secondly, why would you pick a possibility over a sure thing?"

"You do not understand how amazing the city of Atlantis was."

"No, you're right. I don't, and that's why I was leaving the decision up to you. Still, can we not repair the city slowly over time?"

Sela growled and returned her attention to the screen. She didn't change the selected option from the Planetary Ring as the moment stretched. As she continued to deliberate, Rocky saw Derik and Smith enter the top tower tier from the staircase. He turned to them, but was interrupted by Sela hurriedly confirming the Planetary Ring selection. He turned back with a raised eyebrow. She shrugged.

"I did not want the council to get involved," she whispered.

Rocky chuckled and nodded.

The screen morphed again, though, and Rocky held up a hand to the two men, wanting to read the new message first.

Dungeon Rewards
Jormungandr's Golem Heart
Ten Bottles of Gaia's Essence
Jormungandr's Scaled Armor
Jormungandr's Fangs
Earring of the World Serpent

Rocky clicked into each of the options and found that three of the five rewards were crafting materials. The three were the heart, essence, and fangs, but the armor was actually a full set containing boots, pants, belt, chest piece, bracers, and a helmet. Unfortunately, the armor enchantments were locked and a quick scan in his Ether vision told him he didn't recognize a single rune from his enchanting. The same went for the earring, and so Rocky just placed all of the equipment in his bag, making special note of the golem heart.

Adam can use this to recover the Grotto's lost citizens.

The screen changed again and Rocky blinked at it.

Timer to Dungeon Closure Notice
In thirty minutes, this mirrored dimension created by the Godly Prime dungeon will close. All dungeon constructs will begin dissolving shortly. Please exit before the timer elapses.
Time remaining: 29 minutes, 55 seconds.

Rocky was quite distracted when the corpse of Jormungandr vanished from the water's surface and seemed to suddenly appear again in the position Azoth had so elegantly described. Smith and Derik both made surprised gasps.

"Paper cuts and vinegar!"

"Drop bears!"

Both clearly attempted to swear but were filtered by the system. Sela might have been too distracted to report them, however, because she spun around and stared. "Do we have to kill it again?"

Jormungandr
Legendary-Golem Sea Serpent
Level 112
Health Points: Unknown
Active Skills: Unknown
Passive Skills: Unknown
Boss
Converting

Rocky saw the last line of his Analyze and took a closer look at the beast. Tiny white balls of light were wisping off its body, like smoke. The light was being converted from the plastic, and once formed, the ball seemed to blink away, leaving a small trailing line that Rocky thought moved upward. "No, I think it's guarding Atlantis until it's finished converting its body to the Planetary Ring…"

"Do you think we should try to enter Atlantis?" Sela asked without turning back. Rocky did turn back to look at Derik and Smith. He had no clue, maybe they would have a suggestion. They both gave him helpless shrugs.

"I have no idea—"

World Announcement!
Meliora has conquered the World Serpent and been granted access to Atlantis. Their contribution has been awarded with a permanent seat on the Atlantean Council and they will now be pivotal in shaping the direction of Gaia's sapient races.

Meliora will also have exclusive access to the city until Jormungandr finishes converting.

—

World Announcement!
Rockland Barkclay has been granted the title of Humanity's Champion.
All savior quests will now award double Etherience.
Planetary fame rank increased from Baron to Baron II.
Other bastions of humanity may call out to you for aid.

CHAPTER FORTY-EIGHT

Congratulations! You have reached levels 34, 35, 36 and 37.
4 stat points and 4 skill points awarded.
547,276,243 Etherience remaining until level 38.

–

Rockland Barkclay Level 37
Class: Journeyman-Dark Chimera Knight
Level 9 Strategist
Class Skills: Dark Blade, Dark Mend, Soul Blade, Dark Cloak, Shadow Clone, Knight's Resolve, Knight's Quest, Poison Pool, Chimera Bones, Chimera Skin
Health Points = 820 / 820
Dark Ether Pool = 500 / 500
You have 14 stat points and 7 skill points to distribute.
Stamina – 66 (Strength of Body +10) (+4 Stat V)
Strength – 69 (Strength of Arms +20) (+4 Stat V)
Agility – 74 (+4 Stat V)
Dexterity – 69 (+4 Stat V)
Intelligence – 50 (+4 Stat V)
Wisdom – 66 (+4 Stat V)
Charisma – 68 (+4 Stat V)
Luck – 22
Weak Skills
Non-Class Combat Skills: Essence Conversion – 11 (+2), Ether Cleanse – 21
Common Skills: Barter – 8, Fall – 18
Profession Skills: Actor – 5, Cook – 22, Grooming – 21 (+2), Herbalist – 24, Miner – 1, Teacher – 22 (+2), Trader – 5
Moderate Skills

Non-Class Combat Skills: Combatant – 11, Ether Channels – 39 (+5), Ether Manipulation – 39 (+4), Stealth – 51, Swordsmanship – 45 (+1)

Common Skills: Camouflage – 7, Endurance – 19, Perception – 49 (+1), Sneak – 49, Tracker – 39, Trance Meditation – 36 (+3)

Profession Skills: Butcher – 42 (+1), Enchanting – 15, Skinner – 41

Strong Skills

Non-Class Combat Skills:

Common Skills: Analyze – 25 (+3)

Profession Skills:

—

Tier 4

Chimera Blood

Increases all stat points by fifty percent for one hour once every day.

5/5

Skill gained "<u>Chimera Blood.</u>"

—

Unknown Tier

Chimera Transformation

(Requires Chimera Blood, Skin, and Senses)

This skill will grant the Knight all the statistics of their Chimera Familiar and then double the total combined statistics for five minutes. Each transformation is unique to the Knight and not all Knights will survive the outcome.

Automatically granted once the three subskills are completed.

Rocky read over his two new skills, and his mood kept oscillating. He couldn't have even pinpointed his exact emotions. Every time he looked at the extremely powerful Transformation skill his stomach clenched, and his heart rate increased. He tried to look away from the minimized skill and focus on their current task, but walking through the ruins of Atlantis, following Sela, wasn't as riveting as Indiana Jones would have made it.

From afar, the ruins of the city had a shape to it, almost an illusion of fullness. The mounds of white stone and building supports created dense areas where buildings once stood. From up close, it was entirely different. The roads were only distinguishable because they had less rubble, and each 'building' was just a varying-sized pile of white crumbled marble.

The first few collapsed buildings, the group poked through relatively thoroughly, even asking the Golem Knights and Adam's golems to shift fallen marble around to get deeper. After eight empty buildings with nothing but coral, seaweed, and some rotting sea creatures, Sela changed tactics.

"We need to find the central council complex. It surrounded the Godly Tower, and it had the council chambers as well as all of the highly guarded controls," Sela mumbled for what felt like the ninth time and pointed to an area right beside them. Rocky blinked and looked at what might have been a collapsed building, wall, or statue. The only distinguishing feature of this pile of rubble was that the support beams that stood upright were tall, looking like the bones of a high-rise under construction from the world before Ether.

He guessed that the pile of marble was also larger than any other they had seen so far. He sighed. Early on, her pronouncement had been exciting. It didn't feel that way anymore.

It had been about four hours since the end of the fight with the World Serpent, and Rocky swore that Sela was still moving out of pure stubbornness. Part of Rocky's distraction from his new skill was certainly curiosity, but he wasn't above admitting that another part was because of sheer exhaustion. By this point, even the inexhaustible Golem Knights had begged off.

"Sela, maybe it's time to call it a night. It's just me, you, and Zippo left, and I don't think we are going to find it any faster in the darkness," Rocky said for the fifth time.

Zippo started and looked around himself, and Rocky blinked at the young man. Had he been asleep on his feet? Zippo blinked some more and raised his conjured red Fireball a little higher into the air, as if proving that he had been awake and paying attention.

"It should be right here!" Sela pointed right at the unremarkable ruined marble again.

"I'm not saying it isn't, Sela, but even Azoth fell asleep somewhere, about eight blocks back. If we don't at least take the Elixirs of Shortened Sleep and rest for an hour, we're likely to fall asleep standing." Rocky motioned at Zippo and they both looked at him. His chin was on his sternum and his breathing had become more rhythmic. Suddenly his head shot back up and he looked around, not making eye contact with anyone, and not seeming to see the surroundings either. His head slowly fell onto his chest again.

Sela's stubbornness died with a chuckle. "Okay, I can see it is two against one."

"Actually, it's you three against my army," a terrible voice that Rocky knew, but never wanted to hear, called from nearby. Rocky looked behind them to find Frankie by himself and glaring at him. Zippo woke up under the threat that Frankie represented, and it was almost comical to watch the kid come to the same conclusion Rocky had. Frankie had said an army, but he was by himself.

That was when the zombies, skeletal mages, and spitters not only appeared behind him but also climbed over the fallen marble piles of the collapsed buildings all around them. Rocky groaned when the sounds of mechanical booster engines also joined the undead groans. Sure enough, outlines of robotic men backlit by their own engines began filling the starry night sky.

Wait, stars? Hadn't the ruins been eclipsed by the giant head of Jormungandr?

Part of the reason Sela had been so adamant about rushing the exploration of Atlantis was that only the members of Meliora were allowed to enter the city until Jormungandr finished converting to the Planetary Ring. A few pinpricks of light that Rocky had mistaken as stars flew into the sky and he felt his weariness lift for just a moment. With night fallen, the shadow that the World Serpent cast became less noticeable. It was finished converting to the shield, and they were out here all alone.

"We need backup in the ruins immediately!" Sela shouted into her radio, and Rocky pulled out his sword, charging it with five stacks of Dark Blade. This wasn't good.

<Azoth, we are going to need you to get us out of here!> Rocky screamed mentally but didn't feel his pet's reaction. He felt the connection, but it was distant, and Rocky somehow knew that meant Azoth was asleep. He kept up a constant mental scream, hoping it might break through as Frankie began to laugh.

"Did Baron Rocky believe that everything would just go his way? Did you think a fancy title would mean that your enemies gave up?" Frankie crowed.

"Just kill him and be done with it, fool!" Dahrix's voice came from somewhere up above, obviously conveyed through one of his puppets.

The Planetary Ring must be close to completion if Jormungandr isn't here to defend Atlantis anymore… If we hold out, will the Mechanolords regain control?

Rocky's thought was followed by the sound of thousands of engines igniting. Rocky grabbed Sela, and then Zippo's robe, then dove into a caverned space under massive marble slabs. That noise had been the ignition on thousands of missiles. He could recall it vividly from their battle with Jormungandr.

"Put your shield over us," Rocky yelled, hoping Zippo would be fast enough. Explosions began shaking the ground and Rocky interposed his back between the opening he dove through and the two behind him. With his chimera skills, he was the most likely to survive shrapnel.

The first few pieces of stone felt like baseballs hitting his back as they bounced off his armor, but after a sucked in breath, more began punching through the armor and colliding with his skin underneath. He didn't feel the sting of them breaking skin, or the deep numbness of them puncturing into his body, but he had no more time to assess the situation.

They wouldn't survive long in their current situation, and so in desperation Rocky activated Chimera Transformation.

<Arggh!> Rocky heard Azoth exclaim mentally. Was his pet under attack as well?

Then pain unlike anything Rocky felt before crashed into him. Had the shrapnel caused by the explosions ripped him apart? It was hard for him to tell, because his entire body was on fire and getting worse.

The sounds of explosions continued, and spots of orange light started to shine from directions that only darkness had been before. Distantly, Rocky knew that meant the marble above them was almost completely eroded by the bombardment, but that paled in comparison to the shredding pain of the shrapnel destroying him.

He managed to force his head up, and he found both Sela and Zippo staring at him in horror, but thankfully the teenager had placed the shield above them. Rocky smiled sadly at Sela's wide eyed stare. Then he screamed as the searing fire became a cremation chamber.

The pain vanished, as if cut from him with a surgical knife. He would have thought that the wounds would have ached, or that he would have slowly numbed to unfeeling. Instead, he felt like he could jump thousands of feet, crush metal in his hands, and hear conversations from across the globe. It was like an adrenaline kick from his sports days heightened to unimaginable sharpness.

"Why are we here? How did I get here? Stop firing! Why aren't we killing those undead?!"

The sounds of explosions petered out and Rocky looked back up to Sela. She still was wide-eyed, but this time Rocky recognized the stare as something other than concern and desperation. She was shocked. The orange wash over her face vanished, and Rocky spun. He felt his shoulders hit the edges of the space, and his back muscles tweaked, reminding him of the shrapnel wounds that must exist there. The strange sensation was like someone had sunk fish hooks into his ribs and the fishing line was now snagged on something.

He crawled out of the hole, and his back screamed with each movement. The hurt was extrasensory; it radiated up and out from his back. Somehow the damage was so bad that his mind was interpreting the sensation of pain off his body. Like a phantom limb!

The pain dropped away once he was a few feet from the crumbling marble space, and with its disappearance, he found the strength to stand. In fact, he bounced three feet off the ground and landed again. The transformation! It must have increased his statistics. His body felt light, and he looked at his hand. Instead of the familiar sight of fingers opening and closing he found long, scaly, green appendages that looked graceful. And deadly, thanks to the three-inch talons that curled from the end.

Movement caused him to look away, and his eyes found Mechanolords fleeing into the distance or attacking zombies, skeletons, and spitters. At the sight of undead, his mind felt awash with a buzzing annoyance, and thinking was becoming hard. The feeling was familiar and he tried to push through it using his newly acquired outlook that Gary had helped him with.

"Dahrix has lost control! Let's get out of here," an all too familiar voice called from nearby.

It was Frankie's voice, and the kindling anger erupted into an all-consuming rage. Frankie turned to flee, and his movement caught in the corner of Rocky's eye. The rage became a torrent of fury.

"You killed my kit!" Rocky's mouth screamed, but he didn't remember opening it. He also had just enough use of his brain to question the statement itself. He didn't have kits?

As Frankie turned and fled, a group of humans that surrounded him slowly joined him in the action.

A screen popped up in the center of Rocky's vision.

Jack Fan
Master-Mage
Level 15
Health Points: 1,200 / 1,200
Boss

<Prey flees!> something inside of Rocky shouted, and his mouth began to salivate. Without conscious thought, his legs extended and he shot over the ground, almost gliding. A snap of the wind sounded off to his overly sensitive ears and he glanced back, expecting an attack. Two wide raven wings extended from directly above him, and he flinched, crashing into the ground below him. The skin of his shoulder tore away, but then a familiar agony separated from his back, confirmed something that his mind hadn't been willing to accept.

The phantom limbs weren't phantoms at all. He had wings! He leaped back to his feet and jump-glided after the fleeing humans. A few of the remaining Mechanolords attempted to fire at him, but he was moving too fast and erratically. Lasers carved into the stone where he had been, missiles exploded around him, but he kept chasing.

"They're my prey!" he shouted, not knowing where the words came from.

His claws dug into Jack Fan first, and he released a Dark Blade from his claws and Envenom at the same time. The dungeon boss's low health crumpled away in an instant. Rocky moved from fleeing creature to fleeing creature, slashing into black skeletal mages, orcs, half-giants, and humans alike. A few creatures turned to fight, but they seemed to be moving through water, while Rocky had an assisting wind.

A marble wall erected itself between Frankie and him, so Rocky folded his wings. He touched the ground for the barest moment, and then sprang off it with a powerful push of his legs. In a blink, he lowered a shoulder into the wall and shattered it. Then one of his clawed hands crushed down on a raised hand of a feeble human in brown robes. The man screamed out and Rocky headbutted him viciously. No pain came from his forehead, and he raised a lizard hand to his hairline. He found curved and ridged horns.

"So, you've become a monster," Frankie laughed. A ball of black and red light collided with the side of Rocky's head. Rocky felt a slight unease from the collision, but no pain. Yet, his knees buckled under him. "I can use a monster!" Frankie went to the first frail human Rocky had attacked and pulled a red glowing strand from around the neck of the unconscious and misshapen form.

<I will not be controlled!> that same mental scream burst from somewhere inside Rocky. It wasn't his own thought, and he knew that, but his head felt like someone had scooped out the insides and poured in magma instead. A thought would be there, and then just as quickly, it was gone again.

Frankie's eyes widened when he turned back around to find Rocky standing. They widened further when his claw-like hands removed Frankie's hand holding the dragon heartstring. Rocky's second slash used Dark Blade to separate Frankie's black arm at the shoulder. The limb with three heartstrings wrapped around it fell to the ground, and Frankie finally screamed.

Rocky's claw tore out his throat without him even consciously thinking of the action. He stood still for a moment after the attack, but then pain lanced into his side, tracing a line from his hip to his ribs. He looked at the offending spot and found a laser beam. He followed it to its source and then without conscious thought, launched himself at it.

CHAPTER FORTY-NINE

Selaphelia Adensai – Ruins of Atlantis

Sela fought her way through hordes of zombies using her sword, Moon Fire, and her Druidic Vines. She had initially transformed into her Predatory Panther form, but had then been attacked by confused, lingering robo-humans that were currently attacking anything that looked like an enemy. So, she had returned to her human form and shouted warnings at any that would listen. Getting even louder when she saw some attacks land on the shadowed figure that resembled that glimpse she caught of Rockland.

Everything was chaos as Meliora also joined the battle inside the ruins. She could hear people shouting at the rogue and confused Mechanolords not to fire, and she could also hear the Knights in front of her. Gamma was shouting, "Peace, hold your fire, this creature isn't an enemy," and Sela knew Rockland had gone that way.

She broke into a clearing and could see four green golems standing off against ten to twelve unsure metal humans. Sela rushed between them holding up hands.

"These golems aren't enemies either, they are allies!" Sela shouted at them as well and they slowly lowered arms with missiles popping from them. Once the standoff ended, she rushed to the nearest Knight and found herself facing Delta.

"Where is he?" she blurted, and he pointed a finger over his shoulder. She could see a lone Knight standing protectively over something and she hurried on.

"I've tried to wake them both, but they won't even respond to the smell of pizza. Sela, I don't know what else to do!" Omega said in disbelief as she approached. Rockland was atop Azoth, and both were clearly breathing, but also clearly deep in sleep. Or she guessed unconscious if they wouldn't wake with all the noise, and likely jostling that had happened.

After hesitating, she tried poking the manticore, both physically and mentally. Then she tried Rockland with a light shake. She looked up to Omega. "Can you get them back to the guild dome?"

"Totally, dude! But, like, why aren't you coming?" Omega responded in his strange way of speaking that she couldn't place. Rockland claimed it was something popularized by beaches here on Earth before the Ether returned, but she still didn't understand his explanation.

"I found something I need to look into further," she responded, being intentionally vague for now. The ruins Rockland had chosen to hide under had been mostly blasted apart, and thanks to the shifting that occurred, Jason and she found a staircase that led underground. They had not had time to explore it yet, but she had left him there to mark the location for them.

Omega shrugged and then scooped up Rockland in a hand, and Azoth as if the huge manticore was just a large dog. He put Rockland back down to work the larger black chimera onto a shoulder and then lifted the man back up. While Rockland was still nearby, she accessed his bag of holding and took out one of the rewards that Adam needed. The enormous white heart dropped onto the ground in front of her. It was easily as large as Azoth.

"That's all I can carry. These two have been eating a bit too much!" Omega said with a chuckle before turning away. Sela assumed he was heading to the bridge that had appeared from their cliffside and connected to the floating ruins, but her sense of direction felt a little off.

"Jason, Rockland is fine. How are you doing at the staircase?" Sela said into her earpiece radio as she turned back toward the other four Knights.

"Zombies and skeletons are mostly dispatched. I can still hear the crackle of the spitter acid nearby, but I can't see any."

Sela joined the other Knights, who were still looking at the now-growing group of Mechanolords across from them.

"I am sending Omega back to the guild dome. You should probably follow him. Take that huge heart with you to Adam. That will complete his quest once it is placed on the altar back in the Grotto. Okay?"

She shot a quick glare at the robots across from the golems, upset with them for the fact that she could not turn into her raven form and just fly back to find Jason. Who knew what they would do if they saw a massive black bird? The lost imbeciles might think she was not human anymore and resume their attacks on everything around them.

She shook her head and chose the path out of the area that she believed she had taken in. In the end, it took her several minutes to return to Jason, and she was forced to have him send three red Fireballs skyward to mark his location. She asked him to make them small, but they were still quite noticeable. She just hoped that no enemies were paying attention to the display. If there were any left alive in the area, that was.

I should have checked Rockland's notifications! By my great uncle Raguel, I really can only think of one thing at a time!

"So, we are going down there?" Jason asked excitedly.

"Are you going to be able to stay awake?" she countered and lightly punched the young man in the arm. He smiled and laughed, before scratching his neck with only a tiny bit of embarrassment.

With Jason lighting the way, they walked down the marble stone staircase, trying to avoid slipping on the slime and green sludge that must have come from the water beneath them. About eighteen steps down, Sela saw light glinting off something in the air. It took her a moment to catch the blue gleam of a shield under the red wash of Jason's skill. Still, once she saw it, she knew they were in the right place.

She put her hand forward and it passed through the hanging shield without resistance. From one step to the next, the grime and ocean floor debris vanished, and the white marble took on a polished appearance all around them. Two more steps after the shield, a strip of illumination flashed on above her, and she smiled as the bottom of the stairs were suddenly visible another ten steps down. The room beyond flickered, once, twice, and then also began producing a steady light.

Jason's red light slowly shrank as he reabsorbed his Fireball and looked at her with clear excitement. She smiled at him, and they continued down. When the teenager tried to rush by her, she held up an arm. "Careful. I do not know what building this is, and it could be trapped or fall on us."

Jason sobered slightly and they reached the bottom of the stairs. A massive circular chamber of opulent beauty greeted them. In the center of the building, Sela recognized a terminal dais made of marble and covered in snaking blue lines that made patterns she always had thought to be runes. However, now that she knew what runes looked like, she wasn't as certain.

"Is that a computer?" Jason asked from right beside and above her. She jumped slightly, not expecting him to be so close.

"A what, now?"

"Never mind, let's just go check it out!" Jason dodged the question and she shrugged. It was quite possibly what she was looking for, anyway. She glanced at the hallways that led off this central chamber and saw them illuminated. There were at least five of the hallways and she had to wonder what each contained.

Five feet from the dais, it whirred to life, and she heard Jason mutter something that sounded like a confirmation of his earlier statement. Once she stood in front of it, a screen popped up in front of her. This wasn't like the screens of the system, and instead was a localized screen projected by the dais itself. One popped up in front of Jason as well.

Sela's heart hammered in her chest and she started clicking through options on the familiar screens that mimicked the Silver Spires. Beside her, Jason tilted his head. "Does this thing run on DOS? What the *jinkies* is this set up?"

"This is why I keep reporting Rockland. He is a horrible influence to have you swearing as well," she scolded and saw Jason roll his eyes. She wheeled on him and pointed a finger. "I mean it. Kids are not supposed to swear. If you cannot help here, you could *carefully* check the other rooms." She navigated to the map of the structure.

The title of the structure made her smile. 'Atlantean Council and Military Command Complex.'

Jason pointed to the map and winced. "This thing is like two-bit technology. Wow. Alright, I'll try the hangar. If there are ships left, they'll be there."

Sela nodded. "Just take it slow. It seems that everything down here is intact, but no point rushing in. If anything looks unstable or even if you find another shield, turn around and come back. Deal?"

Jason was already leaving and flashed a thumbs-up high over his head in way of an answer. She blinked and returned to the map screen. A red dot showed Jason's location anyway, and since they were the only two down here, she could keep track of him. She opened a second screen to keep the map open, and kept searching through the databases here.

There must be news about the collapse.

She found many options in the dais, but dismissed most of them. Worldwide notices, no. Call the council, no. Adjustments to the EtherNet, no. She paused on the connection to the planetary sky shield and explored. It being here was interesting. Did that mean that Gaia from her time also possessed a sky shield, or was this option here only because she had chosen that option after defeating Jormungandr?

After cataloging the options on the page to her memory, she granted limited access to Algonquin's guild tower. She scrolled through all the communications attempting to enter the planet and discovered only one that wasn't a shop. On the other screen, she pulled up those leaving the planet and found them to be mostly identical. Only one string of letters existed on the entry and not the exit side. '$p3|o' Sela shrugged and granted the Aretrean Bazaar from the Grotto permissions but left all the other shops blocked for now. Once Rockland woke up, she would discuss it with him.

She stumbled onto the security access screen next and found a list of names there that she recognized as Gaian military leaders and sitting council members from her time. Still, right at the top of the screen was Meliora Guild. When she clicked into the name, it gave options that she hurriedly adjusted to ensure only her, Jason, and Rockland could enter past the shielding. Again, that would need to be adjusted later, but for now it would keep people from innocent snooping.

A glance told her Jason arrived in the hangar and she smiled. Hopefully he would find some starships there. She returned to her searching and stumbled onto a page she didn't quite understand.

Current Suspected Gaia
Jophiel Turendal
Previous Gaia
Arrernte Aten

Sela saw that the names on the list went on, but she was stuck on the last name of the 'Current Suspected Gaia.' Turendal was one of the founding families of the Cathodiem Guild. They were a billion years before her time, but if she recalled the history right, the Turendal family had held the highest seat for thousands of years before they suddenly vanished from the guild history. In fact, her great Uncle Raguel had been a Turendal.

There were plenty of theories as to their disappearance, ranging from coups to them forming a new guild, but the truth was lost, despite the extensive writings on the era. Still, her brain was focused heavily on that conundrum to avoid the larger one.

Her brain tried desperately to fit two ill-fitting puzzle pieces together. Gaia was a planetary god, and Jophiel Turendal should have been a human champion. For there to be a list of names of current and previous Gaias... What did that mean?

Do champions become Planetary Gods? Do they take over from previous ones?

Jason's moving dot brought her back to herself, and she shook her head. She could dissect that problem later. Right now, she needed more information on why Ether fled the Sol. She reluctantly closed the current screen and kept searching. Finally, she found the root menu that held the archived minutes from all council meetings. She clicked the final entry and read.

Summary of First Discussion:

The Ether levels on the planet have reached desperate levels. The functionality of most enchantments have begun to fail, and most power converters are running at ten percent efficiency.

Summary of Second Discussion:

Despite numerous studies and inquiries into the source, nothing further has been discovered. This was a weapon that originated on Mars and was triggered by the Martians. The red planet itself has suffered the worst after detonation and the race of Martians have vacated to secondary planets far outside the Sol.

Summary of Third Discussion:

The Cathodiem, Asgardian, Olympus, and Egyptian Guilds have left the Sol and offered refuge to any Gaian who wishes it. They have refused to send representatives back into the system and left within days of the Calamity. Suspicions from the remaining council and military leaders remain unfounded but high.

Summary of Fourth Discussion:

A final decision to evacuate has been made, and planetwide messages have been levied. Some people still refuse to believe the clear science, and the council has decreed that they will only take those willing to leave. No one will be forced to board the final Gaian ships departing.

Sela exited that screen and was about to click the second to last summary notes when the screen flashed red. A message popped up in bright red across the center of the screen.

Access to the Leviathan Pact Chamber has been established. Would Jason Jackson like to become bonded—
Error! Leviathan has broken through.
Error! Leviathan has forced bonding.
Error!

Sela's eyes flew to the hangar. She turned and fled from the room toward it. Jason's dot was still there, but it wasn't moving. She pushed her legs as hard as she could and arrived in the doorway a few seconds later. She found Jason lying on his back near a blue orb, and he was shaking in apparent seizures. She leaped into the room but was blocked by a familiar shape, just shrunken to the size of Azoth.

She was looking at one of the legendary leviathans. Even though she was amazed, her eyes slid to Jason. She Analyzed him.

Jason Jackson
Level 1
Apprentice-Leviathan Space Mage
Health Points: 110 / 110
Ether: Infinite
Skills: 0

Something was still strange. The system always had to give a choice, right? She looked at the leviathan and was forced to step back. She had turned on her Ether sight to ensure Jason was okay. The leviathan looked like a sun condensed down into a black hole. She could feel the power radiating off it.

CHAPTER FIFTY

Adam Weatherbee − Algonquin Grotto

Red Quest
Party Quest − Stone Bender
Rebirth of the Taken
418 people have gone missing from the Territory you reside in. Gaia has cataloged their absence as something that should not have happened and has offered you a quest to help right the balance. You have placed the legendary heart of Jormungandr on the Altar of Michabo. Gaia will grant Rebirth to the souls trapped within.
Rewards:
500,000,000 Etherience
5000 Crystallized Ether
Rebirth of the Citizens
−

Error! Bodies not stored in Altar...
Finding bodies...
Error! Original bodies too far away...
Creating new bodies with available material...
Rebirth successful.

Adam felt the enjoyable rush that told him he added a level or more thanks to the quest. He wondered how many people had managed to level as well thanks to the shared quest and that Etherience surge. That combined with the successful raid of Jormungandr had finally broken his first grind in the Journeyman ranks.

Are those error messages normal?

He closed the window, dismissing it for now, and watched the massive heart begin shrinking in size. It looked like a pile of sand when high tide rolled in, only the massive heart was converting itself into a blue energy that was drunk greedily by the black altar underneath it. He turned to look at Tao, the only Knight he allowed to accompany him up into the control room. Even then, the elevator had creaked and groaned ominously under his weight. At this point, Adam wouldn't have let any of them follow him up, but he had no way of lifting the massive heart without them.

The recent reverence that Epsilon was treating him with was uncomfortable. The others weren't as bad, and Omega was even one of the boys, but unfortunately, he rarely got to hang out with just one of them. It was always 'we're doing it for your protection.' The situation escalated when his higher tier golem puppets were able to say a few words. Adam tried to explain that they were like dogs, and he thought they would never be sapient like the Knights, but that was mostly ignored.

"We must always remember *this too shall pass*. Good and bad times will pass and balance each other. So, let's enjoy this victory with friends, yes?" Tao spoke to the room as a whole. Adam liked the soft-spoken golem. He wasn't sure he understood half the words that came out of his mouth, but that didn't change the vibe he had.

"You think you can sneak me and the A-team some celebratory drinks?" Adam asked the Knight. Tao looked at him and seemed to look away, but Adam saw the wink just before Tao turned.

"The absorption should be done soon, but I'm sorry for the interruption of your work. People will start being reborn once it's done. We might want to get that pink bathrobe up here again, in case they show up naked," Adam joked into the silence of the room.

A few people chuckled and he smiled. It was time to leave them alone and get back to the team. Maybe they could sneak in some dungeon runs tomorrow. At least then the Knights agreed he could be away from them.

The doors at the bottom of the elevator opened to a rather raucous scene. The noise usually wasn't this loud, and Adam exited assuming that people were celebrating the windfall of the quest Etherience. That was when he noticed the absence of Epsilon, Omega, Delta and Gamma. He looked around and noticed the A-team was gone too. He tuned in to what people were saying.

"Golems are coming out of the Grotto walls, get your weapons. The Grotto is under attack!"

Adam and Tao reacted at the same time and rushed down a hallway and out into the Grotto. Adam instinctively took the path that led to the door that held his puppets, and Tao strangely chose the same path. Outside, he found a sight that he couldn't have ever expected.

The Golem Knights were standing in the northern quadrants of the Grotto. Their weapons were drawn but they were facing toward the people of the Grotto.

"What has happened?" Tao asked, and Adam just stared.

Behind the Golem Knights, Adam could make out cowering gray figures. From this distance they looked small, but Adam had learned that almost everything looked that way beside the Knights. Tao started running to his brothers and that got Adam moving again.

Tao was careful with his run, avoiding both buildings and people. Adam wasn't so cautious, but he was soon pulled up short by one of his friends.

"Adam, the Golem Knights are protecting the attacking golems!"

Adam hadn't bothered bringing his puppets along, assuming that the Knights would be more than enough to handle any situation. Now, he took a moment. Was there anyone here who could even hold the Knights off?

"There has to be an explanation!" Adam shouted, and resumed his run.

He reached the group of people who were currently bunched together facing the massive Golem Knights nervously. Adam pushed his way to the front and looked at Epsilon. "What's going on?"

"The people of your Grotto are being reborn," Epsilon said and glanced backward. "But as something new."

World Announcement
Thanks to the actions of Meliora and Adam Weatherbee, a new race has been born on Gaia. Humans of Gaia, welcome the Living Golem race as your younger brothers and sisters.

—

Etherless Void — Guild Collective Armada

"We've lost the signal from your beacons on the target planet, Dahrix. What's happened, child?" Tirahnya the stupid hag demanded, and she called him child again. Dahrix regarded her as coolly as he was able, while his eyes glowed red, and his coolant circulated at speeds that a primitive racer rocket would envy.

"We still have the bearing from the computer, and I'm sure we will be able to get another beacon onto the planet through one of our guilds," Geb responded, and Dahrix turned his head as minimally as possible to regard him. They turned to look at him but he chose to sit statue-still.

<Lieutenant, do you have any idea why the multiple beacons have gone offline?> Dahrix sent, privately. He was even more at a loss for the occurrence than these three were. As he waited, he looked over to Hectar, who was silent for once. The

biologist could perhaps sense the mood of the room, and wisely wasn't interjecting more inane requests for planetary exploration.

Even with his constant searching, they hadn't found anything alive out here. <As far as we can deduce, the signal was severed. If that's the case, the beacons are likely still active.>

<How long would they need to reestablish a connection?> Dahrix responded. Tirahnya puffed her gills out in the equivalent of a human sucking their teeth, and he smiled at her show of emotion. They had no idea how large of a problem might truly exist. They couldn't fathom what he had seen through his—

"Dahrix, why did you have a Kill Stealer title showing earlier when I was aboard your ship?" Hectar spoke for the first time at this meeting. Dahrix's central pump that circulated his coolant seemed to misfire.

"Kill Stealer title?" Tirahnya spat, her blue face flushing a purple as her embarrassment or anger took hold. Dahrix raised a mechanical eyebrow and regarded the young biologist.

"What one does aboard their own ship is their own business. Still, I will answer. I was simply scrolling through my numerous titles to recall their functions. Since you can't seem to keep to yourself aboard my vessel, I am going to remove access." Dahrix hoped that would be the end of that discussion. While the title wasn't exactly something to be proud of, it was still a title and a rather beneficial one at that.

In the future, any kill that he did any damage to would award him full Etherience.

"Why have we never heard of this title before, Dahrix?" Geb asked haughtily.

Dahrix returned to regarding him coolly. "You will recall that the beacons have somehow been disrupted," he answered an earlier question. "The Mechanolords are currently working to reestablish a connection. At present, we don't believe them to be destroyed. I suggest we maintain our current course and wait for the signal to return. Good day."

Dahrix stood and left the chamber, just as his lieutenant responded with a calculated time. <The connection should have already reached us over an hour ago.>

—

Rockland Barkclay – Algonquin Grotto

"Well then." Rocky slowly exhaled into the quiet empty draconic longhouse. "So, this thing is a leviathan?"

"Yeah, it took a Golem Knight restraining it for us to be able to move Zippo here," Adam responded, as he looked between Rocky and the hovering black pod that resembled a seed.

"It didn't attack the Knight when it was restrained?" Rocky asked as he scratched his head, and considered forcing his way by the thing to get to Zippo. Zippo wasn't exactly in danger, but he still hadn't woken up.

"Leviathans have almost no ability to defend themselves," Sela interjected from the doorway Rocky hadn't heard open. "They rely on the mage they are bonded with to provide attack and defense."

He turned and smiled tiredly at her. She was likely here to remind him that he was needed in Atlantis. Meliora had begun searching through the ruins with almost all available resources shortly after the defeat of Jormungandr. While Meliora hadn't found anything useful yet, Sela and Rocky had managed to find at least eight abandoned starships of various classes inside of the Atlantean Council and Military Command Center.

Challenge Issued

A challenge against the city of Atlantis has been issued by Mount Olympus. Would you like to accept this challenge and reap the rewards?
<Yes> | No

"Again?" Sela asked as she saw his screen pop up and likely read it as she approached. He nodded in response and clicked no. "We still have three hallways to explore from the main atrium of the command center. Maybe the answer is in one of them?"

Rocky nodded at Sela's words. "You're sure Zippo is going to be okay, though?"

"Rockland, you know I can't answer that. You've cast Dark Mend, I've used Rejuvenation, and Gary has tried everything he can. It seems that something we can't see or understand is happening to Jason. Our only hope now is to give it more time…"

"And you've already met with Amelia?" Rocky responded, trying to find a reason to stay near Zippo. The first couple days, he had literally sat at his side, using Azoth to wrestle the leviathan away. Yet, it hadn't seemed to help. Sela was right, of course. All they could do was wait and see.

"Yes, I've talked with her, and the seven ships she is building are coming along. She also found some interesting 'ancient' technology in the ships we salvaged, so she's made some modifications. Regardless, she isn't enthusiastic about our chances with less than ten ships against an armada."

"Me either," Rocky murmured as he turned to look at Adam beside him "Keep the peace between the new golems and the humans, okay? I'll be back later tonight."

"Will do," Adam responded, sounding almost as tired as Rocky felt. He nodded to the kid and turned toward the door.

Meliora had just achieved a massive victory, and yet it seemed to just add more problems.

"Let's go figure out what secrets Atlantis is hiding…"

AFTERWORD

We hope you enjoyed Equatorial! Since reviews are the lifeblood of indie publishing, we'd love it if you could leave a positive review on Amazon! Please use this link to go to the Ether Collapse: Equatorial Amazon product page to leave your review: geni.us/EtherCollapse4.

As always, thank you for your support! You are the reason we're able to bring these stories to life.

About Ryan DeBruyn

Ryan has always been a dream chaser. His first career was as a professional athlete, which taught him the dedication and perseverance needed to chase fantastic goals. A devastating injury removed Ryan from this world before his prime, and taught him the value of an education.

His first book began as a hobby project while he attended Georgian College. Using his hard fought lessons, in motivation, discipline and hard work Ryan published his first book in February 2019.

He is a recent graduate in the field of Electrical Engineering and a full-time author.

Here's hoping you enjoy the worlds he creates as much as he does!

Connect with Ryan:
Facebook.com/RyanDeBruyn
Facebook.com/Groups/RyanDeBruyn
RyanDeBruyn.com
Instagram.com/RyRyDubs
Patreon.com/RyanDeBruyn

ABOUT MOUNTAINDALE PRESS

Dakota and Danielle Krout, a husband and wife team, strive to create as well as publish excellent fantasy and science fiction novels. Self-publishing *The Divine Dungeon: Dungeon Born* in 2016 transformed their careers from Dakota's military and programming background and Danielle's Ph.D. in pharmacology to President and CEO, respectively, of a small press. Their goal is to share their success with other authors and provide captivating fiction to readers with the purpose of solidifying Mountaindale Press as the place 'Where Fantasy Transforms Reality.'

Connect with Mountaindale Press:
MountaindalePress.com
Facebook.com/MountaindalePress
Twitter.com/_Mountaindale
Krout@MountaindalePress.com

MOUNTAINDALE PRESS TITLES

GAMELIT AND LITRPG

The Completionist Chronicles Series
The Divine Dungeon Series
Full Murderhobo Series
Year of the Sword Series
By: DAKOTA KROUT

Arcana Unlocked Series
By: GREGORY BLACKBURN

A Touch of Power Series
By: JAY BOYCE

Farming Livia Series
Red Mage Series
By: XANDER BOYCE

Space Seasons Series
By: DAWN CHAPMAN

Ether Collapse Series
Ether Flows Series
By: RYAN DEBRUYN

Dr. Druid Series
By: MAXWELL FARMER

Bloodgames Series
By: CHRISTIAN J. GILLILAND

Threads of Fate Series
By: MICHAEL HEAD

Lion's Lineage Series
By: ROHAN HUBLIKAR AND DAKOTA KROUT

Wolfman Warlock Series
By: JAMES HUNTER AND DAKOTA KROUT

Axe Druid Series
High Table Hijinks Series
Mephisto's Magic Online Series
By: CHRISTOPHER JOHNS

Skeleton in Space Series
By: ANDRIES LOUWS

Dragon Core Chronicles
By: LARS MACHMÜLLER

Chronicles of Ethan Series
By: JOHN L. MONK

Necrotic Apocalypse Series
Pixel Dust Series
By: DAVID PETRIE

Viceroy's Pride Series
By: CALE PLAMANN

Henchman Series
By: CARL STUBBLEFIELD

Artorian's Archives Series
By: DENNIS VANDERKERKEN AND DAKOTA KROUT

Appendix

Adam Weatherbee – A survivor from Kingston who has a unique class giving him the ability to take control of golems. **Apprentice Stone-Summoner**

Adam's Elites – A group of individuals from Kingston that have now formed a group with Adam and his minion Golems.

Alchemy is the Basis of All – Alchemy guild located on Helion Prime. Is studying gasoline which was traded to him by someone in Florida.

Alex Watt – 11-year-old young man that Rocky met while entering Ottawa. Family was massacred by Corsair's goons. **Died during the Ottawa Exodus Struggle**

Altar of Michabo – A place of power that is linked to the Algonquin Guild. This place of power is billions of years old and was created to link another realm (Spirit Realm) to Gaia. This gives the benefit of Rebirth to our hero but at what cost?

Algonquin Grotto – This is where Selaphelia Ardensai chose to start the settlement of survivors. It was chosen because of its natural defenses in the mountains and cliff faces that surround it on three sides. On the fourth side is a large river that runs through Algonquin Park.

Algonquin Park – Is the full Algonquin Park as seen in our current world.

Algonquin Valley – Is the Territory of Rockland Barkclay, and it sits within Algonquin Park. It is quite large but does not encompass the entirety of the current Algonquin Park from present day Earth.

Amber Dell – A member of the A-Team. A muscular Native American woman who is extremely pretty when she smiles. She also seems to take things a little too literally, often forgetting or not understanding the full meaning of things. **Apprentice-Fencer**

Amelia Nanospark – A Helion, who disguises herself as an Iridescent Kobold. Has a unique class of Nanospark that gives her control over her unique nanobots. With it she has created a resistance on Helion Prime against the tyranny of the Guild Collective.

Analyze – A skill that is common for almost all the individuals of the Etherverse. When scrutinizing an object or a person, the system will reveal some information based on your level in the skill. Skill can be countered or obfuscated.

Ancestral Guide – A perk of the Etherverse. Gaia was once predicated on privilege and the power ancestors passed down. Skills, training, gear etc. Ancestral guides were a constant companion that could train the truly fortunate.

Antarctica – A continent on Earth. Google it.

Apep – Essentially a black hole, another form of godly being similar to Gaia but more on par with a Star God. Instead of bringing light to a world, a Void god attempts to subvert worlds away from the light to gain power.

Apep's Void Shoud / Stick – Pieces of gear worn first by the cultists of Apep, but were looted in book 2.

Apothis – One of the countless souls that Apep has at his command. Apep continually spins out his head priest, Apothis, to try to conquer worlds. **Master-Necromonger**

Arbuckle – A very rare metal that can be inscribed with powerful runes, and has the ability to convert hold a large Ether Pool to power them. This metal is required to create a shop, and seed shops. It is somewhat alive and grows more of itself.

Area of Effect (AoE) – A type of skill that creates an effect over a large area. This is usually damage or healing but can be slowing effects or other such effects.

Arena Dungeon – Controlled by the Dungeon core Maximus. This Dungeon becomes the first cardinal Dungeon of the Territory, Algonquin Valley.

Aretrean Bazaar – The Aretrean Bazaar is on Mount Olympus and is the shop our hero has access to currently.

Asgardians – A guild that once resided on Earth but has left when the Ether fled. They are still a powerhouse in the Etherverse.

Astrid – A member of the Territorial Council. Mid-Forties. Tailoress.

Atlantean Academy – A school Selaphelia attended when growing up. This school was attached to Atlantis and held a neutral faction for the guilds. All attendees were either nobility or very skilled.

Atlantean Guild Tower – This is a greater perk that was earned for the cleansing of the nearby Chalk River nuclear meltdown. This is a tower which links up through a satellite to the EtherNet. Thus providing our hero with more information on the current world.

Atrium – The lower levels of the Guild Tower. The Atrium is a massive cathedral that houses Quest Kiosk's a desk that will house assistants, and an elevator that people on the list can use to access the upper tower.

Azoth – Rockland's pet Chimera. Is able to speak and communicate first with Selaphelia and later with Rockland. Through them both is gaining Sapience. **Dread-Chimera**

Azrael – Rockland's ancestor. Azrael was adopted by the Cathodiem guild and never was considered nobility. A new book is on its way with Azrael's coming of age story. **Ether Flows – Tech Duinn**. Keep your eyes peeled.

Bag of Holding – A bag that has been enchanted to contain a massive Ethereal space inside. Our hero lucked into a very large bag of holding from a dungeon early after the crash.

Bailey – A young girl who first got into trouble for enticing young men to steal weapons from the guards. She has now become an adventurer and was captured and detained by LFD along with 400 other citizens. She continued to break free and farm for Etherience.

Bam-Bam – An Ogre boss that attacks the Territory.

Bancroft – Is a town located on the York River in Hastings County in the Canadian province of Ontario.

Bart – A member of the A-Team. Bart looks like a hell's angel with tattoos, long hair and a biker jacket. There is a deep well of kindness in this man as seen through his deeds, from helping people survive to organizing the Territory.

Barry's Bay – Is a community in the township of Madawaska Valley, Ontario, Canada.

Basalt Golem – A golem that converts from the roads. Tar Golem would also be an appropriate name. But Basalt sounds cooler.

Bathilda the Darkscale – Is the dragon under contract with Gaia. She had a necklace that gives her rights to live on Gaia, but she must obey the commands of Gaia to keep the planet in balance. Essentially an all-powerful bouncer who maintains order on the planet.

Batwing Bird – A type of monster that our group faces during the book.

Bear Tribe – Briefly mentioned by Selaphelia. A tribe within the Beastkin.

Beastkin – A race in the Etherverse that contains many tribes of difference beast-humanoids.

Blight Skill / Blighted Bog – A skill Sela learned at the Journeyman ranks.

Bloodlust Aura – A skill released by Bam-bam during combat.

Bone Breast Plate – A breastplate dropped by Rattlegore.

Brent – Is a community on Cedar Lake on the Petawawa River in northern Algonquin Provincial Park.

Bullet – Mutated peregrine falcon that had strong, wind-based skills, and that nearly killed Rocky and the group.

Burks Fall – Is an incorporated village in the Almaguin Highlands region of Parry Sound District, Ontario, Canada.

Canadore – A college / university that resides in North Bay.

Cathodiem Guild – Guild that was situated on Gaia over a billion years ago. Guild was very powerful and had great influence with a seat on the Atlantean Council.

Chain Quest – A type of quest that contains multiple parts.

Chalk River – Is a town in Ontario that is near a nuclear research laboratory. A few days after the Ether crash, the converted golem from the plant melts down, prompting a red quest.

Chidi – An emotional representation of a person. A conflicted chidi often means the person is going through emotional turmoil or is an evil person. Good or bad deeds are often reflected on the chidi. Or emotional struggles as seen by our hero.

Choo Sentani – A type of blanket used by Elven merchants. It interacts with the system in the bazaar and can temporarily transfer items across the shops to be viewed or inspected.

Citizen Accessible Shop – An addon for a shop. This allows an assistant to scan through the merchant's wares that reside in a shop and purchase items on the behest of individuals. This limits interactions and messages that can be transmitted through spies. Still, it doesn't stop them...

Class Ranks – Apprentice, Journeyman, Master, Epic, Legenday (Read Ether Flows to learn more)

Construct Command – A skill that Adam Weatherbee uses to control Golems.

Corsair (Jack Jameson) – Sociopathic leader of the Ottawa Militia. Created an inner group of psychopaths who followed his orders to kill survivors instead of allowing monsters to gain more Etherience. **Died during the Ottawa Exodus Struggle**

Crafter – A skill or class a person can have that is for making equipment or consumables that will aid individuals.

Crom – An ancient being from Gelthisar. Whether it is a god or a very powerful combatant is unclear.

Crystals – Crystallized Ether. Crystals is the short form. A type of currency.

Crushed Ether – A component needed for enchanting. Derived from Crystallized Ether.

Cuppa Macht Leaf – A type of leaf from a Cuppa Macht Tree. It is essentially a collapsible cup that contains a biological reaction to cool liquids. The tree is from a dessert region.

Cursed Regalia – Items with counterproductive enchantments that may hinder the user.

Dahrix – Leader of the Mechano-Lords guild. All black metal with Damascus steel filigree. Despite his mechanical body, he is a hot head.

Dario – The current Guild Prime, who runs the guild collective. It is an elected position and he seems to be a bit too wild to be behind a desk.

Dark Cloak – A skill learned by Rockland Barkclay. This cloak hides our hero in a dark fog and also will help to redirect attacks away from him.

Dark Mend – A skill learned by Rockland Barkclay. It uses shadows and darkness to rearrange broken bones and knit back together flesh.

Debuff – An effect that makes a character weaker: a negative status effect.

Delta – A sapient golem who is a member of the Ottawa Knights. He was created from a historical building known as the Parliament Buildings in Ottawa. An intellectual who prefers logic and deductive reasoning to solve problems. **Master-Knight of Gaia**

Delving Dungeon – A type of dungeon that digs down into the ground creating descending levels with increasing difficulty.

Derik – A devious human who was a member of the initial group that is saved from the Onikuma by Rocky. Rocky banishes Derik during the invasion of the Grotto by Apothis and Frank. Derik's banishment is rescinded and he joins the new council, under probation.

Diamond Chip – A type of currency. This is the lowest form of currency. 10 Diamond Chips = 1 Ruby Mark.

Dmitri Gausse – A Russian mobster stationed at the docks in Florida when the first wave struck. He has been crucial in the Floridians survival. He helps our heroes disable the beacon.

Doran Hetch – A brother who makes a horrible decision to kill humans to save himself. Rocky lets them live but tells them to never be seen again.

Dorset – Is a small community located on the boundary between the Lake of Bays Municipality in Muskoka District and the Algonquin Highlands Township in Haliburton County, Ontario, Canada.

Dragonscale – Usually collected from young dragons and prized for their extreme strength. Dragonscale is considered the strongest bio material in the known Etherverse.

Draksus – Leader of the Ottawa territory. Albino, devastatingly large, and strong.

Dungeon – A creation of Planetary gods to filter Ether to Essence. Each dungeon is rules by a Core that has a personality.

Enchanter's Kit – An item purchased in the shop. Contains a Pen, Mortar and Pestle. This item is a puzzle that Rockland must solve.

Enchanting – A crafting skill that is of immense value. Enchanting uses Glyphs or Runes to circulate Ether and create powerful effects.

Envenom – A skill in the first tier of the Chimera Knight Class.

Epsilon – A sapient golem who appears to be the leader of the Ottawa Knights. He was created from a historical building known as the Parliament Buildings in Ottawa. Extremely devoted to his group of golems and wishes to unite all sapient golems and create a community for them. **Master-Knight of Gaia**

Ernest Ford – Dockmaster. Ernest is in charge of the Floridians and has accepted a Mechanolord conversion seed to help keep them safe. Once he sets up the beacon he is essentially a puppet of Dahrix.

Essence – Essence is the primary resource of a Planetary God. It is filtered from Ether through living beings but can also be recovered from dead organisms. Gaia wakes to find almost all of her vast stores pillaged (oil).

Ether – Cosmic energy of the universe. It is the primary unfiltered raw power that allows life and Planetary Gods to form.

Ether Assisted Protection – A type of protection that helps fledgling Territories. This protection will help turn away powerful monsters.

Ether Converters – A converter that changes Ether into electricity.

Ether Manipulation – A skill that allows individuals to manipulate the Ether internally and externally. Linked with Ether Channels and both have been hidden from Sela during her lifetime.

Ether Pool – A pool of power that skills draw upon to initiate. Synonymous with Mana pool from games.

Ether Tech Helm – A very powerful type of armor. Combines the mechanical advantages of robotic gear with enchantments of Bio Enhanced gear.

Ethernet – A type of global information system used in ancient times. Synonymous with internet.

Exiles – A group of individuals who attacked Rocky during book 2. They were exiled from the Grotto but allowed to hunt in the safety of the Territory.

Fernicular – A type of plant that need Ether to cultivate.

Fire Tornado – A descriptor of the Firestorm skill.

Fireball – A skill Zippo learns in book one.

Firestorm – A skill Zippo learns in book two.

Fennel – A herbalist lady that is mixing ingredients and causes a massive plume of smoke to billow forth outside of the Crafters Hall.

Flatiron – A golem converted from the Flatiron Building in New York.

Florida – A state in the US.

Floridians – The people in the US. As categorized by other humans from earth.

Flow Ridians – The humans of unknown origin as categorized by the Guild Collective.

Flunge – A term used in fencing for a flying lunge.

Frankie Cocozza – Psychologist to the Militiamen on the trip to Algonquin Valley and continues his duties in the Grotto. Turns out he was also the Psychologist for Corsair and his cronies. **Apprentice-Psychologist**

Gaia – Gaia is a Planetary God, specifically the Earth. Each planet is alive and in constant battle with other planets to acquire Essence. What they win if they have the most is still a mystery.

Gaian Plane – The main reality in which our hero resides.

Garnel – A Karacy Salesman in the Aretrean Bazaar. Karacy are often referred to as Dwarfs by other races.

Garry – An older man saved from Kingston. Becomes a member of Adam's Elites off page.

Gamma – A sapient golem who is a member of the Ottawa Knights. He was created from a historical building known as the Parliament Buildings in Ottawa. Hot headed and rash, but also surprisingly good at building. Works hard to help the survivors in the Grotto despite his early complaints to the contrary. **Master-Knight of Gaia**

Gaston – A reluctant healer who wishes to be known as a hero but too scared to actually venture out to fight. He hangs around the military but is not one of them. He also swindles citizens out of Crystals for healing that isn't needed.

Geb – Leader of Bio-Cult and one of the youngest members in a leadership role of a guild on Helion Prime. Likes to call people 'young man' despite her younger age.

Gelthisar – A planetary God.

Gerard – A man from Brent. Some sort of Tank class. Was trapped for most of a week inside LFD.

Glyphs – Another name for Enchanting Runes.

Golden Horseshoe – A term used to describe the Greater Toronto Area. It resembles a horseshoe around Lake Ontario.

Golems – A clever way Gaia has orchestrated to recover a higher percentage of her pillaged Essence. Golems are created from any structure that has no ownership claimed upon it twenty-four hours after the first Ether wave.

Gortuk – A type of monster whose skin was used to create leather that was later turned into a Jerkin of Protection.

Greater Territorial Perk – A benefit that Gaia bestowed for completion of a very difficult Red Quest.

Grotto – Referring to Algonquin Grotto.

Guild Collective – A collection of small guilds that joined together to try to gain a semblance of power that planetary militaries and larger guilds have. They have taken and occupied Helion Prime and are now trying to extend to Gaia.

Guild of Mechano-Lords – Patron of Corsair. Headquarters on Guild Collaborative controlled world of Helion Prime. The leader of the guild is Dahrix.

Guild Prime – Is the leader of the Guild Collective. Currently Dario.

Guild Tent – An item purchased from Garnell. This tent gives a Territory access to guild features at half efficacy without building a true Guild Hall. The guild tower replaces this tent, even skewering it and creating a tent flag for a time.

HALO – High Altitude Low Open

Heartstring – A very powerful item that is created from a Dragon Heart. It can be used to control dungeons, people and is a legendary component.

Hectar – Lieutenant Captain – 'Alchemy is the Basis of All'. Has been running tests on gasoline and his discoveries lead to him being forced to report an emergency finding to the Guild Collaborative prime.

Helion Prime – A planet controlled by the Guild Collective. Originally the home of Amelia Nanospark and her people.

Hollow – A derogatory term used to describe mindless Golems.

Huntsville – Is the largest town in the Muskoka Region of Ontario, Canada.

I-Beam – A metal support beam that looks like an I from the bottom or top.

Initial Increase – A very popular enchantment for tanks. This allows the individual to stand and take a charge from creatures much heavier than themselves.

Initiation Gear – A set of gear that Beastkin use to help them through their trials. All Beastkin must complete the trials to become adults. Due to high death rates this gear was created to increase success rates of participants.

Iridescent Kobold – A race of Kobold's in the Ether Verse. Kobolds are small dragonkin or lizardfolk.

Jack Wareham – A member of the A-Team. A rotund man who is constantly jolly and supportive. He unfortunately dies at the hands of Rockland, when no other options are left to him. **Apprentice-Trapper**

Jason Jackson – 15-year-old young man that Rocky met while entering Ottawa. Family was massacred by Corsair's goons. Has become a member of the party and is fixated on getting stronger. Changes his name to Zippo to distance himself from the tragedy. **Red-Fire Mage**

Jessibihr Windfall – A merchant in the Aretrean Bazaar. Sells skill scrolls primarily. Rockland dislikes him from his actions in book one. Ripped off Rockland in book one.

Joe Flacca – Member of the Ottawa Militia. Becomes its General after the fall of Corsair. Quickly becomes Zippo's best friend but dies sacrificing himself for Rocky. **Special-Trooper. Died during the Place of Power Contestation.**

Joaquim Smith – Joaquim Smith is an initial survivor that was in Algonquin Park during the crash. His group of fifteen is lucky

enough to be saved by Rocky from a giant Onikuma.
Apprentice-Medicine Man

Jorge – A member of the Grotto Council. Hooded and shadowed. Not very talkative.

Karacy – A race native to Gelthisar. Also termed Dwarf.

Karl Keerdint – An engineer who was constructing the crafters hall. Highly attentive to detail and not afraid of authority.

Kata – A Japanese word that refers to patterns of movement. It is often used to teach proper styles for sword and martial arts.

Kingsbraid – A plant that needs Ether to cultivate.

Knight's Action – A skill that Rockland can acquire in the Chimeran Knight class.

Knight's Resolve – A skill that Rockland can acquire in the Chimeran Knight class.

Knowledge Tablet – A tablet that has access to books that are stored in the EtherNet or purchased from other areas of the Ether Verse.

Kodo's Jacket – A piece of Cursed Regalia picked up by our hero during book 3.

Lacy Obs – Rockland's sister.

Letoya Deckman – A friend of Victoria Faris. A member of the Grotto Military and a combat classer.

Lillian Meghan Wright Centre – A educational building inside York Univeristy.

Lingren – An elven merchant inside the Aretrean Bazaar. Somewhat honest but currently disliked by Rockland for his racist slurs and remarks.

Loincloth – An item dropped by Ogres. Ogres use the skin of their strongest foe to craft a loincloth.

Long Forgotten Dungeon (LFD) – Rocky and the gang hide in this Dungeon on the way to Ottawa. Rocky makes a deal with LFD, which he terms Little Friendly Dungeon. LFD will help keep the devastation caused by a nuclear meltdown at bay and, in time, help Rocky's settlement level.

Louisville Slugger – A popular type of wooden bat.

M3 – Is an American .45-caliber submachine gun.

Mages Guild – Guild located on Helion Prime. A guild that is entirely comprised of Mage classes.

Mageleaf – A type of plant that needs Ether to cultivate.

Madawaska – Is an incorporated township in Renfrew County in Eastern Ontario, Canada.

Marcel Grey – A dishwasher in the Mess Hall who has a Geologist class. Gets directed to go to morning trainings and strengthen himself.

Martian Hive – A guild that originated on Mars. Fled when Ether vanished. Still a powerful entity in the Ether Verse.

Maximus – An arena dungeon inside of Algonquin Valley.

McDougall – Is a township in central Ontario, Canada.

Mechanolord – An individual who has been converted into a machine hybrid. They often gain significant power but miss out on a great deal of skill building.

Mechanolords Conversion Seeds – An item that converted biological beings into Mechanolords.

Melee Weapon – A weapon that is used in close quarters.

Meliora Guild – The guild created by Rockland and Sela for the people of the Grotto.

Michabo – A Native American man that resides in the Spirit Realm. He is half rabbit and half man. Extremely old and possibly deceitful.

Minions – A servile dependent, follower or underling.

Minion Golems – Golems controlled by others.

Monsters Bane – An enchantment on an item.

Montessori – The Montessori Method of Education is a individual-centered education approached based on scientific observations of children. Often the teachers learn the materials before sharing it with their pupils. This creates a joint learning environment.

Mortar and Pestle – A bowl and a rod that are used in conjunction to pulp seeds into powders or liquids.

Mr. Pips – A member of the A-Team. Tall wiry man with very blonde hair, and needs food immediately… according to Rocky.

Nadine Shealds – Rockland's mother.

Nanoweave Under Armor – A piece of gear worn by the hero. It is form fitting, self-cleaning, and climate controlled by the nanobots inside.

Nebula – Nebula is a giant cloud of gas in space. This can be caused by explosions of stars or the formation of new stars.

Nipissing – A university / college in the town of North Bay.

North Bay – is a city in Northeastern Ontario, Canada.

NPCs – Non-Power Classes

Odin – The name of the Star God. Otherwise known as the Sun.

Oliver Grees – 13-year-old young man that Rocky met while entering Ottawa. Family was massacred by Corsair's goons. **Died during the Ottawa Exodus Struggle.**

Other Planetary Gods (spoken of) – Mars, Gelth, Krond, Sinfath, Helion Prime (Planet)

Omega – A sapient golem who is a member of the Ottawa Knights. He was created from a historical building known as the Parliament Buildings in Ottawa. A California beach bum

personality that wants to try all the comforts of the old world.
Master-Knight of Gaia

Ottawa Knights – See Tao, Epsilon, Gamma, Delta and Epsilon.

Pan's Cloak – A piece of Cursed Regalia that may billow in unseen winds. It may even pull the user off their feet for no reason. This item was given to Victoria.

Pangaea – Was a supercontinent that existed during the late Paleozoic and early Mesozoic eras.

Parliament Knight Golems – The Parliament golems are five knight brothers that are sapient. They wish to make a place for golems in this new world.

Pebbles – An Ogre boss that controls time magic.

Perception Skill – A skill that highlights things that you might not notice otherwise.

Phalanx – A body of troops standing in close formation. In this book, an inverted triangle formation to break a charge.

Planetary Essence – The secondary tier of energy need by Dungeons and Planetary gods.

Planetary Leaderboards – A feature listing the strongest in multiple categories. Part of the connection to the EtherNet.

Plasma Grenade/Mine – A grenade/mine that uses a Plasma reaction to create a miniature sun.

Poison Pool – A part of the Envenom skill. Our hero can collect poisons and secrete a venom of his own based on the potency of his Poison Pool.

Quests – Can be issued by Gaia directly (Red) or can be issued by Atlantean Net which is the system put in place by ancient Gaians to improve leveling and compatibility with Gaia and Ether.

Questing – Accepting quests and completing them for Etherience. This is a common way to quickly increase levels within the Etherverse.

Radar Globe – A device on Dahrix's Battleship that he destroys with his laser ports.

Ragnar – Another soul devoured by Apep, and is continually spun out to do his bidding. This individual is far less willing than Apothis and Rattlegore and resists the power of the Void god. His corpse is currently stored in Rocky's Bag of Holding. **Journeyman-Vanir**

Ragnar's Longsword – A sword used by Ragnar and looted after his death. It is later unlocked by Zippo.

Rat Hide Helm – An item that is dropped by the Rat Wolf's and Bat Birds in book 3.

Rattleshirt – Slightly manic soul devoured by Apep. Rattlegore can create a type of skeletal creature that is extremely powerful but territorial. The bones of the creatures he creates are extremely strong and don't burn. **Journeyman–Master of Bones**

Rattleshirt Breastplate – The official name of an item dropped by Rattlegore in Book 2.

Rattlegore – Is a transformation of Rattleshirt using a special Skill and consuming all of Rattleshirt's summoned creatures, however, Rocky and company mostly prevented this.
Journeyman – Obsidian Bone Apostle

Rebirth – A way to return an individual's spirit to a living body. Requires high amounts of Territorial Etherience but can save a person from dying. Often a broken body can be healed to working order after severe damage. The return of the spirit will then revitalize the body and make it useable. Does not need to be the owner's soul to be Reborn.

Red Quest – A quest issued by Gaia herself. These quests are of utmost importance and often return balance to the world.

Research Ships – A ship in the Guild Armada that is meant to research areas they pass through.

Revenant Class – The Apprentice Class of Rockland Barclay.

Richard Sun – The leader of the Nippissing and Canadore survivors. He was a coach and professor at the schools and lead a great deal of kids to survive the Apocalypse.

Rictus – A nightmarish race that Rockland runs into outside of Garnell's shop, inside the Aretrean Bazaar. Sela mocks Rockland for his fear.

Rockland Barclay – Distant relative of Azrael, General of the Darkest Night, General of Cathodiem Guild. The main character of the story. If you don't know that, you haven't been paying attention. **Dark-Revenant - Dark-Chimera Knight**

Rune of Protection – An enchanting Rune or Glyph that increases the inherent Ether defence of an item. This helps protect people from damage.

Ryerson – A University in Toronto, Ontario.

Selaphia Ardensai – Granddaughter of Selaphiel. Captain of Cathodiem Guild. Captain of a Century during the War on Mars. Ancestral guide to Rockland Barkclay but not blood related. **Dark-Druid**

Seraphim Seven – A term for a powerful group of individuals in the Etherverse. Likely a guild and could be the remnants of the Cathodiem Guild.

Shadow Clone – A skill Rockland gained in the Apprentice Ranks. Creates a copy of himself out of smoke that he can utilize in combat or reconnaissance.

Shaman Class – A class that uses totems and often has a bloodlust ability. Assumed base class of Bam-bam the Ogre boss.

Silver Spires – A territory that Sela grew up in. The home town of the Cathodiem Guild and a very beautiful place.

Simon Hetch – A brother who makes a horrible decision to kill humans to save himself. Rocky lets them live but tells them to never be seen again.

Skandranon – Summoned Chimera to serve as Leader of Chimera Roost, which has now become Algonquin Valley. Progenitor of Azoth.

Smith – A nickname for Joaquim Smith.

Snollygoster – Slang. A politician who is guided by personal advantage rather than by a consistent, respectable principle.

Soul Blade – A weapon that is spiritually bound to the user. Gains power and is able to level up. Seems to change as it levels. Currently seems alive in Rockland's hands.

Sphinx – A mythical creature that is immensely powerful and often asks a riddle.

Sphinx Golden Armor – Armor dropped by the Puzzle dungeon. This set is great for tanking and was given to Victoria.

Spirit Realm – A realm that is outside of reality and houses Michabo. Our heroes end up there at the end of Book 2. This Realm was created as part of some long term plan to vanquish an evil.

Stalwart – A class skill learned by Rockland in Book 3.

Stealth Skill – A skill that Rockland learns in Book 1. He purchases it as a scroll in the Aretrean Bazaar.

Steel – Leader of the Steel Wolfpack. Extremely large boss monster who evolved beside an iron mine, which led him to have fur with the tensile strength of steel.

Taskmasters – Sapient Golems that are in charge of teams of slaves inside of New York. Some of the taskmasters are brutal.

Tao – A sapient golem who is a member of the Ottawa Knights. He was created from a historical building known as the Parliament Buildings in Ottawa. Extremely wise and well-versed in some of the mysteries of the Etherverse. Where he gets his knowledge is a mystery but he is soft spoken and takes over morning training for combat and Meditation. **Master-Knight of Gaia**

Territory – A Territory is a piece of land that will level along with the leader who owns it. The Territory conveys many bonuses to the inhabitants and stabilizes Ether flow, making the immediate area more structured for monster growth.

Territorial Inventory Space (Reserve) – This is a Ethereal Space that is linked to a Territory. It can only be accessed in the Territory and acts like a safe with levels of access.

Territorial Sphere – An item that is created when a Territory is broken down. This sphere can be used to increase an existing Territory size, create a new Territory or sold for a great deal of Crystals.

The Grind – A term used to describe the end of Ranks when the Etherience needed to progress is so high that levels are very hard to come by.

The Scourge – A ship that Amelia traded to the Grotto for allies and information.

Tirahnya – A leader of the Biology Guild in the Guild Collective.

Toronto – A massive city in Southern Ontario, Canada.

Totems – A skill that creates objects with an Area of Effect. The effects vary, but include, shielding, healing, speed and others.

University – The Canadian Equivalent of an American College.

Uplink – A communications link to a satellite.

Victoria Faris – A character introduced in Book 3. A member of the Grotto Military and a tank class. She is powerful and becomes critical to the group's success throughout the book as parties begin to form.

Void God – Opposite of a Sun God. The equivalent to a blackhole that is constantly trying to suck in more Sun Gods and Planetary Gods.

William Shakespeare Statue – A golem that is converted from the Statue in New York.

Did **you** find a word with an X?

Yin-Yang golem – First sapient golem Rocky runs into. This golem is a little bit insane due to its nature.

York University – A University in Toronto.

Yuri – A member of the Grotto Council. A smith who was voted in by the people for all of their hard work in making the Grotto liveable.

Zippo – Nickname for Jason Jackson.

www.ingramcontent.com/pod-product-compliance
Lightning Source LLC
Chambersburg PA
CBHW051937020726
47501CB00001B/163